Paul Ambrose Bigandet

The Life, or Legend, of Gaudama, the Buddha of the Burmese

With annotations. The ways to neibban, and Notice on the phongyies, or Burmese

monks. Vol. 1

Paul Ambrose Bigandet

The Life, or Legend, of Gaudama, the Buddha of the Burmese
With annotations. The ways to neibban, and Notice on the phongyies, or Burmese monks.
Vol. 1

ISBN/EAN: 9783337246426

Printed in Europe, USA, Canada, Australia, Japan

Cover: Foto ©Andreas Hilbeck / pixelio.de

More available books at **www.hansebooks.com**

THE LIFE OR LEGEND

OF

GAUDAMA

THE BUDDHA OF THE BURMESE.

With Annotations.

THE WAYS TO NEIBBAN, AND NOTICE ON THE PHONGYIES OR BURMESE MONKS.

BY THE

RIGHT REVEREND P. BIGANDET,

BISHOP OF RAMATHA,
VICAR APOSTOLIC OF AVA AND PEGU.

IN TWO VOLUMES.

VOL. I.

Third Edition.

LONDON:
TRÜBNER & CO., LUDGATE HILL
1880.

ADVERTISEMENT TO THIRD EDITION.

THE origin of the present work dates back to the years 1852, 1853, 1854, and 1855, when portions of it appeared in the "Journal of the Indian Archipelago and Eastern Asia," edited by J. R. Logan of Penang (vols. vi., vii., viii., and ix.). The first complete edition was printed at Rangoon in Burmah in 1858, and a second, much enlarged, at the same place in 1866.

Very few copies of either of these editions reached Europe, and both are entirely out of print. The present third edition—a faithful reprint of the second—issued, with Bishop Bigandet's sanction, for the benefit of European and American scholars and readers, will, therefore, it is hoped, be gladly received.

Buddhism and Gautama, the faith and its founder, whose followers are between four and five hundred millions of the human race, were comparatively unknown in Europe but a generation ago, and yet this great faith had continued for four and twenty centuries to spread over the vast lands of the East, taking deep and enduring root in all, from Bhotan, Nepaul, and Ceylon, over Further

India to China Proper, Mongolia, Mantchooria, Tibet, and Japan.

Buddhism, as it is found in Burmah, has a particular claim to the attention of a diligent and attentive observer. We there have that religious creed or system as pure from adulteration as it can be after a lapse of so many centuries. Philosophy never flourished in Burmah, and, therefore, never modified the religious systems of the country. Hinduism never exercised any influence on the banks of the Irrawaddy. Chinese and Burmese have often met on battlefields, but the influence of the Middle Kingdom has never established itself in Burmah. In other words, Chinese Buddhism has never been able to penetrate into the customs and manners of the people, and has not attempted to communicate its own religion to its southern neighbours. It would seem that the true form of Buddhism is to be found in Burmah, and that a knowledge of that system can only be arrived at by the study of the religious books of Burmah, and by attentively observing the religious practices and ceremonies of the people. This is what Bishop Bigandet has endeavoured to do throughout his work.

Mr. Alabaster, the author of a very popular work on Siamese Buddhism, testifies to the great value of the Bishop's work, which, he remarks, is in one sense complete, for whereas the Siamese manuscript concludes with the attainment of omniscience, the Bishop had materials which enabled him to continue the story to the death of Nirwana (Neibban in the Burmese Pali form). He might have added that the work modestly entitled "Life of Gaudama" is a complete exposition of the great system of Eastern Asia. The metaphysical part, which is the very essence of the system, has received a due consideration, and the priesthood has been fully described. Moreover, the foot-notes help the ordinary reader in understanding clearly the text of the Legend.

Professor Albrecht Weber speaks also of the Bishop's work in terms of high commendation (see "Literarisches Centralblatt," 1870, No. 29, reprinted in "Indische Streifen," vol. iii.), whilst a still further testimony is accorded to its importance in the recent appearance of a French translation by Lieutenant Victor Gauvain.

LONDON, *December* 1879.

PREFACE TO THE FIRST EDITION.

WHETHER Buddhism be viewed in its extent and diffusion, or in the complex nature of its doctrines, it claims the serious attention of every inquiring mind.

In our own days it is, under different forms, the creed prevailing in Nepaul, Thibet, Mongolia, Corea, China, the Japanese Archipelago, Anam, Cambodia, Siam, the Shan States, Burmah, Arracan, and Ceylon. Its sway extends over nearly one-fourth of the human race.

Though based upon capital and revolting errors, Buddhism teaches a surprising number of the finest precepts and purest moral truths. From the abyss of its almost unfathomable darkness it sends forth rays of the brightest hue.

To the reflecting mind, the study of this religious system becomes the study of the history of one of the greatest religious enterprises that has ever been undertaken to elevate our nature above its low level, by uprooting the passions of the heart and dispelling the errors of the mind. A serious observer sees at a glance the dark and humiliating picture of the sad and barren results of the greatest and mightiest efforts of human wisdom, in its endeavours to find out the real cause of all human miseries, and to provide the remedies to cure the moral distempers to which our nature is subject. The fact of man's wretched and fallen condition was clearly perceived by the Buddhist philosopher, but he failed in his attempts to help man out of the difficulties which encompass him in all directions, and to bring him back to the path of truth and salvation. The efforts begun on the banks of the Ganges at an early period, and carried on with the greatest ardour and perseverance, have proved as abortive as those made at a later period throughout Greece and Italy by the greatest and brightest geniuses of antiquity. What a grand and irresistible demonstration both of the absolute inability of man to rescue from evil and attain good, and of the indispensable necessity of divine interference to help him in accomplishing that twofold achievement!

It may be said in favour of Buddhism, that no philosophico-religious system has ever upheld, to an equal degree, the notions of a saviour and deliverer, and of the necessity of his mission for procuring the salvation, in a Buddhist sense, of man. The *rôle* of Buddha, from beginning to end, is that of a deliverer, who preaches a law designed to secure to man deliverance from all the miseries under which he is labouring. But by an inexplicable and deplorable eccentricity, the pretended saviour, after having taught man the way to deliver himself from the tyranny of his passions, only leads him, after all, into the bottomless gulf of total annihilation.

Buddhism, such as we find it in Burmah, appears to have retained, to a great extent, its original character and primitive genuineness, exhibiting, as it does, the most correct forms and features of that Protean creed. At the epoch the Burmans left the northern valleys and settled in the country they now inhabit, they were a half-civilised Mongolian tribe, with no kind of worship, except a sort of geniolatry, much similar to what we see now existing among the various tribes bordering on Burmah. They were in the same condition when the first Buddhist missionaries arrived among them. Deposited in this almost virginal soil, the seed of Buddhism grew up freely without encountering any obstacle to check its growth.

Philosophy, which, in its too often erratic rambles in search of truth, changes, corrects, improves, destroys, and, in numberless ways, modifies all that it meets, never flourished in these parts ; and, therefore, did not work on the religious institutions, which accordingly have remained up to this day nearly the same as they were when first imported into Burmah. The free discussion of religious and moral subjects, which constituted the very life of the Indian schools, and begat so many various, incoherent, and contradictory opinions on the most essential points of religion and philosophy, is the sign of an advanced state of civilisation, such as does not appear to have ever existed on the banks of the Irrawaddy.

Owing to its geographical position, and perhaps, also, to political causes, Burmah has ever remained out of the reach of Hindu influence, which in Nepaul has coloured Buddhism with Hindu myths, and habited it in gross forms of idolatry. In China, where there already subsisted at the time of the arrival of the preachers of the new doctrine the worship of heroes and ancestors, Buddhism, like an immense parasitic plant, extended itself all over the institutions which it covered rather than destroyed, allowing the ancient forms to subsist under the disguise it afforded them. But such was not the state of Burmah when visited by the first heralds of Buddhism.

The epoch of the introduction of Buddhism in Burmah has hitherto been a matter of conjecture. According to Burmese annals, Boudha-gautha, at the end of the fourth century of our era, brought from Ceylon a copy of the scriptures, and did for Burmah what Fa-Hian, the Chinese pilgrim, accomplished a few years afterwards in India and Ceylon for the benefit of his country. But Burmans maintain that they were followers of Buddha long before that epoch. If an inference may be drawn from analogy, it is probable that they are right in their assertion. China is fully as far from the ancient seat of Buddhism as Burmah. Yet it appears from the Chinese annals that the doctrines of the Indian philosopher were already propagated in some parts of that empire in the middle of the first century of our era, and probably at an earlier date. There is no improbability in concluding that, at least at the same time, Buddhist missionaries had penetrated into this country to propagate their tenets. According to Buddhistic annals, it was after the holding of the 3d Council, 236 after Gaudama's death, 207 B.C., that two missionaries carried religion to Thaton, the ruins of which are still to be seen between the mouths of the Tsitang and Salween rivers, and established Buddhism in Pegu. Be that as it may, we know, from the magnificent Buddhist monuments of Pagan, that that religion had reached, in the eleventh and twelfth centuries, a degree of splendour that has never since been equalled.

The Buddhist scriptures are divided into three great parts, the Thoots or instructions, the Wini or discipline, and the Abidama or metaphysics. Agreeably to this division, the matter of the following pages is arranged under three heads. The Life of Buddha, with some portions of his preaching, will convey notions of his principal teachings and doctrines. It is accompanied with copious annotations intended to explain the text, and to convey detailed notices of the system of Buddhism in general, and particularly as it is found existing in Burmah. We have added a few small dzats, or accounts of some of the former existences of Gaudama, and the summary of two large ones.

In the Notice on the Phongyies will be found the chief points of discipline fully explained and developed. We have endeavoured to render as complete as possible the account of the Buddhist Religious, or Phongyies. It is an exposition and practical illustration of the highest

results that can be obtained under the influence of the
doctrines of the Indian philosopher.

In the Ways to Neibban an attempt has been made to
set forth and unfold the chief points of metaphysics upon
which hinges the whole religious system. We confess
that the summary of metaphysics is rather concise. We
were reluctant to proceed too far in this subject, which,
to the generality of readers, is an uninviting one.

A suggestion from Captain H. Hopkinson, Commissioner
of the Martaban and Tenasserim Provinces, has induced
us to add a few remarks on the names and situations of
the principal towns and countries mentioned in the
Legend, with the view of identifying them with modern
sites and places.

It is hardly necessary to state here that the writer,
when he undertook this work, had no other object in view
than that of merely expounding the religious system of
Buddhism as it is, explaining its doctrines and practices as
correctly as it was in his power to do, regardless of their
merits and demerits. His information has been derived
from the perusal of the religious books of the Burmans,
and from frequent conversations on religion, during several
years, with the best informed among the laity and the
religious whom he has had the chance of meeting.

The surest way perhaps of coming to at least an exact
and accurate knowledge of the history and doctrines of
Buddhism would be to give a translation of the Legends
of Buddha, such as they are to be met with in all countries
where Buddhism has established its sway, and to accompany these translations with an exposition of the various
doctrinal points, such as they are held, understood, and
believed by these various nations. This has already been
done by eminent Orientalists, on Thibetan, Sanscrit, Cingalese, and Chinese originals. A similar work, executed
by competent persons among the Shans, Siamese, Cam-
bodians, and Cochin Chinese, would considerably help the

savans in Europe, who have assumed the difficult task of expounding the Buddhist system in its complex and multifarious forms, to give a full, general, and comprehensive view of that great religious creed with all its variations.

The best way to undermine the foundations of a false creed and successfully attack it, is to lay it open to the eyes of all and exhibit it as it really is. Error never retains its hold over the mind except under the mask of truth which it contrives to assume. When deprived of the mask that has covered its emptiness and unreality, it vanishes away as a phantom and an illusion.

We are happy in having an opportunity of returning publicly our thanks to the worthy Commissioner of Pegu, Major A. P. Phayre, for his kind exertions in furthering the publication of this work. Not only is he an eminent Oriental scholar, and profoundly versed in all that has reference to Buddhism, but his great delight is to encourage every effort that tends to unfold and explain a creed which, despite all that has been written about it in the several countries where it flourishes, still contains many mysteries in the parts relating to its history and doctrines that require clearing up.

We have, with a deeply-felt distrust of our poor abilities, taken the best portion out of our limited stock of information concerning the Buddhist system as it exists in these parts, and, with a willing heart, presented it to the public. We hope that our example may induce others, whose stores of knowledge on this subject are fuller and richer than ours, to act in a similar spirit in aid of the prosecution of a great object, viz., the acquisition of a correct knowledge of the religion of nearly 300,000,000 of our fellow-men.

RANGOON, *October* 1858.

PREFACE TO THE SECOND EDITION.

THE First Edition of the Life of Gaudama being out of print for the last five or six years, we have, at the request of several highly esteemed persons, come to the determination of publishing a second and much-enlarged edition of the same Work. In carrying on the plan of improvement which we had in contemplation, we have been favoured by a happy circumstance. We have, after much labour, found and procured, in the Burmese capital, a very rare palm-leaf manuscript, the contents of which have supplied us with copious and interesting details respecting the sayings and doings of Gaudama.

The book is known under the Pali name of Tatha-gatha-oudana, the meaning of which is Joyful Utterance, or Praises, of the Tatha-gatha. The latter expression is one of the many titles given to Gaudama: it means, he who has come like all his predecessors. In the opinion of Buddhists, the Buddhas who appear throughout the duration of a world, or in the various series of succeeding worlds, have all the same mission to accomplish; they are gifted with the same perfect science, and are filled with similar feelings of compassion for and benevolence towards all beings. Hence the denomination which is fitly given to Gaudama, the last of them.

In the course of the Work will be found some particulars

concerning the author of the manuscript referred to, and the place where it was composed. We have only to state here that we have gathered therefrom much information on the condition of Gaudama, previous to his last existence, on the origin of the Kapilawot country, where he was born, and on the kings he has descended from. We have also met with many new details on the great intellectual working of Gaudama's mind, during the forty-nine days he spent in meditation around the Bodi-tree, particularly on the important theory of the twelve Nidanas, or causes and effects, which, with the four sublime truths, constitutes the very essence of the system. We have also found many important particulars concerning the whereabouts of Gaudama during the first twenty years of his public life, and the conversions he effected whilst engaged in the work of an itinerant preacher. Here, too, we have gleaned and selected a few of the instructions he delivered to the people that crowded about him. The story of Dewadat is narrated at great length. We have carefully written down what is said of the three Assemblies, or Councils, held at Radzagio, Wethalie, and Pataliputra, and what is mentioned of the kings who reigned in Magatha from Adzatathat to Dammathoka. We have mentioned the great fact of the spread of Buddhism beyond the boundaries of Magatha after the holding of the third Council, taking care to relate what we have found stated concerning its diffusion in Pegu and Burmah.

Numerous notes have been added to those of the First Edition, for the purpose of elucidating and explaining, as far as we are able, the principles of Buddhism and whatever is connected with that religious system.

RANGOON, *May* 1866.

CONTENTS.

VOL. I.   *b*

CHAPTER IV

CHAPTER V.

CHAPTER VI.

CHAPTER VII.

CHAPTER XI.

CHAPTER XII.

LEGEND OF THE BURMESE BUDDHA,

CALLED

GAUDAMA.

—◆◆—

CHAPTER I.

Invocation of the Burmese translator—Slow but steady progress of Phra-laong towards the Buddhaship—Promise made to him by the Buddha Deipinkara—Origin and beginning of the Kapilawot country and of its Rulers—Birth of Thoodaudana—His marriage with the Princess Maia—Rumour of the coming birth of a Buddha—Phralaong in the seat of Nats—Dream of Maia—Conception of Phralaong—Wonders attending that event.

I ADORE[1] Buddha who has gloriously emerged from the bottomless whirlpool of endless existences, who has extinguished the burning fire of anger and other passions, who

---

[1] All Buddhistic compositions are invariably prefaced with one of the following formulas of worship, always used by writers on religious subjects. The one relates to Buddha alone, and the other to the three most excellent things, ever deserving the highest veneration. The first, always written in Pali, beginning with the words *Namau tassa*, may be translated as follows : I adore thee, or rather adoration to, the blessed, perfect, and most intelligent. Here are proposed to the faith, admiration, and veneration of a true Buddhist, the three great characteristics of the founder of his religion, his goodness and benevolence, his supreme perfection, and his boundless knowledge. They form the essential qualifications of a being who has assumed to himself the task of bringing men out of the abyss of darkness and ignorance, and leading them to deliverance. Benevolence prompts him to undertake that great work, perfection fits him for such a high calling, and supreme science enables him to follow it up with a complete success. They are always held out to Buddhists as the three bright attributes and transcendent qualities inherent in that exalted personage, which are ever to attract and concentrate upon him the respect, love, and admiration of all his sincere followers.

The second formula may be considered as a short act of faith often repeated by Buddhists. It consists in saying—I take refuge in Buddha,

VOL. L   A

has opened and illuminated the fathomless abyss of dark ignorance, and who is the greatest and most excellent of all beings.

---

the Law, and the Assembly. This short profession of faith is often much enlarged by the religious zeal of writers and the fervent piety of devotees. From the instance of this legend we may remark how the compiler, with a soul warmed by fervour, is passing high encomiums upon each of the three sacred objects of veneration, or the sacred asylums wherein a Buddhist delights to dwell. There is no doubt that this formula is a very ancient one, probably coeval with the first age of Buddhism. The text of this legend bears out the correctness of this assertion. It appears that the repetition of this short sentence was the mark that distinguished converts. Ordinary hearers of the preachings of Buddha and his disciples evinced their adhesion to all that was delivered to them by repeating the sacred formula. It was then, and even now it is to Buddhists, what the celebrated Mahomedan declaration of faith—there is but one God, and Mahomed is his prophet—is to the followers of the Arabian Prophet. It is extremely important to have an accurate idea of the three sacred abodes in which the believer expects to find a sure shelter against all errors, doubts, and fears, and a resting-place where his soul may securely enjoy the undisturbed possession of truth. They constitute what is emphatically called the three precious things.

Phra and Buddha are two expressions which, though not having the same meaning, are used indiscriminately to designate the almost divine being, who after having gone, during myriads of successive existences, through the practice of all sorts of virtues, particularly self-denial and complete abnegation of all things, at last reaches to such a height of intel-lectual attainment that his mind becomes gifted with a perfect and universal intelligence or knowledge of all things. He is thus enabled to see and fathom the misery and wants of all mortal beings, and to devise means for relieving and filling them up. The law that he preaches is the wholesome balm designed to cure all moral distempers. He preaches it with unremitting zeal during a certain number of years, and commissions his chosen disciples to carry on the same benevolent and useful undertaking. Having laid on a firm basis his religious institution, he arrives at the state of Neibban. Buddha means wise, intelligent. Phra is an expression conveying the highest sense of respect, which was applied originally only to the author of Buddhism, but now, through a servile adulation, it is applied to the king, his ministers, all great personages, and often by inferiors to the lowest menials of Government. The word Phra, coupled with that of Thaking, which means Lord, is used by Christians in Burmah to express the idea of God, the supreme being.

From the foregoing lines the reader may easily infer that the author of Buddhism is a mere man, superior to all other beings, not in nature, but in science and perfection. He lays no claim whatever to any kind of superiority in nature; he exhibits himself to the eyes of his disciples as one of the children of men, who has been born and is doomed to die. He carries his pretensions no farther. The idea of a supreme being is nowhere mentioned by him. In the course of his religious disputations with the Brahmins, he combats the notion of a god, coolly establishing the most crude atheism. No one, it is true,

I adore the Law which the most excellent Buddha has published, which is infinitely high and incomparably profound, exceedingly acceptable, and most earnestly wished-

---

can deny that in certain Buddhistic countries the notion of an Adibudha, or supreme being, is to be found in writings as well as popular opinions, but we know that these writings are of a comparatively recent date, and contain many doctrines foreign to genuine Buddhism. This subject will, however, receive hereafter further developments.

The Law, the second object of veneration, is the body of doctrines delivered by Buddha to his disciples during the forty-five years of his public career. He came to the perfect knowledge of that law when he attained the Buddhaship under the shade of the Bodi tree. At that time his mind became indefinitely expanded; his science embraced all that exists; his penetrating and searching eye reached the farthest limits of the past, saw at a glance the present, and fathomed the secrets of the future. In that position, unclouded truth shone with radiant effulgence before him, and he knew the nature of all beings individually, their condition and situation, as well as all the relations subsisting between them. He understood at once the miseries and errors attending all rational beings, the hidden causes that generated them, and the springs they issued from. At the same time he perceived distinctly the means to be employed for putting an end to so many misfortunes, and the remedies to be used for the cure of those numberless and sad moral distempers. His omniscience pointed out to him the course those beings had to follow in order to retrace their steps back from the way of error, and enter the road that would lead to the coming out from the whirlpool of moral miseries in which they had hitherto wretchedly moved during countless existences. All that Gaudama said to the foregoing effect constitutes the law upon which so many high praises are lavished with such warm and fervent earnestness. A full and complete knowledge of that law, in the opinion of Buddhists, dispels at once the clouds of ignorance, which, like a thick mist, encompass all beings, and sheds bright rays of pure light which enlighten the understanding. Man is thus enabled to perceive distinctly the wretchedness of his position, and to discover the means wherewith he may extricate himself from the trammels of the passions and finally arrive at the state of Neibban, which is, as it shall be hereafter fully explained, exemption from all the miseries attending existence. The whole law is divided into three parts; the Abidama or metaphysics, Thouts or moral instructions, and the Wini or discipline. According to the opinion of the best informed among Buddhists, the law is eternal, without a beginning or an author that might have framed its precepts. No Buddha ever considered himself, or has ever been looked upon by others, as the inventor and originator of the law. He who becomes a Buddha is gifted with a boundless science that enables him to come to a perfect knowledge of all that constitutes the law: he is the fortunate discoverer of things already existing, but placed far beyond the reach of the human mind. In fact, the law is eternal, but has become, since the days of a former Buddha, obliterated from the minds of men, until a new one, by his omniscience, is enabled to win it back and preach it to all beings.

The third object of veneration is the Thanga, or Assembly. The meaning

for by Nats and men, capable to wipe off the stains of concupiscence, and is immutable.

I adore the Assembly of the Perfect, of the pure and illustrious Ariahs in their eight sublime states, who have overcome all the passions that torment other mortals, by eradicating the very root of concupiscence, and who are famous above all other beings.

I undertake to translate from the Pali[2] text the history

---

of the Pali word Thanga is nearly equivalent to that of church or congregation. In the time Gaudama lived the assembly was composed of all individuals who, becoming converts, embraced the mode of living of their preacher, and remained with him, or if they occasionally parted from him for a while, always kept a close intercourse with him, and spent a portion of their time in his company. Having left the world, they subjected themselves to certain disciplinary regulations, afterwards embodied in the great compilation called Wini. The members of the Assembly were divided into two classes; the Ariahs or venerables, who by their age, great proficiency in the knowledge of the law, and remarkable fervour in the assiduous practice of all its ordinances, occupied deservedly the first rank amongst the disciples of Buddha, and ranked foremost in the Assembly. The second class was composed of the Bickus, or simple mendicant Religious. It is difficult to assert with any degree of probability whether the Upasakas, or ordinary hearers, have ever been regarded as members of the Thanga, and forming a portion thereof. The Upasakas were believers, but continued to live in the world, and formed, as it were, the laity of the Buddhistic church. According to the opinion of Buddhists in these parts, the laity is not considered as forming or constituting a part of the Thanga; those only who abandon a secular life, put on the yellow canonical dress,

and endeavour to tread in the footsteps of their great teacher, are entitled to the dignity of members of the Assembly, to which a veneration is paid similar to that offered to Buddha and the law. The Ariahs, or venerables, are divided into four classes, according to their greater or less proficiency in knowledge and moral worth. They are called Thotapan, Thakadagan, Anagam, and Arahat. In the class of Thotapan are included the individuals who have entered into the current, or stream, leading to deliverance, or, in other terms, who have stepped into the way of perfection. The Thotapan is as yet to be born four times ere he can obtain the deliverance. Those who belong to the second class glide rapidly down the stream, following steadily the way leading to perfection, and are to be born once more in the condition of Nat, and once in that of man. Those of the third class are to be born once in the condition of Nats. Finally, those of the fourth class have gone over the fourth and last way to perfection, reached the summit of science and spiritual attainments, and are ripe for the state of Neibban, which they infallibly obtain after their death. The Ariahs are again subdivided into eight classes, four of which include those who are following the four ways of perfection; the four others comprehend those who enjoy the reward of the duties practised in following the ways of perfection.

[2] The Burmese translator of the

of our most excellent Phra, from the period he left Too-cita,[3] the fourth abode of Nats, to the time he entered into the state of Neibban.

Pali text gives us to understand that his intention is not to give the history of our Buddha during the countless existences that have preceded the last one, when he obtained the supreme intelligence. Buddhists keep five hundred and ten histories or legends of Buddha, purporting to give an account of as many of his former existences; and to enhance the value of such records, the contents are supposed to have been narrated by Buddha himself to his disciples and hearers. I have read most of them. Two hundred of these fabulous narrations are very short, and give few particulars regarding our Phra when he was as yet in the state of animal, man, and Nat. They are, except the heading and the conclusion, the very same fables and *contes* to be met with amongst all Asiatic nations, which have supplied with inexhaustible stores all ancient and modern fabulists. The last ten narratives are really very complete and interesting stories of ten existences of Buddha preceding the one we are about to describe, during which he is supposed to have practised the ten great virtues, the acquisition of which is an indispensable qualification for obtaining the exalted dignity of Phra. Some of these legends are really beautiful, interesting, and well-composed pieces of literature.

[3] Toocita, or the joyful abode, is one of the seats of the Nats. But in order to render more intelligible several passages of this work, it is almost indispensable to have an idea of the system adopted by Buddhists in assigning to rational beings their respective seats or abodes. There are thirty-one seats assigned to all beings, which we may suppose to be disposed on an immense scale, ex-

tending from the bottom of the earth to an incommensurable height above it. At the foot we find the four states of punishment, viz., hell, the states of Athourikes, Preithas, and animals. Next comes the abode of man. Above it are the six seats of Nats. These eleven seats are called the seats of passion, or concupiscence, because the beings residing therein are still subject to the influence of that passion, though not to an equal degree. Above the abodes of Nats we meet with the sixteen seats, called Rupa, disposed perpendicularly one above the other to an incalculable height. The inhabitants of those fanciful regions are called Brahmas, or perfect. They have freed themselves from concupiscence and almost all other passions, but still retain some affection for matter and material things. Hence the denomination of Rupa, or matter, given to the seats. The remaining portion of the scale is occupied by the four seats called Arupa or immaterials, for the beings inhabiting them are entirely delivered from all passions. They have, as it were, broken asunder even the smallest ties that would attach them to this material world. They have reached the summit of perfection; one step farther, and they enter into the state Neibban, the consummation, according to Buddhists, of all perfection. To sum up all the above in a few words: there are four states of punishment. The seat of man is a place of probation and trial. The six abodes of Nats are places of sensual pleasures and enjoyments. In the sixteen seats of Rupa are to be met those beings whose delights are of a more refined and almost purely spiritual nature, though retaining as yet some slight

Previous, however, to commencing the work, I will relate succinctly what is found in our books respecting the great Being who, by a slow but sure process, was qualifying himself for his great and high destiny. It is stated that all the following particulars were narrated by Gaudama himself to the great disciple Thariputra.

For seven thingies of worlds, he who was to become a Buddha felt, during that immense number of revolutions of nature, a thought for the Buddhaship awakening in his soul. This thought was succeeded by a wish, a desire, and a longing for that extraordinary calling. He began to understand that the practice of the virtues of the highest order was requisite to enable him to attain the glorious object of his ardent wishes, and no less than 125,000 Buddhas appeared during that space of time.

When the above period had at last come to an end, the inward workings of his soul prompted him to ask openly for the Buddhaship. The period of asking lasted nine thingies of worlds. It was brightened and illustrated by the successive manifestation of 987,000 Buddhas. In the beginning of this latter period, the future Gaudama was a prince of the name of Laukatara, ruler of the Nanda country. At that time there appeared in the country of Kapilawot a Buddha called Thakiamuni Paurana Gaudama. As he happened to travel through the Nanda country, with the twofold object of preaching the law and begging for his food, the ruler Laukatara made great offerings to him. Meanwhile, with a marked earnestness, he solicited at the feet of Thakiamuni the favour of becoming, at some future time, a Buddha like himself. He expressed the wish to be born in the same country, from the same father and mother, to have for his wife the very same queen, to ride the same horse, to be attended by the

---

affections for matter. In the four seats of Arupa are located those beings who are wholly disentangled from material affections, who delight only in the sublimest contemplation, soaring, as it were, in the boundless regions of pure spiritualism.

same companions and the same two great disciples on the right and on the left. To this request Thakiamuni replied in the affirmative, but he added that an immense length of time had still to elapse ere the objects of his petition could be fully granted. A similar application was repeatedly made to all the other succeeding Buddhas, and a like promise was held out to him.

The third period of four thingies of worlds was remarkable for the complete absence of all that could enlighten or illustrate the various states of existence. A complete moral and intellectual darkness was spread over all beings, and kept them wrapped up in utter darkness. No Buddhas, no Pitzekabuddhas appeared to illuminate by their doctrine and science the minds of men. No Tsekia-wade, or king of the world, made his appearance to infuse life and energy in the midst of the universal slumbering.

But the hundred thousand revolutions of nature that followed were more fortunate. There flourished no less than twenty-seven Buddhas, from Tahingara, the first in the series, to Kathaba, the last one immediately preceding Gaudama.

During the period when the Buddha named Deipinkara was the teacher of all beings, our future Gaudama was born in the country of Amarawatti, from illustrious and rich parents belonging to the caste of Pounhas.

While still a youth, he lost both his parents and inherited their property.

In the midst of pleasure and plenty he one day made this reflection :—The riches that I now possess were my parents' property, but they have not been able to save them from the miseries attending death. They will not, alas! afford to me a better and more secure fate. When I go into the grave, they will not come along with me. This bodily frame I am clad in is not worthy to be pitied. Why should I bestow signs of compassion upon it? Filled with impurities, burdened by rottenness, it has all the elements of destruction in the compounded parts of its existence. Towards Neibban I will turn my regards; upon it my eyes shall be riveted. There is the tank in which all the impurities of passion may be washed away. Now I will forsake everything, and go forthwith in search of a teacher that will point out to me the way that leads to the state Neibban.

Full of these thoughts, the young man gave away to the needy all that he possessed, reserving nothing to himself. Freed from the trammels of riches, he withdrew into a lonely place, where the Nats had prepared beforehand all that was necessary to minister to his wants. He embraced the profession or mode of life of a Rahan, or perfect. Attired in the dress of his new profession, he lived for some time on this spot under the name of Thoomeda. Displeased, however, with the too easy mode of life he was leading, he left that spot, and contented himself with dwelling under the shade of trees. He, however, went forth from time to time in quest of his food.

A few years previous to the retirement of Thoomeda into solitude, he who was to be the Buddha Deipinkara migrated from one of the Nats' seats, and was incarnated in the womb of the Princess Thoomeda, wife of Thoodewa, king of the Ramawatti country. Subsequently he was married to the Princess Padouma, who bore unto him a son, named Oothabakanda. On the same year in which the child was born, the king left his palace on an elephant's back, withdrew into some lonely place, practised during ten months all sorts of self-inflicted penances, and, under the shade of the tree Gniaong Kiat, became a Buddha. On that occasion the earth quivered with great violence, but the hermit Thoomeda, being in ecstasy at that moment, knew nothing of the extraordinary occurrence.

On a certain day, Deipinkara was travelling through the country for the twofold purpose of preaching the law and collecting his food. Arrived near a place where the road was very bad, he stopped for a while until the road should be made passable. The people hastened from all parts to

come and prepare the road for Deipinkara and his followers. Thoomeda, gifted with the privilege of travelling through the air, happened to pass over the spot where
crowds of people were busily engaged in preparing and
levelling a road. The hermit alighted on that spot, and
inquired of the people what was the reason of their busy
exertions. They told him that the most excellent Deipinkara was expected with a large retinue of disciples, and
that they strained every nerve to have the road ready
for them. Thoomeda begged to be permitted to bear a
part in the good work, and asked that a certain extent
of the road be assigned to him as his task. His request
was granted, and he forthwith set to work with the
greatest diligence. It was all but finished when Buddha
Deipinkara, followed by forty thousand disciples, made his
appearance. Thoomeda, actuated by an ardent desire of
testifying his respect to the holy personage, without a
moment's hesitation flung himself into the hollow that
was as yet not filled, and lying on his belly, with his back
upwards, bridged the place, and entreated the Buddha and
his followers to cross the hollow by trampling over his
body. Great and abundant shall be the merits that I,
said he within himself, shall gain by this good work. No
doubt I will receive from the mouth of Deipinkara the
assurance that I shall, hereafter, obtain the Buddhaship.
The Buddha, standing over him, admired the humble and
fervent devotedness of Thoomeda. With one glance he
perceived all that was going on in the hermit's mind, and
with a loud voice, that could be heard by all his disciples,
he assured him that four thingies and one hundred thousand worlds hence he would become a Buddha, the fourth
that would appear during the world, called Badda. He
went on to describe minutely the principal events that
were to illustrate his future career. No sooner was this
revelation made to him than Thoomeda hastened back to
his forest. Sitting at the foot of a tree, he encouraged
himself by fine comparisons to the practice of those vir-

tues that were best suited to weaken in him the influence of the passions.

In the different existences that followed, Thoomeda, at all the periods of the appearance of some Buddhas, received a confirmation of the promise he had had from the lips of Deipinkara.

This present world we live in has been favoured above all others. Already three Buddhas have appeared, viz., Kaukkasan, Gaunagong, and Kathaba. These all belonged to the caste of Pounhas, and he who was to be hereafter our Gaudama, during the many existences he passed through, at the time of the manifestations of those three Buddhas, was always born of the same caste. Kathaba is said to have lived and preached during the ninth andrakap. It was he who, for the last time, assured the future Gaudama that he would obtain the Buddhaship during the tenth andrakap.

We will only mention his last existence in the seat of man, previous to the one in which he was to obtain the great prize he had laboured for with so much earnestness during innumerable existences. He became prince under the name of Wethandra, and practised to an eminent, nay heroic, degree the virtues of liberality and charity. To such an extent did he obey the dictates of his liberal heart, that, after having given away all the royal treasures, his white elephant, &c., he did not shrink from parting with his own wife, the Princess Madi, and his two children, Dzali and Gahna. He then died and migrated to the Toocita seat, and enjoyed the blissfulness and felicity of Nats, under the name of Saytakaytoo, during fifty-seven koudes of years.

The origin and beginning of the Kapilawot country, as well as of its rulers, are to be alluded to as briefly as possible. In the country of the middle, Mitzimadesa, the kings that ruled from the time of Mahathamadat to that of Ookakaritz, king of Benares, were 252,556 in number. The last-named monarch was married to five wives, and had children by them all. The first queen happening to die, the king became passionately enamoured of a young woman, whom he married. She soon presented him with a son, whom the king, pressed by his young wife's solicitations, declared heir-apparent, to the prejudice of his elder sons. As might have been expected, the four elder sons loudly complained of the preference given to their younger brother. To put an end to these domestic disputes, the king called his four sons and their five sisters, gave them a large retinue, and bade them go in a northerly direction, in search of a spot favourable for building a new city. They followed their father's advice. After long wandering through the forests, they came to a place where lived the Rathee Kapila, who, becoming acquainted with the object of their errand, desired them to stay with him and found a city. He also wished that on the very spot where his hut stood the king's palace should be erected. He predicted that this city would become great, powerful, and illustrious; that it would be a city of peace, since the animals in the forests lived peaceably, without ever attempting to inflict harm on each other. The proposal was cheerfully accepted. All the people set to work with great earnestness. When the work was completed, they offered the new city to Kapila, who was made their teacher. Hence the name of Kapila-wottoo, or Kapilawot.

The four princes, finding that among their followers there were no daughters of the royal race whom they could marry, resolved, in order to keep pure the blood-royal, to marry their four younger sisters. The eldest one was raised to the dignity of queen-mother. Ookamukka, the eldest of the brothers, was the first king of Kapilawot. Whilst these things were taking place, the king of Benares, having been attacked with leprosy, had left his throne and retired to a forest north of his capital. There he found his cure under the shade of the kalau tree. At the same time the eldest sister, named Peya, who had become queen-mother, was seized with the same distemper, and went into the same forest. She met with the king, whom she knew not. By his advice she sat under the kalau tree, and the beneficent smell of the leaves soon worked a perfect cure. They were subsequently married, and had a numerous progeny. They settled on this spot, and built the city of Kaulya. The small river Rohani flowed between Kaulya and Kapilawot.*

From Ookamukka, the first king of Kapilawot, to Prince Wethandra, there are but seven successive kings. From Dzali, the son of Wethandra, to Dzeyathena, the great-grandfather of Gaudama, there were 82,002 kings. Let it be borne in mind, that, during that period of time, our Phralaong, or future of Gaudama, was in one of the Nats' seats. The princes of Kapilawot were wont to go and sport on the water of a lake somewhat distant from the

---

* When laying before the reader a short and concise account of the being who was to become the Buddha called Gaudama, the writer deems it necessary to make a general observation, which, he hopes, will greatly help the reader to understand correctly several passages of the following pages. Gaudama was a Hindu, brought up by Hindu masters, and initiated in all the knowledge possessed by the society he lived in. He accepted the fabulous genealogies of kings such as they were found in the writings of his days. The same may be said of the erroneous notions respecting our globe, the size and motions of the sun and the moon and other heavenly bodies, the explanations of many natural phenomena, the description of hell, of the seats of reward, &c. Teacher as he was of moral precepts, based upon metaphysical principles, Gaudama concerned himself very little about these things, which, in his eyes, were not worth the consideration of a sage. But he, or more probably his disciples, availed themselves of these notions for resting upon them some portions of their system, and giving them such developments as best suited their views. These notions, though wedded to the religious system originated by Gaudama, do not, strictly speaking, belong to it. They existed before his appearance in the schools of philosophy; they formed a part of the stock of knowledge possessed by the society in which he was reared. To account properly for these particulars and many others belonging to the disciplinary regulations, recourse must be had to the study of the ancient religion of the Hindus, Brahminism.

In the account of the foundation of the Kapilawot city, we find that the practice of leaving the eldest sister unmarried, and of the princes marrying their own sisters, is up to this day observed by the royal family of Burma. The eldest daughter of the reigning monarch is to remain unmarried during her parents' life, and the first queen is often, if not always, the sister or half-sister of the king. The same unnatural practice prevailed in the royal family of the ancient Persians.

city. They at first erected a temporary place of residence in the vicinity of that sheet of water, and finally built a city which received the name of Dewaha. It had likewise its kings of the same Thagiwi race. Dzeyathena, the king of Kapilawot, had a son named Thiahanoo, and a daughter named Yathaudara. Aukaka, king of Dewaha, his contemporary, had also a son and a daughter, Eetzana and Kitzana. Thiahanoo was married to Kitzana, who bore unto him five sons, Thoodaudana, Kanwaudana, Thoukkaudana, Thekkaudana, and Amittaudana; and two daughters, Amita and Pilita. Eetzana, the son of the king of Dewa, married Yathaudara, daughter of Dzeyathana, king of Kapilawot. From this marriage were born two sons, Thoopabuddha and Dantapani, and two daughters, Maia and Patzapati.

When Eetzana became king of Dewaha, a considerable error had crept into the calendar. A correction was deemed necessary. There lived a celebrated hermit, or Rathee, named Deweela, well versed in the science of calculation. After several consultations held on this important subject in the presence of the king, it was agreed that the Kaudza era of 8640 years should be done away with on a Saturday, the first of the moon of Tabaong, and that the new era should be made to begin on a Sunday, on the first day of the waxing moon of the month Tagoo. This was called the Eetzana era.

On the 10th of the new era, Thoodaudana was born in the city of Kapilawot; and on the twelfth year, Maia was born at Dewaha. In the days of the Buddha Wipathi, the future Maia was then the daughter of a Pounha. Her father, who tenderly loved her, gave her one day a fine nosegay with a great quantity of the choicest perfumes and essences. The young girl, delighted with these articles, hastened to the place where lived Wipathi, and with pious and fervent earnestness laid at his feet all that she had received from her father. Wipathi, admiring the fervent liberality of the damsel, assured her that she would hereafter become the mother of a Buddha, who was to be called Gaudama.

When Thoodaudana was eighteen years of age, his father, King Thiahanoo, called eight Pounhas skilled in the science of astrology, and directed them to go with a large retinue and splendid presents in search of a royal princess to be married to his son. The eight Pounhas departed. They visited several countries, but all in vain; they could not find one princess worthy of their master's son. At last they came to the city of Dewaha. They had no sooner arrived in sight of it than they saw many signs which prognosticated that in the city would be found an accomplished princess, in every respect qualified to become the wife of the heir to the throne of Kapilawot. At that time the young Maia had gone to enjoy herself in a garden outside the city. It was situated on a gently sloping ground, covered with all sorts of the finest and rarest trees. A small brook, winding its course in various directions, shed on every hand, from its gently murmuring waters, a delicious freshness. Thither the royal messengers resorted. They found the princess in the midst of her companions, outshining them all in beauty, like the moon among the stars. Admitted into her presence, the head of the deputation attempted to speak and explain the object of his visit; but he was so much overwhelmed by the beauty and the graceful and dignified appearance of the princess, that his voice failed him, and he fainted three times in succession. As each fit came on him several damsels ran to his assistance with pitchers of fresh water, and brought him back to his senses. Having recovered his spirits, the chief Pounha felt encouraged by some graceful and kind words from the lips of the princess. He explained to her, in the choicest expressions, the object of his mission; and with a faltering and timid tone of voice stated to her that he had come to entreat her to accept presents from, and the hand of, Prince Thoodaudana. Meanwhile he poured at her feet the brightest jewels and rarest articles. The princess, with a sweet voice, modestly replied that she was under the protection and care of her beloved parents, whose will she never resisted; that it was to them that this affair should be referred. For her own part, she had but one thing to do—to abide by her parents' wishes.

Satisfied with the answer, the Pounhas retired, and hastened to the palace of King Eetzana, to whom they related all that had just happened. The king graciously agreed to the proposal, and, in proof of his perfect satisfaction, sent in return a deputation with many presents to Prince Thoodaudana and his father. As might be expected, the royal messengers were well received at Kapilawot. Thiahanoo and his son set out with a countless retinue for the city of Dewaha. In a grove of mango-trees an immense building was erected, out of the city, for their reception and accommodation; and in the middle of that building a spacious hall was arranged with infinite art for the marriage ceremony. When all the preparations were completed, the bridegroom, attended by his father, King Thiahanoo and the chief of Brahmas, went out to meet the bride, who was coming from the garden, accompanied by her mother and the wife of the great Thagia. Both advanced towards the centre of the hall, near a stand raised for the occasion. Thoodaudana first stretched forth his hand and laid it over that place. Maia gracefully did the same. They then took each other's hands, in token of the mutual consent. At that auspicious moment all the musical instruments resounded, and proclaimed in gladdening airs the happy event. The Pounhas, holding the sacred shell in their hands, poured the blessed water over their heads, uttering all sorts of blessings. The parents and relatives joined in invoking upon the young couple the choicest benedictions. The king, princes, Pounhas, and nobles vied with each other in making presents, and wishing them all sorts of happiness.

When the festival was over, Thiahanoo desired to go back to his country with his son and daughter-in-law.

This was done with the utmost pomp and solemnity. On his return, he continued to govern his people with great prudence and wisdom, and at last died and migrated to one of the Nats' seats. He was succeeded by his son Thoodaudana, who, with his amiable wife, religiously observed the five precepts and the ten rules of kings. By his beneficence and liberality to all, he won the sincere affection of his people. It was on the twenty-eighth year of the new era that he was married. Soon after, he took for his second wife, Patzapati, the younger sister of Maia. Thoodaudana's sister, Amitau, was married to Thouppabuddha, the son of king Eetzana.

About four thingies,[4] an hundred thousand worlds ago,[5] the most excellent Buddha, who is infinitely wise

---

[4] Thingie is a number represented by a unit, followed by sixty-four ciphers; others say, one hundred and forty.

[5] Buddhists have different ways of classifying the series of worlds, which they suppose to succeed to each other, after the completion of a revolution of nature. As regards Buddhas, who appear at unequal intervals for illuminating and opening the way to deliverance to the then existing beings, worlds are divided into those which are favoured with the presence of one or several Buddhas, and those to which so eminent a benefit is denied. The present revolution of nature, which includes the period in which we live, has been privileged above all others. No less than five Buddhas, like five shining suns, are to shoot forth rays of incomparable brilliancy, and dispel the mist of thick darkness that encompasses all beings, according to their respective laws of demerits. Of these five, four, namely, Kaukassan, Gaunagong, Kathaba, Gaudama, have already performed their great task. The fifth, named Aremideia, is as yet to come. The religion of Gaudama is to last five thousand years, of which two thousand four hundred and eight are elapsed. The names of the twenty-eight last Buddhas are religiously preserved by Buddhists, together with their age, their stature, the names of the trees under which they have obtained the universal intelligence, their country, the names of their father and mother, and those of their two chief disciples. Deinpakara occupies the fourth place in the series. He is supposed to have been eighty cubits high, and to have lived one hundred thousand years.

It is not without interest to examine whether there have existed Buddhas previous to the time of Gaudama, and whether the twenty-eight Buddhas above alluded to are to be considered as mythological beings who have never existed. It cannot be denied that mention of former Buddhas is made in the earliest sacred records, but it seems difficult to infer therefrom that they are real beings. 1st. The circumstances respecting their extraordinary longevity, their immense stature, and the myriads of centuries that are supposed to have elapsed from the times of the first to those of Gaudama, are apparently conclusive proofs against

and far superior to the three orders of beings, the Brahmas, the Nats,[6] and men, received at the feet of the Phra Deipinkara the assurance that he would afterwards become

---

the reality of their existence. 2d. The names of those personages are found mentioned in the preachings of Gaudama, together with those individuals with whom he is supposed to have lived and conversed during former existences. Who has ever thought of giving any credence to those fables? They were used by Gaudama as so many means to give extension and solidity to the basis whereupon he intended to found his system. 3d. There are no historical records or monuments that can give countenance to the opposite opinion. The historical times begin with Gaudama, whilst there exist historical proofs of the existence of the rival creed of Brahminism anterior to the days of the acknowledged author of Buddhism.

It cannot be doubted that there existed in the days of Buddha, in the valley of the Ganges and in the Punjaub, a great number of philosophers, who led a retired life, devoting their time to study and the practice of virtue. Some of them occasionally sallied out of their retreats to go and deliver moral instructions to the people. The fame that attended those philosophers attracted round their lonely abodes crowds of hearers, eager to listen to their lectures and anxious to place themselves under their direction for learning the practice of virtue. In the pages of this legend will be found passages corroborating this assertion. Thence arose those multifarious schools, where were elaborated the many systems, opinions, &c., for which India has been celebrated from the remotest antiquity. The writer has had the patience to read two works full of disputations between Brahmins and Buddhists, as well as some books of the ethics of the latter. He

has been astonished to find that in those days the art of arguing, disputing, defining, &c., had been carried to such a point of nicety as almost to leave the disciples of Aristotle far behind. It has been said that the gymnosophists whom Alexander the Great met in India, were Buddhist philosophers. But the particulars mentioned by Greek writers respecting their manners and doctrines contradict such a supposition. They are described as living in a state of complete nakedness, and as refusing to deliver instructions to the messenger of Alexander, unless he consented to strip himself of his clothes. On the other hand, we know that Buddha enjoined a strict modesty on his religious, and in the book of ordinations the candidate is first asked whether he comes provided with his canonical dress. The gymnosophists are represented as practising extraordinary austerities, and holding self-destruction in great esteem. These and other practices are quite at variance with all the prescriptions of the Wini, or book of discipline. It is further mentioned that the Macedonian hero met with other philosophers living in community; but whether these were Buddhists or not, it is impossible to decide. It can scarcely be believed that Buddhism in the days of Alexander could have already invaded the countries which the Grecian army conquered.

[6] Nat in Pali means Lord. Its signification is exactly equivalent to that of Dewa, Dewata. The Nats are an order of beings in the Buddhistic system, occupying six seats or abodes of happiness, placed in rising succession above the abode of man. They are spirits endowed with a body of so subtle and ethereal nature as

himself a Buddha. At this time he was a Rathee,[7] under the name of Thoomeda. During that immense space of time, he practised in the highest degree the ten great

to be able to move with the utmost rapidity from their seat to that of man, and *vice versa.* They play a conspicuous part in the affairs of this world, and are supposed to exercise a considerable degree of influence over man and other creatures. Fear, superstition, and ignorance have peopled all places with Nats. Every tree, forest, fountain, village, and town has its protecting Nat. Some among the Nats having lost their high station through misconduct, have been banished from their seats and doomed to drag a wretched existence in some gloomy recess. Their power for doing evil is supposed to be very great. Hence the excessive dread of those evil genii entertained by all Buddhists. A good deal of their commonest superstitious rites have been devised for propitiating those enemies to all happiness, and averting the calamitous disasters which they seem to keep hanging over our heads.

Though the Nats' worship is universal among the Buddhists of all nations, it is but fair to state that it is contrary to the principles of genuine Buddhism and repugnant to its tenets. It is probable that it already existed among all the nations of Eastern Asia at the time they were converted to Buddhism.

The tribes that have not as yet been converted to Buddhism have no other worship but that of the Nats. To mention only the principal ones, such as the Karens, the Khyins, and the Singphos, they may differ in the mode of performing their religious rites and superstitious ceremonies, but the object is the same, honouring and propitiating the Nats. This worship is so deeply rooted in the minds of the wild and half-civilised tribes of Eastern Asia, that it has been, to a great extent, retained by the nations that have adopted Buddhism as their religious creed. The Burmans, for instance, from the king down to the lowest subject, privately and publicly indulge in the Nats' worship. As to the tribes that have remained outside the pale of Buddhism, they may be styled Nats' worshippers. Hence it may be inferred that previous to the introduction or the preaching of the tenets of the comparatively new religion in these parts, the worship of Nats was universal and predominating.

[7] Raci or Rathee means an hermit, a personage living by himself in some lonely and solitary recess, far from the contagious atmosphere of impure society, devoting his time to meditation and contemplation. His diet is of the coarsest kind, supplied to him by the forests he lives in; the skins of some wild animals afford him a sufficient dress. Most of those Rathees having reached an uncommon degree of extraordinary attainment, their bodies become spiritualised to a degree which enables them to travel from place to place by following an aerial course. In all Buddhistic legends, comedies, &c., they are often found interfering in the narrated stories and episodes.

There is no doubt but those devotees who, in the days of Buddha, spent their time in retreat, devoted to study and meditation, were Brahmins. In support of this assertion we have the highest possible native authority, the Institutes of Menoo, compiled probably during the eighth or ninth century before Christ. We find in that work, minutely described, the mode of life becoming a true Brahmin. During the third part of his life, a Brahmin must live as an anchorite in the woods. Clad in the bark of trees or the skins of animals,

virtues, the five renouncings, and the three mighty works of perfection.[8] Having become a great prince[9] under the name of Wethandra, he reached the acme of self-abnegation and renouncement to all the things of this world. After his death, he migrated to Toocita, the fourth abode of Nats. During his sojourn in that happy place, enjoying the fulness of pleasure allotted to the fortunate inhabitants of those blissful regions, a sudden and uncommon rumour, accompanied with an extraordinary commotion, proclaimed the gladdening tidings that a Phra was soon to make his appearance in this world.*

On hearing that a Phra was soon to make his appear-

---

with his hair and nails uncut, having no shelter whatever but that which is afforded him by the trees of the forest, keeping sometimes a strict silence, living on herbs and roots, he must train himself up to bearing with entire unconcern the cold of winter and the heat of summer. Such is the course of life, according to the Vedas, which the true Brahmin is bound to follow during the third portion of his existence. Some Buddhistic zealots have sometimes endeavoured to emulate the ancient Rathees in their singular mode of life. It is not quite unfrequent in our days to hear of some fervent Phongies who, during the three months of Lent, withdraw into solitude, to be more at liberty to devote their time to study and meditation. This observance, however, is practised by but very few individuals, and that, too, with a degree of laxity that indicates a marked decline of the pristine fervour that glowed in the soul of primitive Buddhists.

[8] The three great works are; the assistance afforded to his parents and relatives, the great offerings he had made, coupled with a strict observance of the most difficult points of the law, and benevolent dispositions towards all beings indiscriminately.

[9] This extraordinary monarch, called Tsekiawade, never makes his appearance during the period of time allotted to the publication and duration of the religious institutions of a Buddha.

---

* *Remark of the Burmese translator.*—There are three solemn occasions on which this great rumour is noised abroad. The first, when the Nats, guardians of this world, knowing that 100,000 years hence the end of this world is to come, show themselves amongst men with their heads hanging down, a sorrowful countenance, and tears streaming down their faces. They are clad in a red dress, and proclaim aloud to all mortals the destruction of this planet 100,000 years hence. They earnestly call upon men to devote themselves to the observance of the law, to the practice of virtue, the support of parents, and the respect due to virtuous personages. The second occasion is, when the same Nats proclaim to men that a thousand years hence a Buddha or Phra will appear amongst them; and the third is, when they come and announce to men that within a hundred years there will be in this world a mighty prince, whose unlimited sway shall extend over the four great islands.

ance amongst men, all the Nats, the peaceful inhabitants of the fortunate abode of Toocita, assembled in all haste and crowded around Phralaong,[10] eagerly inquiring of him, who was the fortunate Nat to whom was reserved the signal honour of attaining the incomparable dignity of Buddha. The reason which directed their steps towards Phralaong, and suggested their inquiry, was, that in him were already to be observed unmistakable signs, foreshadowing his future greatness.

No sooner did it become known that this incomparable destination was to be his happy lot, than Nats from all parts of the world resorted to the abode of Toocita, to meet Phralaong and to congratulate him upon this happy occasion. "Most glorious Nat," did they say to him, "you have practised most perfectly the ten great virtues;[11] the time is

---

[10] Here I make use of the expression Phralaong, or more correctly Phraalaong, to designate Buddha before he obtained the supreme knowledge, when he was, as it were, slowly and gradually gravitating towards the centre of matchless perfection. In that state it is said of him that he is not yet ripe.

This word involves a meaning which ought to be well understood. No single expression in our language can convey a correct idea of its import, and for this reason it has been retained through these pages. *Alaong* is a derivative from the verb *laong*, which means to be in an incipient way, in a way of progression towards something more perfect. A Buddha is at first a being in a very imperfect state; but passing through countless existences, he frees himself, by a slow process, from some of his imperfections; he acquires merits which enable him to rise in the scale of progress, science, and perfection. In perusing the narrative of the five hundred and ten former existences of Gaudama which have come down to us, we find that, when he was yet

in the state of animal, he styled himself Phralaong. The Burmese have another expression of similar import to express the same meaning. They say of a being as yet in an imperfect condition that he is soft, tender as an unripe thing; and when he passes to the state of perfection, they say that he is ripe, that he has blossomed and expanded. They give to understand that he who is progressing towards the Buddhaship has in himself all the elements constitutive of a Buddha lying as yet concealed in himself; but when he reaches that state, then all that had hitherto remained in a state of unripeness bursts suddenly out of the bud and comes to full maturity. Similar expressions are often better calculated to give a clear insight into the true and real opinions of Buddhists than a lengthened and elaborate dissertation could do.

[11] The ten great virtues or duties are, liberality, observance of the precepts of the law, retreat into lonely places, wisdom, diligence, benevolence, patience, veracity, fortitude, and indifference. The five renounce-

now come for you to obtain the sublime nature of Buddha. During former existences, you most rigidly attended to the observance of the greatest precepts, and walked steadily in the path of the highest virtues ; you then sighed after and longed for the happiness of Nats and Brahmas; but now you have most gloriously achieved the mightiest work, and reached the acme of perfection. It remains with you only to aspire at the full possession of the supreme intelligence, which will enable you to open to all Brahmas, Nats, and men the way to the deliverance from those endless series of countless existences [12] through which they are doomed

ments are, renouncing children, wife, goods, life, and one's self.

[12] Metempsychosis is one of the fundamental dogmas of Buddhism. That continual transition from one existence to another, from a state of happiness to one of unhappiness, and *vice versa*, forms a circle encompassing the Buddhist in every direction. He is doomed to fluctuate incessantly on the never-settled waters of existence. Hence his ardent wishes to be delivered from that most pitiable position, and his earnest longings for the ever-tranquil state of Neibban, the way to which Buddha alone can teach him by his precepts and his examples.

This dogma is common both to Brahmins and Buddhists. The originator and propagator of the creed of the latter found it already established; he had but to embody it among his own conceptions, and make it agree with his new ideas. His first teachers were Brahmins, and under their tuition he learned that dogma which may be considered as the basis on which hinge both systems. In fact, the two rival creeds have a common object in view, the elevating of the soul from those imperfections forced upon her by her connection with matter, and the setting of her free from the sway of passions, which keep her always linked to this world.

According to the votaries of both creeds, transmigration has for its object the effecting of those several purposes. There is a curious opinion among Buddhists respecting the mode of transmigrations, and there is no doubt it is a very ancient one, belonging to the genuine productions of the earliest Buddhism. Transmigration, they say, is caused and entirely controlled by the influence of merits and demerits, but in such a way that a being who has come to his end transmits nothing of his entity to the being to be immediately reproduced. The latter is a being apart, independent of the former, created, it is true, by the influence of the late being's good or bad deeds, but having nothing in common with him. They explain this startling doctrine by the comparison of a tree successively producing and bearing fruits, of which some are good and some bad. The fruits, though coming from the same tree, have nothing in common, either with each other or with those that were previously grown, or may afterwards grow out of the same plant ; they are distinct and separate. So they say, *kan*, or the influence of merits and demerits, produces successively beings totally distinct one from the other. This atheistic or materialistic doctrine is not generally known by the common people, who practically hold

to pass. Now the light of the law is extinguished, a universal darkness has overspread all minds. Men are more than ever slaves to their passions; there is a total lack of love among them; they hate each other, keep up quarrels, strifes and contentions, and mercilessly destroy each other. You alone can free them from the vicissitudes and miseries essentially connected with the present state of all beings. The time is at last come, when you are to become a Buddha."

Unwilling to return at once a positive answer, Phralaong modestly replied that he wanted some time to inquire particularly into the great circumstances always attending the coming of a Buddha in this world, viz., the epoch or time when a Buddha appears, the place which he chooses for his apparition or manifestation, the race or caste he is to be born from, and the age and quality of her who is to be his mother. As regards the first circumstance, Phralaong observed that the apparition of a Buddha could not have taken place during the previous period[13] of 100,000 years

that transmigration is effected in the manner professed and taught by Pythagoras and his school.

If between the adherents of the two creeds there is a perfect agreement respecting the means to be resorted to for reaching the point when man becomes free from miseries, ignorance, and imperfections, they are at variance as to the end to be arrived to. The Brahmin leads the perfected being to the supreme essence, in which he is merged as a drop of water in the ocean, losing his personality, to form a whole with the Divine substance. This is Pantheism. The Buddhist, ignoring a supreme being, conducts the individual that has become emancipated from the thraldom of passions to a state of complete isolation, called Neibban. This is, strictly speaking, Annihilation.

[13] The duration of a revolution of nature, or the time required for the formation of a world, its existence

and destruction, is divided into four periods. The fourth period, or that which begins with the apparition of man on the earth until its destruction, is divided into sixty-four parts, called andrakaps. During one andrakap, the life of man increases gradually from ten years to an almost innumerable number of years; and having reached its maximum of duration, it decreases slowly to its former short duration of ten years. We live at present in that second part of an andrakap when the life of man is on the decline and decrease. If my memory serve me right, we have reached at present the ninth or tenth andrakap of the fourth period. Should the calculation of Buddhists ever prove correct, the deluded visionaries who look forward to an approaching Millennium, have still to wait long ere their darling wishes be realised.

Though it be somewhat tiresome and unpleasant to have to write down

and more that had just elapsed, because during that period the life of men was on the increase. The instructions on birth and death, as well as on the miseries of life, which

the absurd and ridiculous notions Burmans entertain respecting the organisation of matter, the origin, production, existence, duration, and end of the world, it appears quite necessary to give a brief account, and sketch an outline of their ideas on these subjects. The reader will then have the means of tracing up to their Hindu origin several of the many threads that link Buddhism to Brahminism, and better understand the various details hereafter to be given, and intended for establishing a great fact, viz., the Brahminical origin of the greater part of the Buddhistic institutions. He will, moreover, have the satisfaction of clearly discovering, buried in the rubbish of fabulous recitals, several important facts recorded in the Holy Scriptures.

Matter is eternal, but its organisation and all the changes attending it are caused and regulated by certain laws co-eternal with it. Both matter and the laws that act upon it are self-existing, independent of the action and control of any being, &c. As soon as a system of worlds is constituted, Buddhists boldly assert and perseveringly maintain that the law of merit and demerit is the sole principle that regulates and controls both the physical and moral world.

But how is a world brought into existence? Water, or rather rain, is the chief agent, operating in the reproduction of a system of nature. During an immense period of time rain pours down with an unabating violence in the space left by the last world that has been destroyed. Meanwhile strong winds, blowing from opposite directions, accumulate the water within definite and certain limits until it has filled the whole space. At last appears on the surface of water,

floating like a greasy substance, the sediment deposited by water. In proportion as the water dries up under the unremitting action of the wind, that crust increases in size, until, by a slow, gradual, but sure process, it invariably assumes the shape and proportion of our planet, in the manner we are to describe. The centre of the earth, indeed of a world or system of nature, is occupied by a mountain of enormous size and elevation, called Mienmo. This is surrounded by seven ranges of mountains, separated from each other by streams, equalling, in breadth and depth, the height of the mountain forming its boundaries in the direction of the central elevation. The range nearest to the Mienmo rises to half its height. Each successive range is half the height of the range preceding it. Beyond the last stream are disposed four great islands, in the direction of the four points of the compass. Each of those four islands is surrounded by five hundred smaller ones. Beyond those there is water, reaching to the farthest limits of the world. The great island we inhabit is the southern one, called Dzampoudipa, from the Jambu, or Eugenia tree, growing upon it.

Our planet rests on a basis of water double the thickness of the earth; the water itself is lying on a mass of air that has a thickness double that of water. Below this aërial stratum is *laha*, or vacuum.

Let us see now in what manner our planet is peopled, and whence came its first inhabitants. From the seats of Brahmas which were beyond the range of destruction when the former world perished, three celestial beings, or, according to another version, six, came on the earth, remaining on it in a state of perfect happiness, occasion-

form the true characteristics of Buddha's law, would not then be received with sufficient interest and attention. Had any attempt been made at that time to preach on

ally revisiting, when it pleased them, their former seats of glory. This state of things lasts during a long period. At that time the two great luminaries of the day and the stars of night have not as yet made their appearance, but rays of incomparable brightness, emanating from the pure bodies of those new inhabitants, illuminate the globe. They feed at long intervals upon a certain gelatinous substance, of such a nutritious power that the smallest quantity is sufficient to support them for a long period. This delicious food is of the most perfect flavour. But it happens that at last it disappears, and is successively replaced by two other substances, one of which resembles the tender sprout of a tree. They are so nutritious and purified that in our present condition we can have no adequate idea of their properties. They too disappear, and are succeeded by a sort of rice called *Tha-le.* The inhabitants of the earth eat also of that rice. But alas! the consequences prove as fatal to them as the eating of the forbidden fruit proved to the happy denizens of Eden. The brightness that had hitherto encircled their bodies and illuminated the world vanishes away, and, to their utmost dismay, they find themselves, for the first time, sunk into an abyss of unknown darkness. The eating of that coarse food creates fæces and evacuations which, forcing their way out of the body, cause the appearance of what marks the distinction of the sexes. Passions, for the first time, burn and rage in the bosom of those hitherto passionless beings. They are deprived of the power to return to their celestial seats. Very soon jealousy, contentions, &c., follow in the train of the egotistical distinction of *mine* and *thine.* Finding them-

selves in the gloom of darkness, the unhappy beings sigh for and long after light, when, on a sudden, the sun, breaking down the barrier of darkness, bursts out, rolling, as it were, in a flood of light, which illuminates the whole world; but soon disappearing in the west below the horizon, darkness seems to resume its hold. New lamentations and bewailings arise on the part of men, when in a short time appears majestically the moon, spreading its silvery and trembling rays of light. At the same time the planets and stars take their respective stations in the sky, and begin their regular revolutions. The need of settling disputes that arise is soon felt by the new inhabitants; they agree to elect a chief, whom they invest with a sufficient authority for framing regulations which are to be obligatory on every member of society, and power for enforcing obedience to those regulations. Hence the origin of society.

Men, at first practising virtue, enjoyed a long life, the duration of which reached to the almost incredible length of a thingie. But they having much relaxed in the practice of virtue, it lessened proportionably to their want of fervour in the observance of the law, until, by their extreme wickedness, it dwindled to the short period of ten years. The same ascending and descending scale of human life, successively brought in by the law of merit and demerit, takes place sixty-four times, and constitutes an andrakap, or the duration of a world.

It remains only to mention rapidly some particulars regarding the end of a revolution of nature. The cause of such an event is the influence of the demerits, prevailing to such an extent as to be all-powerful in working out these three great topics, the men of those days, to whom those great events would have appeared so distant, could not have been induced to look upon them with sufficient attention ; the four great truths would have made no impression on their minds ; vain and fruitless would have been the efforts to disentangle them from the ties of passions, then encompassing all beings, and to make them sigh after the deliverance from the miseries entailed upon mankind by birth, life, and death. The period when human life is under a hundred years' duration cannot at all be the proper period for such an important event, as the passions of men are then so many and so deeply rooted that Buddha would in vain attempt to preach his law. As the characters which a man traces over the smooth surface of unruffled water instantly disappear without leaving any mark behind, so the law and instructions that one should attempt to spread on the hardened hearts of men would make no lasting impression upon them. Hence he concluded that the present period, when the life of men was of about a hundred years' duration, was the proper one for the apparition of a Buddha. This first point having been disposed

destruction. Two solemn warnings of the approaching dissolution of our planet are given by Nats, one nearly 100,000 and the other 100 years before that event. The bearers of such sad news make their appearance on earth with marks of deep mourning, as best suited to afford additional weight to their exhortations. They earnestly call on men to repent of their sins and amend their lives. These last summonses are generally heeded by all mankind, so that men, when the world is destroyed, generally migrate, together with the victims of hell who have atoned for their past iniquities, to those seats of Brahmas that escape destruction. There are three great principles of demerit, concupiscence, anger, and ignorance. The world also is destroyed by the action of three different agents, fire, water, and wind. Concupiscence is the most common, though the less heinous of the three. Next comes anger, less prevailing, though it is more heinous ; but ignorance is by far the most fatal of all moral distempers. The moral disorder then prevailing causes destruction by the agency that it sets in action. Concupiscence has for its agency fire ; anger, water ; ignorance, wind ; but in the following proportion. Of sixty-four destructions of this world, fifty-six are caused by conflagration, seven by water, and one by wind. Their respective limits of duration stand as follows : conflagration reaches to the five lowest seats of Brahmas ; water extends to the eighth seat, and the destructive violence of the wind is felt as far as the ninth seat.

of, Phralaong examined in what part of the globe a Buddha was to appear.

His regards glanced over the four great islands [14] and the 2000 small ones. He saw that the island of Dzapoudiba, the southern one, had always been the favourite place selected by all former Buddhas; he fixed upon it, too, for himself. That island, however, is a most extensive one, measuring in length 300 youdzanas, in breadth 252, and in circumference 900. He knew that on that island former Buddhas and semi-Buddhas, the two great Rahandas,[15] or disciples of the right and left, the prince whose sway is universal, &c., had all of them invariably fixed upon and selected that island, and, amidst the various countries on the island, that of Mitzima, the central one, where is to be found the district of Kapilawot. "Thither," said he, "shall I resort, and become a Buddha."

Having determined the place which he was to select for his terrestrial seat, Phralaong examined the race or caste from which he was to be born. The caste of the people

---

[14] Our planet or globe is composed, according to Buddhists, of the mountain Mienmo, being in height 82,000 youdzanas (1 youdzana is, according to some authorities, equal to little less than 12 English miles) above the surface of the earth, and in depth equal to its height. Around this huge and tall elevation are disposed the four great islands, according to the four points of the compass; and each of these again is surrounded by 500 small islands. The countries south of the great chain of the Himalaya are supposed to form the great island lying at the south.

It would be easy to give, at full length, the ridiculous notions entertained by Buddhists of these parts on geography and cosmography, &c., &c.; but the knowledge of such puerilities is scarcely worth the attention of a serious reader, who is anxious to acquire accurate information respecting a religious system, which was designed by its inventor to be the vehicle of moral doctrines, with but very few dogmas. Those speculations upon this material world have gradually found their place in the collection of sacred writings, but they are no part of the religious creed. They are of a Hindu origin, and convey Indian notions upon those various topics. These notions even do not belong to the system as expounded in the Vedas, but have been set forth at a comparatively modern epoch.

[15] A Rahanda is a being very far advanced in perfection, and gifted with high spiritual attainments, which impart to his mortal frame certain distinguished prerogatives, becoming almost spirits. Concupiscence is totally extinguished in a Rahanda; he may be said to be fit for the state Neibban. Several classes are assigned to Rahandas alone, according to their various degrees of advancement in the way of perfection.

and that of merchants appeared too low, and much wanting in respectability, and, moreover, no Buddha had ever come out therefrom. That of the Pounhas was in former times the most illustrious and respected, but that of princes, in those days, far surpassed it in power and consideration. He therefore fixed his choice upon the caste of princes, as most becoming his future high calling. " I choose," said he, " prince Thoodaudana for my father. As to the princess who is to become my mother, she must be distinguished by a modest deportment and chaste manners, and must never have tasted any intoxicating drink. During the duration of 100,000 worlds she must have lived in the practice of virtue, performing with a scrupulous exactitude all the rules and observances prescribed by the law. The great and glorious Princess Maia is the only person in whom all these conditions are to be found. Moreover, the period of her life shall be at an end ten months and seven days hence; [16] she shall be my mother."

Having thus maturely pondered over these four circumstances, Phralaong, turning to the Nats that surrounded him, anxiously expecting his answer, plainly and unreservedly told them that the time for his becoming Buddha had arrived, and bade them forthwith communicate this great news to all the Brahmas and Nats. He rose up, and, accompanied by all the Nats of Toocita, withdrew into the delightful garden of Nandawon. After a short sojourn in that place, he left the abode of Nats, descended into the seat of men, and incarnated in the womb of the glorious

---

[16] It is an immutable decree that she on whom has been conferred the singular honour of giving birth to a mortal who, during the course of his existence, is to become a Buddha, dies invariably seven days after her delivery, migrating to one of the delightful seats of Nats. The Burmese translator observes that a womb that has been, as it were, consecrated and sanctified by the presence of a child of so exalted a dignity, can never be- come afterwards the hidden abode of less dignified beings. It must be confessed that the conception of Phralaong in his mother's womb is wrapped up in a mysterious obscurity, appearing as it does to exclude the idea of conjugal intercourse. The Cochin-Chinese in their religious legends pretend that Buddha was conceived and born from Maia in a wonderful manner, not resembling at all what takes place according to the order of nature.

Maia, who at once understood that she was pregnant with a boy who would obtain the Buddhaship. At the same moment also the Princess Yathaudara, who was to be the wife of the son of Maia, descended from the seats of Nats, and was conceived in the womb of Amitau, the wife of Prince Thouppabuddha.

At that time the inhabitants of Kapilawot were busily engaged in celebrating, in the midst of extraordinary rejoicings, the festival of the constellation of Outarathan (July–August). But the virtuous Maia, without mixing amidst the crowds of those devoted to amusements, during the seven days that preceded the full moon of July, spent her time among her attendants, making offerings of flowers and perfumes. The day before the full moon she rose up at an early hour, bathed in perfumed water, and distributed to the needy four hundred thousand pieces of silver. Attired in her richest dress, she took her meal, and religiously performed all the pious observances usual on such occasions. This being done, she entered into her private apartment, and, lying on her couch, fell asleep and had the following dream :—

Four princes of Nats, of the abode of Tsadoomarit, took the princess with her couch, carried it to the Mount Himawonta,[17] and deposited it on an immense and magnificent rock, sixty youdzanas long, adorned with various colours, at the spot where a splendid tree, seven youdzanas high, extends its green and rich foliage. The four queens, wives of the four princes of Tsadoomarit, approaching the couch where Maia was reclining, took her to the banks of the lake Anawadat, washed her with the water of the lake, and spread over the couch flowers brought from the abode of Nats. Near the lake is a beautiful mountain of a silvery appearance, the summit whereof is crowned with a magni-

---

[17] The Mount Himawonta is famous in all Buddhistic compositions, as the scene where great and important events have happened. It is in all probability the Himalaya, as being the highest range of mountains ever known to Indian Buddhists.

ficent and lofty palace. On the east of the palace, in the side of the mount, is a splendid cave. Within the cave, a bed similar to that of the Nats was prepared. The princess was led to that place and sat on the bed, enjoying a delicious and refreshing rest. Opposite this mount, and facing the cave where Maia sat surrounded by her attendants, rose another mount, where Phralaong, under the shape of a young white elephant, was roaming over its sides in various directions. He was soon seen coming down that hill, and, ascending the one where the princess lay on her bed, directed his course towards the cave. On the extremity of his trunk, lifted up like a beautiful string of flowers, he carried a white lily. His voice, occasionally resounding through the air, could be heard distinctly by the inmates of the grotto, and indicated his approach. He soon entered the cave, turned three times round the couch whereupon sat the princess, then, standing for a while, he came nearer, opened her right side, and appeared to conceal himself in her womb.

In the morning, having awoke from her sleep, the queen related her dream to her husband. King Thoodaudana sent without delay for sixty-four Pounhas.[18] On a

---

[18] Pounhas are the Brahmins who, even in those days of remote antiquity, were considered as the wisest in their generation. They had already monopolised the lucrative trade of fortune-tellers, astrologers, &c., and it appears that they have contrived to retain it up to our own days. During my first stay in Burmah I became acquainted with a young Pounha, wearing the white dress, and getting his livelihood by telling the horoscopes of newly-born infants, and even grown-up people. I learned from him the mode of finding out by calculation the state of the heavens at any given hour whatever. This mode of calculation is entirely based on the Hindu system, and has evidently been borrowed from that people.

Though Brahmins in those days, as in our own, worked on popular ignorance and credulity in the manner abovementioned, we ought not to lose sight of the great fact, borne out by this legend in a most distinct and explicit way, that many among them devoted all their time, energies, and abilities to the acquirement of wisdom, and the observance of the most arduous practices. Their austere mode of life was to a great extent copied and imitated by the first religious of the Buddhist persuasion. Many ordinances and prescriptions of the Wini agree, in a remarkable degree, with those enforced by the Vedas. In the beginning, the resemblance must have been so great as to render the discrepancies scarcely perceptible, since

ground lined with cow-dung, where parched rice, flowers, and other offerings were carefully deposited and profusely spread, an appropriate place was reserved for the Pounhas. Butter, milk, and honey were served out to them in vases of gold and silver; moreover, several suits of apparel and five cows were offered to each of them as presents, as well as many other articles. These preliminaries being arranged, the prince narrated to them the dream, with a request for its explanation.

"Prince," answered the Pounhas, "banish from your mind all anxious thoughts, and be of a cheerful heart; the child whom the princess bears in her womb is not a girl but a ' boy. He will, after growing up, either live amongst men, and then become a mighty ruler, whose sway all the human race will acknowledge; or, withdrawing from the tumult of society, he will resort to some solitary place, and there embrace the profession of Rahan. In that condition he will disentangle himself from the miseries attending exist-ence, and at last obtain the high dignity of Buddha." Such was the explanation of the dream. At the moment Phra-laong entered into Maia's womb, a great commotion was felt throughout the four elements, and thirty-two wonders simultaneously appeared. A light of an incomparable brightness illuminated suddenly ten thousand worlds. The blind, desirous, as it were, to contemplate the glorious dignity of Phralaong, recovered their sight; the deaf heard distinctly every sound; the dumb spoke with fluency; those whose bodies were bent stood up in an erect position; the lame walked with ease and swiftness; prisoners saw their fetters unloosed, and found themselves restored to liberty; the fires of hell were extinguished; the ravenous cravings of the Preithas[19] were satiated; animals were

---

we read in this very work of an in-junction made to the early converts, to bestow alms on the Pounhas as well as on the Bickus or mendicant religious, placing them both on a foot-ing of perfect equality.

[19] Preitba is a being in a state of pun-ishment and sufferings on account of sins committed in a former existence. He is doomed to live in the solitary recesses of uninhabited mountains, smarting under the pangs of never-

exempt from all infirmities; all rational beings uttered but
words of peace and mutual benevolence; horses exhibited
signs of an excessive joy; elephants, with a solemn and
deep voice, expressed their contentment; musical instruments resounded of themselves with the most melodious
harmony; gold and silver ornaments, worn at the arms and
feet, without coming in contact, emitted pleasing sounds;
all places became suddenly filled with a resplendent light;
refreshing breezes blew gently all over the earth; abundant
rain poured from the skies during the hot season, and
springs of cool water burst out in every place, carrying
through prepared beds their gently murmuring streams;
birds of the air stood still, forgetting their usual flight;
rivers suspended their course, seized with a mighty astonishment; sea water became fresh; the five sorts of lilies were
to be seen in every direction; every description of flowers
burst open, displaying the richness of their brilliant colours;
from the branches of all trees and the bosom of the hardest
rocks, flowers shot forth, exhibiting all around the most
glowing, dazzling, and varied hues; lilies, seemingly rooted
in the canopy of the skies, hung down, scattering their
embalmed fragrance; showers of flowers poured from the
firmament on the surface of the earth; the musical tunes
of the Nats were heard by the rejoiced inhabitants of our
globe; hundreds of thousands of worlds[20] suddenly approached each other, sometimes in the shape of an elegant
nosegay, sometimes in that of a ball of flowers or of a
spheroid; the choicest essences embalmed the whole
atmosphere that encompasses this world. Such are the
wonders that took place at the time Phralaong entered his
mother's womb.

---

satiated hunger. His body, and particularly his stomach, are of gigantic
dimensions, whilst his mouth is so
small that a needle could scarcely be
shoved into it.

[20] In the Buddhistic system of cos-
mogony, 100,000 worlds form one
system, subject to the same immutable changes and revolutions as affect
this one which we inhabit. They
admit, indeed, that the number of
worlds is unlimited, but they assert
that those forming one system are
simultaneously destroyed, reproduced
and perfected, by virtue of certain
eternal laws inherent in matter itself.

When this great event happened, four chiefs of Nats, from the seat of Tsadoomarit,[21] armed with swords, kept an uninterrupted watch round the palace, to avert any accident that might prove hurtful to the mother or her blessed fruit. From 10,000 worlds, four Nats from the same seat were actively engaged in driving away all Bilous[22] and other monsters, and forcing them to flee and hide themselves at the extremity of the earth. Maia, free from every disordered propensity, spent her time with her handmaids in the interior of her apartments. Her soul enjoyed, in a perfect calm, the sweetest happiness; fatigue and weariness never affected her unimpaired health. In his mother's womb, Phralaong appeared like the white thread passed through the purest and finest pearls; the womb itself resembled an elegant Dzedi.[23] *

---

[21] Tsadoomarit is the first of the six abodes of Nats. The description of the pleasures enjoyed by the inhabitants of that seat is replete with accounts of the grossest licentiousness.

[22] A Palou, or rather Bilou, is a monster with a human face, supposed to feed on human flesh. His eyes are of a deep red hue, and his body of so subtle a nature as never to project any shadow. Wonderful tales are told of this monster, which plays a considerable part in most of the Buddhistic writings.

[23] A Dzedi is a religious edifice of a conical form, supported on a square basis, and having its top covered with what the Burmese call an umbrella, resembling in its shape the musical instrument vulgarly called *chapeau chinois* by the French. On each side of the quadrangular basis are opened four niches, in the direction of the four cardinal points, destined to receive statues of Buddha. This monument is of every dimension in size, from the smallest, a few feet high, to the tallest, of one or two hundred feet high. It is to be seen in every direction, and in the neighbourhood of towns every elevation is crowned with one or several Dzedis.

The word Dzedi means a sacred depository, that is to say, a place where relics of Buddha were enshrined. The word has been extended since to places which have become

---

* *Remark of the Burmese Translator.*—It is to be borne in mind that mothers of Buddhas having had the singular privilege of giving birth to a child of so exalted a dignity, it would not be convenient or becoming that other mortals should receive life in the same womb; they therefore always die seven days after their delivery and migrate to the abode of Nats, called Toocita. It is usual with other mothers to be delivered, lying in an horizontal position, and sometimes before or after the tenth month. But with the mother of a Buddha the case is not the same; the time of her confinement invariably happens at the beginning of the tenth month, and she is always delivered in an erect and vertical position.

With the solicitous care and vigilant attention with which one carries about a thabeit [24] full of oil, the great Maia watched all her movements, and during ten months unremittingly laboured for the safe preservation of the precious fruit of her womb.

---

receptacles of the scriptures, or of the relics of distinguished religious, who had acquired eminence by their scientific and moral attainments. In the beginning, those Dzedis were a kind of *tumuli*, or mounds of earth or bricks, erected upon the shrine wherein relics were enclosed. In proportion as the followers of the Buddhistic faith increased in number, wealth, and influence, they erected Dzedis on a grander scale, bearing always a great resemblance in shape and form to the primitive ones. The stupas or topes discovered in the Punjaub, and in other parts of the Indian Peninsula, were real Buddhistic tumuli or Dzedis.

During succeeding ages, when relics could not be procured, the faithful continued to erect Dzedis, the sight of which was intended to remind them of the sacred relics, and they paid to those relics and monuments the same veneration as they would have offered to those enriched with those priceless objects. In Burmah, in particular, the zeal, or rather the rage, for building Dzedis has been carried to a degree scarcely to be credited by those who have not visited that country. In the following pages there will be found an attempt to describe the various forms given to those monuments.

[24] The thabeit is an open-mouthed pot, of a truncated spheroidical form, made of earth, iron, or brass, without ornaments, used by the Buddhist monks when going abroad, in their morning excursions, to receive the alms bestowed on them by the admirers of their holy mode of life.

CHAPTER II.

Birth of Buddha in a forest—Rejoicings on that occasion—Kaladewila—Prediction of the Pounhas—Vain efforts of Thoodaudana to thwart the effect of the Prediction.

THE time of her approaching confinement being close at hand, the princess solicited from her husband, King Thoodaudana, leave to go to the country of Dewah,[1] amongst her friends and relatives. As soon as her request was made known, the king ordered that the whole extent of the road between Kapilawot and Dewah should be per-

[1] This country of Dewah is one of the sixteen countries, so much celebrated in the Buddhistic annals, where the greatest religious events have taken place. They are placed in the centre, north, and north-west portions of Hindustan. In this place was born the celebrated Dewadat, who became brother-in-law to Buddha himself. But notwithstanding the close ties of relationship that united him to so saintly a personage, Dewadat is represented as the incarnation of evil, ever opposed to Buddha in his benevolent designs in favour of human kind. At last, in an attempt against his brother-in-law's life, he met with a condign punishment. The earth burst open under his feet, and, surrounded by devouring flames, he rolled down to the bottom of the lowest hell, acknowledging, however, in the accents of a true but tardy repentance, his errors and the unconquerable power of Buddha. Three red-hot iron bars transfix him perpendicularly, hanging him in an erect position, whilst three other bars pierce him through the shoulders and the side. For his repentance he is to be delivered hereafter from those torments, and restored to earth, in order to acquire merits that may entitle him to a better place in future existences. Some accounts mention that he is to become a Pietzega Buddha. This story respecting Dewadat has given rise in Burmah to a very strange misconception. The Burmese, with their usual thoughtlessness, on hearing of the particulars respecting the sufferings and mode of death of our Saviour, concluded that he must have been no other but Dewadat himself, and that, for holding opinions opposite to those of Buddha, he suffered such a punishment. The writer was not a little surprised to find in the writings of the old Barnabite missionaries a lengthened confutation of this erroneous supposition.

fectly levelled, and lined on both sides with plantain trees, and adorned with the finest ornaments. Jars, full of the purest water, were to be deposited all along the road at short intervals. A chair of gold was made ready for conveying the queen ; and a thousand noblemen, attended by an innumerable retinue, were directed to accompany her during the journey. Between the two countries an immense forest of lofty Engyin trees extends to a great distance. As soon as the *cortège* reached it, five water-lilies shot forth spontaneously from the stem and the main branches of each tree, and innumerable birds of all kinds, by their melodious tunes, filled the air with the most ravishing music. Trees, similar in beauty to those growing in the seats of Nats, apparently sensible of the presence of the incarnated Buddha, seemed to share in the universal joy.

On beholding this wonderful appearance of all the lofty trees of the forest, the queen felt a desire to approach nearer and enjoy the marvellous sight offered to her astonished regards. Her noble attendants led her forthwith a short distance into the forest. Maia, seated on her couch, along with her sister Patzapati, desired her attendants to have it moved closer to an Engyin tree (*shorea robusta*), which she pointed out. Her wishes were immediately complied with. She then rose gently on her couch ; her left hand, clasped round the neck of her sister, supported her in a standing position. With the right hand she tried to reach and break a small branch, which she wanted to carry away. On that very instant, as the slender rattan, heated by fire, bends down its tender head, all the branches lowered their extremities, offering themselves, as it were, to the hand of the queen, who unhesitatingly seized and broke the extremity of one of the young boughs. By virtue of a certain power inherent in her dignity, on a sudden all the winds blew gently throughout the forest. The attendants, having desired all the people to withdraw to a distance, disposed curtains all round the place the queen was standing on. Whilst she was in that position, admiring the slender bough she held in her hands, the moment of her confinement happened, and she was delivered of a son.*

Four chief Brahmas[2] received the new-born infant on a golden net-work, and placed him in the presence of the happy mother, saying, "Give yourself up, O Queen, to joy

---

* On the same day a son was born to Amitaudana, called Ananda. The wife of Thouppaboudha of Dewah was delivered of a daughter, called Yathaudara, who became afterwards the wife of Phralaong. Anouroudha, the son of Thookkaudana, was ushered into existence on the same solemn occasion. The above-named Ananda was first cousin to the Buddha, and subsequently became the amiable, faithful, and devoted disciple who, during twenty-five years, attended on the person of Buddha, and affectionately ministered to all his wants. After the death of his mother Maia, Phralaong was nursed and brought up with the greatest care by his aunt Patzapati, sometimes called Gautamee.

---

[2] According to Buddhistic notions, Buddha labours during his mortal career for the benefit of all living beings. His benevolent and compassionate heart, free from all partiality, feels an ardent desire of opening before them the way that leads to deliverance from the miseries of every succeeding existence, and of bringing them finally to the never troubled state of Neibban. Such a generous and benevolent disposition constitutes the genuine characteristic of Buddha. The Brahmas, inhabiting the sixteen seats of Rupa, are all but ripe for obtaining the crowning point of Buddhistic perfection. They only wait for the presence of a Buddha to unloose, by his preachings, the slender ties that keep them still connected with this material world.

The Nats, though far less advanced in merits and perfection, eagerly look forward for the apparition of that great personage, who is to point out to them the means of freeing themselves from the influence of passions, and thereby destroying in them the principle of demerits. Men, also, in their state of probation and trial, want the mighty aid of a Buddha, who will enable them by his transcendent doctrine to advance in merits, so as either to arrive at once at the ever-quiescent state of Neibban, or progress gradually on the way. Hence, on his birth, Buddha is ministered to by those three sorts of intelligent beings, who are particularly destined to share in the blessings his coming is designed to shower on them.

The mission of a Buddha is that of a saviour. His great object, to make use of a Buddhistic expression, is, during his existence, to procure the deliverance of all the beings that will listen to his instructions and observe the precepts of the law. He is distinguished by feelings of compassion and an ardent love for all beings, as well as by an earnest desire of labouring for their welfare. These are the true characteristics of his heart. In this religious system mention is often made of Pitzegabuddhas, who have all the science and merits of a Buddha, but they are deficient in the above-mentioned qualities, which form, as it were, the essence of a true and genuine Buddha. They are never therefore honoured with the noble appellation of Buddha.

and rejoicing; here is the precious and wonderful fruit of your womb." *

From the hands of the four chiefs of Brahmas, four chiefs of Nats received the blessed child, whom they handed over to men, who placed him on a beautiful white cloth. But to the astonishment of all, he freed himself from the hands of those attending upon him, and stood in a firm and erect position on the ground, when casting a glance towards the east, more than one thousand worlds appeared like a perfectly levelled plain. All the Nats inhabiting those worlds made offerings of flowers and perfumes, exclaiming with exultation, "An exalted personage has made his appearance;—who can ever be compared to him? who has ever equalled him? He is indeed the most excellent of all beings." Phralaong looked again towards the three other directions. Raising his eyes upwards, and then lowering them down, he saw that there was no being equal to him. Conscious of his superiority, he jumped over a distance of seven lengths of a foot, in a northern direction, exclaiming,—" This is my last birth; there shall be to me no other state of existence; I am the greatest of all beings."[3] He then began to walk steadily in the same

---

* *Remarks of the Burmese Translator.*—When children are born they appear in this world covered all over their bodies with impure and disgusting substances. But an exception was made in favour of our infant Phralaong. He was born without the least stain of offending impurity; he was ushered into this world, pure and resplendent, like a fine ruby placed on a piece of the richest cloth of Kathika. He left his mother's womb with his feet and hands stretched out, exhibiting the dignified countenance of a Pundit descending from the place where he has expounded the law. Though both mother and child were exempt from the humiliating miseries common to all other human beings, there came down from the skies upon both, by way of a respectful offering, gentle showers of cold and warm water, succeeding each other alternately in a regular order.

[3] The Chinese, Cochin-Chinese, Cingalese, and Nepaulese Legends all agree in attributing to Phralaong the use of reason from the moment he was born, as well as the power of uttering with a proud accent the following words: "I am the greatest of all beings; this is my last existence." To his own eyes he must have appeared in this world without any competitor, since he knew already that he was destined to release countless beings from the trammels of existence, and lead them to a state of

direction.   A chief of Brahmas held over his head the
white umbrella.[4]   A Nat carried the golden fan.   Other
Nats held in their hands the golden sword, the golden
slippers, the cope set with the rarest precious stones, and
other royal insignia.[*]

---

perfect rest, screened for ever from
the incessant action of merits and
demerits.   He alone whose mind is
deeply imbued with Buddhistic notions can boast exultingly that he has
at length arrived at his last existence,
and that, within a few years, he will
escape out of the whirlpool of endless
existences, wherein he has been turning and fluctuating from a state of
happiness to one of wretchedness.
This perpetual vicissitude is to him
the greatest evil, the opposite of
which is, therefore, the greatest good.
No wonder, then, to hear our Phralaong, who was better acquainted
with the miseries attending existence
than any one else, exclaiming with
the accents of a complete joy—"This
is my last existence."

The Burmese translator seems delighted to remark that on two former
occasions Phralaong, then an infant,
had spoken distinct words, which he
addressed to his mother.   This happened in the beginning of the two
existences during which he practised
two of the ten great virtues.   It took
place first on the day he was born to
that existence, when, under the name
of Mahauthata, he displayed consummate skill and wisdom.   The legend
of Mahauthata is a very amusing performance, written in a very pure language, and relating stories about as
credible as those we read in the Arabian Tales of a Thousand and One
Nights.   What surprised the writer
not a little, was to find, in perusing
that composition, a decision given by
our Mahauthata, in a case perfectly
similar to that which showed forth,
in the presence of all Israel, the
incomparable wisdom of Solomon.
When Phralaong practised the last

and most perfect of virtues, liberality,
carried to its farthest limits, ending
in perfect abnegation of self, and renouncing all that he possessed, he
entered, too, into this world with the
faculty of speech, and became a prince
under the name of Wethandra.   The
legend of Wethandra is by far the
best of all.   Taking it as a mere ro-
mance, it is replete with circumstan-
tial details well calculated to excite
the finest emotions of the heart.   The
latter part, in particular, can scarcely
be read without heart-moving feelings
of pity and commiseration, on beholding our Phralaong parting willingly
with all his property, with his wife
and his lovely children, and finally
offering his own person, to satisfy the
ever-renewed calls on his unbounded
generosity.

[4] In Burmah the use of the white
umbrella is limited to the king and
idols.   The former can never move
without having some one to hold over
his head this distinguishing mark of
royalty.   Any one who has been introduced into the palace of Amera-
poora will not have forgotten how
great was his satisfaction on beholding the white umbrella towering above
the sides of passages, and moving in
the direction he was sitting in.   He
knew that the time of his expectation
was at an end, and that in a moment
he would behold the golden face.

---

[*] *Remarks of the Burmese Translator.*—In former existences, our Phralaong is said to have spoken a few
words immediately after his birth,
viz., when he was Mahauthata and
Wethandra.   In the first, he came
into this world holding in his hands a
small plant, which a Nat had brought

Thirty-two mighty wonders had proclaimed the incarnation of Phralaong in his mother's womb, and the same number of wonders announced his birth to the earth. Moreover, in that same moment were born the beautiful Yathaudara, Ananda, the son of Amitaudana, the noblemen Tsanda and Kaludari, and the horse Kantika. The great tree Bodi also sprung from the ground, in the forest of Oorouwela, about two youdzanas distant from the city of Radzagio, and in a north-easterly direction from that place, and the four golden vases suddenly reappeared.

The inhabitants of Dewah, joining those of Kapilawot, set out for the latter country with the newly-born infant, to whom they rendered the greatest honours. The Nats of the seat of Tawadeintha, on hearing that a son was born to King Thoodaudana, and that under the shade of the tree Bodi[5] he would become a true Buddha with a per-

and placed in his tender hands at that very moment. He showed it to his mother, who asked him what it was. "This is a medicinal plant," replied he, to his astonished mother. The plant was cast into a large jar full of water, and the virtualised liquid ever retained the power of curing every kind of bodily distemper. When he was born, or rather began the existence in which he was called Wethandra, he stretched out his hands asking something from his mother which he might bestow on the needy. The mother put at his disposal one thousand pieces of silver.

[5] In glancing over the genealogy of the twenty-eight last Buddhas, the writer has observed that every Buddha has always obtained the supreme intelligence under the shadow of some trees. Our Phralaong, as will be seen hereafter, attained to the exalted dignity of Buddha under the tree Baudhi (*ficus religiosa*), which grew up spontaneously at the very moment he was born. The writer has never been able to discover any well-grounded reason to account for this remarkable circumstance, so carefully noted down, relating the particulars attending the elevation of a being to this high station. For want of a better one, he will be permitted to hazard the following conjecture. Our Phralaong, previous to his becoming a Buddha, withdrew into solitude for the purpose of fitting himself for his future calling, in imitation of all his predecessors, leading an ascetic life, and devoting all his undivided attention and mental energies to meditation and contemplation, coupled with works of the most rigorous mortification. The senses, he knew well, were to be submitted to the uncontrolled sway of reason, by allowing to himself only what was barely requisite for supporting nature. Regardless of every comfort, his mind was bent upon acquiring the sublime knowledge of the principle and origin of all things, on fathoming the miseries of all beings, and on endeavouring to discover the most efficacious means of

fect knowledge of the four great truths, gave full vent to their boundless joy, hoisting unfurled flags and banners in every direction, in token of their indescribable rejoicings.

There was a celebrated Rathee, named Kaladewila, who had passed through the eight degrees of contemplation, and who was in the habit of resorting daily to the prince's palace for his food. On that very day, having taken his meal as usual, he ascended to the seat of Tawadeintha,[6] and found the fortunate inhabitants of that seat giving themselves up to uncommon rejoicings. He asked them the reason of such an unusual display of enrapturing transports of exultation. "It is," replied they to the inquiring Rathee, "because a son is born to King Thoodaudana, who will soon become a true Buddha. Like all former Buddhas, he will preach the law and exhibit in his person and throughout his life the greatest wonders and a most accomplished pattern of the highest virtues. We will hear the law from his very mouth."

On hearing the answer of the Nats, Kaladewila immediately left the seat of Tawadeintha, and directed his

---

affording them a thorough relief, by pointing out to them the road they had to follow in order to disentangle themselves from the trammels of existence, and arrive at a state of perfect rest. In common with all other ascetics, our Phralaong had no other shelter against the inclemency of the seasons but the protecting shadow of trees. It was under the cooling and refreshing foliage of the trees of the forests, that he spent his time in the placid and undisturbed work of meditation, acquiring gradually that matchless knowledge and consummate wisdom which he needed for carrying on to perfection the benevolent undertaking he had in contemplation.

[6] It is a maxim generally received amongst Buddhists, that he who has far advanced in the way of perfection acquires extraordinary privileges both in his soul and his body. The latter obtains a sort of spiritualised nature, or rather matter becomes so refined and purified that he is enabled to travel over distances with almost the rapidity of the thought of the mind. The former, by the help of continual meditation on the causes and nature of all things, enlarges incessantly its sphere of knowledge. The remembrance of the past revives in the mind. From the lofty position such a being is placed in, he calmly considers and watches the movement of events that will take place in future times. The more his mind expands, and the sphere of his knowledge extends, the greater are the perfections and refinements attending the coarser part of his being.

aërial course towards the palace of Thoodaudana. Having entered into the palace and occupied the place prepared for him, he conveyed to the king the good tidings of a son having been born unto him.

A few days after this message, the royal child was brought into the presence of his rejoicing father. Kaladewila was present on the occasion. Thoodaudana ordered that the child should be attired with the finest dress, and placed in the presence of the Rathee, in order to pay him his respects. But the child rose up and set his two feet on the curled hair of the venerable personage. The persons present on the occasion, not knowing that a Buddha in his last existence never bows down to any being, thought that the head of the imprudent child would be split into seven parts as a punishment for his unbecoming behaviour. But Kaladewila, rising up from his seat, and lifting up his hands to his forehead, bowed respectfully to the infant Phralaong. The king, astonished at such an unusual condescension from so eminent a personage, followed his example, and out of respect prostrated himself before his son.

By virtue of his great spiritual attainments, Kaladewila could recollect at once all that had taken place during the forty preceding worlds, and foresee all that would happen during the same number of future revolutions of nature. On seeing the high perfections shining forth in our Phralaong, he considered attentively whether he would become a Buddha or not. Having ascertained that such a dignity was reserved for him, he wished to know if the remaining period of his own existence would permit him to witness the happy moment when he would be a Buddha. To his deep regret, he foresaw that the end of his life would come before the occurrence of that great event, and that he would have then migrated to one of the seats of Arupa, and be, therefore, deprived of the favour of hearing the law from his mouth. This foresight caused a profound sadness in his heart, and abundant tears flowed from his eyes. But when he reflected on the future destiny of the blessed child, he could not contain within himself the pure joy that overflowed his soul. The people present on the occasion soon observed the opposite emotions which alternately affected the soul of Kaladewila. They asked him the reason of such an unusual occurrence. " I rejoice," said he, " at the glorious destiny of that child ; but I feel ·sad and disconsolate when I think that it will not be given to me to see and contemplate him clothed with the dignity of Buddha. I bewail with tears my great misfortune."

With a view of assuaging his sorrow, Kaladewila, casting another glance towards future events, eagerly sought to discover if, among his relatives, there would not be at least one who would be so fortunate as to see Phralaong in the nature of Buddha. He saw with inexpressible delight that his nephew Nalaka would enjoy the blessing denied to himself. Thereupon he went in all haste to his sister's house, inquiring about her son. At his request the lad was brought into his presence. " Beloved nephew," said the venerable Rathee, "thirty-five years hence,[7] the son

---

[7] According to the prophecy of Kaladewila, Phralaong is to become Buddha when thirty-five years old. The total duration of his life being eighty years, it follows that he has lived as Buddha forty-five years. The advice of the old Rathee to his nephew Nalaka, to become a Rahan in order to better dispose himself to welcome the coming of Buddha, and listen with greater benefit to his preachings, leads me to make a remark and write down an observation that has been already alluded to. From this passage and many others which the reader will easily notice hereafter, as well as from the example of Buddha himself, one must suppose that at the time Phralaong was born, some institutions, the most important one at least, viz., that of the Rahans, recluses, or monks, already existed in a more or less perfect state. Relying solely on the authority of this Legend, no attempt at denying this supposition can ever be made. Kaladewila speaks of the order of Rahans as of a thing well known. Nalaka sends to the bazaar for the purchase of the dress and other articles he wanted for his new mode of life. Phralaong, on his way to his garden, sees a Rahan, whose habits and manners are described to him by his coachman. Having become Buddha, he meets with ascetics and recluses living in community, leading a life much resembling that which he is supposed to have hereafter instituted, holding but few opinions, which, according to his own standard, were heretical. From these facts flows the natural conclusion that Gaudama is not the inventor or originator of all the Buddhistic disciplinary institutions. He found

of King Thoodaudana will become a Buddha; you will contemplate him in that sublime and exalted nature. From this day, therefore, you shall embrace the profession of Rahan." The young man, who descended from a long succession of wealthy noblemen, said within himself, "My uncle, indeed, never says anything but under the impulse of irresistible and cogent motives. I will follow his advice and will become a recluse." He immediately ordered the purchase of the insignia of his new profes-fession, a patta, a thingan,[8] and other articles. His head was shaved, and he put on the yellow garb. Attired in his new dress, he looked all round, and saw that, amongst

---

among the multifarious sects of Brahminism many practices and ordi-nances which he approved of and incorporated or embodied in his new system. This is another proof, amounting to a demonstration, that Buddhism is an offshoot of the great Hindu system. In this respect, Gaudama borrowed largely from what he found existing in his own days, iu the schools he resorted to, and re-echoed many tenets upheld by the masters under whom he studied the sciences and the training to morals and virtue. He enlarged and deve-loped certain favourite theories and principles which had found favour with him; at the same time, for the purpose of leading his disciples to perfection, he enforced many discip-linary regulations, almost similar to those he had been subjected to dur-ing the years of his probation. He was certainly an ardent promoter of the perfected and improved system he endeavoured to introduce.

[8] The Thingan or Tsiwaran is com-posed of three parts—the thinbaing, resembling an ample petticoat, bound up to the waist, with a leathern girdle, and falling down to the heels; the kowot, which consists of a sort of cloak of a rectangular shape, covering the shoulders and breast, and reach-ing somewhat below the knee; and the dougout, which is a piece of cloth of the same shape, folded many times, thrown over the left shoulder when going abroad, and used to sit on when no proper seat has been prepared. The colour of these three pieces, con-stituting the dress of a recluse, is invariably yellow. The jack-tree sup-plies the material for dyeing the cloth yellow. In order to maintain a spirit of perfect poverty among the members of the order of the recluse, the Wini prescribes that the tsiwaran ought to be made up with rags picked up here and there, and sewed together. The rule, in this respect, at least as far as its spirit goes, is thoroughly disre-garded, and has become almost a dead letter.

The hairs of the head and the beard, being too often objects which vanity turns to its own purposes, are, to say the least, mere superfluities. A stern contemner of worldly things must, of course, do away with things which may prove temptations to him, or at least afford him unnecessary trouble. Hence no layman can ever aspire to become a Rahan unless he has pre-viously submitted to the operation of a complete shaving of the head, in-cluding even the eye-brows.

all beings, the Rahans are by far the most excellent. Then turning towards the place which Phralaong occupied, he prostrated himself five successive times in that direction, rose up, placed the patta in its bag, threw it over his shoulder, and directed his steps towards the solitude of Himawonta, where he devoted himself to all the exercises of his profession. At the time Phralaong became a Buddha, our hermit went to that great master, learnt from him the works that lead to the state of perfect stability of mind, returned back to his solitude, and attained to the perfection of Rahanda by the practice of the eminent works. Seven months after his return, the end of his existence arrived, when, disentangled from all the ties that had hitherto kept him in the world of passions, he reached the happy state of Neibban.

CHAPTER III.

A Name is given to the child—Prediction of the Pounhas respecting the child—Death of Maia—Miraculous occurrence at the child's cradle —Adolescence of the Phralaong—He sees the four signs—Return from the garden to the royal city.

FIVE days after the birth of Phralaong took place the ceremony of washing the head and giving him a name. In the apartment of the palace several kinds of perfumed wood and essences, such as sandal-wood, lignum, aloes, camphor, &c., were strewed profusely, as well as the most exquisitely scented flowers and parched rice. The nogana (a sort of beverage made of milk, sugar, and honey) was prepared in great abundance. One hundred and eighty Pounhas,[1] the most versed in the science of astrology, were

---

[1] Which of the two systems, Buddhism or Brahminism, is the most ancient? This is a question which learned Orientalists have in former days variously answered. If, however, some credit is to be given to this Legend, and the hero thereof is to be regarded as the author of Buddhism, the solution of that much-controverted question is comparatively easy, and seems to admit of no doubt. Priority of antiquity is decidedly in favour of Brahminism. At the time Buddha was born, and in his own country, we find already subsisting the great politico-religious fabric of Hinduism. The distinction of caste is already mentioned in several passages. We find the Pounhas or Brahmins already monopolising the lucra- tive trade of soothsaying, and re- garded as the best informed among their countrymen. They are treated with great respect and consideration even by proud monarchs, who testify their regard for them by costly pre- sents and every possible mark of dis- tinction. It is true that their caste is not always spoken of with great regard by Buddhist authors; but this is to be attributed to the deadly en- mity that prevailed at a later period between those two great rival sects, which have so long struggled for supremacy over the Indian Peninsula. The Brahminical creed is spoken of in very disparaging terms by Buddh- ists; and, as a matter of course, they have been reciprocally handled severely by their opponents. To

invited to partake of a splendid entertainment in the palace. The king made to every one of them costly presents, and desired them to examine carefully all the signs, prognosticating the future destiny of his son. Amidst that crowd of soothsayers, eight Pounhas were present, who explained the dream that Maia had in the beginning of her pregnancy. Seven of them, lifting up the index [2] of each hand of the child, were amazed at the wonderful signs their eyes met. " If this child," said they, " remain in the society of men, he will become a mighty ruler that will bring all nations under his sway; but if he embrace the profession of recluse, he will certainly become a Buddha." They began to foretell the incomparable glory and high honours that would attend his universal reign. The eighth Pounha, named Kauntagnia, the descendant of the celebrated son of Thoodata, and the youngest of all, raised up the index of one hand of the child. Struck with

---

those who feel inclined to regard Buddha as but a great reformer of a religious system already existing, the question will not appear cleared of all difficulty. But upon them rests the task of establishing on uncontrovertible grounds their hypothesis, ere any serious attention can be paid to the conclusion they would fain infer in favour of the superior antiquity of Buddhism. As for us, we believe Buddha to be the real author of the great religious system under examination. But, at the same time, we readily concede that many elements found existing in those days were seized upon by Buddha, and skilfully arranged so as to harmonise well with his plans.

[3] Superstition and ignorance seem to have been in all ages and under every climate the prolific source of human follies and mental delusions. Man has always been and will ever be the same ridiculously superstitious being, as long as his mind is left to itself, unenlightened by revelation.

With few exceptions, the greatest men of Italy and Greece were as superstitious as the *vulgus*, to whom, in every other respect, they were so superior. The resemblance error bears to truth, when human passions have some interest at stake, deceives many; under deceitful appearances it finds its way to the mind, and then clings to the heart. There is in man an innate desire of tearing asunder the thick veil that hides from him the knowledge of future events. Unable to comprehend the perfect economy of an all-wise Providence in the disposition and management of the affairs of this world, he has recourse to the most absurd means for satiating the cravings of his inordinate curiosity. Hence the prevailing superstition of those days, which induced men to believe that Brahmins, on inspecting the inner part of the hand, could discover certain signs, foreshowing the good or bad destiny of every individual.

the wonderful and unmistakable signs that forced themselves on his view, he exclaimed, " No! this child will not
remain long in the society of men; he will free himself
from the vicissitudes [3] and miseries attending the existence of all beings, and will finally become a Buddha." As
the child was to be the instrument for promoting the
welfare and merits of all mortals, they gave him the name
of Theiddat.

Seven days after her confinement Maia died, and by the
virtue of her merits migrated to the seat of Toocita, and
became the daughter of a Nat.[*] Her death was not the
result of her delivery, but she departed this world because
the term of her life had come. On their return to their
home, the Pounhas assembled their children and said to
them. " We are already advanced in years. We dare not
promise to ourselves that we will ever see the son of King

---

[3] Metempsychosis, or the transmigration of the soul from one state of
existence into another in the same
world, is one of the leading dogmas
of Buddhism. Many passages of the
present work, or rather the Buddhistic system as a whole, can never be
understood unless this tenet be
always borne in mind. It is by passing through countless existences that
a being is slowly purified of his imperfections, and gradually advances
in the way of merits and perfection.
The sacred writings of Buddhists
mention that our Phralaong had to
range, during innumerable existences,
the whole series of the animal kingdom, from the dove to the elephant,
ere he could be born in the state of
man, when, in this condition, he, as
stated by himself, went often into
hell to atone for certain trespassings.
Pythagoras had likely borrowed, and
received directly or indirectly from
the East, this doctrine, which his
school re-echoed throughout Greece
and Italy. The end of metempsychosis is, according to Buddhists, the
state of Neibban. On this point the
author of Buddhism has been at variance with other religious schools,
which in his own days held and professed the dogma of transmigration.

[*] Maia was confined in the beginning of the third age. This expression is rather a very loose and general
one, and is far from indicating, with
any approach to accuracy the period
of Maia's age when she was delivered
of her son. The age of man is divided
into three parts. The first extends
from birth to the sixteenth or eighteenth year; the second goes to the
forty-fifth year or thereabout; and
the third, from the forty-fifth year to
the end of life. Phralaong was born
on the 68th year of the Eatzana era,
on the 6th after the full moon of the
month Katsong. Maia was therefore
fifty-six years old. The author of
this work strives hard to prove this
the age, apparently advanced of Maia,
was the best fitted for securing the
safety and perfection of the fruit of
her womb.

Thoodaudana become a Buddha; but to you such a favour is reserved. Listen respectfully to all his instructions, and endeavour to enter the profession of Rahan without delay, and withdraw into solitude. Let us also all join you in that holy vocation." Three Pounhas refused the invitation, and would not enter the profession. The five others cheerfully gave up everything and became distinguished members of the ascetic body.

King Thoodaudana, hearing of the explanation given by the Pounhas, inquired whether his son was really to become a Rahan. Having been assured that all the signs predicted the future destiny of his son to such a calling, he desired to know what those signs were. He was told that the four following things were the very signs foreshowing the future career of his son, viz., an old man, a sick man, a dead man, and a recluse.[4] As soon as his son should

---

[4] The three first allegorical omens or signs which, according to the foretelling of the Pounhas, were to be seen and observed hereafter by Phralaong, are designed to mean and express the compound of all miseries attending human existence, from the moment man crosses the threshold of life to that of death. The view of these objects was intended to make him disgusted with a state necessarily accompanied with such an amount of wretchedness. He was soon induced by reflection to hold in contempt the things of this world, and consequently to seek with ardour some means of estranging himself from all visible and material objects. The fourth sign, that is to say, the view of a Rahan, or a contemner of this world, aspiring to perfect disengagement from the trammels of passion, and shaping his course towards Neibban, was the very pattern he had to imitate and follow for arriving to that state of perfection, which he felt a strong, though as yet somewhat confused, desire of possessing.

The Nats or Dewatas are the ever-ready ministers for affording to Phralaong the assistance he requires to reach in safety the Buddhaship. They rejoice at the news of his approaching conception in the womb of Maia; they watch over the mother who is to give birth to so blessed a child; they receive the newly-born infant, and hand him over to men; they baffle, by their almost supernatural power, the obstacles which the worldly-minded Thoodandana tries to throw in the way of his son's vocation; in a word, their angelical ministrations are always at hand to help and protect our Phralaong, and enable him to reach that state wherein he shall be fully qualified for announcing to men the law of deliverance. The belief in the agency of angels between heaven and earth, and their being the messengers of God for conveying, on solemn occasions, his mandates to men, is coeval, according to sacred records, with the appearance of man in this world. Innumerable are the instances of angelical ministrations mentioned in the holy writ. We look upon angels as mere

successively remark those four signs, he would immediately come to the conclusion that the state of Rahan alone is worthy of the warm admiration and eager wishes of a wise man.

King Thoodaudana, who ardently wished to see his son become a great monarch, whose sway would extend over the four great islands and the two thousand smaller ones, gave the strictest orders that none of the four omens should ever meet his eyes. Guards were placed in every direction at distances of a mile, charged with but one care, that of keeping out of his son's sight the appearance of these fatal omens.

On that day eighty thousand noblemen, who were present at the great rejoicings, pledged themselves each one to give one of his male children to attend on the royal infant. "If he become," said they, "a mighty monarch, let our sons be ever with him, as a guard of honour to confer additional lustre on his wonderful reign. If he be ever elevated to the sublime dignity of Buddha, let our children enter the holy profession of recluse, and follow him whithersoever he may direct his steps."

Thoodaudana, with the tender solicitude of a vigilant father, procured for his beloved offspring nurses exempt from all corporeal defects, and remarkable for their beautiful and graceful appearance.

---

spiritual substances, assuming a human form, when, by the command of God, they have to bring down to men some divine message. In the system of the Buddhists, Nats are described as having bodies indeed, but of such a pure nature, particularly those inhabiting the superior seats, that they are not only not subjected to the miseries inherent in our nature, but are moreover gifted with such superior attainments as almost to enjoy the perfections and qualifications inherent in the nature of spirits. On this occasion the Nats are endeavour- ing to make virtue triumph over vice; but, in the course of this legend, we will have several opportunities of remarking a counteraction worked up by evil or wicked Nats for upholding the reign of passion or of sin. In this system the two contending elements of good and evil have each its own advocates and supporters. A Hindu Milton might have found two thousand years ago a ready theme for writing, in Sanscrit or Pali, a poem similar to that more recently composed by the immortal English bard.

D

The child grew up, surrounded with a brilliant retinue of numerous attendants.

On a certain day happened the joyful feast of the ploughing season. The whole country, by the magnificence of the ornaments that decorated it, resembled one of the seats of Nats. The country people without exception, wearing new dresses, went to the palace. One thousand ploughs and the same number of pairs of bullocks were prepared for the occasion. Eight hundred ploughs, less one, were to be handled and guided by noblemen. The ploughs, as well as the yokes and the horns of the bullocks, were covered with silver leaves. But the one reserved for the monarch was covered with leaves of gold. Accompanied by a countless crowd of his people, King Thoodaudana left the royal city and went into the middle of extensive fields. The royal infant was brought out by his nurses on this joyful occasion. A splendid jambu tree (*Eugenia*), loaded with thick and luxuriant green foliage, offered on that spot a refreshing place under the shade of its far-spreading branches. Here the bed of the child was deposited. A gilt canopy was immediately raised above it, and curtains, embroidered with gold, were disposed round it. Guardians having been appointed to watch over the infant, the king, attended by all his courtiers, directed his steps towards the place where all the ploughs were held in readiness. He instantly put his hands to his own plough; eight hundred noblemen, less one, and the country people followed his example. Pressing forward his bullocks, the king ploughed to and fro through the extent of the fields. All the ploughmen, emulating their royal lord, drove their ploughs in a uniform direction. The scene presented a most animated and stirring spectacle on an immense scale. The applauding multitude filled the air with cries of joy and exultation. The nurses, who kept watch by the side of the infant's cradle, excited by the animated scene, forgot the prince's orders, and ran near to the spot to enjoy the soul-stirring sight displayed before their admiring eyes. Phralaong, casting a glance all round, and seeing no one close by him, rose up instantly, and, sitting in a cross-legged position, remained absorbed as it were in a profound meditation. The other nurses, busy in preparing the prince's meal, had spent more time than was at first contemplated. The shadow of the trees had, by the movement of the sun, turned in an opposite direction. The nurses, reminded by this sight that the infant had been left alone, and that his couch was exposed to the rays of the sun, hastened back to the spot they had so imprudently left. But great was their surprise when they saw that the shadow of the jambu tree had not changed its position, and that the child was quietly sitting on his bed. The news of that wonder was immediately conveyed to King Thoodaudana, who came in all haste to witness it. He forthwith prostrated himself before his son, saying, " This is, beloved child, the second time that I bow to you."

Phralaong[5] having reached his sixteenth year, his father ordered three palaces to be built for each season of the year. Each palace had nine stories; and forty thousand maidens, skilful in playing all sorts of musical instruments, were in continual attendance upon him, and charmed all his moments by uninterrupted dances and music. Phra-

---

[5] From what has been already mentioned of the life of our Phralaong, we may see that many particulars regarding his birth and his childhood have been described with sufficient accuracy; but little or nothing is said of his adolescence, at least until the age of sixteen, when he gets united to the famous and youthful Yathaudara. In common with many other great men, almost all the years of the private life of this celebrated and extraordinary personage are wrapped up in a complete obscurity. We may conclude from his great proficiency in the knowledge of those sciences and attainments befitting his high situation, he was not remiss, since he was enabled to set at defiance the greatest masters of those days. In the midst of pleasures he knew how to devote the best part of his time to study, unless we suppose that science was infused into his mind by no exertion of his own. The Burmese have a regular mania for dividing with a mathematical precision what at first appears to admit of no such division. Virtues, vices, sciences, arts, &c., all, in a word, are subjected to a rigorous division, which, if arbitrary in itself, has the great advantage of conferring a substantial help to the memory.

laong appeared among them with the beauty and dignity of a Nat, surrounded with an immense retinue of daughters of Nats. According to the change of seasons he passed from one palace into another, moving as it were in a circle of ever-renewed pleasures and amusements. It was then that Phralaong was married to the beautiful Yathaudara, his first cousin, and the daughter of Thouppabudha and of Amitau. It was in the eighty-sixth year of his grandfather's era that he was married, and also consecrated Prince royal by the pouring of the blessed water over his head.

Whilst Phralaong was spending his time in the midst of pleasures, his relatives complained to the king of the conduct of his son. They strongly remonstrated against his mode of living, which precluded him from applying himself to the acquisition of those attainments befitting his exalted station. Sensible of these reproaches, Thoodaudana sent for his son, to whom he made known the complaints directed against him by his relatives. Without showing any emotion, the young prince replied, " Let it be announced at the sound of the drum throughout the country, that this day week I will show to my relatives in the presence of the best masters that I am fully conversant with the eighteen sorts of arts and sciences." On the appointed day he displayed before them the extent of his knowledge; they were satisfied, and their doubts and anxieties on his account were entirely removed.

On a certain day Phralaong, desiring to go and enjoy some sports in his garden, ordered his coachman to have his conveyance ready for that purpose. Four horses, richly caparisoned, were put to a beautiful carriage, that resembled the dwelling-place of a Nat. Phralaong having occupied his seat, the coachman drove rapidly towards the garden. The Nats, who knew that the time was near at hand when Phralaong would become a Buddha, resolved to place successively before his eyes the four signs foreshowing his future high dignity. One of them assumed

the form of an old man, the body bending forward, with
grey hairs, a shrivelled skin, and leaning languidly on a
heavy staff. In that attire, he advanced slowly, with
trembling steps, towards the prince's conveyance. He
was seen and remarked only by Phralaong and his coachman. " Who is that man ? " said the prince to his driver;
" the hairs of his head, indeed, do not resemble those of
other men." " Prince," answered the coachman, " he is an
old man. Every born being is doomed to become like
him; his appearance must undergo the greatest changes,
the skin by the action of time will shrivel, the hairs turn
grey, the veins and arteries, losing their suppleness and
elasticity, will become stiff and hardened, the flesh will
gradually sink and almost disappear, leaving the bare
bones covered with dry skin." " What ? " said to himself
the terrified prince ; " birth is indeed a great evil, ushering
all beings into a wretched condition, which must be
inevitably attended with the disgusting infirmities of old
age ! " His mind being taken up entirely with such considerations, he ordered his coachman to drive back to
the palace. Thoodaudana, having inquired from his courtiers what motive had induced his son to return so soon
from the place of amusement, was told that he had seen an
old man, and that he entertained the thought of becoming
a Rahan.* " Alas ! " said he, " they will succeed in

---

* In the course of this work
the word Rahan is often used. It
is of the greatest importance that
the reader should firmly seize the
meaning that it is designed to convey. We find it employed to designate, in general, the religious belonging either to the Buddhistic or
Brahminical sects. When Buddhists
happen to mention their brethren of
the opposite creed, who have renounced the world and devoted
themselves to the practice of religious
duties, they invariably call them
Rahans. When they speak of Pounhas or Brahmins, who are living in
the world, leading an ordinary secular
mode of life, they never style them
Rahans. Thence we may safely infer
that the individuals to whom this
denomination was applied formed a
class of devotees quite distinct from
the laymen.
That class, it appears, comprised
all the individuals who lived either
in community under the superintendence and guidance of a spiritual
superior, or privately in forests under the protecting shade of trees, and
in lonely and solitary places. The

thwarting the high destiny of my son. But let us try now every means to afford him some distraction, so that he may forget the evil idea that has just started up in his mind." He gave orders to bring to his son's palace the prettiest and most accomplished dancing-girls, that, in the midst of ever renewed pleasure, he might lose sight of the thought of ever entering the profession of Rahan. The guard surrounding his palace was doubled, so as to preclude the possibility of his ever seeing the other signs.

On another day, Phralaong, on his way to his garden, met with the same Nat under the form of a sick man, who appeared quite sinking under the weight of the most loathsome disease. Frightened at such a sight, Phralaong, hearing from the mouth of his faithful driver what this disgusting object was, returned in all haste to his palace. His father, more and more disturbed at the news conveyed to him, multiplied the pleasures and enjoyments destined for his son, and doubled the number of guards that had to watch over him. On a third occasion, whilst the prince was taking a walk, the same Nat, assuming the shape of a dead man, offered to the astonished regards of the prince

---

latter religious are, however, generally designated by the appellation of Ascetics and Rathees. They were the forefathers of those fanatics who up to our days have appeared through the breadth and length of the Indian Peninsula, practising penitential deeds of the most cruel and revolting description. They are described by Buddhists as wearing curled and twisted hair, clad in the skins of wild beasts, and not unfrequently quite destitute of any sort of clothing, and in a state of complete nakedness.

The former, who lived in community, did not lead the same course of life. We find some communities, the three, for instance, under the guidance of the three Kathabas, in the Ouroowela forest, not far from Rad-zagio, whose inmates are called either Rahans or Rathees. This indicates that their mode of life partook both of the common and hermitical life, resembling, to a certain extent, that which was observed by the Christian communities of cenobites established in the desert of Upper Egypt during the first ages of our era.

Those communities appear to have been the centres in which principles were established, opinions discussed, and theories elaborated. The chiefs enjoyed high reputation for learning. Persons desirous to acquire proficiency in science resorted to their abode, and, under their tuition, strove to acquire wisdom. The following pages of this work will afford several striking illustrations of the views just sketched out.

the shocking sight of a corpse. Trembling with fear, the young prince came back forthwith to his residence. Thoo-daudana, being soon informed of what had taken place, resorted to fresh precautions, and extended to the distance of one youdzana the immense line of countless guards set all round the palace.

On a fourth occasion, the prince, driving rapidly to-wards his garden, was met on his way by the same Nat under the meek form of a Rahan. The curiosity of the prince was awakened by the extraordinary sight of that new personage: he asked his coachman what he was. " Prince," answered the coachman, " he is a Rahan." At the same time, though little acquainted with the high dignity and sublime qualifications of a recluse, he was enabled, by the power of the Nats, to praise and extol in dignified language the profession and merits of Rahans. The prince felt instantaneously an almost irresistible incli-nation to embrace that attractive mode of life. He quietly went as far as his garden.

The whole day was spent in all sorts of rural diversions. Having bathed in a magnificent tank, he went a little before sunset to rest awhile on a large well-polished stone table, overshaded by the far-spread branches of beautiful trees hanging above it, waiting for the time to put on his richest dress. All his attendants were busily engaged in preparing the finest clothes and most elegant ornaments. When all was ready, they stood silent round him, waiting for his orders. Perfumes of every description were dis-posed in a circular row with the various ornaments on the table whereon the prince was sitting.

At that very moment a chief Thagia was quietly enjoy-ing a delicious and refreshing rest on the famous stone table, called Pantoo Kambala. On a sudden, he felt his seat as it were getting hot. " Lo! what does this mean?" said the astonished Thagia; " am I doomed to lose my happy state?" Having recollected himself, and reflected a while on the cause of such a wonderful occurrence, he soon knew that

Phralaong was preparing to put on for the last time his princely dress. He called to him the son of a Nat, named Withakioon, and said to him, " On this day, at midnight, Prince Theiddat is to leave his palace and withdraw into solitude. Now he is in his garden, preparing to put on his richest attire for the last time. Go, therefore, without a moment's delay to the place where he is sitting, surrounded by his attendants, and perform to him all the required services. Bowing respectfully to the chief of Thagias, Withakioon obeyed, and by the power inherent in the nature of Nats, he was in an instant carried to the presence of Phralaong. He assumed the figure of his barber, and immediately set to work to arrange the turban with as much taste as art round his head. Phralaong soon found out that the skilful hand which disposed the folds of his head-dress was not that of a man, but of a Nat. One fold of the turban appeared like one thousand, and ten folds like ten thousand folds, offering the magical *coup-d'œil* of as many different pieces of cloth, arranged with the most consummate skill. The extremity of the turban, which crossed vertically the whole breadth of the countless folds, appeared covered with a profusion of shining rubies. The head of Phralaong was small, but the folds of the turban seemed numberless. How could that be so ? It is a wonder surpassing our understanding; it would be rashness and temerity to allow our mind to dwell too much upon it.

Having completely dressed, Phralaong [6] found himself

---

[6] The triumphant return of Phralaong from his garden to the city, when he is attired with the richest dress, is commemorated by Buddhists, at least in Burmah, on the day a young boy is preparing to enter into a monastery of recluses for the purpose of putting on the yellow robe, and preparing himself to become afterwards a member of the order, if he feel an inclination to enlist in its ranks.

Phralaong was bidding a last farewell to the world, its pomps and vanities. So the youthful candidate is doing who is led processionally through the streets, riding a richly-caparisoned horse, or sitting on an elegant palanquin, carried on the shoulders of men. A description of this ceremony will be found in the notice on the Buddhistic monks or Talapoins.

I am obliged to confess that I have

surrounded by all sorts of musicians, singers, and dancers, vieing with each other in their endeavours to increase the rejoicing. The Pounhas sang aloud his praise. " May he

---

found it somewhat difficult to discover any connection between the expressions made use of by Keissa Gautami and the inference drawn therefrom by Phralaong. The explanation of the difficulty may be, however, stated as follows :—Gautami bestows the epithet happy or blessed upon the father and mother as well as on the wife of Prince Theiddat, because she remarked and observed in him those qualities and accomplishments befitting a worthy son and a good husband. The words blessed and happy struck the mind of the future Buddha, attracted his attention, and drew forth his exertions to find out their true import. He asks himself, In what consists true and real happiness? Where is it to be found? By what means can such an invaluable treasure be procured? Can it be conferred upon man by the possession of some exterior object? Can his parents or wife be really happy by the mere accidental ties that connect them with his person? No, answers our young philosopher to himself : Happiness can be procured but by waging war against passions, and carrying it on until their total destruction. Then the victorious soul, sitting calmly on the ruins of her deadly opponents, enjoys in the undisturbed contemplation of truth an indescribable happiness. In this we clearly perceive the unmistakable bearing of Buddhistic morals. It is as it were the embryo of the whole system.

King Thoodandana, influenced by worldly considerations, eagerly wished his son to become a great monarch instead of a poor and humble recluse, even a Buddha. This alone suggests the idea that in those days the *rôle* of a Buddha was not held in so great

an esteem and veneration as it was afterwards. Had it been otherwise, the most ambitious father might have remained well satisfied with the certainty of seeing his own son becoming a personage before whom the proudest monarchs would one day lower to the dust their crowned heads.

At that time a Buddha, or the personage honoured with that title, was looked upon as a mere sage, distinguished among his fellow-men by his great wisdom and eminent proficiency in the study of philosophy. It is highly probable that this name had been bestowed upon a great many illustrious individuals who lived before the days of Gaudama. Hence the fabricated genealogy of twenty-eight former Buddhas, supposed to have lived myriads of years and worlds previously, including the three that have preceded him during the continuance of this system of nature. Here a superstitious and ill-judged enthusiasm has raised up heaps of extravagancies, setting up a ridiculous theory, designed to connect the *rôle* of the present Buddha with those of a fabulous antiquity, and give additional lustre to it. There is no doubt that the glowing halo of sacredness and glory, encircling now the name of Buddha, has never adorned that of any former one. It has been created by the extraordinary progress his doctrines made at first in the Indian Peninsula, and next throughout eastern Asia, and kept up by the fervent admiration of his enthusiastic followers.

The means resorted to by Thoodaudana to retain his son in the world of passions, and thereby thwart his vocation, could not, we hardly need mention, be approved of by any moralist of even the greatest elasti-

conquer and triumph! May his wishes and desires be ever fulfilled!" The multitude repeated incessantly in his honour stanzas of praises and blessings. In the midst of universal rejoicings, Phralaong ascended his carriage. He had scarcely seated himself on it, when a message, sent by his father, conveyed to him the gladdening tidings that Yathaudara had been delivered of a son. "That child," replied he with great coolness, "is a new and strong tie that I will have to break." The answer having been brought to his father, Thoodaudana could not understand its meaning. He, however, caused his grandson to be named Raoula. Phralaong, sitting in his carriage, surrounded by crowds of people, who rent the air with cries of joy and jubilation, entered into the city of Kapilawot. At that moment a princess, named Keissa Gautami, was contemplating from her apartments the triumphant entrance of Phralaong into the city. She admired the noble and graceful deportment of Prince Theiddat, and exclaimed with feelings of inexpressible delight, "Happy the father and mother who have such an incomparable son! happy the wife who is blest with such an accomplished husband!" On hearing those words, Phralaong desired to understand their meaning and know their bearing. "By what means," said he to himself, "can a heart find peace and happiness?" As his heart was already disentangled from the thraldom of passions, he readily perceived that real happiness could be found but in the extinction of concupiscence, pride, ignorance, and other passions. He resolved henceforth to

---

city of conscience and principles; but they were eminently fitted to try the soundness of Phralaong's calling, and the strong and tenacious dispositions of his energetic mind. They set out in vivid colours the firmness of purpose and irresistible determination of his soul in following up his vocation to a holier mode of life; and what is yet more wonderful, the very objects that were designed to enslave him became the instruments which helped him in gaining and ascertaining his liberty. Magnificent, indeed, is the spectacle offered by a young prince remaining unmoved in the midst of the most captivating, soul-stirring, and heart-melting attractions; sitting coolly on his couch, and looking with indifference, nay, with disgust, on the crowd of sleeping beauties.

search ardently for the happy state of Neibban, by quitting the world that very night, leaving the society of men, and withdrawing into solitude. Detaching from his neck a collar of pearls of immense value, he sent it to Keissa Gautami, as a token of gratitudé for the excellent lesson she had given him by the words which she had uttered in his praise. The young princess received it as a mark of favour which she imagined Prince Theiddat intended to pay her. Without further notice of her, he retired into his own apartment to enjoy some rest.

CHAPTER IV.

Phralaong leaves his palace, the royal city, and retires into solitude, amidst the plaudits of the Nats—He cuts his fine hair with a stroke of his sword, and puts on the habit of Rahan—He begs his food at Radzagio —His interview with the ruler of that place—His studies under two Rathees—His fast and penances in the solitude of Oorouwela during six years.

PHRALAONG had scarcely begun to recline on his couch, when a crowd of young damsels, whose beauty equalled that of the daughters of Nats, executed all sorts of dances to the sound of the most ravishing symphony, and displayed in all their movements the graceful forms of their elegant and well-shaped persons, in order to make some impression upon his heart. But all was in vain; they were foiled in their repeated attempts. Phralaong fell into a deep sleep. The damsels, in their disappointment, ceased their dances, laid aside their musical instruments, and, soon following the example of Phralaong, quietly yielded to the soporific influence caused by their useless and harassing exertions. The lamps, lighted with fragrant oil, continued to pour a flood of bright light throughout the apartments. Phralaong awoke a little before midnight, and sat in a cross-legged position on his couch. Looking all around him, he saw the varied attitudes and uninviting appearance of the sleeping damsels. Some were snoring, others gnashing their teeth, others had their mouths wide open; some tossed heavily from the right to the left side, others stretched one arm upwards and the other downwards; some, seized as it were with a frantic pang, suddenly coiled up their legs for a while, and with the same violent motion again pushed them down. This unexpected exhibition made a strong impression on Phralaong; his heart was set, if possible, freer from the ties of concupiscence, or rather he was confirmed in his contempt for all worldly pleasures. It appeared to him that his magnificent apartments were filled with the most loathsome and putrid carcasses. The seats of passions, those of Rupa and those of Arupa, that is to say, the whole world, seemed, to his eyes, like a house that is a prey to the devouring flames. " All that," said he to himself, " is most disgusting and despicable." At the same time his ardent desires for the profession of Rahan were increasing with an uncontrollable energy. " On this day, at this very moment," said he with an unshaken firmness, " I will retire into a solitary place." He rose instantly and went to the arched door of his apartment. " Who is here watching ? " said he to the first person he met. " Your servant," replied instantly the vigilant nobleman Tsanda. " Rise up quickly," replied the prince ; " now I am ready to retire from the world and resort to some lonely place. Go to the stable and prepare the fastest of my horses." Tsanda bowed respectfully to his master, and executed his orders with the utmost celerity. The horse Kantika, know- ing the intentions of the prince, felt an inexpressible joy at being selected for such a good errand, and he testified his joy by loud neighs ; but, by the power of the Nats, the sound of his voice was silenced, so that none heard it.

While Tsanda, in compliance with the orders he had received, was making the necessary preparations, Phra- laong desired to see his newly born son Raoula. He opened gently the door of the room where the princess was sleeping, having one of her hands placed over the head of the infant. Phralaong, stopping at the threshold, said to himself :—" If I go farther to contemplate the child, I will have to remove the hand of the mother ; she may be awakened by this movement, and then she will prove a great obstacle to my departure. I will see the child

after I have become a Buddha." He then instantly shut
the door and left the palace. His charger was waiting for
him. "To your swiftness," said Phralaong to Kantika,
"do I trust for executing my great design. I must become
a Buddha, and labour for the deliverance of men and Nats
from the miseries of existence, and lead them safely to
the peaceful shores of Neibban." In a moment he was on
the back of his favourite horse. Kantika was a magnificent animal; his body measured eighteen cubits in length,
with which his height and circumference were in perfect
proportion. The hair was of a beautiful white, resembling
a newly cleaned shell; his swiftness was unrivalled, and
his neighings could be heard at a very great distance;
but on this occasion the Nats interfered, no sound of his
voice was heard, and the noise of his steps was completely
silenced. Having reached the gate of the city, Phralaong
stopped for a while, uncertain as regarded the course he
was to follow. To open the gate, which a thousand men
could with difficulty cause to turn upon its hinges, was
deemed an impossibility. Whilst he was deliberating
with his faithful attendant Tsanda, the huge gate was
silently opened by the Nats, and a free passage given to him
through it. It was in the year 97 when he left Kapilawot.

Phralaong had scarcely crossed the threshold of the
gate when the tempter endeavoured to thwart his pious
design. Manh [1] Nat resolved to prevent him from retir-

---

[1] Phralaong having overcome with
uncommon fortitude the numberless
obstacles which he had encountered
on the part of men, will have now to
meet another foe, perhaps more formidable, a wicked Nat, or demon.
His name, according to its orthography, is Mar or Mara, but the
Burmese call him Manh, which means
pride. Manh is, therefore, the evil
spirit of pride, or rather personified
pride, and the enemy of mankind,
ever ready to oppose the benevolent
designs and generous efforts of
Buddha in carrying on his great
undertaking, conceived to benefit
humanity, by teaching men the way
that leads to deliverance from all
miseries. The first plan concocted
by Manh for stopping, at the very
outset, the progress of Phralaong,
was to flatter his ambition by promising him *all the kingdoms of this
world and their glory.* From that
day the tempter never lost sight of
the benevolent Buddha, but followed
him everywhere, endeavouring to
prevent the immense success that

ing into solitude and becoming a Buddha. Standing in
the air, he cried aloud, " Prince Theiddat, do not attempt
to lead the life of a recluse ; seven days hence you will
become a Tsekiawaday ; your sway shall extend over the
four great islands ; return forthwith to your palace."
" Who are you ? " replied Phralaong.   " I am Manh Nat,"
cried the voice.   " I know," said Phralaong, " that I can
become a Tsekiawaday, but I feel not the least inclination
for earthly dignities ; my aim is to arrive at the nature of
Buddha."   The tempter, urged onward by his three wicked
propensities, concupiscence, ignorance, and anger, did not
part for a moment from Phralaong ; but as the shadow
always accompanies the body, he too, from that day, always
followed Phralaong, striving to throw every obstacle in
his way towards the dignity of Buddha.   Trampling down
every human and worldly consideration, and despising a
power full of vanity and illusion, Phralaong left the city
of Kapilawot, at the full moon of July under the constellation Oottarathan.   A little while after, he felt a strong
desire to turn round his head and cast a last glance at the
magnificent city he was leaving behind him ; but he soon
overcame that inordinate desire and denied himself this
gratification.   It is said that on the very instant he was
combating the rising sense of curiosity the mighty earth
turned with great velocity, like a potter's wheel, so that
the very object he denied himself the satisfaction of contemplating came of itself under his eyes.   Phralaong
hesitated a while as to the direction he was to follow, but
he resolved instantly to push on straight before him.

His progress through the country resembled a splendid

was to attend his future mission.
The evil propensities which constitute, as it were, the very essence of
Manh's nature, are concupiscence,
envy, and an irresistible proneness to
do harm. The devil indeed could
hardly be made up of worse materials.

It is really interesting through the

course of this Legend to read of the
uninterrupted efforts made by the
personification of evil to thwart
Buddha in all his benevolent designs.
The antagonism begins now, but it
will be maintained with an obstinate
and prolonged activity during the
whole life of Buddha.

triumphal ovation. Sixty thousand Nats marched in front of him, an equal number followed him, and as many surrounded him on his right and on his left. All of them carried lighted torches, pouring a flood of light in every direction; others again spread perfumes and flowers brought from their own seats. All joined in chorus, singing the praises of Phralaong. The sound of their united voices resembled loud peals of continued thunder, and the resounding of the mighty waves at the foot of the Mount Oogando. Flowers, shedding the most fragrant odour, were seen gracefully undulating in the air, like an immense canopy, extending to the farthest limits of the horizon. During that night, Phralaong, attended with that brilliant retinue, travelled a distance of thirty youdzanas, and arrived on the banks of the river Anauma. Turning his face towards Tsanda, he asked what was the river's name. "Anauma is its name," replied his faithful attendant. "I will not," said Phralaong to himself, "show myself unworthy of the high dignity I aspire to." Spurring his horse, the fierce animal leaped at once to the opposite bank. Phralaong alighted on the ground, which was covered with a fine sand resembling pearls, when the rays of the sun fell upon it in the morning. On that spot he divested himself of his dress, and calling Tsanda to him, he directed him to take charge of his ornaments, and carry them back with the horse Kantika to his palace. For himself, he had made up his mind to become a Rahan. "Your servant too," replied Tsanda, "will become also a recluse in your company." "No," said the prince, "the profession of Rahan does not at present befit you." He reiterated this prohibition three times. When he was handing over to Tsanda his costly ornaments, he said to himself, "These long hairs that cover my head, and my beard too, are superfluities unbecoming the profession of Rahan." Whereupon with one hand unsheathing his sword, and with the other seizing his comely hairs, he cut them with a single stroke. What remained of his hairs on the head measured about one inch and a half in length. In like manner he disposed of his beard. From that time he never needed shaving; the hairs of his beard and those of the head never grew longer during the remainder of his life.[2] Holding his hairs and turban together, he cried aloud, " If I am destined to become a Buddha, let these hairs and turban remain suspended in the air; if not, let them drop down on the ground." Throwing up both to the height of one youdzana, they remained suspended in the air, until a Nat came with a rich basket, put them therein, and carried them to the seat of Tawadeintha. He there erected the Dzedi Dzoulamani, wherein they were religiously deposited. Casting his regards on his own person, Phralaong saw that his rich and shining robe did not answer his purpose, nor appear befitting the poor and humble profession he was about to embrace. While his attention was taken up with this consideration, a great Brahma, named Gatigara, who in the days of the Buddha Kathaba had been an intimate friend of our Phralaong, and who, during the period that elapsed between the manifestation of that Buddha to the present time, had not grown old, discovered at once the perplexity of his friend's mind. " Prince Theiddat," said he, " is preparing to become a Rahan, but he is not supplied with the dress and other implements essentially required for his future calling. I will provide him now with the thinbaing, the kowot, the dugout, the patta, the leathern girdle, the hatchet, the needle, and filter.[3] He took with him all

---

[2] This circumstance explains one peculiarity observable in all the statues representing Buddha. The head is invariably covered with sharp points, resembling those thorns with which the thick envelope of the durian fruit is armed. Often I had inquired as to the motive that induced native sculptors to leave on the head of all statues that sort of inverted nails, without ever being able to obtain any satisfactory answer. It was only after having read this passage of the life of Buddha that I was enabled to account for this apparently singular custom, which is designed to remind all Buddhists of the ever-continued wonder whereby the hairs which remained on Buddha's head never grew longer from the day he cut them with his sword.

[3] Every talapoin or recluse must

these articles, and in an instant arrived in the presence of Phralaong, to whom he presented them. Though unacquainted with the details of that dress, and untrained in the use of those new implements, the prince, like a man who had been a recluse during several existences, put on with a graceful gravity his new dress. He adjusted the thinbaing round his waist, covered his body with the kowot, threw the dugout over his shoulders, and suspended to his neck the bag containing the earthen patta. Assuming the grave, meek, and dignified countenance of a Rahan, he called Tsanda and bade him go back to his father and relate to him all that he had seen. Tsanda, complying with his master's request, prostrated himself three times before him; then, rising up, he wheeled to the right and departed. The spirited horse, hearing the last words of Phralaong, could no more control his grief.[4]

be provided with one needle, wherewith he is to sew his dress, one hatchet to cut the wood he may be in need of, either for erecting a shelter for himself or for other purposes, and one filter to strain the water he intends to drink, that it might be cleared from all impurities, but chiefly of insects or any living body that might be in it, which would expose the drinker thereof to the enormous sin of causing the death of some animal.

[4] The various accounts that are given of the horse Kantika, and the grief he feels at parting with his master, grief which reaches so far as to cause his death, may appear somewhat extraordinary, puerile, and ridiculous to every one except to Buddhists. One great principle of that religious system is that man does not differ from animals in nature, but only in relative perfection. In animals there are souls as well as in men, but these souls, on account of the paucity of their merits and the multiplicity of their demerits, are yet in a very imperfect state.

When the law of demerits grows weak, and that of merits gathers strength, the soul, though continuing to inhabit the body of animals, has the knowledge of good and evil, and can attain to a certain degree of perfection. Buddhistic writings supply many instances of this belief. Whilst Buddha was in the desert, an elephant ministered to all his wants. As a reward for such a series of services, Buddha preached to him the law, and led him at once to the deliverance, that is to say, to the state of Neibban. When one animal has progressed so far in the way of merits as to be able to discern between good and bad, it is said that he is ripe, or fit to become man. The horse Kantika seems to have reached that state of full ripeness, since, after his death, he passed to the state of Nat. This peculiar tenet of Buddhistic faith accounts for the first of the five great commands, which extends the formal injunction of "thou shalt not kill" to animals. When a candidate is admitted, according to the prescriptions contained in the sacred

" Alas ! " said he, " I will see no more my master in this world." His sorrow grew so great that his heart split into two parts, and he died on the spot.

After his death, he became a Nat in the seat of Tawadeintha. The affliction of Tsanda at parting with his good master was increased by the death of Kantika. The tears that streamed down his cheeks resembled drops of liquid silver.

Phralaong, having thus begun the life of a recluse, spent seven days alone in a forest of mango trees, enjoying in that retirement the peace and happiness of soul which solitude alone can confer. The place, in the neighbourhood of which he began his religious life, is called Anupyia, in the country belonging to the Malla princes. He then started for the country of Radzagio, travelling on foot a distance of thirty youdzanas. Arrived near the gate of the royal city, Phralaong stopped for a while, saying within himself, " Peimpathara, the king of this country, will no doubt hear of my arrival in this place. Knowing that the son of King Thoodaudana is actually in his own royal city, he will insist upon my accepting all sorts of presents. But now, in my capacity of Rahan, I must decline accepting them, and by the rules of my profession I am bound to go and beg along the streets, from house to house, the food necessary for my support." He instantly resumed his journey, entered the city through the eastern gate, the patta hanging on his side, and followed the first row of houses, receiving the alms which pious hands offered him. At the moment of his arrival the whole city was shaken by a mighty commotion, like that which is felt in the seat of Thoora when the Nat Athoorein makes his apparition in it. The inhabitants, terrified at such an ominous sign, ran in all haste to the palace. Admitted into the presence of the

---

Kambawa, into the order of Rahans, he is expressly and solemnly commanded to refrain from committing four sins, which would deprive him *de facto* of the dignity he has been elevated to. The taking away willingly of the life of anything animated is one of these four trespassings.

monarch, they told him that they knew not what sort of being had just arrived in the city, walking through the streets and begging alms. They could not ascertain whether he was a Nat, a man, or a Galong. The king, looking from his apartments over the city, saw Phralaong, whose meek deportment removed all anxiety from his mind. He, however, directed a few of his noblemen to go and watch attentively all the movements of the stranger. "If he be," said he, "a Bilou, he will soon leave the city and vanish away; if a Nat, he will raise himself in the air; if a Naga, he will plunge to the bottom of the earth." Phralaong, having obtained the quantity of rice, vegetables, &c., he thought sufficient for his meal, left the city through the same gate by which he had entered it, sat down at the foot of a small hill, his face turned towards the east, and tried to make his meal with the things he had received. He could not swallow the first mouthful, which he threw out of his mouth in utter disgust. Accustomed to live sumptuously and feed on the most delicate things, his eyes could not bear even the sight of that loathsome mixture of the coarsest articles of food collected at the bottom of his patta. He soon, however, recovered from that shock; and gathered fresh strength to subdue the opposition of nature, overcome its repugnance, and conquer its resistance. Reproaching himself for such an unbecoming weakness:—"Was I not aware," said he, with a feeling of indignation against himself, "that when I took up the dress of a mendicant such would be my food? The moment is come to trample upon nature's appetites." Whereupon he took up his patta, ate cheerfully his meal, and never afterwards did he ever feel any repugnance at what things soever he had to eat.

The king's messengers, having closely watched and attentively observed all that had happened, returned to their master, to whom they related all the particulars that they had witnessed. "Let my carriage be ready," said the king, "and you, follow me to the place where this stranger is resting." He soon perceived Phralaong at a distance, sit. ting quietly after his refection. Peimpathara alighted from his conveyance, respectfully drew near to Phralaong, and, having occupied a seat in a becoming place, was over- whelmed with contentment and inexpressible joy to such an extent, indeed, that he could scarcely find words to give utterance to his feelings. Having at last recovered from the first impression, he addressed Phralaong in the follow- ing manner :—"Venerable Rahan, you seem to be young still, and in the prime of your life ; in your person you are gifted with the most attractive and noble qualities, indicat- ing surely your illustrious and royal extraction. I have under my control and in my possession a countless crowd of officers, elephants, horses and chariots, affording every desirable convenience for pleasure and amusement of every description. Please to accept of a numerous retinue of attendants, with whom you may enjoy yourself whilst remaining within my dominions. May I be allowed to ask what country you belong to, who you are, and from what illustrious lineage and descent you are come ?" Phralaong said to himself :—"It is evident that the king is un- acquainted with both my name and origin ; I will, how- ever, satisfy him on the subject of his inquiry." Pointing out with his hand in the direction of the place he had come from, he said :—" I arrive from the country which has been governed by a long succession of the descendants of Prince Kothala. I have, indeed, been born from royal progenitors, but I have abandoned all the prerogatives attached to my position, and embraced the profession of Rahan. From my heart I have rooted up concupiscence, covetousness, and all affections to the things of this world." To this the king replied :—"I have heard that Prince Theiddat, son of King Thoodaudana, had seen four great signs, portending his future destiny for the profession of Rahan, which would be but a step to lead him to the exalted dignity of a Buddha. The first part of the prediction has been already fulfilled. When the second shall have received its accomplishment,

I beg you will show your benevolence to me and my people. I hope my kingdom will be the first country you will direct your steps to, after having acquired the supreme science." To this Phralaong graciously assented.

Phralaong, having left the king, resumed his journey, and fell in with a Rathee,[5] or hermit, named Alara, and

---

[5] The fact of Buddha placing himself under the tuition of two masters or teachers, leading an ascetic life, to learn from them notions of the most abstruse nature, establishes, beyond all doubt, the high antiquity of the existence in India of a large number of individuals, who, living in some retired spot, far from the tumult of society, endeavoured, by constant application, to dive into the deepest recesses of morals and metaphysics. The fame of the learning of many among them attracted to their solitude crowds of disciples, anxious to study under such eminent masters. Hence we see some of these Rathees at the head of four or five hundred disciples. There is no doubt that the most distinguished Rathees became the founders of many of those philosophico-religious schools for which India was renowned from the remotest antiquity. Like many others who thirsted for knowledge, Phralaong resorted to the schools of the Rathees, as to the then most celebrated seats of learning.

From this fact we may be allowed to draw another inference, which may be considered as a consequence of what has been stated in a foregoing note, regarding the superior antiquity of Brahminism over Buddhism. Phralaong was brought up in the bosom of a society regulated and governed by Brahminical institutions. He must have been imbued from the earliest days of his elementary education with the notions generally taught, viz.: the Brahminical ones. When he grew up and began to think for him-

self, he was displeased with certain doctrines which did not tally with his own ideas. Following the example of many that had preceded him in the way of innovation, he boldly shaped his course in a new direction, and soon arrived at a final issue on many points, both with his teachers and some of the doctrines generally received in the society in which he had been brought up. We may, therefore, safely conclude that the doctrines supposed to have been preached by the latest Buddha are but an off-shoot of Brahminism. This may serve to account for the great resemblance subsisting between many doctrines of both creeds. The cardinal points on which these two systems essentially differ are the beginning and the end of living beings. Between these two extremes there is a multitude of points on which both systems so perfectly agree that they appear blended together.

The Rathees seem, according to the institutes of Menoo, to have been first in observing two practices, much enforced by the Wini in subsequent times. They were supported by the alms bestowed on them by their disciples and the admirers of their singular mode of life. They were courted and esteemed by the world, in proportion to the contempt they appeared to hold it in. Denying to themselves the pleasures which were opposed to their austere life, they observed, as long as they remained Rathees, the rules of the strictest celibacy.

Phralaong, preparing himself for

inquired about the several Dzans. Alara satisfied him on four kinds of Dzans, but as regards the fifth, he was obliged to refer him to another Rathee, named Oudaka, who gave him the necessary explanations. Having nothing more to learn from these masters, Phralaong said to himself, " The knowledge I have thus acquired is not sufficient to enable me to obtain the dignity of Buddha." Whereupon he resolved to devote himself to the Kamatan[6] or meditation on the instability and nothingness of

---

his future high calling, began to study the science of *Dzan* under distinguished masters. What is meant by Dzan? This Pali word means thought, reflection, meditation. It is often designed by the Burmese to mean a peculiar state of the soul that has already made great progress in the way of perfection. Phralaong intended, by placing himself under the direction of those eminent teachers, to learn the great art of training his mind for the obtaining, by constant and well-directed meditations, of high mental attainments. In the book of Buddhistic metaphysics, I have found the science of Dzan divided into five parts, or rather five steps, which the mind has to ascend successively ere it can enjoy a state of perfect quiescence, the highest point a perfected being can arrive at before reaching the state of Neibban. In the first step the soul searches after what is good and perfect, and having discovered it, turns its attention and the energy of its faculties towards it. In the second, the soul begins to contemplate steadily what it has first discovered, and rivets upon it its attention. In the third stage, the soul fondly relishes, and is, as it were, entirely taken with it. In the fourth, the soul calmly enjoys and quietly feasts on the pure truths it has loved in the former state. In the fifth, the soul, perfectly satiated with the knowledge of truth, remains in a

state of complete quietude, perfect fixity, unmoved stability, which nothing can any longer alter or disturb. The Burmese and all Buddhists, always fond of what is wonderful, attribute supernatural perfections to those who have so far advanced in mental attainments. Their bodies become, as it were, half-spiritualised, so that they can, according to their wishes, carry themselves through the air from one place to another, without the least hindrance or difficulty.

[6] Kamatan means the fixing of the attention on one object, so as to investigate thoroughly all its constituent parts, its principle and origin, its existence and its final destruction. It is that part of metaphysics which treats of the beginning, nature, and end of beings. To become proficient in that science, a man must be gifted with a most extensive knowledge and an analysing mind of no common cast. The process of Kamatan is as follows. Let it be supposed that man intends to contemplate one of the four elements, fire, for instance; he abstracts himself from every object which is not fire, and devotes all his attention to the contemplation of that object alone; he examines the nature of fire, and finding it a compound of several distinct parts, he investigates the cause or causes that keep those parts together, and soon discovers that they are but accidental ones, the action whereof may be impeded or destroyed

all that exists. To effectuate thoroughly his purpose, he repaired to the solitude of Oorouwela, where he devoted all his time to the deepest meditation. On a certain day it happened that five Rahans, on their way to a certain place to get their food, arrived at the spot where Phralaong lived and had already entered on the course of his penitential deeds. They soon became impressed with the idea that our hermit was to become a Buddha. They resolved to stay with him and render him all the needful services, such as sweeping the place, cooking rice, &c.

---

by the occurrence of any sudden accident. He concludes that fire has but a fictitious ephemeral existence. The same method is followed in examining the other elements, and gradually all other things he may come in contact with, and his final conclusion is, that all things placed without him are destitute of real existence, being mere illusions, divested of all reality. He infers, again, that all things are subjected to the law of incessant change, without fixity or stability. The wise man, therefore, can feel no attachment to objects which, in his own opinion, are but illusions and deception : his mind can nowhere find rest in the midst of illusions always succeeding to each other. Having surveyed all that is distinct of self, he applies himself to the work of investigating the origin and nature of his body. After a lengthened examination, he arrives, as a matter of course, at the same conclusion. His body is a mere illusion without reality, subjected to changes and destruction. He feels that it is as yet distinct from self. He despises his body, as he does everything else, and has no concern for it. He longs for the state of Neibban, as the only one worthy of the wise man's earnest desire. By such a preliminary step, the student, having estranged himself from this world of illusions, advances towards the study of the excellent works which will pave the way to Neibban. The Burmese reckon forty Kamatana. They are often repeated over by devotees, whose weak intellect is utterly incapable of understanding the meaning they are designed to convey to the mind.

Notwithstanding his singular aptitude in acquiring knowledge, Phralaong devoted six whole years, in the solitude of Oorouwela, busily engaged in mastering the profound science he aimed at acquiring. It was during that time that he received the visits of five Rahans, whose chief was named Koondanha. They were very probably, like so many of their profession, travelling about in search of knowledge. They placed themselves under the direction of Phralaong, and in exchange for the lessons they received from him, they served him as humble and grateful disciples are wont to attend on a highly esteemed teacher. In this, as well as many other circumstances, we see that, previous to Gaudama's preachings, there already existed in India an order of devotees or enthusiasts, who lived secluded from the world, devoted to the study of religious doctrines and the practice of virtues of the highest order. The order of Buddhistic monks or talapoins, which was subsequently established by the author of Buddhism, is but a modification of what actually subsisted in full vigour in his own country and in his own time.

The time for the six years of meditation was nearly over, when Phralaong undertook a great fast,[7] which was carried to such a degree of abstemiousness that he scarcely allowed to himself the use of a grain of rice or sesame a day, and finally denied himself even that feeble pittance. But the Nats, who observed his excessive mortification, inserted Nat food through the pores of his skin. Whilst Phralaong was thus undergoing such a severe fasting, his face, which was of a beautiful gold colour, became black; the thirty-two marks indicative of his future dignity disappeared. On a certain day, when he was walking in a much enfeebled state, on a sudden he felt an extreme weakness, similar to that caused by a dire starvation. Unable to stand up any longer, he fainted and fell on the ground. Among the Nats that were present, some said, " The Rahan Gaudama is dead indeed; " some others replied, " He is not dead, but has fainted from want of food." Those who believed he was dead hastened to his father's palace to convey to him the sad message of his son's death. Thoodaudana inquired if his son died previous to his becoming a Buddha. Having been answered in the affirmative, he refused to give credit to the words of the Nats. The reason of his doubting the accuracy of the report was, that

---

[7] In a Buddhistic point of view the only reason that may be assigned for the extraordinary fast of Phralaong is the satisfaction of showing to the world the display of wonderful action. Fastings and other works of mortification have always been much practised by the Indian philosophers of past ages, who thereby attracted the notice, respect, admiration, and veneration of the world. Such rigorous exercises, too, were deemed of great help for enabling the soul to have a more perfect control over the senses, and subjecting them to the empire of reason. They are also conducive towards the calm and undisturbed state in which the soul is better fitted for the arduous task of constant meditation. The fast of Gaudama, preparatory to his obtaining the Buddhaship, recalls to mind that which our Lord underwent ere He began His divine mission. If the writer, in the course of this work, has made once or twice a remark of similar import, he has done so, not with the intention of drawing a parallel as between facts, but to communicate to the reader the feelings of surprise and astonishment he experienced when he thought he met with circumstances respecting the founder of Buddhism which apparently bore great similarity to some connected with the mission of our Saviour.

he had witnessed the great wonders prognosticating his son's future dignity that had taken place, first when Phralaong, then an infant, was placed in the presence of a famous Rathee, and secondly, when he slept under the shade of the tree Tsampoo-thabia. The fainting being over, and Phralaong having recovered his senses, the same Nats went in all haste to Thoodaudana, to inform him of his son's happy recovery. "I knew well," said the king, "that my son could not die ere he had become a Buddha." The fame of Phralaong's having spent six years in solitude, addicted to meditation and mortification, spread abroad like the sound of a great bell,[8] hung in the canopy of the skies.

---

[8] Bells are common in Burmah, and the people of that country are well acquainted with the art of casting them. Most of the bells to be seen in the pagodas are of small dimensions, and differing in shape somewhat from those used in Europe. The inferior part is less widened, and there is a large hole in the centre of the upper part. No tongue is hung in the interior, but the sound is produced by striking with a horn of deer or elk the outward surface of the lower part. No belfry is erected for the bells; they are fixed on a piece of timber, laid horizontally, and supported at its two extremities by two posts, at such a height that the inferior part of the bell is raised about five feet above the ground.

The largest specimens of Burmese art in casting bells of great weight are the two bells to be seen, the one in the large pagoda of Rangoon, called Shway Dagon, and the other at Mingon, about twelve or fifteen miles north of Amerapoura, on the western bank of the Irrawaddy. The first, in the town of Rangoon, was cast in 1842, when King Tharawaddy visited the place, with the intention of founding a new city, more distant from the river, and nearer to the mount upon which rises the splendid Shway Dagon. In its shape and form it exactly resembles the kind of bells above described. Here are some particulars respecting that large piece of metal, collected from the inscription to be seen upon it. It was cast on the fifth day of the full moon of Tabodwai (February), 1203 of the Burmese era. The weight of metal is 94,682 lbs.; its height 9½ cubits; its diameter 5 cubits; its thickness 20 fingers or 15 inches. But during the process of melting, the well-disposed came forward and threw in copper, silver, and gold in great quantities. It is supposed, says the writer of the inscription, that in this way the weight was increased one-fourth.

The bell of Mingon was cast in the beginning of this century. In shape and form it resembles our bells in Europe. It is probable that some foreigner residing at Ava suggested the idea of giving such an unusual form to that monumental bell. Its height is 18 feet, besides 7 feet for hanging apparatus. It has 17 feet in diameter, and from 10 to 12 inches in thickness. Its weight is supposed to exceed two hundred thousand English pounds.

In the interior large yellowish and

Phralaong soon remarked that fasting and mortification were not works of sufficient value for obtaining the dignity of Buddha; he took up his patta and went to the neighbouring village to get his food. Having eaten it, he grew stronger; his beautiful face shone again like gold, and the thirty-two signs reappeared.[9] The five Rahans that had lived with him said to each other—" It is in vain that the Rahan Gaudama has, during six years of mortification and

---

greyish streaks indicate that considerable quantities of gold and silver had been thrown in during the process of melting. No idea can at present be had of the power of the sound of that bell, as its enormous weight has caused the pillars that support it partially to give way. To prevent a fatal disaster, the orifice of the bell has been made to rest on large short posts, sunk in the ground and rising about three feet above it. In no respect can these bells bear any comparison with those of Europe. They are mightily rough and rude attempts at doing works on a scale far surpassing the abilities of native workmen, who otherwise succeed tolerably well in casting the comparatively small bells commonly met with in the courtyards of pagodas.

[9] One of the genuine characters of Buddhism is correctly exhibited in this observation of Phralaong's respecting fasts, mortifications, and other self-inflicted penances. They are not looked upon as the immediate way leading to perfection, nor as *a portion* or a part of perfection itself. Such deeds are but means resorted to for weakening passions and increasing the power of the spiritual principle over the natural one : they are preparatory to the great work of meditation or the study of truth, which is the only high-road to perfection. To the sage that has already begun the laborious task of investigating truth, such practices are of no use, and are nowhere insisted on as

necessary, or even useful. In the book of discipline, no mention is made of them. The life of the initiated is one of self-denial; all superfluities and luxuries are strictly interdicted ; all that is calculated to minister to passions and pleasure is carefully excluded. But the great austerities and macerations practised by the religious of the Brahminical sect are at once rejected by the Buddhist sages as unprofitable and unnecessary to them. The inmates of the Buddhist monasteries in our days are never seen indulging in those cruel, disgusting, and unnatural practices performed from ‸time immemorial by some of their brethren of the Hindu persuasion. This constitutes one of the principal differences or discrepancies between the two systems. With the founder of Buddhism fasts and penitential deeds are of great concern to him who is as yet in the world, living under the tyrannical yoke of passions and the influence of the senses. By him they are viewed as powerful auxiliaries in the spiritual warfare for obtaining the mastery over passions. This point once gained, the sage can at once dispense with their aid as being no longer required. The follower of the Hindu creed looks upon those practices as *per se* eminently meritorious and capable of leading him to perfection; hence the mania for carrying those observances to a degree revolting to reason, and even to the plain good sense of the people.

sufferings, sought the dignity of Buddha; he is now compelled to go out in search of food; assuredly, if he be
obliged to live on such food, when shall he ever become a
Buddha? He goes out in quest of food; verily, he aims
at enriching himself. As the man that wants drops of
dew or water to refresh and wash his forehead, has to look
for them, so we have to go somewhere else to learn the
way to, and the merit of, Dzan, which we have not been
able to obtain from him." Whereupon they left Phralaong, took up their pattas and tsiwarans, went to a distance of eighteen youdzanas, and withdrew into the forest
of Migadawon, near Baranathee.

CHAPTER V.

AT that time, in the solitude of Oorouwela, there lived in a village a rich man, named Thena. He had a daughter named Thoodzata. Having attained the years of puberty, she repaired to a place where there was a gniaong tree, and made the following prayer to the Nat guardian of the place[1]:—" If I marry a husband that will prove a suitable

---

[1] The Nats or Dewatas play a conspicuous part in the affairs of this world. Their seats are in the six lower heavens, forming, with the abode of man and the four states of punishment, the eleven seats of passions. But they often quit their respective places, and interfere with the chief events that take place among men. Hence we see them ever attentive in ministering to all the wants of the future Buddha. Besides, they are made to watch over trees, forests, villages, towns, cities, fountains, rivers, &c. These are the good and benevolent Nats. This world is also supposed to be peopled with wicked Nats, whose nature is ever prone to the evil. A good deal of the worship of Buddhists consists in superstitious ceremonies and offerings made for propitiating the wicked Nats, and obtaining favours and temporal advantages from the good ones. Such a worship is universal, and fully countenanced by the talapoins, though in opposition to the real doctrines of genuine Buddhism. All kinds of misfortunes are attributed to the malignant interference of the evil Nats. In cases of severe illness that have resisted the skill of native medical art, the physician gravely tells the patient and his relatives that it is useless to have recourse any longer to medicines, but a conjuror must be sent for to drive out the malignant spirit, who is the author of the complaint. Meanwhile directions are given for the erection of a shed, where offerings intended for the inimical Nat are deposited. A female relative of the patient begins dancing to the sound of musical instruments. The dance goes on, at first in rather a quiet manner, but it gradually grows more animated until it reaches the acme of animal frenzy.

.match, and the first fruit of our union be a male child, I will spend annually in alms deeds 100,000 pieces of silver, and make an offering at this spot." Her prayer was heard,

---

At that moment the bodily strength of the dancing lady becomes exhausted; she drops on the ground in a state of apparent faintness. She is then approached by the conjuror, who asks her if the invisible foe has relinquished his hold over the diseased. Being answered in the affirmative, he bids the physician give medicines to the patient, assuring him that his remedies will now act beneficially for restoring the health of the sick, since their action will meet no further opposition from the wicked Nat.

Ignorance brings everywhere superstition in its train. When man is unacquainted with the natural cause that has produced a result, or an effect, which attracts powerfully his mind's attention and affects him to a great degree, he is induced by his own weakness to believe in the agency of some unknown being, to account for the effect that he perceives. He devises the most ridiculous means for expressing his gratitude to his invisible benefactor, if the result be a favourable one; and has recourse to the most extravagant measures to counteract the evil influence of his supposed enemy, if the result be fatal to him. Having once entered into the dark way of superstition, man is hurried on in countless false directions by fear, hope, and other passions, in the midst of the daily occurrence of multifarious and unforeseen events and circumstances. Hence the expression or manifestation of his superstition assumes a variety of forms, and undergoes changes to an extent that baffles every attempt at either counting their numberless kinds or following them up through their ever-changing course. In addition to the stores of superstitions bequeathed by the generation that has preceded him, man has those of his own creation; and the latter, if the thought of his mind and the desires of his heart could be analysed, would be found far exceeding the former in number. Having spent many years in a country where Buddhism has prevailed from time immemorial, and observed the effects of superstition over the people in their daily doings, the writer has come to the conclusion that there is scarcely an action done without the influence of some superstitious motive or consideration. But the most prolific source of superstition is the belief in the existence of countless good and evil Nats, with whom the imagination of Buddhists has peopled this world.

It can scarcely be understood how the followers of an atheistical creed can make, consistently with their opinions, an attempt at prayer. Such an act of devotion implies the belief in a being superior to men, who has a controlling power over them, and in whose hands their destinies are placed. With a believer in God, prayer is a sacred, nay, a natural duty. But such cannot be the case with atheists. Despite the withering and despairing influence of atheism, nothing can possibly obliterate from the conscience and heart of man that inward faith in a supreme being. The pious Thoodzata has in view the attainment of two objects: she prays, without knowing to whom, that by the agency of some one she might obtain the objects of her petition; she is anxious to show her gratitude when she sees that her prayer has been heard. Her faith in the *quasi* omnipotence of the genii makes her address thanks to them. The Nat is

and its twofold object granted. When Phralaong had ended the six years of his fasting and mortification, on the day of the full moon of the month Katson, Thoodzata was preparing to make her grateful offering to the Nat of the place. She had been keeping one thousand cows in a place abounding with sweet vines; the milk of those thousand was given to five hundred cows; these again fed with their own milk two hundred and fifty others, and so on, in a diminishing proportion, until it happened that sixteen cows fed eight others with their milk. So these eight cows gave a milk, rich, sweet, and flavoured beyond all description.

On the day of the full moon of Katson,[2] Thoodzata rose at an early hour to make ready her offering, and disposed everything that the cows should be simultaneously milked. When they were to be milked, the young calves of their own accord kept at a distance; and as soon as the vessels were brought near, the milk began to flow in streams from

---

not the person to whom her prayer appears directed, but he is rather a witness of her petition. The Burmese, in general, under difficult circumstances, unforeseen difficulties, and sudden calamities, use always the cry, *Phra kaiba* — God assist me — to obtain from above assistance and protection. Yet that Phra cannot be their Buddha, though he be in their opinion the Phra *par excellence*, since they openly declare that he in no way interferes in the management of this world's affairs. Whence that involuntáry cry for assistance, but from the innate consciousness that above man there is some one ruling over his destinies? An atheistical system may be elaborated in a school of metaphysics, and forced upon ignorant and unreflecting masses, but practice will ever belie theory. Man, in spite of his errors and follies, is naturally a believing being; his own weakness and multiplied wants ever compel

him to have recourse to some great being that can help and assist him, and supply, to a certain extent, the deficiency which, in spite of himself, he is compelled to acknowledge existing in him as a stern and humiliating reality.

[2] The Burmese, like all transGangetic nations, divide the year into twelve lunar months of twenty-nine and thirty days alternately. Every third year they add one month, or as they say, double the month of Watso (July). The year begins on, or about, the 12th of April. The days of worship are the days of the four quarters of the moon; but the days of the new and full moon seem to have preference over those of the two other quarters, which latter are scarcely noticed or distinguished from common days. It was on the day of the full moon of April that Thoodzata made her grand offering.

the udders into the vessels. She took the milk and poured it into a large caldron, set on the fire which she had herself kindled. The milk began to boil; bubbles formed on the surface of the liquid, turned on the right and sunk in, not a single drop being spilt out; no smoke arose from the fireplace. Four kings of Nats watched about while the caldron was boiling; the great Brahma kept open an umbrella over it; a Thagia brought fuel and fed the fire. Other Nats, by their supernatural power, infused honey into the milk, and communicated thereto a flavour, such as the like is not to be found in the abode of men. On this occasion alone, and on the day Phralaong entered the state of Neibban, the Nats infused honey into his food. Wondering at the so many extraordinary signs which she saw, Thoodzata called her female slave, named Sounama, related to her all that she had observed, and directed her to go to the gniaong tree, and clear the place where she intended to make her offering. The servant, complying with her mistress' direction, soon arrived at the foot of the tree.

On that very night Phralaong had had five dreams.[3]

---

[3] The Burmese translator, not having given in his remarks the explanation or interpretation of Phralaong's five dreams, it seems rather presumptuous to attempt doing a thing, the neglect of which, on the part of the author, may be attributed either to voluntary omission or to incapacity and inability. Let us try to make up, in part, for the deficiency. The first dream prognosticated the future greatness of Phralaong, whose sway, by the diffusion of his doctrines throughout the world, was to be universal, extending from one sea to the other sea. The grass growing out of his navel and reaching to the sky was indicative of the spreading of his law, not only amongst the beings inhabiting the seat of men, but also amidst those dwelling in the abodes of Nats and Brahmas. The ants covering his legs offer an enigma, the explanation of which is reserved to some future Œdipus. As to the birds of various colours, gathering round him, from the four points of the compass, and on a sudden becoming all white, by their contact with him, they represent the innumerable beings that will come to hear the preaching of the future Buddha with divers dispositions, and different progress in the way of merits, and will all be perfected by their following the true way to merit, that he will point out to them. The fifth dream in which Phralaong thought he was walking on a mountain of filth, without being in the least contaminated by it, foreshowed the incomparable perfection and purity of Buddha, who, though remaining in the world of passions, was no more to be affected by their influence.

1st, It appeared to him that the earth was his sleeping place, with the Himawonta for his pillow. His right hand rested on the western ocean, his left on the eastern ocean, and his feet on the southern ocean. 2d, A kind of grass, named Tyria, appeared to grow out of his navel and reach to the skies. 3d, Ants of a white appearance ascended from his feet to the knee and covered his legs. 4th, Birds of varied colour and size appeared to come from all directions and fall at his feet, when, on a sudden, they all appeared white. 5th, It seemed to him that he was walking on a mountain of filth, and that he passed over it without being in the least contaminated.

Phralaong, awaking from his sleep, said to himself, after having reflected for a while on those five dreams,—"To-day I shall certainly become a Buddha." Thereupon he rose instantly, washed his hands and face, put on his dress, and quietly waited the break of day, to go out in quest of his food. The moment being arrived to go out, he took up his patta, and walked in the direction of the gniaong tree. The whole tree was made shining by the rays which issued from his person; he rested there for a while. At that very moment arrived Sounama, to clear, according to her mistress' orders, the place for her offering. As she approached, she saw Phralaong at the foot of the tree. The rays of light which beamed out of his person were reflected on the tree, which exhibited a most splendid and dazzling appearance. On observing this wonder, Sounama said to herself: "Of course the Nat has come down from the tree to receive the offering with his own hands." Overcome with an unutterable joy, she immediately ran to her mistress and related her adventure. Thoodzata was delighted at this occurrence, and wishing to give a substantial proof of her gratitude for such good news, she said to Sounama: "From this moment you are no more my servant; I adopt you for my elder daughter." She gave her instantly all the ornaments suitable to her new position. It is customary for all the l'hralaongs to be provided, on the day they are to become Buddha, with a gold cup of an immense value. Thoodzata ordered a golden vessel to be brought, and poured therein the nogana or boiled milk. As the water glides from the leaf of the water-lily without leaving thereon any trace, so the nogana slided from the pot into the golden cup and filled it up. She covered this cup with another of the same precious metal, and wrapped up the whole with a white cloth. She forthwith put on her finest dress, and, becomingly attired, she carried the golden cup over her head; and with a decent gravity walked towards the gniaong tree. Overwhelmed with joy at seeing Phralaong, she reverentially advanced towards him, whom she mistook for a Nat. When near him, she placed gently the golden vessel on the ground, and offered him in a gold basin scented water to wash his hands. At that moment, the earthen patta offered to Phralaong by the Brahma Gatikara disappeared. Perceiving that his patta had disappeared, he stretched forth his right hand, and washed it in the scented water; at the same time Thoodzata presented to him the golden cup containing the nogana. Having observed that she had caught the eyes of Phralaong, she said to him: "My Lord Nat, I beg to offer you this food, together with the vessel that contains it." Having respectfully bowed down to him, she continued: "May your joy and happiness be as great as mine; may you always delight in the happiest rest, ever surrounded by a great and brilliant retinue." Making then the offering of the gold cup, worth 100,000 pieces of silver, with the same disinterestedness as if she had given over only the dry leaf of a tree, she withdrew and returned to her home with a heart overflowing with joy.

Phralaong rising up took with him the golden cup, and having turned to the left of the gniaong tree, went to the bank of the river Neritzara, to a place where more than 100,000 Buddhas had bathed, ere they obtained the supreme intelligence. On the banks of that river is a bathing-place. Having left on that spot his golden cup, he undressed himself, and descended into the river. When he had bathed, he came out and put on his yellow robe, which in shape and form resembled that of his predecessors. He sat down, his face turned towards the east; his face resembled in appearance a well-ripe palm fruit. He divided his exquisite food into forty-nine mouthfuls, which he ate entire, without mixing any water with it. During forty-nine days he spent round the Bodi tree, Buddha never bathed, nor took any food, nor experienced the least want. His appearance and countenance remained unchanged; he spent the whole time absorbed, as it were, in an uninterrupted meditation. Holding up in his hands the empty golden vessel, Phralaong made the following prayer: "If on this day I am to become a Buddha, let this cup float on the water and ascend the stream." Whereupon he flung it into the stream, when, by the power and influence of Phralaong's former good works, the vessel, gently gliding towards the middle of the river, and then beating up the stream, ascended it with the swiftness of a horse to the distance of eighty cubits, when it stopped, sunk into a whirlpool, went down to the country of Naga, and made a noise, on coming in contact with and striking against the three vessels of the three last Buddhas, viz.: Kaukathan, Gaunagong, and Kathaba. On hearing this unusual noise, the chief of Nagas awoke from his sleep, and said: "How is this? yesterday, a Buddha appeared in the world; today, again, there is another." And in more than one hundred stanzas he sung praises to Buddha.

On the banks of the river Neritzara there is a grove of Sala trees, whither Phralaong repaired to spend the day under their cooling shade. In the evening he rose up and walked with the dignified and noble bearing of a lion, in a road eight oothabas wide, made by the Nats, and strewed with flowers, towards the gniaong tree. The Nats, Nagas, and Galongs joined in singing praises to him, playing instruments, and making offerings of the finest flowers and most exquisite perfumes, brought from their own seats. The same rejoicings took place in ten thousand other worlds. Whilst on his way towards the tree, he met with a young man, just returning with a grass-load he had cut in the fields. Foreseeing that Phralaong might require some portion of it for his use, he presented him an offering of eight handfuls of grass, which were willingly accepted.

Arrived close to the gniaong tree,[4] Phralaong stopped

---

[4] We have now reached the most interesting episode of Phralaong's life. He is to become a perfected Buddha under the shade of the gniaong or banyan tree (*ficus indica, ficus religiosa*). There are two circumstances attending that great event, deserving peculiar notice. The first is the preference given to the east over the three other points of the compass, and the second, the mighty combat that takes place between Phralaong and the wicked Nat Manh, or Mar. I notice the first circumstance because it agrees with the tradition prevailing amongst most nations previous to or about the coming of our Lord, that from the east there was to come an extraordinary personage, who would confer on the human race the greatest benefits, and cause the return of happy times, like the golden age so much celebrated by poets. The Roman historian Suetonius bears testimony to the existence of that tradition as being universally known in his own days. It is not impossible that the same notion, not unknown in the far east, might have induced Phralaong to look towards the east at the supreme moment when perfect intelligence was to become his happy lot. It may be said in opposition to this supposition, that the splendour and magnificence of the sun, emerging from the bosom of night, and dispelling darkness by pouring a flood of light on the face of the earth, restoring nature to life and action, was a sufficient inducement to Phralaong

for giving preference to the east. But to an ascetic like him, who is convinced that this world is a mere illusion, such a consideration would weigh very little on his mind, and would not be a sufficient motive to induce him to give so marked a preference to the east.

The second circumstance remarkable for the time it occurred, is the great combat between Phralaong and Manh. The first is the personification of goodness and benevolence towards all beings; the second is the personification of consummate wickedness. The contest is to take place between the good principle on the one hand, and the evil one on the other. Phralaong, on his becoming Buddha, will preach a law designed to dispel mental darkness, to check vicious passions, to show the right way to perfection, to unloose the ties that keep beings in the wretched state of existence, and enable them to reach safely the peaceful shores of Neibban. Manh, the devil himself, the father of darkness, of lies and deceit, delights in seeing all beings plunged into the abyss of vices, carried out of the right way by the impetuous and irresistible torrent of their passions, and doomed to turn for ever in the whirlpool of endless existences. He looks upon himself as the king of this world, and proudly exults in contemplating all beings bending their neck under his tyrannical yoke, and acknowledging his undisputed power. Now the moment approaches when a

at the south of the tree, his face turned towards the north, when, on a sudden, the southern point of the globe seemed to lower down to the hell Awidzi, the lowest of all, whilst

mighty antagonist will contend with him for the empire of the world. His mission will be to labour incessantly for the delivery of all beings from the grasp of their mortal enemy, and set them free from the tyranny of passions. Manh is enraged at the audacious pretensions of Phralaong. Hence the gigantic efforts he makes to maintain his rights, and retain possession of his empire. At the time Phralaong left the world to become a Rahan, Manh endeavoured to dissuade him from attempting such a design. But on this occasion, the tempter summons all his forces to avert, by an irresistible attack, the deadly blow soon to be levelled at him. It is needless to add that the reader, in perusing the detailed account of the attack of Manh against Phralaong, ought to bear in mind that it exhibits throughout but an allegory of the opposition of evil to good. The victory of Phralaong over Manh exemplifies the final triumph of truth over error.

When the contest was nearly over, Phralaong objected to the claims of Manh to the possession of his throne, on the ground that he never had practised the ten great virtues, nor performed works of kindness, charity, and benevolence, which alone can entitle a being to obtain the Buddhaship. It is to be borne in mind that these qualifications form the real characteristics of a Buddha, together with the possession of the supreme intelligence. In this system, they admit that there exist certain beings called Pitzega-Buddhas, who possess all the knowledge and science of a genuine Buddha, but as they are divested of those benevolent feelings, which induce the former to labour earnestly for the benefit and salvation of all beings, they cannot be

assimilated to the real Buddhas. The cross-legged position which our Buddha is always taken in preference to any other, whilst he spent forty-nine days at the foot of and in various places round the Bodi tree, is, as every one knows, peculiar to and a favourite with all Asiatics. But with him, it is the fittest position for meditation and contemplation. Hence most of the statues or images of Gaudama exhibit or represent him in the cross-legged position which he occupied when he attained the Buddhaship. As this event is by far the most important of his life, it is but natural that this great occurrence should ever be forced upon the attention and memory of his followers, by objects representing him on that most important stage of his last existence. It is not unusual to meet with statues of Gaudama, sometimes of colossal dimensions, representing him in a reclining position. This is the peculiar situation he occupied when he died. Hence those two most common images of Gaudama are designed to remind his followers of the two greatest circumstances of his life, viz., his becoming Buddha, and his entering the state of Neibban.

Here again one is forcibly compelled to reflect on the singular *rôle* attributed to those Pitzega Buddhas. They possess all the science of a Buddha, but are deficient in that kindness, benevolence, and zeal which prompt the real Buddhas to labour so strenuously for the deliverance of all beings. They appear only in those ages of darkness and ignorance which are not to be brightened and enlightened by the presence of a Buddha. They are like smaller luminaries, shedding a pale light among men, to prevent their sinking into an unthe northern one appeared to reach the sky. Then he said, "Verily this is not the place where I shall become a Buddha." Thence Phralaong went on his right side towards the east of the tree, and standing up, his face turned towards the west, he said, "This is indeed the place where all the preceding Buddhas have obtained the supreme intelligence. Here, too, is the very spot whereupon I shall become a Buddha, and set up my throne." He took, by one of their extremities, the eight handfuls of grass and scattered them on the ground, when, on a sudden, there appeared emerging, as it were, from the bottom of the earth, a throne fourteen cubits high, adorned with the choicest sculptures and paintings, superior in perfection to all that art could produce. Phralaong, then facing the east, uttered the following imprecation: "If I am not destined to become a Buddha, may my bones, veins, and skin remain on this throne, and my blood and flesh be dried up." He then ascended the throne, with his back turned against the tree, and his face towards the east. He sat down in a cross-legged position, firmly resolved never to vacate the throne, ere he had become a Buddha. Such firmness of purpose, which the combined elements could not shake for a moment, no one ought to think of ever becoming possessed of.

Whilst Phralaong was sitting on the throne in that cross-legged position, Manh Nat said to himself, "I will not suffer Prince Theiddat to overstep the boundaries of my empire." He summoned all his warriors and shouted to them. On hearing their chief's voice, the warriors gathered thick round his person. His countless followers

---

fathomable abyss of ignorance ; they maintain on earth some sparks of the knowledge of fundamental truths, which otherwise would be completely obliterated from the memory of men. Not unlike the prophets of old, they prepare men in an indirect manner for the coming of the future deliverer. Their mission being at an end, when a Buddha is to come among men, they disappear, and none of them is to be seen either in the days of Buddha or during all the time his religion is to last.

in front, on his right and on his left, reached to the distance of eighteen youdzanas, and above him to that of nine only. Behind him, they extended to the very limits of the world. The cries of that immense multitude were re-echoed at a distance of ten thousand youdzanas, and resembled the roaring of the mighty sea. Manh Nat rode the elephant Girimegala, measuring in length five youdzanas. Supplied with one thousand right arms, he wielded all sorts of the most deadly weapons. His countless warriors, to avoid confusion, were all disposed in ranks, bearing their respective armour. They appeared like immense clouds, slowly rolling on and converging towards Phralaong.

At that time, Nats surrounded Phralaong, singing praises to him; the chief Thagia was playing on his conch, whereof a single blowing resounds for four entire months; the chief Naga was uttering stanzas in his honour; a chief Brahma held over him the white umbrella. On the approach of Manh Nat's army, they were all seized with an uncontrollable fear, and fled to their respective places. The Naga dived into the bottom of the earth, to a depth of five hundred youdzanas, and covering his face with his two wings, fell into a deep sleep. The Thagia, swinging his conch upon his shoulders, ran to the extremity of the world. The Brahma, holding still the umbrella by the extremity of the handle, went up to his own country. Phralaong was, therefore, left alone. Manh Nat, turning to his followers, cried to them, "There is, indeed, no one equal to the Prince Theiddat; let us not attack him in front, but let us assail him from the north side."

At that moment, Phralaong, lifting his eyes, looked on his right, left, and front, for the crowd of Nats, Brahmas, and Thagias that were paying him their respects. But they had all disappeared. He saw the army of Manh Nat coming thick upon him from the north, like a mighty storm. "What!" said he, "is it against me alone that such a countless crowd of warriors has been assembled? I have no one to help me, no father, no brothers, no sisters, no friends, and no relatives. But I have with me the ten great virtues which I have practised; the merits I have acquired in the practice of these virtues will be my safeguard and protection; these are my offensive and defensive weapons, and with them I will crush down the great army of Manh." Whereupon he quietly remained meditating upon the merits of the ten great virtues.

Whilst Phralaong was thus absorbed in meditation, Manh Nat began his attack upon him. He caused a wind to blow with such an extraordinary violence that it brought down the tops of mountains, though they were one or two youdzanas thick. The trees of the forests were shattered to atoms. But the virtue of Phralaong's merits preserved him from the destructive storm. His tsiwaran itself was not agitated. Perceiving that his first effort was useless, Manh caused a heavy rain to fall with such violence that it tore the earth, and opened it to its very bottom. But not even a single drop touched Phralaong's person. To this succeeded a shower of rocks, accompanied with smoke and fire; but they were changed into immense masses of flowers, which dropped at Buddha's feet. There came afterwards another shower of swords, knives, and all kinds of cutting weapons, emitting smoke and fire. They all fell powerless at the feet of Phralaong. A storm of burning ashes and sand soon darkened the atmosphere, but they fell in front of him like fragrant dust. Clouds of mud succeeded, which fell like perfumes all round and over Phralaong. Manh caused a thick darkness to fill the atmosphere, but to Phralaong it emitted rays of the purest light. The enraged Manh cried to his followers, "Why do you stand looking on? Rush at once upon him and compel him to flee before me." Sitting on his huge elephant, and brandishing his formidable weapons, Manh approached close to Phralaong and said to him, "Theiddat, this throne is not made for you; vacate it forthwith; it is my property." Phralaong calmly answered, "You have not as yet practised the ten great virtues, nor gone through the five acts of self-denial; you have never devoted your life to help others to acquire merits; in a word, you have not yet done all the needful to enable you to obtain the supreme dignity of Phra. This throne, therefore, cannot be yours." Unable to control any longer his passion, Manh threw his formidable weapons at Phralaong; but they were converted into garlands of beautiful flowers, that adapted themselves gracefully round his body. His sword and other weapons, that could cut at once through the hardest rocks, were employed with no better success. The soldiers of Manh, hoping that their united efforts would have a better result, and that they could thrust Phralaong from his throne, made a sudden and simultaneous rush at him, rolling against him, with an irresistible force, huge rocks, as large as mountains; but by the virtue of their opponent's merits, they were converted into fine nosegays, that gently dropped at his feet.

At that time the Nats, from their seats, looked down on the scene of the combat, suspended between hope and fear. Phralaong at that moment said to Manh: "How do you dare to pretend to the possession of this throne? Could you ever prove, by indisputable evidence, that you have ever made offerings enough to be deserving of this throne?" Manh, turning to his followers, answered: "Here are my witnesses; they will all bear evidence in my favour." At the same moment they all shouted aloud, to testify their approval of Manh's words. "As to you, Prince Theiddat, where are the witnesses that will bear evidence in your favour and prove the justness of your claim to the possession of this throne?" Phralaong replied: "My witnesses are not like yours, men or any living beings.[5] The earth

---

[5] The witness whom Phralaong summoned in support of his claim to the undisturbed possession of the throne was the earth itself. It may be from the example that was set on this occasion that Buddhists have borrowed the habit of calling the earth as a witness of the good works they have done or are doing. I will briefly relate what is done and said

itself will give testimony to me. For, without alluding even to those offerings I have made during several previous existences, I will but mention the forty-seven great ones I made whilst I lived as Prince Wethandra." Stretching out his right hand, which he had kept hitherto under the folds of his garment, and pointing to the earth, he said with a firm voice : " Earth, is it not true that at the time I was Prince Wethandra I made forty great offerings ? " The earth replied with a deep and loud roaring, resounding in the midst of Manh's legions, like the sound of countless voices, threatening to spread death and destruction in their ranks. The famous charger of Manh bent his knees, and paid homage to Phralaong. Manh himself, disheartened and discomfited, fled to the country of Watha-watti. His followers were so overpowered by fear that they flung away all that could impede their retreat, and ran away in every direction. Such was the confusion and disorder that prevailed that two warriors could not be seen following the same course in their flight.

Looking from their seats on the defeat of Manh and the

---

on such occasions. During my former residence in Burmah I observed on a certain occasion, when taking my evening walk, about ten or twelve persons of both sexes assembled on a rather retired spot in the vicinity of a pagoda. As they appeared all quite attentive, I came near to them to see what was the cause that had brought them thither, and what occurrence seemed to rivet their attention. As I was known to some of them, they were not frightened by my sudden apparition. On my asking them the motive of their assembling here at a late hour, they said that, having buried yesterday a child two years old, they came to make some offerings of boiled rice, plantains, and other fruits, to propitiate the Nat of the place. Having asked them to repeat the formula they had uttered on the occasion,

they kindly complied with my request. Here is the substance of that formula. "Believing in the three precious things, Buddha, the Law, and the Assembly of the perfect, I make this offering, that I may be delivered from all present and future miseries. May all beings existing in the four states of punishment reach the fortunate seats of Nats. I wish all my relatives and all men inhabiting this and other worlds to have a share in this meritorious work. O earth and you Nats, guardians of this place, be witness to the offering I am making." On uttering these last words, the offerer of the present, or a talapoin, sent for this purpose, pours down some water on the ground.

* As the Nats and all other beings are to be benefited by the preachings of Buddha, it is but natural that they

glorious victory of Phralaong, the Nats[6] rent the air with shouts of exultation. The Brahmas, Nagas, and Galongs joined the Nats in celebrating his triumph over his enemies. They all hastened from more than ten thousand worlds to pay their respects and offer their felicitations, presenting him with flowers and perfumes, saying: "Victory and glory to Phralaong! Shame and defeat to the infamous Manh!"

It was a little while before sunset when Phralaong had achieved his splendid victory over his proud foe. At that time he was wrapped up, as it were, in the profoundest meditation. The extremities of the branches of the Bodi tree[7] fell gently over him, and, by their undulations,

---

all join in singing his praises and exalting his glorious achievements. The Nagas and Galongs are fabulous animals, which are often mentioned in the course of this Legend. It has been observed in a former note that, according to the Buddhistic notions, animals are beings in a state of punishment, differing from man, not in nature, but in merits. Some of them, having nearly exhausted the sum of their demerits, begin to feel the influence of former merits. They are supposed to have, to a certain extent, the use of reason. No wonder if they rejoice at seeing the triumph of him who is to help them in advancing towards a condition better than their present one.

[7] The banyan tree, at the foot of which Phralaong obtains perfect intelligence, is occasionally called throughout this narrative the Bodi tree. The word Bodi means wisdom, science, or knowledge. The Burmese, in their sacred writings, always mention the tree by that name, because, under its shade, perfect science was communicated to Phralaong. It is supposed to occupy the very centre of the island of Dzampudiba. During all the while Phra or Buddha (let us call him now by that name) re-

mained under that tree his mind was engaged in the most profound meditation, which the gigantic efforts of his enemy could scarcely interrupt. It is not to be inferred from the narrative in the text that supreme intelligence was communicated suddenly or by miraculous process to our Buddha. He was already prepared, by former mental labours, for that grand result; he had previously capacitated himself, by studies and reflection, for the reception of that more than human science; he required but a last and mighty effort of his intelligence to arrive finally at the acme of knowledge, and thereby to become a perfect Buddha. That last effort was made on this occasion, and crowned with the most complete success. He gained the science of the past, present, and future.

It would be somewhat curious to investigate the motives that have determined Buddhists to give to that sacred tree the name of Bodi. At first sight one will infer that such a name was given to the tree because, under its refreshing and cooling shade the Bodi, or Supreme intelligence, was communicated to Phralaong. The occurrence, however extraordinary it be, is scarcely suffi-

seemed caressing, as it were, his tsiwaran ; they resembled
so many beautiful nosegays of red flowers that were
offered to him. At the first watch of the night Phralaong applied all the energies of his powerful mind to
ascertain the laws of the causes and effects, in order to
account for all that is in existence. He argued in the
following manner : " Pain and all sorts of miseries do exist
in this world. Why do they exist ? Because there is
birth. Why is there birth ? Because there is conception.
Now conception does take place, because there is existence,
or that moral state produced by the action or influence of
merits and demerits. Existence is brought in by *Upadan,*
or the combining of affections calculated to cause the
coming into existence. The latter has for its cause the
desire. The desire is produced by sensation. The latter
is caused by the contact. The contact takes place because
there are the six senses. The six senses do exist, because
there is name and form, that is to say, the exterior sign
of the ideal being and the type of the real being. Name
and form owe their existence to erroneous knowledge ;
the latter in its turn is produced by the imagination,
which has for its cause ignorance.[8]

Having followed in his mind the succession of the

cient to account for such an appellation. Bearing in mind the numerous
and striking instances of certain re-
vealed facts and truths, offered to
the attention of the reader of this
Legend, in a deformed but yet recognisable shape, it would not be quite
out of the limits of probability to
suppose that this is also a remnant
of the tradition of the tree of knowledge that occupied the centre of the
garden of Eden.

[8] The theory of the twelve causes
and effects is, in itself, very abstruse,
and almost above the comprehension
of those uninitiated in the metaphysics of Buddhists. I will attempt
to analyse it in as simple and clear a
way as possible. This theory is very
ancient, probably coeval with the
first ages of Buddhism. It forms
this basis of its ontology and metaphysics, in the same manner as the
four great and transcendent truths
are the foundation whereupon rests
the system of morals. It is probable
that Gaudama, in his preachings,
which were very simple, and within
the reach of ordinary minds, never
formulated his doctrine on this essential point in such a dry and concise
manner. But the seed was sown,
and the germ deposited here and there
in his instructions. His immediate
disciples, in endeavouring to give a
distinct shape to their master's doc-

twelve causes and effects, and reached the last link of that chain, Phralaong said to himself: " Ignorance, or no science, is the first cause which gives rise to all the phe-

trines, gradually framed the formula or theory just stated. It, in fact, presents the very characteristics of a system elaborated in a philosophical school.

In taking our departure from the first cause, which is *Awidza*, or ignorance, or the wanting in science, or no knowledge, we have to follow the different stages and conditions of a being until it reaches decrepitude, old age, and death. When we speak of ignorance, or no science, we must not suppose the material existence of a being that ignores. But we must take ignorance in an abstract sense, deprived of forms, and subsisting in a manner very different from what we are wont to consider ordinary beings. A European has a great difficulty in finding his way through a process of reasoning so extraordinary, and so different from that positivism which he is used to. But with the Buddhist the case is widely different. He can pass from the abstract to the concrete, from the ideal to the real, with the greatest ease. But let us follow the scale of the causes and effects, upon which there are twelve steps.

From ignorance comes *Sangkara*, that is to say conception or imagination, which mistakes for reality what is unreal, which looks on this world as something substantial, whilst it is, indeed, nothing but shadow and emptiness, assuming forms which pass away as quick as the representations of theatrical exhibitions. Sangkara, in its turn, begets *Wignian*, or knowledge, attended with a notion of sentiment, implying that of soul and life, in an abstract sense. From Wignian proceeds *Namrup*, the name and form, because knowledge can have for its object but name and

form, &c., or, to speak in the language of Buddhists, things that are external and internal. But let it be borne in mind that what is herein meant is but the individuality of an ideal being.

The name and form give birth to the *Chayatana*, six senses, or seats of the sensible qualities. To our division of the five ordinary senses Buddhists add the sixth sense of Mano, or the heart, the internal sense. Through the senses we are put in communication or contact with all objects; hence the six senses give rise to the sixth cause *Pasa*, which means, properly speaking, contact. From this cause flows the seventh one, called *Wedana*, or sensation, or, more generally still, sensibility. In fact, there can be no contact from which there will not result some sensation, either pleasant or unpleasant. *Wedana* gives infallibly rise to *Tahna*, or passion, or desire, or inclination. From this point the series of causes and effects is comparatively easy, because it presents conditions essentially connected with a material object. By Tahna we ought not to understand only the mere inclination that the sexes have one for the other, but the general propensity created in a being by any contact whatever, or perhaps, as usual with Buddhists, the desire taken in an abstract sense.

The immediate result from Tahna is *Upadan*, the attachment, or the conception. It is that state in which the desire adheres to something, assumes a shape. It is, in fact, the being conceived. From the state of conception the being passes into that of *Bawa*, or existence, or that condition which is created and made by the influence of former good or bad deeds preceding birth, which is but

nomena I have successively reviewed. From it springs the world and all the beings it contains. It is the cause of that universal illusion in which man and all beings are miserably lulled. By what means can this ignorance be done away with? Doubtless by knowledge and true science. By means of the light that science spreads I clearly see the unreality of all that exists, and I am freed from that illusion which makes other beings to believe that such thing exists, when, in reality, it does not exist. The imagination, or the faculty to imagine the existence of things which do not exist, is done away with. The same fate is reserved to the false knowledge resulting therefrom to the name and form, to the six senses, to contact, to sen-

---

the apparition of the being into this world. *Dzati*, or birth, is the eleventh cause. It is the nshering of a being into the world. There are six ways by which a being comes into this world, viz., those of Nat, Man, Assura, Preitta, animal, and the inhabitant of hell. Birth is accomplished in four different manners, by humidity, an egg, a mattrice, and metamorphosis.

The twelfth and last step in the ladder of the causes and effects is decrepitude and death. In fact, every being that is born must grow old, decay, and finally die.

Such is the process followed by Buddhists in attempting to account for all that exists. What effect could such a reasoning have over the mind of the generality of hearers it is difficult to say. But we may rest assured that, though these principles existed, as an embryo, in the discourses of the author of Buddhism, they were never laid before the generality of hearers in that crude scholastic form. Such abstruse ideas, when analysed and commented upon by Buddhist doctors, gave rise to the most opposite conclusions. The materialist school based its revolting doctrines upon that theory; we may

add that the opinions of that school are generally held in Burmah, and by the great mass of Buddhists. Some other doctors reasoned in the following manner: Ignorance supposes two things, a being ignoring and a thing ignored, that is to say, man and the world. They admitted the eternity of a soul which had to pass through the series above enumerated. With them metempsychosis was a process exactly similar to that imagined by the Brahmins. As to the world, it was, to them, an unreality. Knowledge enabled them to come to the position of understanding and believing that there is no such thing as what we by mistake call world. The latter opinion, which seems to admit of a principle existing distinct from matter, is opposed to the former and general one, which supposes that spirit is but a modification of matter. We deliberately make use of the doubt, implying expression, at the head of the preceding sentence, respecting the real opinions of the latter school, because, in their way of arguing, it is impossible not to come to the painful conclusion that they ignore, or do not admit, a distinction between spirit and matter.

sation, to desire, to conception, to existence, to birth, and to pain or miseries."

Then Phralaong says to himself : "The knowledge of the four great truths is the true light that can dispel ignorance and procure the real science, whereby the coming out from the whirlpool of existences, or from the state of illusion, can be perfectly effected. These four truths are : 1, The miseries of existence; 2, The cause productive of misery, which is the desire, ever-renewed, of satisfying oneself without being able ever to secure that end; 3, The destruction of that desire, or the estranging oneself from it, is the important affair deserving the most serious attention; 4, The means of obtaining the individual annihilation of that desire is supplied solely by the four Meggas, or highways, leading to perfection. But these Meggas can be followed only by those who have a right intention, a right will, and who, throughout life, exert themselves to regulate their action, conduct, language, thought, and meditations. It was then that the heart of Phralaong acquired an unshakable firmness, a perfect purity or exemption from all passions, an unalterable meekness, and a strong feeling of tender compassion towards all beings.

When these fundamental truths had been known, felt, and relished,[9] Phralaong's mind, casting a glance over the

---

[9] In a work different from that which has been translated is found a more developed exposition of the four great and sublime truths. We think that the reader will like to see in what manner Buddhists themselves understand this important subject, which is, with them, the foundation of their doctrine on morals.

There are four great truths: pain, the production of pain, the destruction of pain, and the way leading to that destruction. What is pain, which is the first of the great truths? It is birth, old age, sickness, death, the coming in contact with what we dislike, the separation from what we feel an attachment for, the illusion which begets false knowledge. All that is pain. What is the production of pain, the second sublime truth? It is the desire which incessantly longs for an illusory satisfaction, which can never be obtained. That desire is a perpetually renewed craving, coveting objects here and there, and never satiated. Such is the cause productive of pain; such is the prolific source of all miseries. What is the destruction of pain, which is

past, was able to discover at once all that had taken place during the countless states of his former existences. He recollected the name he had borne, those of his parents, the places he had seen and visited, the caste he had belonged to, and all the chief events that had marked the course of his progress through the continual migrations. He likewise saw reflected, as in a mirror, the former conditions of existence of all other beings. The immense development and expansion of his mind, which enabled him to fathom the depth of the past, happened during the first watch of the night.

. He applied now all the expanded powers of his incomparable mind to take a correct survey of all the beings now in existence. He glanced over all those that were in hell, and the other three states of punishment, those living on earth, and those dwelling in the twenty-six superior seats. He at once understood distinctly their state, condition,

---

the third great truth? It is the doing away with that desire which always shows itself, searches after this or that object, is always attended with feelings of pleasure, or some other sensations. It is the perfect and entire stifling of that craving which always covets, and is never satiated. The estranging oneself from that desire and that craving, the complete destruction of both, constitutes the third great truth. What is the way leading to the destruction of that desire, which is the fourth great truth? The way which one has to follow, in order to obtain that most desirable result, is that which the wise man invariably follows, when he is with an intention, will, diligence, action, life, language, thought, and meditation, always pure and correct.

The four truths are exceedingly praised by Buddhists. They constitute what is emphatically called the law of the wheel, incessantly revolving upon itself, and always presenting successively those four points to the attentive consideration and affectionate piety of the faithful. They are the offensive weapons wherewith passions are attacked and destroyed : they are the sword that cuts asunder the link that retains a being in the circle of existences. The revelation, or manifestation of those truths, is the great work that a Buddha has to perform. When it is made, all beings in their respective seats rejoice in an extraordinary manner. Inanimate nature even partakes in the universal joy. The earth shakes with a great violence, and the greatest prodigies proclaim aloud the fortunate manifestation of a law, which opens to all beings the way leading to deliverance. The preaching of that doctrine took place for the first time in the forest of Migadawon, not far from Baranathee, in the presence and for the benefit of the five Rahans, who had attended on Buddha, during the six years of mortification which he spent to prepare and qualify himself for the Buddhaship.

merits, demerits, and all that appertained to their physical and moral constitutive parts. This labour occupied his mind up to midnight.

Urged by the merciful and compassionate dispositions of his soul, Phralaong often revolved within himself the following: "All is misery and affliction in this world; all beings are miserably detained in the vortex of existences; they float over the whirlpool of desire and concupiscence; they are carried to and fro by the fallacious cravings of a never-obtained satisfaction. They must be taught to put an end to concupiscence by freeing themselves from its influence. Their minds must be imbued with the knowledge of the four great truths. The four ways that I have discovered shall inevitably lead men and Nats to that most desirable end. These ways ought to be pointed out to them, that, by following them, men and Nats may obtain the deliverance."

Whilst these thoughts thronged through his mind, a little before break of day, in the 103d year of the Eatzana era, on the day of the full moon of Katson, the perfect science broke at once over him: he became the Buddha.

When this great wonder took place, ten thousand worlds were shaken twelve times with such a violence as to make hairs stand on one end. These words, "most excellent being," were heard throughout the same series of worlds. Magnificent ornaments decorated all places. Flagstaffs appeared in every direction, adorned with splendid streamers. Of such dimensions were they that the extremities of those in the east reached the opposite side of the west; and those in the north, the southern boundary. Some flags, hanging from the seats of Brahmas, reached the surface of the earth. All the trees of ten thousand worlds shot out branches, loaded with fruits and flowers. The five sorts of lilies bloomed spontaneously. From the clefts of rocks beautiful flowers sprang out. The whole universe appeared like an immense garden, covered with flowers; a vivid light illuminated those places, the darkness of which could not be dispersed by the united rays of seven suns. The water, which fills the immensity of the deep, at a depth of eighty-four thousand youdzanas, became fresh and offered a most agreeable drink. Rivers suspended their course; the blind recovered their sight, the deaf could hear, and the lame were able to walk freely. The captives were freed from their chains and restored to their liberty. Innumerable other wonders took place at the moment Phralaong received the supreme intelligence. He said then to himself, "Previous to my obtaining the supreme knowledge, I have, during countless generations, moved in the circle of ever-renewed existences and borne-up misery. Now I see this distinctly. Again, I perceive how I can emancipate myself from the trammels of existence, and extricate myself from all miseries and wretchedness attending generation; my will is fixed on the most amiable state of Neibban. I have now arrived to that state of perfection that excludes all passions."

It was at the full moon of the month Katson, when these memorable occurrences took place, and it was daylight when Phralaong at last obtained the fulness of the Buddhaship. After this glorious and triumphant achievement, Phralaong, whom from this moment we must call Phra or Buddha, continued to remain on the throne, in a cross-legged position, with a mind absorbed in contemplation during seven days. Mental exertion and labour were at an end. Truth in its effulgent beauty encompassed his mind and shed over it the purest rays. Placed in that luminous centre, Phra saw all beings entangled in the web of passions, tossed over the raging billows of the sea of renewed existences, whirling in the vortex of endless miseries, tormented incessantly and wounded to the quick by the sting of concupiscence, sunk into the dark abyss of ignorance, the wretched victims of an illusory, unsubstantial, and unreal world. He said then to himself: "In all the worlds there is no one but me who knows how to break through the web of passions, to still the waves that waft beings

from one state into another, to save them from the whirlpool of miseries, to put an end to concupiscence and break
its sting, to dispel the mist of ignorance by the light of
truth, to teach all intelligent beings the unreality and non-
existence of this world, and thereby lead them to the true
state of Neibban." Having thus given vent to the feelings
of compassion that pressed on his benevolent heart, Phra,
glancing over future events, delighted in contemplating the
great number of beings who would avail themselves of his
preachings, and labour to free themselves from the slavery
of passions. He counted the multitudes who would enter
the ways that lead to the deliverance, and would obtain
the rewards to be enjoyed by those who will follow one of
those ways. The Baranathee country would be favoured
first of all with the preaching of the law of the wheel.
He reviewed the countries where his religion would be
firmly established. He saw that Maheinda, the son of
king Asoka, would carry his law to Ceylon, two hundred
and thirty-six years after his Neibban.

When these and other subjects were fully exhausted,
the most excellent Phra came down from his throne and
went to a distance of ten fathoms from the Bodi tree, in a
north-east direction. There he stood, his eyes fixedly
riveted on the throne, without a single wink, during seven
consecutive days, given up to the most intense and undisturbed meditation. The Nats, observing this extraordinary posture, imagined that he regretted the throne he had
just vacated, and that he wanted to repossess himself of it.
They concluded that, such being the case, Prince Theiddat
had not as yet obtained the Buddhaship. When the
period of seven days was over, Buddha, who knew the innermost thoughts of the Nats, resolved to put an end to
their incredulous thinking respecting his person. For that
purpose, he had recourse to the display of miraculous
powers.[10] He raised himself high up in the air, and, to

---

[10] Buddhists allow to their Buddha miracles. How is this power con-
the power of working wonders and ferred upon him? This is a difficulty

their astonished regards, he wrought at once more than a thousand wonders, which had the immediate effect of silencing all their doubts, and convincing them that he was indeed the Buddha.

Having come down to the place which he had started from, for the display of prodigies, Buddha went to the north of the tree Bodi at a distance of only two fathoms from it. He spent this time in walking to and fro from east to west, during seven days, over a road, prepared for that purpose by the Nats. He was engaged all the while in the work of the sublimest contemplation.

He then shaped his course in a north-west direction, at a distance of thirteen fathoms from the sacred tree. There stood a beautiful house, shining like gold, resplendent with precious stones. It was a temporary residence, purposely prepared for him by the Nats. Thither he repaired, and sat down in a cross-legged position during seven days. He devoted all his time to meditating on the Abidamma, or the most excellent science. This science is divided into seven books. Phra had already gone over the six first and fully mastered their contents, but the six glories had not as yet shot forth from his person.

It was only after having mastered the contents of the last division, named Pathan, divided into twenty-four parts, that the six glories appeared. Like the great fishes that delight to sport only in the great ocean, the mind of Buddha expanded itself with undescribable eagerness, and delighted to run unrestrained through the unbounded

---

they cannot explain satisfactorily. The science of Buddha makes him acquainted with all the laws regulating nature, that is to say, the *ensemble* of the animate and inanimate beings constituting a world; but one is at a loss to find the origin of that power which enables him, as often as he likes, to suspend the course of those laws. Be that as it may, certain it is that Buddha resorted always, during the course of his preachings, to miracles, in order to convince those who seemed to listen with rather an incredulous ear to his doctrines. Miracles were used successfully, as powerful and irresistible weapons, against certain heretics, the Brahmins, in particular, who taught doctrines opposed to his own. They often accompanied his preachings, for increasing faith in the heart of his hearers.

field opened before him by the contents of that volume. Brown rays issued from his hairs, beard, and eyelids. Gold-like rays shot forth from his eyes and skin ; from his flesh and blood dashed out purple beams, and from his teeth and bones escaped rays, white like the leaves of the lily ; from his hands and feet emanated rays of a deep-red colour, which, falling on the surrounding objects, made them appear like so many rubies of the purest water. His forehead sent forth undulating rays, resembling those reflected by cut crystal. The objects which received those rays appeared as mirrors, reflecting the rays of the sun. Those six rays of various hues caused the earth to resemble a globe of the finest gold. Those beams at first penetrated through our globe, which is eighty-two thousand youdzanas thick, and thence illuminated the mass of water which supports our planet. It resembled a sea of gold. That body of water, though four hundred and eighty thousand youdzanas thick, could not stop the elastic projection of those rays, which went forth through a stratum of air nine hundred and sixty thousand youdzanas thick, and were lost in the vacuum. Some beams, following a vertical direction, rushed through the six seats of Nats, the sixteen of Brahmas, and the four superior ones, and thence were lost in vacuum. Other rays following a horizontal direction, penetrated through an infinite series of worlds. The sun, the moon, the stars appeared like opaque bodies, deprived of light. The famous garden of Nats, their splendid palace, the ornaments hanging from the tree Padetha were all cast into the shade and appeared obscure, as if wrapped up in complete darkness. The body of the chief Brahma, which sends forth light through one million of systems, emitted then but the feeble and uncertain light of the glowworm at sunrise. This marvellous light, emanating from the person of Buddha, was not the result of vowing or praying : but all the constituent parts of his body became purified to such an extent by the sublime meditation of the most excellent law that they shone with a matchless brightness.

Having thus spent seven days in that place, close to the Bodi tree, he repaired to the foot of another gniaong tree, called atzapala, or the shepherds' tree, so called because, under its cooling shade, shepherds and their flocks of goats rested during the heat of the day. It was situated at the east of the Bodi, at a distance of thirty fathoms. There he sat in a cross-legged position, during seven days, enjoying the sweetness of self-recollection. It was near to that place that the vile Manh, who, since his great attack on Buddha, had never lost sight of him, but had always secretly followed him with a wicked spirit, was compelled to confess that he had not been able to discover in that Rahan anything blamable, and expressed the fear of seeing him at once pass over the boundaries of his empire. The tempter stooped in the middle of the highway, and across it drew successively sixteen lines, as he went on reflecting on sixteen different subjects. When he had thought over each of the ten great virtues, he drew, first, ten lines, saying: "The great Rahan has indeed practised to a high degree those ten virtues. I cannot presume to compare myself to him." In drawing the eleventh, he confessed that he had not, like that Rahan, the science that enabled to know the inclinations and dispositions of all beings. In drawing the twelfth, he said that he had not as yet acquired the knowledge of all that concerns the nature of the various beings. Drawing the four remaining lines, he confessed successively that he did not feel, like that Rahan, a tender compassion for the beings yet entangled in the miseries of existence, nor could he perform miracles, nor perceive everything, nor attain to the perfect and supreme knowledge of the law. On all these subjects he avowed his decided inferiority to the great Rahan.

Whilst Manh was thus engaged with a sad heart in meditating over those rather humiliating points, he was at last found out by his three daughters, Tahna,[11] Aratee, and Raga, who had for sometime been looking after him. When they saw their father with a downcast countenance, they came to him, and inquired about the motive of his deep affliction. " Beloved daughters," replied Manh, " I see this Rahan escaping from my dominion, and notwithstanding my searching examination, I have not been able to detect in him anything reprehensible. This is the only cause of my inexpressible affliction." " Dear father," replied they, " banish all sorrows from your mind, and be of a good heart ; we will very soon find out the weak side of the great Rahan, and triumphantly bring him back within the hitherto unpassed limits of your empire." " Beware of the man you will have to deal with," replied Manh. " I believe that no effort, however great, directed against him, will ever be rewarded with success. He is of a firm mind and unshaken purpose. I fear you shall never succeed in bringing him back within my dominions." " Dear father," said they, " we women know how to manage such affairs ; we will catch him like a bird in the net of concupiscence ; let fear and anxiety be for ever dispelled from your heart." Having given this assurance, forthwith they went to Buddha, and said to him, " Illustrious Rahan, we approach you respectfully and express the wish of staying with you, that we may minister to all your wants." Without in the least heeding their words, or even casting a glance at them, the most excellent Buddha remained un-

---

[11] The great tempter had been foiled in all his attempts to conquer Buddha. In the sadness of his heart he was compelled to acknowledge the superiority of his opponent and confess his defeat. His three daughters came to console him, promising that they would, by their united efforts, overcome the firmness of the great Rahan, by awakening in his heart the fire of concupiscence. The names of those three daughters of Manh denote concupiscence. These new enemies of Buddha, therefore, are mere personifications of the passion of lust. Pride, personified in Manh, had proved powerless against the virtue of Buddha ; he is now assailed from a different quarter ; the attack is to be directed against the weakest side of human nature. But it is as successless as the former one : it affords to Buddha another occasion for a fresh triumph.

moved, enjoying the happiness of meditation. Knowing that the same appearance, face, and bodily accomplishments might not be equally pleasing, they assumed, one the appearance of a heart-winning young girl, another that of a blooming virgin, and the third that of a fine middle-aged beauty.' Having thus made their arrangements, they approached Buddha, and several times expressed to him the desire of staying with him and ministering to his wants. Unmoved by all their allurements, Buddha said to them, " For what purpose do you come to me ? You might have some chance of success with those that have not as yet extinguished the fire of passion, and rooted it from their heart ; but I, like all the Buddhas, my predecessors, have destroyed in me concupiscence, passion, and ignorance. No effort, on your part, will ever be able to bring me back into the world of passions. I am free from all passions, and have obtained supreme wisdom. By what possible means could you ever succeed in bringing me back into the whirlpool of passions ? " The three daughters of Manh, covered with confusion, yet overawed with admiration and astonishment, said to each other, " Our father forsooth had given us a good and wise warning. This great Rahan deserves the praises of men and Nats. Everything in him is perfect : to him it belongs to instruct men in all things they want to know." Saying this, they, with a downcast countenance, returned to their father.

It was in that very same place, at the foot of the adzapala gniaong, that a heretic Pounha, named Mingalika, proud of his caste, came with hasty steps, speaking loudly, and with little respect approached the spot where Buddha was sitting.[12] Having entered into conversation with him,

[12] In Burmah the originator of the great Buddhistic system is called Gaudama, and this appellation, according to many, appears to be his family name. When he is called Rahan Gaudama, it means the ascetic belonging to the family of Gaudama. In Nepaul, the same personage is known under the name of Thakiamuni, that is to say, the ascetic of the Thakia family. Those who refused to believe in Buddha and his

the Pounha heard from his mouth instructions worthy of being ever remembered. He said to Buddha, " Lord Gaudama, I have two questions to put to you. Whence comes the name Pounha ? What are the duties to be performed in order to become a real Pounha ? " Buddha penetrating with the keen eye of wisdom into the innermost soul of

doctrines, those who held tenets disagreeing with his own, and professed what, in the opinion of their adversaries, was termed a heretical creed, invariably called Buddha by his family name, placing him on the same level with so many of his contemporaries who led the same mode of life. The Siamese give the appellation of Sammana Khodom to their Buddha, that is to say, Thramana Gaudama, or Gautama. The Sanscrit word Thramana means an ascetic who has conquered his passions and lives on alms. Gaudama belonged to the Kchatria caste. Kings and all royal families in those days came out of the same caste. Hence his father Thoodaudana was king of the country of Kapilawot, anciently a small state, north of Goruckpore.

The young Pounha, not unlike the young man mentioned in the gospel, had, by the preachings of Gaudama, become acquainted with all the laws and practices relating to the general duties and obligations incumbent on men in general. He might have perhaps added that he had observed all those precepts from his youth, or, at least, that he was sure now, with the additional light he had received from his eminent teacher, to observe faithfully all the injunctions mentioned in the course of the lecture : but he was not satisfied with an ordinary proficiency in virtue and observances ; he aimed at superior attainments ; he wished to obtain the greatest perfection, that is to say, that of Brahmas. In what does such a perfection consist ? The book of metaphysics in-

forms us that the five states of Dzan, or contemplations, are enjoyed by the beings located in the sixteen seats of Brahmas, in the following order. The first state, or that of consideration, is shared by all the beings inhabiting the three first seats of Brahmas. Their occupation is to consider the various subjects the mind has to dwell on. The second Dzan, or reflection, is reserved for the beings occupying the next three seats. Those beings have no more to look out for subjects of meditation. Their sole occupation is to dive into truth and fathom its depth and various bearings. The third state of Dzan procures the pleasure which is derived from the contemplation of truth, and belongs to the beings of the three seats, superior to those just alluded to ; in the fourth Dzan is enjoyed a placid happiness, which is the result of the possession of truth ; it is reserved for the beings of the three next seats. The fifth Dzan, or perfect stability, is the happy lot of the beings living in the five last seats. Those fortunate inmates are so entirely rooted in truth, and so perfectly exempt from all that causes mutability, that they arrive at a state of complete fixity, the whole of their soul being riveted on truth.

Apology is certainly due to the reader, who is but slightly initiated in such abstruse subjects, for laying before him particulars with which he is so unfamiliar ; but this trouble must be borne up by him who desires to obtain access into the gloomy sanctuary of Buddhism.

his interlocutor, answered, " The real and genuine Pounha is he who has renounced all passions, put an end to concupiscence, and has entered the ways leading to perfection. But there are others, who are proud of their origin, who walk hastily, speak with a loud voice, and who have not done what is needful to destroy the influence of passions. These are called Pounhas because of their caste and birth. But the true sage avoids everything that is rash, impetuous or noisy: he has conquered all his passions, and put an end to the principle of demerits. His heart loves the repetition of formulas of prayers, and delights in the exercise of meditation. He has reached the last way to perfection. In him there is no longer wavering, or doubt, or pride. This man really deserves the name of Pounha, or pure: he is indeed the true Pounha according to the law." The instruction being finished, the Pounha rose respectfully from his place, wheeled to the right and departed.

Buddha continued the sublime work of contemplating pure truth through the means of intense reflection. Having remained seven days in that position, Buddha arose in an ecstasy and went to the south-eastern side of the Bodi tree, to a distance of an oothaba (1 oothaba = to 20 tas, 1 ta = to 7 cubits), on the sixth day after the full moon of Nayon. On that spot there was a tank called Hidza-lee-dana. On the bank of that tank he sat, under the shade of the Kiin tree, in a cross-legged position during seven days, enjoying the delight of meditation. During those seven days rain fell in abundance, and it was very cold. A Naga, chief of that tank, would have made a building to protect Buddha against the inclemency of the weather, but he preferred, in order to gain greater merits, to coil himself up sevenfold round his person, and to place his head above him, with his large hood extended. When the seven days were over and the rain had ceased, the Naga quitted his position; then assuming the appearance of a young man, he prostrated himself before Buddha and worshipped him. Buddha said: " He who aims at obtaining the state of Neibban ought to possess the knowledge of the four roads leading thereto, as well as that of the four great truths and of all laws. He ought to bear no anger towards other men, nor harm them in any way soever. Happy he who receives such instructions."

Buddha moved from that place, and went to the south of the Bodi tree, to a distance of forty fathoms. At the foot of the linloon tree he sat in a cross-legged position, having his mind deeply engaged in the exercise of the sublimest contemplation. In that position he spent seven entire days, which completed the forty-nine days which were to be devoted to reflection and meditation around the Bodi tree. When this period of days was over, at day-break, on the fifth day after the full moon of Watso, he felt the want of food. This was quickly perceived by a Thagia, who hastened from his seat to the spot where Buddha was staying, and offered him some Thit khia fruits, others say Kia-dzoo fruits, to prepare his system to receive more substantial food. After he had eaten them, the same celestial attendant brought him some water to rinse his mouth, and to wash his face and hands. Buddha continued to remain in the same position, under the cooling and protecting shade of the linloon tree.

To consecrate, as it were, and perpetuate the remembrance of the seven spots occupied by Buddha during the forty-nine days that he spent round the tree Bodi, a Dzedy was erected on each of those seven places. King Pathanadi Kosala surrounded them with a double wall, and subsequently King Dammathoka added two others. There were only three openings, or gates, to penetrate into the enclosed ground, one on the north, another on the east, and the third on the south. The river Neritzara rolls its deep blue waters in a south-eastern direction from the Bodi tree, to a distance of eight oothabas from it. On the eastern bank of that stream another Dzedy has been erected on the spot where, previous to his becoming a Buddha, he had eaten the forty-nine mouthfuls of the delicious Nogana offered to him by the pious Thoodzata.

Whilst Buddha was sitting in a cross-legged position under the linloon tree, two brothers named Tapoosa and Palekat, merchants by profession, arrived with five hundred carts in the Oorouwela forest, at the very place where Buddha was staying. They had sailed from their native town, called [13] Oukkalaba, which lies in a south-eastern direction from the Mitzima country, bound for the port of

---

[13] The episode of these two merchants is well known to the inhabitants of the Irrawaddy valley. In three different manuscripts which the writer has had in his hands, he has found it related with almost the same particulars. Oukkalaba, the place the two young men started from, was situated probably on the spot now occupied by the village of Twaintay, or not far from it. How far that place was from the sea in those remote times it is not possible to ascertain with precision. Certain it is, that it was a port from which vessels sailed across the Bay of Bengal. The port of Eedzeitha has not as yet been identified with any known locality. It was situated in all probability between the mouth of the Krichna and that of the Hoogly. One of the manuscripts mentions that when Gaudama handed over to the two merchants eight hairs of his head, he bade them, on their arrival in their country, deposit the hairs on a small hill called Seingouttara, where the relics of the three former Buddhas of our period had been enshrined. They were twenty-seven days in reaching Maudin or Cape Negrais, rather a long voyage. Having come to their own place, they related to the governor all the particulars of their interesting journey. The latter, without loss of time, assembled the people and set out in search of the Seingouttara mount. All the eminences were cleared of their brushwood, but the mount could not be discovered. Not knowing what to do, they consulted the Nats on that affair. At last, through their assistance, the mount was found out. But when they inquired about the place of the relics of the three former Buddhas, the Nats of Yesapan, Inandra, and Gauveinda confessed that they knew nothing on the subject, but referred the inquirers to other Nats older than they, viz.: those of Deckina, Ynubani, Maubee, Ameisa, and Tsoolay, who at once pointed out the spot which they were so eagerly searching after. This spot is no other than the one over which stands and towers the lofty and massive Shoay Dagon. They erected a Dzedy, in which they enshrined the relics they had brought with them, the eight hairs of Buddha. This story is doubtless the foundation on which rests the popular belief that those very hairs are to this day in the interior of that monument, and the true source from which has originated the profound veneration which, in our own days, Buddhists, from all parts of Burmah, Siam, and the Shan states, pay by their pilgrimages and offerings to the Dagon Pagoda.

Adzeitta. After landing, they hired five hundred carts to carry their goods to a place called Soowama. They were on their way to their destination when they arrived in the Oorouwela forest. Great was their surprise when they saw on a sudden all their carts unable to move, and arrested by some invisible power.

A Nat who had been formerly their relative stopped by his power the wheels of the carriages. Surprised at such a wonder, the merchants prayed to the Nat who was guardian of that place. The Nat, assuming a visible shape, appeared before them and said to them: " The illustrious Buddha who by the knowledge of the four great truths has arrived to the nature of Phra, is now sitting at the foot of the linloon tree. Go now to that place, and offer him some sweet bread and honey; you shall derive therefrom great merits for many days and nights to come." The two brothers, joyfully complying with the Nat's request, prepared the sweet bread and honey, and hastened in the direction that had been indicated to them. Having placed themselves in a suitable position and prostrated themselves before Buddha, they said: " Most glorious Phra, please to accept these offerings; great merits doubtless will be our reward for many days to come." Buddha had no patta to put those offerings in, for the one he had received from the Brahma Gatigara had disappeared when Thoodzata made him her great offerings. Whilst he was thinking on what he had to do, four Nats came and presented him each with one patta, made of nila or sapphire stone. Phra accepted the four pattas, not from motives of covetousness, but to let each Nat have an equal share in such meritorious work. He put the four pattas one in the other, and by the power of his will they on a sudden became but one patta, so that each Nat lost nothing of the merit of his offerings. Buddha received the offerings of the two merchants in that patta, and satisfied his appetite. The two brothers said to Buddha : " We have on this day approached you, worshipped you, and respectfully listened to your instructions; please to consider us as your devoted followers for the remainder of our lives." [14] They obtained the position of Upathaka. They continued addressing Buddha and said: " What shall we henceforth worship ? " Buddha, rubbing his hand over his head, gave them a few of the hairs that had adhered to his fingers, bidding them to keep carefully those relics. The two brothers, overjoyed at such a valuable present, most respectfully received it, prostrated themselves before Buddha, and departed.

---

[14] Upasaka is a Pali word which is designed to mean those persons who, having heard the instructions of Buddha, and professed a faith or belief in him and his doctrines, did not enter the profession of Rahans. Hence they are quite distinct from the Bikus or mendicants, who formed the first class of the hearers of Buddha, and renounced the world in imitation of their great master. The Upasakas were therefore people adhering to the doctrines of Buddha, but as yet remaining engaged in the ordinary pursuits of life. The two brothers became disciples of Buddha, but not of the first class, since they did not embrace the more perfect mode of life of the ascetics.

This is the first instance in this legend of an allusion being made to relics, that is to say, to objects supposed to be surrounded with a certain amount of sacredness, and esteemed on that account to be worthy of receiving from devotees respect and veneration. The two young converts, not as yet confirmed in the new faith they had embraced, thought they wanted some exterior object to which they might hereafter direct their homage and offer their respects. They were as yet far from being acquainted with the sublime science of their eminent teacher, who, disregarding matter and all its modifications, could not but feel quite indif-ferent respecting the pretended value of relics of even the most sacred character. How is it that the stern moralist, the contemner of this illusory world, could think of giving a few hairs of his head to two new young converts, that they might use them as objects of worship? Buddha doubtless knew exactly and appreciated admirably the wants and necessities of human nature as it is, and will very likely ever be to the end of ages. Men are led, actuated, impressioned, and influenced by the senses; in fact, it is through their senses that the knowledge of things is conveyed to their minds. He gave to his imperfectly instructed disciples a thing that would serve to vivify and reanimate in their memory the remembrance of Buddha, and of the instructions they had heard from him. Those grossly-minded hearers asked for an object they might carry about with them and worship. Buddha, out of deference for their weak intellect, gave them a few hairs of his head, the sight of which was designed to maintain in their souls a tender affection for the person of him these things had belonged to. This subject will receive hereafter the further treatment it deserves when we come to examine the nature of the worship paid by Buddhists to the images of Gaudama, and to the relics and Dzedia.

CHAPTER VI.

Buddha hesitates to undertake the task of preaching the law—The great Brahma entreats him to preach the law to all beings—His assent to the entreaties—Journey towards Migadawon—He meets Ouppaka—His first preachings—Conversion of a young nobleman named Ratha, followed by that of his father and other relatives—Conversion of several other noblemen—Instructions to the Rahans—Conversion of the three Kathabas.

HAVING come to the end of his great meditations,[1] Buddha left this spot and returned to the place called Adzapala, where he revolved the following subject in his mind:— "The knowledge," said he, "of the law and of the four great truths, which I alone possess, is very hard to be had.

---

[1] I have, except on one occasion, always made use of the terms meditation and contemplation to express the inward working of Buddha's mind during the forty-nine days he spent at the foot of the banyan tree. But the Burmese translator most commonly employs a much stronger expression, conveying the idea of trance and ecstasy. Hence after having remained seven days on the same spot, deeply engaged in considering some parts of the law he was soon to preach, it is said of him that he comes out from a state of perfect ecstasy. This expression implies a state of complete mental abstraction, when the soul, disentangled from the trammels of sense, raises itself above this material world, contemplates pure truth and delights in it. All her faculties are taken up with the beauty and perfection of truth ; she clings to it with all her might, regardless of all the illusions this world is filled with. This situation of the soul is much esteemed by all fervent Buddhists. It is the lot of but a few privileged Rahans, who have made great progress in perfection, and obtained an almost entire mastery over their passions and senses. This great gift is, as one may well imagine, ardently coveted by many, who, though not possessing it, lay claim to it on false pretences. This being a sin devotees who relish a contemplative life are very liable to, which the framer of the regulations of the Buddhist monks has pronounced as *ipso facto* excluding from the society all those who would falsely claim the possession of uncommon spiritual attainments which they have not. In the book of ordination used for the admission of candidates to the order of Rahans or talapoins, this sin is the last of the four offences which deprive a member of the order of his dignity, and cause his expulsion from the society.

The law is deep; it is difficult to know and understand it; it is very sublime, and can be comprehended only by the means of earnest meditation. It is sweet, filling the soul with joy, and accessible only to the wise. Now all beings are sunk very low by the influence of the five great passions; they cannot free themselves from their baneful operation, which is the source of all mutability. But the law of mutability is the opposite of the law of Neibban or rest. This law is hard to be understood. If I ever preach that law, beings will not be able to understand me, and from my preaching there will result but a useless fatigue and unprofitable weariness. Buddha thus remained almost disinclined to undertake the great duty of preaching the law. The great Brahma, observing what was taking place in Buddha's soul, cried out: "Alas! all mankind are doomed to be lost. He who deserves to be worshipped by all beings now feels no disposition to announce the law to them." He instantly left his seat, and having repaired to the presence of Phra, his cloak over his shoulders with one extremity hanging backward, he bent his knee, lifted up his joined hands to the forehead before the sage, and said to him: "Most illustrious Buddha, who art adorned with the six glories, do condescend to preach the most excellent law; the number of those buried under the weight and filth of passions is comparatively small; if they do not listen to the law there will be no great loss. But there is an immense number of beings who will understand the law. In this world there are beings who are moderately given up to the gratification of sensual appetites; and there are also a great many who are following heretical opinions to whom the knowledge of truth is necessary, and who will easily come to it. Lay now open the way that leads to the perfection of Ariahs; those perfections are the gates to Neibban." Thus he entreated Buddha. This Brahma had been in the time of Buddha Kathaba a Rahan, under the name of Thabaka, and was transferred to the first seat of Brahma for the duration of a world.

On hearing the supplications of that Brahma, Buddha began to feel a tender compassion for all beings. With the keen eyes of a Buddha he glanced over the whole world. He discovered distinctly those beings who were as yet completely sunk in the filth of passions, those who were but partly under the control of passions, and those whose dispositions seemed to be more promising. He then made to the chief of Brahmas the solemn promise that he would preach his law to all beings. Satisfied with the answer he had received, the chief rose up, withdrew respectfully at a proper distance, and turning on the right, left the presence of Buddha and returned to his own seat.

Another thought preoccupied the mind of Buddha. " To whom," said he, " shall I announce the law ? " Having pondered a while over this subject, he added : " The Rathee Alara of the Kalama race is gifted with wisdom and an uncommonly penetrating mind; passions have scarcely any influence over him. I will first preach to him the most excellent law." A Nat then said to Phra that Alara had died seven days ago. Buddha, to whom the past is known, had already seen that Alara was dead. He said : " Great indeed is the loss Alara has met with; he would have doubtless been able to understand right well the law I intended to preach to him. To whom shall I go now ? " Having paused a while, he added : " The Rathee Oodaka, son of Prince Rama, has a quick perception ; he will easily understand my doctrine ; to him I will announce the law." But the same Nat told him that Oodaka had died the night before last, at midnight. " O ! great is the loss that has come upon Oodaka; he would have easily acquired the knowledge of the perfect law." Buddha considered a third time, and said to himself : " To whom shall I go to preach the law ? " After a moment's delay he added : " Many are the services I received in the wilderness from the five Rahans who lived with me.[2] I will repay

---

[2] The five Rahans alluded to are the very same individuals who met VOL. I. Phral-iong in the solitude at the time he was undergoing a great fast and H

their good offices to me, by preaching to them the law, but where are they now? His penetrating regards soon discovered them in the solitude of Migadawon. Having

performing all sorts of works of self-denial and corporal austerities in the most rigorous manner. During all the time he spent in those hard exercises of strict mortification, to conquer his passions and secure the complete triumph of the mind over the senses, he was assisted in all his wants by those five Rahans, who rendered to him the usual services disciples are wont to perform to their teacher. When they saw Phralaong at the end of his mighty efforts in that great struggle resuming the habits of a mendicant, they left him at once, unwilling to believe that he would ever become a Buddha. Our Phra, not unmindful of the good services he had received from them, resolved to impart first to them the blessings of his preachings. Alara and Oodaka, his two first teachers in the science of Dzan, were destined to be the first who would have heard the good news had they not been dead. Gratitude seems to have been the first and main motive that induced him to select as the first objects of his mission the very same persons who had been instrumental in furthering his efforts to acquire the Buddhaship.

The unpleasant epithet of heretic is given to those five Rahans, as well as to another named Upaka, as designed to mean that they held tenets at variance with those of Buddha, and refused to acknowledge him as possessed of the perfect intelligence. Buddhists, in their writings, invariably call their opponents by the name of holders of false doctrines. The Brahmins or Pounhas who refused to seek refuge in Buddha, his law, and the assembly of his disciples, are spoken of as professors of heterodoxical doctrines.

From the narrative of this legend we may conclude, with a probability amounting almost to certitude, that Buddha in his preachings addressed himself first to the Brahmins, as being by their caste the most influential portion of the Hindu community. Those that are called by the name of Pounhas are the Brahmins living in the world and following the ordinary pursuits of life. Those that are mentioned by the names of Rahans and Rathees are probably Brahmins, or at least belong to some other distinguished caste like that of the Kchatrias, but are members of some religious order or ascetics. They were in those days men whom, in imitation of the ancient Greeks, we may call philosophers, and who belonged to one or other of the branches into which the great Indian school was divided. We may conjecture that at that time India exhibited a scene much resembling that which Greece subsequently offered to the eyes of the observer in the days of Socrates and Plato, when schools of philosophy were to be met with in every direction. The Hindu philosophers, favoured by climate and their ardent imagination, carried much farther than the Greek wise men, both in theory and practice, the discussion of dogmas and the fervour of religious practices. If credit is to be given to our Legend in a historical point of view, we may safely conclude that such was the state of India when Buddha began his preachings. His first hearers were Rahans, Rathees, and Pounhas, that is to say, the most learned and wisest men in those days. The latter in particular seemed at first disinclined to offer opposition to Buddha; they listened to him as to a distinguished philosopher; his arguments were examined, discussed, and

enjoyed himself in the place Adzapala, Buddha went on towards the country of Baranathee. All the former Buddhas travelled through the air, but our Buddha, who had merciful designs over Upaka, went on foot. On his way to the village of Gaya, at a distance of three gawots from the Bodi tree, Buddha went to rest, at midday, for a while under the cooling shade of a tree. There he was seen by the heretic Rahan Upaka, who, approaching near him, said, " O Rahan, all your exterior bespeaks the most amiable qualities ; your countenance is at once modest and beautiful. Under what teacher have you become a Rahan ? To what law or doctrine have you given preference in your arduous studies ?" Buddha answered " Upaka, I have triumphed over all the laws of mutability ; I am acquainted with all the laws that rule this universe, and the beings existing therein ; from concupiscence and other passions I am wholly disengaged. I have come to preach the most excellent law to all beings, and teach them the four great truths I alone am acquainted with. I will beat

---

answered by them in the best way they could. In that polemical warfare, arguments were at first the only offensive and defensive weapons used and handled by the combatants on both sides. Buddha's two favourite doctrines of Atheism and Neibban, which established the two broad lines of separation between the two systems, begat much discussion and created some animosity between him and his adversaries. But what widened the gap between the two parties, and placed them in a hostile array against each other, was the broad principle of equality amongst men, latent in the bosom of Buddha's doctrines, and levelled at the distinction of castes. Buddha preached to men of all conditions without exception ; he opened before all the ways that lead to Neibban ; made no distinction between man and man, except that which is drawn by virtue and vice,

merits and demerits. He allowed every one to approach him and take rank among his disciples ; faith in his doctrine entitled any man to be numbered amidst his followers ; the entrance into the order of Rahans or perfect was open to all those who, by their meritorious actions and renouncing the world, qualified themselves for this dignity. This principle which put on a footing of equality men of all castes and nations, and recognised no real superiority but that which is conferred by virtue and merit, could not prove agreeable to the proud Brahmins. It provoked, by its gradual development, the animosity of the opponents of Buddha's doctrines. The battle of arguments, after having raged with various success, was afterwards converted into one of a bloody character, which ended in the total extermination or expulsion of the Buddhists from the Indian peninsula.

the great drum of the law. I have no teacher, and among
Nats and men there is none equal to me. Because of my
victory, I have been named Zeena. Now I am proceeding to the country of Baranathee, for the sake of preaching
the law." Upaka replied, " You are certainly the illustrious Gaudama." He then shook his head, turned away
from the road, and went to the village of Wingaha. The
instructions, however, germinated as good seed in the soul
of Upaka, and were the foundation of his subsequent conversion, which happened as follows :—After this interview
with Gaudama, Upaka dwelt as a hermit in the village of
Wingaha, where a shed was erected for his dwelling. A
hunter brought him support. It happened that the hunter
being engaged in a hunting excursion, his daughter went
to the hermit's cell, to carry him his food. Upaka was
smitten by the beauty of the damsel. He stretched himself on his belly and said to himself, " I will take no food,
nor change this position, unless I obtain the object of my
wishes." He stayed for several days in that position
without uttering a word, or making a single movement, or
taking any food. At last the hunter returned and went
forthwith to the hermit's cell to inquire about the cause of
his strange behaviour. He pulled him by the feet, calling
him aloud by the name of hermit; after a while a sepul-
chral groan was heard, indicating that he was still alive.
The good hunter affectionately entreated him to mention
to him what he wanted; that he was ready to give him
anything that he would ask. The hermit a second time
made a prolonged groan, as a man endeavouring to gather
strength. He then mentioned to the hunter the passion
he had for his daughter, and swore that he would die on
the spot if his demand were rejected. The father having
given his consent, Upaka rose up, and was soon married
to Tsawama, who after due time presented him with a son.
It happened that Tsawama soon began to dislike her
husband, and poured upon him on every occasion all sorts
of abuse. Unable to bear any longer the unpleasant

behaviour of his wife, Upaka said to himself, " I have here neither friend nor supporter: I will go to my friend Dzina; he will receive me with kindness." Hereupon he departed, inquiring everywhere about his friend Dzina. At last he arrived at the place where Buddha was staying with his disciples. Some of them, hearing Upaka inquiring with a loud voice about his friend Dzina, took him into the presence of Buddha, who, understanding at once the sad and painful state of the old man, kindly asked what he wanted. Upaka replied that he desired to become a Samanay under his direction. Buddha, to try his disposition, said to him, " You are too old, Upaka, to enter upon the course of the severe life of a Samanay, and conform to the enjoined practices." But the latter renewing his entreaties, he was admitted among the members of the assembly. He became an Anagam, died and migrated to one of the seats of Brahmas. After a short stay up there, he obtained the deliverance. His son was Thoobadda, who became afterwards an illustrious convert. Buddha continued his way towards Baranathee, and soon reached the solitude of Migadawon, a little distant from Baranathee, and went to the place where lived the five unbelieving Rahans. When they saw him coming at a distance, they said to each other, " The Rahan Gaudama is in search after disciples; he has just performed penitential deeds, and he is looking out for alms and clothes. Let us pay no respect to him in the way of going out to meet him, of receiving the tsiwaran from his hands, of presenting him water to wash his feet and preparing a place to sit on; let him sit wherever he pleases." Such was the plan they concerted among themselves. But when Buddha drew near, they could adhere no longer to their resolution. They rose up and went out to welcome his arrival. One took the tsiwaran from his hands, another the patta, a third one brought water for the washing of the feet, and a fourth one prepared a becoming place to rest. Buddha sat in the place that had been prepared for him. They called him by the name of Gaudama and other appellations, usually bestowed on ordinary Rahans. Buddha meekly replied to them, " Do not call me any longer by the name of Gaudama, or any other title bestowed on an ascetic. I have become a Rahanda; I alone am acquainted with the four fundamental truths. Now I am come to preach to you the true law. Listen, O Rahans, to my words; I will lead you to the true state of Neibban. My law will make you acquainted not only with the truths to be known, but at the same time point out to you the duties you have to perform, in order to obtain the state of Arahat. There are four ways leading to perfection. He who steadily follows them will enjoy the rewards and merits gained by his exertions. In that position he will see distinctly his own self; the light of Neibban will break forth upon him. But in order to obtain the great results I set forth before you, he must forsake his house and the world, and become a Rahan."

The unbelieving Rahans persisted in not acknowledging him as a Buddha, and reproached him with going about in search of disciples and in quest of alms. The same preaching was repeated by Buddha, and the same answer was returned by his incredulous hearers. At last Buddha, assuming a lofty and commanding tone, said to them, " I declare unto you that I am a Buddha, knowing the four great truths and showing the way to Neibban." The hitherto unbelieving ascetics humbled themselves, and declared their belief in him and in all that he had taught. From that moment they entered on the four ways of perfection. The day was that of the full moon of Watso. The preaching began at the moment when half the disc of the sun was visible on the western horizon, and half that of the moon was above the eastern horizon. When completed, the sun had just disappeared, and the moon's entire globe was visible on the horizon. The five first converts were named Kautagnya, Baddiha, Wappa, Mahanan, and Asadzi.

The Nats, guardians of the country of Baranathee[3] and Migadawon, hearing the sublime instructions delivered by Buddha on this occasion, cried aloud, "The law which the most excellent Buddha preaches is such as no man, Pounha or Brahma, can teach." Their united voices were heard in the lowest seat of Nats; the inhabitants of that seat, catching their words, repeated them, and they were heard by those of the next seat, and so on, until they reached the seats of Brahmas, and were re-echoed through 10,000 worlds. A mighty commotion was felt all over these worlds.

The five at first unbelieving, but now believing Rahans obtained the perfection of Thautapati. Buddha often repeated to those that approached him, "Come to me; I preach a doctrine which leads to the deliverance from all the miseries attending existence." On that day, being the full moon of Watso, eighteen koodes (18,000,000,000) of Nats and Brahmas who had heard his preachings obtained

---

[3] The mission of Buddha is not, as previously observed, confined to men living on earth, but it extends its beneficial action over all the beings inhabiting the six seats of Nats and sixteen of Brahmas. Those beings, the latter in particular, are much advanced in perfection, but they are not yet ripe for the sublime state of Neibban. Though freed, at least the Brahmas, from the influence of passions, they retain as yet some inclination for matter; they want the help of a Buddha to break at once the few slender ties that retain them in the state of existence.

The first preaching of Buddha was rewarded with the conversion of five Rahans, and of a countless number of Nats and Brahmas. Such a plentiful harvest he could scarcely anticipate to reap; and the beginning of his career, attended with such wonderful success, amply repaid him for the extraordinary exertions he made in order to qualify himself for the

Buddhaship. The author of the Legend remarks, with an unfeigned pleasure, that owing to the conversion of the five Rahans, the worlds witnessed the beautiful sight of six Rahandas congregated on the same spot. The Rahanda has attained the summit of perfection; he has arrived at the last existence; his death will relieve him from the burden of existence, and open to him the way leading to perfect rest, to complete abstraction—in a word, to Neibban. The Rahandas rank first among the disciples and hearers of Buddha; they constitute the *élite* of his followers, and form the most distinguished portion of the assembly or congregation of the perfect. We have already stated that the members composing the assembly of the hearers were divided into distinct sections, and formed different degrees, according to the difference of their respective progress on the way of perfection.

the deliverance.   The conversion of those five Rahans exhibited to the world the splendid and wonderful sight of six Rahandas assembled in the same place.

At that time, whilst Buddha was in the Migadawon grove, the memorable conversion of a young layman took place.   There was in the country of Baranathee the son of a rich man, named Ratha.   He was of very gentle and amiable disposition.   His father had built for him three palaces for each season of the year.   A crowd of young damsels, skilful in the art of playing on all sorts of musical instruments, attended him in each of those palaces. Ratha spent his time in the midst of pleasure and amusements.   On a certain day, while surrounded with female dancers and singers, he fell into a deep sleep.   The musicians, following his example, laid aside their instruments, and fell asleep too.   The lamps, filled with oil, continued to pour a flood of light throughout the apartments.   Awaking sooner than usual, Ratha saw the musicians all asleep round him in various and unseemly situations.   Some slept with wide-opened mouths, some had dishevelled hair, some were snoring aloud, some had their instruments lying on themselves, and others by their side.   The whole exhibited a vast scene of the greatest confusion and disorder.   Sitting on his couch in a cross-legged position, the young man silently gazed with amazement and disgust over the unseemly spectacle displayed before him; then he said to himself, "The nature and condition of the body constitute indeed a truly heavy burden; that coarser part of our being affords a great deal of trouble and affliction." Whereupon he instantly arose from his couch, put on his gilt slippers, and came down to the door of his apartment. The Nats, who kept a vigilant watch, lest any one should oppose him in the execution of his holy purpose, kept open the door of the house, as well as the gate of the city. Ratha, free from all impediments, directed his steps towards the solitude of Migadawon.   At that time Buddha who had left his sleeping place at a very early hour, was walking in front of the house. He saw at a distance a young man coming in the direction he was in. He instantly stopped his pacing, and going into his own apartment, sat as usual on his seat, awaiting the arrival of the young stranger, who soon made his appearance and stated modestly the object of his visit. Buddha said to him, "O Ratha! the law of Neibban is the only true one: alone it is never attended with misery and affliction. O Ratha! come nearer to me; remain in this place; to you I will make known the most perfect and valuable law." On hearing these kind and inviting expressions, Ratha felt his heart overflow with the purest joy. He instantly put off his slippers, drew nearer to Buddha, bowed down three times before him, withdrew then to a becoming distance, and remained in a respectful attitude. Buddha began to preach the law, unfolding successively the various merits obtained by alms-giving, by a strict performance of all duties and practices of the law, and, above all, by renouncing the pleasures of this world. During all the while the heart of the young visitor expanded in a wonderful manner: he felt the ties that hitherto had bound him as it were to the world gradually relaxing and giving way before the unresisting influence of Buddha's words. The good dispositions of the young hearer were soon remarked by Buddha, who went on explaining all that related to the miseries attending existence, the passions tyrannising over the soul, the means wherewith to become exempt from those passions, and the great ways leading to perfection. After having listened to that series of instructions, Ratha, like a white cloth that easily retains the impressions of various colours printed upon it, felt himself freed from all passions, and reached at once the state of Thautapati.

Ratha's mother, not meeting her son early, went up as usual to his apartment, and, to her great surprise, found him gone; moreover she observed unmistakable marks of his sudden and unexpected departure. She ran forthwith to her husband, and announced to him the sad tidings.

On hearing of such an unlooked-for event, the father sent messengers in the direction of the four points of the compass, with positive orders to search incessantly after his son, and leave no means of inquiry untried. As to himself he resolved to go to the solitude of Migadawon, in the hope of finding out some track of his son's escape. He had scarcely travelled a limited distance, when he observed on the ground the marks of his son's footsteps. He followed them up and soon came in sight of Buddha's resting-place. Ratha was at the time listening with deepest attention to all the words of his great teacher. By the power of Buddha he remained hidden from the eyes of his father, who came up, and, having paid his respects to Gaudama, eagerly asked him if he had not seen his son. Gaudama bade him sit down and rest after the fatigue of his journey. Meanwhile he assured him that he would soon see his son. Rejoiced at such an assurance, Ratha's father complied with the invitation he had received. Buddha announced his law to this distinguished hearer, and soon led him to the perfection of Thautapati. Filled with joy and gratitude, the new convert exclaimed, "O illustrious Phra, your doctrine is a most excellent one; when you preach it, you do like him who replaces on its basis an upset cup; like him, too, who brings to light precious things, which had hitherto remained in darkness; like him who points out the right way to those that have lost it; who kindles a brilliant light in the middle of darkness; who opens the mind's eyes that they might see the pure truth. Henceforth I adhere to you and to your holy law; please to reckon me as one of your disciples and supporters." This was the first layman that became a disciple of Gaudama, in the capacity of Upasaka.[4]

---

[4] It may be interesting to give an abridgment of an instruction or sermon delivered by Gaudama to a Nat. It will be as a fair specimen of other similar performances. The Nat made his appearance at nightfall, and respectfully entreated Buddha to deliver certain instructions which would enable men to come to the understanding of many points of the law on which they had hitherto fruitlessly meditated. Buddha was then in the

Whilst Buddha was busily engaged in imparting instruction to Ratha's father, the young man had entered into a deep and solemn meditation over some of the high-

---

monastery of Dzetawon, in the country of Thawattie. This sermon is supposed to have been repeated by Ananda, who had heard it from the mouth of Buddha himself. It is, according to the Burmese, the most excellent sermon; it contains thirty-eight points.

"Young Nat," said Buddha, "here are the most excellent things men and Nats ought to attend to, in order to capacitate themselves for the state of Neibban: to shun the company of the foolish; to be always with the wise; to proffer homage to those that are deserving of it; to remain in a place becoming one's condition; to have always with one's self the influence of former good works; steadily to maintain a perfect behaviour; to be delighted to hear and see much, in order to increase knowledge; to study all that is not sinful; to apply one's self to acquire the knowledge of Wini. Let every one's conversation be regulated by righteous principles; let every one minister to the wants of his father and mother; provide all the necessaries for his wife and children; perform no action under the evil influence of temptation; bestow alms; observe the precepts of the law; assist one's relatives and friends; perform no actions but such as are exempt from sin; be ever diligent in such avoiding, and abstain from intoxicating drink. Let no one be remiss in the practice of the law of merits. Let every one bear respect to all men; be ever humble; be easily satisfied and content; gratefully acknowledge favours; listen to the preaching of the law in its proper time; be patient; delight in good conversation; visit the religious from time to time; converse on religious subjects; cultivate the virtue of mor-

tification; practise works of virtue; pay attention always to the four great truths; keep the eyes fixed on Neibban. Finally, let one in the middle of the eight afflictions of this world be, like the Rahanda, firm, without disquietude, fearless, with a perfect composure. O young Nat, whoever observes these perfect laws shall never be overcome by the enemies of the good: he shall enjoy the peace of Ariaha."

Within a narrow compass, Buddha has condensed an abridgment of almost all moral virtues. The first portion of these precepts contains injunctions to shun all that may prove an impediment to the practice of good works. The second part inculcates the necessity of regulating one's mind and intention for a regular discharge of the duties incumbent on each man in his separate station. Then follows a recommendation to bestow assistance on parents, relatives, and all men in general. Next to that, we find recommended the virtues of humility, resignation, gratitude, and patience. After this, the preacher insists on the necessity of studying the law, visiting religious, conversing on religious subjects. When this is done, the hearer is commanded to study with great attention the four great truths, and keep his mind's eye ever fixed on the happy state of Neibban, which, though as yet distant, ought never to be lost sight of. Thus prepared, the hearer must be bent upon acquiring the qualifications befitting the true sage. Like the one mentioned by the Latin poet, who would remain firm, fearless, and unmoved, even in the midst of the ruins of the crumbling universe, the Buddhist sage must ever remain calm, composed, and unshaken among all the

est maxims he had heard from his great teacher. He was calmly surveying, as it were, all the things of this world; the more he progressed in that great work, the more he felt there was in himself no affection whatever for any-thing. He had not yet become a Rahan, nor put on the Rahan's dress. Phra, who attentively watched all the movements of his pupil's mind, concluded from his present dispositions that there could be no fear of his ever return-ing into the world of passions. He suddenly caused by his mighty power the son to become visible to his father's eyes. The father, perceiving on a sudden his son sitting close by him, said, "Beloved son, your mother is now bathed in tears, and almost sinking under the weight of affliction caused by your sudden departure; come now to her, and by your presence restore her to life, and infuse into her desolated soul some consolation." Ratha, calm and unmoved, made no reply, but cast a look at his master. Buddha, addressing Ratha's father, said to him, "What will you have to state in reply to what I am about to tell you? Your son knows what you know; he sees what you see; his heart is entirely disentangled from all attachment to worldly objects; passions are dead in him. Who will now ever presume to say that he ought to subject himself again to them and bend his neck under their baneful in-fluence?" "I have spoken rashly," replied the father; "let my son continue to enjoy the favour of your society; let him remain with you for ever and become your dis-ciple. The only favour I request for myself is to have the satisfaction of receiving you in my house with my son attending you, and there to enjoy the happiness of supply-ing you with your food." Buddha by his silence assented to his request. No sooner had his father departed than Ratha applied for the dignity of Rahan, which was forth-with conferred upon him. At that time there were in the world seven Rahandas.

---

vicissitudes of life. Here is again clearly pointed out the final end to be arrived at, viz., that of perfect mental stability. This state is the foreshadowing of that of Neibban.

On the following morning, Gaudama, putting on his yellow tsiwaran, and carrying the patta under his arm, attended by the Rahan Ratha, sallied from his house, and went, according to his promise, to the place of Ratha's father, to receive his food. He had scarce entered the house and occupied the seat prepared for him, when the mother of the new Rahan and she who was formerly his wife came both to pay him their respects. Buddha preached to them the law, explaining in particular the three [5] principal observances becoming their sex and con-

---

[5] From the perusal of this legend, it can be remarked that Buddha, in the course of his preachings, withheld from no one the knowledge of his doctrine, but, on the contrary, aimed at popularising it in every possible way. In this respect he widely differed from the Brahmins, who enveloped their tenets in a mysterious obscurity, and even in that state of semi-incomprehensibility, condescended to offer them to the consideration of but a few selected adepts. But Buddha followed quite an opposite course. He preached to all without exception. On this occasion we see him engaged in explaining to the mother and wife of Ratha duties truly becoming their sex and position. He warned them against the danger of speaking too much, or speaking hastily and with a tone of dissatisfaction. He desired them to be always cool and moderate in their conversation, and to take a pleasure in conversing on religious topics, such as the practice of the ten great duties, the merits of almsgiving, and on the other precepts of the law. He showed to them the unbecomingness of inconsistency in speaking, and finally concluded by exhorting them to allow wisdom to guide them in the right use of the faculty of speech. Every one will agree in this that the lecture was a very appropriate one, and would suit women of our days as well as those of Buddha's times.

It is not easy to determine whether these two female converts became Rabanesses by forsaking the world and devoting all their time to religious observances, or simply believed in Buddha's doctrines and continued to live in the world. The Burmese translator makes use of expressions liable to both interpretations. I feel inclined to adopt the second supposition. They became female Upasakas, and continued to live in the world. We shall see, hereafter, that Gaudama's aunt, Patzapati, was the first, after much entreating, who was allowed to become a Rahaness.

The great former of the Buddhistic disciplinary regulations has also laid down rules for the institution and management of an order of female devotees, to match, as it were, with that of talapoins. Hence in almost all countries where Buddhism flourishes, there are to be met houses and monasteries which are the abodes of those pious women, who emulate Rahans in the strict observance of practices of the highest order. Their dress, except the colour, which is white, is quite similar to that of talapoins; their head is shaved; they live in strict continence as long as they continue to wear the dress of their profession. They have certain formulas of prayer to repeat every day several times. Their diet is the same as that of talapoins; they are forbidden to take any food after midday. I am not

dition. The effect of the preaching was immediate and irresistible: they became exempt from all sins, and attained the state of the perfect, of Thautapati, and became, among the persons of their sex, the first Upasakas. They desired to be ranked among his disciples, and devoted themselves to his service. They were the first persons of their sex who took refuge in the three precious things, Buddha, his law, and the assembly of the perfect. Gaudama and his faithful attendant, having eaten the excellent and savoury food prepared for them, departed from the house and returned to the monastery.

Four young men [6] belonging to the most illustrious

---

aware that they render any service to society in the way of keeping schools for the benefit of female children. They live on alms freely bestowed on them by their co-religionists. The Burmese honour them with the title of Mathi-la-shing, which means ladies of the religious duties. The order of those female devotees is now much on the decline; the iumates of houses are but few, enjoying a very small share of public esteem and respect. They are generally looked upon with feelings akin to those entertained towards beggars.

In the Wini, or book of discipline, the relations that are allowed to subsist between the two orders of male and female devotees are minutely described and clearly laid down, so as to prevent the evils that might result from a familiar and unnecessary intercourse. Thoroughly acquainted with the weakest side of human nature, the author of the Wini has legislated on that subject with the utmost circumspection. He allowed rather aged Rahans to be the spiritual advisers of the Rahanesses, but he denies them the leave of ever going to their houses under any pretext whatever. When the latter want to hear preaching or receive some advice from the Rahans, they resort in broad daylight to the monastery, are permitted to stay in a large hall open to the public, at a considerable distance from him whom they desire to consult. Having briefly and with becoming reverence made known the object of their visit, and received some spiritual instructions, they immediately return to their own place.

The same reflection may be applied to the conversion of Ratha's father. It is said that he was the first convert out of the body of laymen. He does not appear to have forsaken the world and become a first-class convert. He became a Thautapati, and at once entered one of the four ways leading to perfection, but remained in the world.

[6] The conversion of Ratha and of his young friends shows to us distinctly the tendency of Buddha's preachings, and their effect over those who believed in him. Ratha is represented as a young worldly-minded man, who, in the midst of riches, has denied himself to no kind of pleasure. He feels that the enjoyments he was so fond of can in no manner satisfy the cravings of his heart: he is disgusted at them, and resolves to withdraw into solitude, with the intention of placing himself under the direction of some eminent teacher, and

families of Baranathee, and formerly connected with Ratha by the ties of intimate friendship, having heard that their friend had shaved his head and beard, had put on a yellow dress and become a Rahan, said among themselves: "Our friend has withdrawn from the society of men, given up all pleasures, and has entered into the society of Rahans. There can be no doubt but the law of Wini [7] is most ex-

learn from him the way to happiness. He hopes that the study of philosophy will lead him to true wisdom and the acquirement of the means that may render him happy. He luckily falls in with Buddha, who explains to him that the senses are the instruments through which passions act upon and tyrannise over the soul, by keeping it in a painful subjection to matter. He points out to him the necessity of freeing himself from their control. This principle of Buddhism, which aims at disengaging the soul from matter, isolating it from all that proves a burden to it, and delivering it from the tyrannical yoke of concupiscence, is in itself perfectly correct, but, carried beyond its legitimate consequences, it becomes false and absurd. According to Buddhists, the soul, disentangled from all that exists, finds itself alone without any object it can adhere to; folding itself up into its own being, it remains in a state of internal contemplation, destitute alike of all active feelings of pleasure and pain. This doctrine was known in the time of Buddha, as far as the principle is concerned. The Rathees and other sages in those days upheld it both in theory and practice; but, on the consequences, the originator of Buddhism was at issue with his contemporaries, and struck out a new path in the boundless field of speculative philosophy.

[7] The Wini is one of the great divisions of Buddhistic sacred writings. The Pitagat, or collection of all the Scriptures, is divided into three parts—the Thouts, containing the preachings of Buddha, the Wini, or book of the discipline, and the Abidama, or the book of Metaphysics. That compilation is supposed to embody the doctrines of Buddha in a complete manner. These books have not been written by Buddha himself, since it is said of him that he never wrote down anything. The first Buddhistic compositions were certainly written by the disciples of Phra, or their immediate successors. But there arose some disputes among the followers of Buddha, as to the genuineness of the doctrines contained in the various writings published by the chief disciples. To settle the controversy, an assembly or council of the most influential members of the Buddhistic creed, under the presidency of Kathaba, was held about three months after Gaudama's demise. The writings regarded as spurious were set aside, and those purporting to contain the pure doctrines of Phra were collected into one body, and formed, as it were, the canon of sacred books. The matter so far was settled for the time being, but the human mind, when unrestrained by authority, acted in those days with the same result as it does in our own times. Various and different were the constructions put on the same text by the expounders of the Buddhistic law. All parties admitted the same books, but they dissented from each other in the interpretation. Some of the books hitherto regarded as sacred were

cellent and sublime, and the profession of Rahan most perfect." Whereupon they came to the place their friend resided in, prostrated themselves before him, as usual in such circumstances, and sat down at a respectful and becoming distance. Ratha took them before Buddha, praying him to deliver to those who had been his friends in the world the same instructions he had received from him. Gaudama willingly assented to his request, and forthwith began to explain to them the nature and abundance of merits derived from almsgiving. He initiated them into the knowledge of the chief precepts and observances of the law. These young hearers received with a cheerful heart his instructions, and felt within themselves an unknown power, dissolving gradually all the ties that had hitherto retained them in the world of passions. Delighted at remarking so good dispositions in those young men, Gaudama explained to them the higher doctrine of the four great and fundamental truths which lead to perfection.[8]

---

altered or rejected altogether to make room for the works of new doctors. Confusion prevailed to such an extent, that an hundred years later a second council was assembled for determining the authenticity of the real and genuine writings. A new compilation was made and approved of by the assembly. The evil was remedied ; but the same causes that had exercised so baneful an influence previously to the time of the second council soon worked again and produced a similar result. Two hundred and thirty-five years after Gaudama's death a third council was assembled. The books compiled by the second council were revised and apparently much abridged, and with the sanction of the assembled fathers a new canon of scriptures was issued. The Pitagat in its present shape is regarded as the work of this last assembly. All the books are written in the Pali or Magatha language. In

the beginning of the fifth century of our era, according to our author's computation, a learned man, named Boudagautha, went to Ceylon, and brought back to Burmah a copy of the collection of the Pitagat. Then he introduced into this country the alphabet now in use, and translated into the vernacular a portion of the scriptures. This important subject shall receive hereafter fuller development.

[8] The four principles or truths so often alluded to in the course of this work ought to be well understood, in order to get a clear insight into the system under consideration. These four truths are as follows:—1. There are afflictions and miseries attending the existence of all beings. 2. There are passions and, in particular, concupiscence, which are the causes of all miseries. 3. There is Neibban, which is the exemption of all passions, and, consequently, the deliver-

When the preaching was over, they applied for and obtained the dignity of Rahans. There were at that time eleven Rahandas in the whole world.

Fifty other young men of good descent, who had been the companions of Ratha while in the world, having heard that their friend had left the world, had put on the yellow

ance from all miseries. 4. There are the four ways or high roads leading to Neibban. Here is the summary of the sublime knowledge and transcendent science possessed by a Buddha: these four fundamental truths form the four features or characteristics of his law; they safely guide man in the way to deliverance. The Buddhist sage, who longs to become perfect, must study with attention the position of all beings in this world, survey with a patient regard their diversified conditions, and fathom the depth of the abyss of miseries in which they are miserably sunk. A vague, general and superficial knowledge of these miseries is insufficient to create that perfect acquaintance with human wretchedness. He ought to examine one after the other those series of afflictions, until he feels, as it were, their unbearable weight pressing over his soul. This first step having been made by the means of reflection, meditation, and experience, the sage, standing by the side of all miseries that press upon all beings, as a physician, by the bed of a patient, enquires into the cause of such an awful moral disorder. He soon discovers the generating causes of that universal distemper; they are the passions in general; or rather, to speak more in accordance with Buddhistic expressions, concupiscence, anger, and ignorance are the springs all demerits flow from, are the impure sources wherefrom originate all the miseries and afflictions this world is filled with. The destruction of those passions is the

main and great object he has in view. He, therefore, leaves the world and renounces all pleasures and worldly possessions, in order to extinguish concupiscence; he practises patience under the most trying circumstances, that anger may no longer have any power over him; he studies the law, and meditates on all its points, in order to dispel the dark atmosphere of ignorance by the bright light of knowledge.

Having advanced so far, the sage has not yet reached the final object of his desires; he has not yet attained to the end he anxiously wishes to come to. He is just prepared and qualified for going in search of it. Neibban, or the *absolute* exemption and *permanent* deliverance from the four causes productive of existence, or of a state of being, is the only thing he deems worthy to be desired and earnestly longed for. The sage, perceiving such a desirable state, sighs after it with all the powers of his soul. Neibban is to him what the harbour is to the storm-beaten mariner, or deliverance to the worn-out inmate of a dark dungeon. But such a happy state is, as yet, at a great distance; where is the road leading thereto? This is the last truth the sage has to investigate. The four roads to perfection are opened before him. These he must follow with perseverance; they will conduct him to Neibban. They are a perfect belief, a perfect reflection, a perfect use of speech, and a perfect conduct.

garb and become Rahan, said to each other: "The law which our friend listened to may not be a bad one; the profession he has entered into may not be as despicable as many people are wont to assert." They resolved to judge for themselves and to be eye-witnesses to all that had been said on the subject. They set out for the monastery Ratha was living in, came into his presence, paid their respects to him, and stopped at a proper distance in a respectful posture. Ratha led them to his great teacher, humbly craving for his former friends the same favour he had done to him. Buddha graciously assented to the request, and imparted instruction to his young hearers, with such a happy result that they instantly applied for admittance to the dignity of Rahans. This favour was granted to them. The total number of Rahandas was thereby raised to sixty-one.

On a certain day, Gaudama called his disciples into his presence,[9] and said to them: "Beloved Rahans, I am

---

[9] Buddha, having trained up his disciples to the knowledge of his doctrines as well as to the practice of his ordinances, elevates them to the dignity of preachers, or, to be more correct, makes them fellow-labourers in the arduous task of imparting to mankind the wholesome knowledge of saving truths. An unbounded field is opened before him; the number of beings who are designed to partake of the blessings of his doctrines is incalculably great. His own efforts will not prove adequate to the difficulties such a mighty undertaking is encompassed with; he joins to himself fervent disciples that have reached all but the farthest limit of perfection by the thorough control they have obtained over their passions; he considers them as instruments well fitted for carrying into execution his benevolent designs, and entrusts them with the mission he has entered upon. By adopting such a step, the wise founder of Buddhism establishes a regular order of men, whom he commissions to go and preach to all living creatures the doctrines they have learnt from him. The commission he imparted to them was evidently to be handed down to their successors in the same office. He may now die, but he is sure that the work he has begun shall be carried on with zeal and devotedness by men who have renounced the world and given up all sorts of enjoyments, that they might engage in the great undertaking with a heart perfectly disentangled from all ties and impediments of every description.

In entrusting his disciples with the important duty of teaching mankind, Buddha, obeying the impulse of his universal charity, desires them to go all over the world and preach all the truth to all mortals. He distinctly charges them to announce openly and unreservedly all that they have heard

exempt from the five great passions which, like an immense net, encompass men and Nats. You too, owing to the instructions you have received from me, enjoy the same glorious privilege. There is now incumbent on us a great duty, that of labouring effectually in behalf of men and Nats, and procuring to them the invaluable blessing of the deliverance. To the end of securing more effectually the success of such an undertaking, let us part with each other and proceed in various and opposite directions, so that not two of us should follow up the same way. Go ye now and preach the most excellent law, expounding every point thereof, and unfolding it with care and attention in all its bearings and particulars. Explain the beginning, the middle, and the end of the law to all men, without exception; let everything respecting it be made publicly known and brought to the broad daylight. Show now to men and Nats the way leading to the practice of pure and meritorious works. You will meet, doubtless, with a great number of mortals, not as yet hopelessly given up to their passions, and who will avail themselves of your preaching

---

from him. In these instructions the plan of Buddha is clearly laid down, and the features of the mission he assumes distinctly delineated. His object is to spread his doctrines all over the world and to bring all beings under his moral sway. He makes no distinction between man and man, nation and nation. Though belonging by birth to a high caste, he disregards at once those worldly barriers whereby men are separated from each other, and acknowledges no dignity but that which is conferred by virtue. Bold, indeed, was the step that he took in a country where the distinction of caste is so deeply rooted in the habits of the people, that all human efforts have, hitherto, proved abortive in destroying it. It has already been hinted in a foregoing note that Gaudama placed himself on a new ground, in opposition to the Brahminical doc-trines. He, doubtless, cautiously avoided to wound directly the feelings of his antagonists; but, at the same time, he adroitly sowed the seed of a mighty revolution, that was to change, if left to grow freely, the face of the Indian peninsula. His doctrine bore two characteristics, that were to distinguish it essentially from that of his adversaries; it was popular and universal, whereas that of his opponents was wrapped up in a mysterious obscurity, and unfolded completely only to a privileged caste. Another great difference between the two systems is this: Buddha paid little attention to the dogmatical portion of religion, but laid the greatest stress on morals. The dogmas are few and little insisted on. He aimed at correcting the vices of the heart, but exerted himself little to redress the errors of the mind.

for reconquering their hitherto forfeited liberty, and freeing themselves from the thraldom of passions. For my
own part, I will direct my course towards the village of
Thena, situated in the vicinity of the solitude of Ooroowela."

At that time the wicked Nat Manh came into the presence of Buddha, and tempted him in the following manner:—"Men and Nats," said he, "have the five senses;
through those five senses passions act upon them, encompass their whole being, and finally keep them bound up
with the chains of an unresistible slavery. As to you,
Rahan, you are not an exception to that universal condition, and you have not yet outstepped the boundaries of
my empire." Phra replied: "O vile and wretched Nat!
I am well acquainted with the passions men and Nats are
subjected to. But I have freed myself from them all, and
have thereby placed myself without the pale of your empire; you are at last vanquished and conquered." Manh,
yet undismayed, replied: "O Rahan, you may be possessed
of the power of flying through the air; but even in that
condition, those passions which are inherent in the
nature of mortal beings will accompany you, so that you
cannot flatter yourself of living without the boundaries of
my empire." Phra retorted, "O wicked Nat, concupiscence and all other passions I have stifled to death in me,
so that you are at last conquered." Manh, the most
wretched among the wretched, was compelled to confess
with a broken heart that Phra had conquered him, and he
instantly vanished away.

Full of fervour in preaching the law, the Rahans saw
themselves surrounded with crowds of converts, who asked
for the dignity of Rahan. They poured in daily from all
parts, into the presence of Buddha, to receive at his hands
the much-longed-for high dignity.[10] Buddha said to them,

---

[10] In these new instructions delivered to the Rahans, Buddha gives
them the power of receiving into
the ranks of the assembly those of
their converts who should prove foremost in understanding the law and
observing its highest practices. He
empowers them to confer on others

"Beloved Rahans, it is painful and troublesome both to you and to those who desire to be admitted into our holy brotherhood to come from such a great distance to me. I

the dignity of Rahans, and admit them to the various steps that lead to that uppermost one. To observe uniformity in the reception of candidates to the various orders, Buddha laid down a number of regulations embodied in the Kambawa, or book used as a sort of ritual on the days of admission of candidates to the dignity of Patzins and Rahans. The contents of this small· but interesting work may be seen in the notice on the order of talapoins, or Buddhist monks, inserted at the end of this volume. That the reader may have now an idea of the general purpose and object of these regulations, I will sketch a slight outline of them. The candidate, who seeks for admission among the members of the order, has to appear before an assembly of Rahans, presided over by a dignitary. He must be provided with the dress of the order, and a patta or the pot of a mendicant. He is presented to the assembly by a Rahan, upon whom devolves the important duty of instructing him in all that regards the profession he is about to embrace, and lead him through the ordeal of the ceremony. He is solemnly interrogated before the assembly on the several defects and impediments which incapacitate an individual for admission into the order. On his declaring that he is free from such impediments, he is, with the consent of the assembled fathers, promoted to the rank of Patzin. But before he is allowed to take his place among his brethren, he is instructed in the four principal duties he will have to observe, and warned against the four capital sins, the commission of which would deprive him of his high and holy character, and cause his expulsion from the society.

It is supposed that the candidate, previous to his making application for obtaining the dignity of Rahan, has qualified himself by study and a good life for admittance among the perfect. By surrounding the admission of candidates into the ranks of the order with a display of ceremonies, the shrewd framer of these regulations intended to encircle the whole body with a halo of dignity and sacredness, and at the same time to provide, as far as human wisdom allows, against the reception of unworthy postulants.

Hitherto Buddha had reserved to himself alone the power of elevating hearers or converts to the dignity of Rahans; now he transfers to his disciples that power and bids them use it as they had seen him do, in behalf of those whom they deem worthy applicants. He has established a society, and striven to infuse·into it all the elements necessary for keeping it up hereafter, and securing its existence and permanency. He sets up a kind of ecclesiastical hierarchy, which is to be perpetuated during the ages to come by the same means and power that brought it into existence.

Having put such a power into the hands of his disciples, Buddha very properly exhorts them to emulate him in his efforts to become perfect. He sets himself as a pattern of perfection, and bids them all imitate the examples he places before them. He shows briefly to them by what means he has attained the state of Arahatapho, and stimulates them to the adopting of similar means. The word Arahatapho is composed of two words —arahat, which means perfect, and pho or phola, as the orthography indicates, which means reward, merit. The state of Arahatapho is that in which a man enjoys the merits or

now give to you the power of conferring the dignity of Patzin and Rahan on those whom you may deem worthy to receive it. This is the summary way you will have to follow on such occasions. Every candidate shall have his hair and beard shaved, and shall be provided with the tsi-waran of yellow colour. These preliminaries being arranged, the candidate, with the extremities of the kowot thrown over his shoulders, shall place himself in a squatting position, his joined hands raised to the forehead, repeating three times, 'I adhere to Buddha, to the law, and to the assembly of the perfect.'"

Gaudama, assembling again round him the Rahans, said to them, "Beloved Rahans, it is owing to my wisdom, aided by constant reflection and meditation, that I have at last reached the incomparable state of Arahatapho; endeavour all of you to follow my example, and arrive at last at the same state of excellence and perfection."

The vile and wretched Nat Manh appeared again before Buddha, striving to tempt him in the same manner as before. Buddha, discovering the snares laid down by the tempter, returned the same reply. Finding himself discovered, Manh vanished from his presence.

Having spent his first lent [11] in the solitude of Migada-

---

reward of perfection, which he has reached by the practice of virtue, and particularly the acquirement of wisdom or knowledge of the highest points of the law. It is used often in opposition to the word Arahata-megata, which signifies the ways or roads leading to perfection.

[11] I have translated by *lent* the Burmese expression Watso, which is but the Pali term Wasa, Burmanised. The word "lent," which has been adopted, is designed to express not the real meaning of Wasa, but to convey to the reader's mind the idea of a time devoted to religious observances. Wasa means a season, but it is intended to designate the rainy season, which in those parts of the Peninsula where Buddha was residing begins in July and ends in November. During that period the communications between villages and towns are difficult, if not impossible. The religious mendicants were allowed in former times, very likely from the very days of Buddha, to retire into the houses of friends and supporters, from which they went forth occasionally begging their food. In the beginning, those who were admitted in the society did not live in community, as was afterwards done in those countries where Buddhism has been of a long time in a flourishing condition. They were allowed to with-

won, Phra shaped his course in the direction of the forest of Oroowela. On his way to that place he stopped for a while in a jungle, and sat under a tree, to enjoy some rest

draw into solitude, and lead an ascetic life, or to travel from one place to another to preach the law and make converts. This work could not be well done during the rainy season. Hence the disciples, while as yet few in number, gathered round their master during that period to hear instructions from him, and practise virtue under his immediate superintendence. They lived with him during all the time the rainy season lasted. This was called to spend the season. In the course of this Legend, the same expression is often met with. It is said of Buddha that he spent a season in such a place, another in another place, to indicate that he stayed in one place during the rainy season, which precluded the possibility of doing the duties of an itinerant preacher.

When the religious order became regularly constituted, and the basis it was to stand on was fairly laid down, the ever-increasing number of members made them feel the want of secluded places where they could live in community, and at the same time quite retired from the world. Houses or monasteries were erected for receiving the pious Rahans. The inmates of those dwellings lived under the direction of a superior, devoting their time to study, meditation, and the observances of the law. They were allowed to go out in the morning very early, to beg and collect the food they wanted for the day. Such is the state the religious are living in up to our own time in Burmah, Ceylon, Thibet, Siam, and in the other countries where Buddhism has been firmly established.

The religious season, or lent, lasts three months. It begins in the full moon of Watso (July) and ends at the full moon of Thadinkiout (October). The keeping of the season in Burmah is as follows:—On the days of the new and full moon crowds of people resort to the pagodas, carrying offerings of flowers, small candles, oil, &c. A great many are found to spend the night in the bungalows erected, chiefly for that purpose, in their immediate vicinity. Women occupy bungalows separated from those of men. It must be admitted that there, as in churches, they far outnumber the men. On such occasions, religion appears to be rather the pretext than the real object of such assemblies. With the exception of old men and women, who are heard to converse on religious topics, and repeat some parts of the law, or recite some praises in honour of Buddha, the others seem to care very little for religion. The younger portion of the weaker sex freely indulge in the pleasure of conversation. It is quite a treat to them to have such a fine opportunity of giving full ·scope to their talkative powers. During that season the pious faithful are charitably inclined to bestow alms on the Rahans. All the necessaries of life pour with abundance and profusion into the monasteries. Besides almsgiving and resorting to the pagodas, some fervent laymen practise abstinence and fastings to a certain extent; these, however, are but few. During that period the Buddhist recluses are often invited to go to certain places, prepared for the purpose, to preach the law to and receive alms from crowds of hearers who are gathered thither on such occasions. Talapoins are generally seated on an elevated platform, facing the congregation; they keep their large fans before the face through modesty, to

under its cool shade. At that time thirty young noblemen had come to the jungle to indulge in sports and diversions. Each of them had brought his wife, with the exception of one, who, having no wife, was accompanied by a harlot. During the night the harlot rose up unperceived, picked up the best articles belonging to the parties, and carrying them with her, took to her heels through the dense forest. In the morning the thirty young noblemen, rising up, soon perceived the havoc made in the richest articles of their dress, and set out in search of her who they suspected had done the mischief. They came by chance to the spot where Gaudama was sitting in a cross-legged position, and inquired from him whether he had seen a woman passing by. Buddha said to them, " Which, in your opinion, is the best and most advantageous thing, either to go in search of yourselves or in search of a woman ?" They replied, " Of course it is preferable to look after ourselves." " If so," replied Buddha, " stay with me for a while ; I will preach my law to you, and, with its help, you will arrive at the knowledge of self, and thence at perfection." They cheerfully assented to his request, listened attentively to his instructions, and obtained the state of perfect believers, but in various degrees, according to their respective dispositions. They gave up the habit of drunkenness they had hitherto indulged in, and persevered in the observance of the five great precepts.

[It is to be remarked, adds the Burmese translator, that this happy result was secured to the fortunate hearers by

---

save themselves from the danger of looking on some tempting object. They repeat in chorus certain passages of the life of Buddha, enumerate the five great precepts and other observances of the law. The whole preaching generally goes on in Pali, that is to say, in a language unknown to the congregation. When they have done their duty they withdraw, followed by a great number of their disciples, carrying back to the monasteries all the offerings made by the faithful. It happens also, although but seldom in our days, that some fervent recluses withdraw during the whole or a part of the lent season into solitary places, living by themselves, and devoting all their time to reading the books of the law, and meditating on the most important points and maxims of religion.

the influence of good works made during former existences.[12]]

Gaudama, having so happily completed the conversion

---

[12] The remarks of the Burmese translator afford me an opportunity of explaining one of the leading tenets of the Buddhistic creed. All beings in this world are subjected to the double influence of their merits and demerits. The good influence pre-dominates when the sum of merits surpasses that of demerits, and it is superseded by the latter when the contrary takes place. This principle once admitted, Buddhists explain the good or evil that befalls every individual in every conceivable state of existence. Is a man dead, he is at-tended on his way to another state of being both by his merits and demerits, who, like two inseparable companions, follow him whithersoever he goes. Should the sum of demerits prove greater, he is forced into hell, or into some other state of punishment, to bear sufferings proportionately to his offences, until he has fully paid off his debt, or, to speak the language of Buddhists, until the sum of his de-merits be quite exhausted. If, on the contrary, at the moment of his death the influence of merits be the strongest, he is directed into a state of happiness, pleasure, and enjoyment, say in one of the seats of Nats or Brahmas, and remains there as long as the action of the good influence lasts. When it is over he comes again into the abode of man, or in a state of probation, when he has to labour anew for amassing new and greater merits, that will hereafter entitle him to a higher reward than the one he had previously enjoyed. From the foregoing observations it is evident that the idea of a Supreme Being rewarding the good and punish-ing the wicked is carefully excluded, and all foreign interference on this subject entirely done away with.

Another conclusion flowing from the same source is, that there is no eternity of reward or punishment, but both last for a longer or shorter period, in proportion to the sum of merits and demerits, and consequently to the power of each influence respec-tively.

It may be asked what becomes of the sum of demerits and its conse-quent evil influence, whilst the superior good influence prevails? The sum of demerits remains all the while entire and undiminished; the operation of the evil influence is sus-pended, and has no power whatever, its own being checked by a greater one. But the sum of merits being exhausted, and its inherent action at an end, the opposite one is set at liberty, and acts on the individual proportionately to its own strength, and lasts until it is all exhausted. As man can never be without some merits or demerits, good or bad deeds, he must be either in a state of reward or punishment; this is, if I may say so, the mainspring that moves all beings into the whirlpool of countless existences, wherein they meet happi-ness or unhappiness according to their deserts. The being that tends strongly and perseveringly through his various existences towards perfection, weakens gradually, and finally destroys in him-self the law of demerits; he ascends steadily the steps of the ladder of perfection by the practice of the highest virtues. Having reached its summit, there is no more reason for his going through other existences, and he steps at once into the state of Neibban.

On the above principle Buddhists account for all the various phases of human existence. Is a child born from rich, great, and distinguished

of those young noblemen, rose up and continued his journey in the direction of the forest of Ooroowela. At that time there were three distinguished and far-famed teachers who presided over a vast number of Rathees or disciples leading an ascetic life. They were named Ooroowela Kathaba, Nadi Kathaba, and Gaya Kathaba. The first had under him five hundred disciples, the second three hundred, and the third two hundred. Buddha went up to the monastery of Ooroowela Kathaba, and said to him, "I carry but a few articles with me, and need but a small place to rest in ; I beg of you to be allowed to spend the night only in your kitchen." Kathaba answered: "Since you have so few things with you, I willingly allow you to accommodate yourself in the best way you can in the cook-room; but I must inform you that the Naga guardian of the place is an animal of a very wicked temper, powerfully strong, and having a most deadly venom." "I fear not the Naga," replied Buddha ; "I am well satisfied with your allowing me a place in the cook-room." Whereupon he entered into the kitchen, sat down in a cross-legged position, and, keeping his body in an erect posture, remained absorbed, as it were, in the deepest contemplation. The Naga soon appeared, and irritated at seeing that a stranger presumed to remain in a place committed to his care, resolved to drive out the intruder. He began to vomit a cloud of

---

parents, does he become a wealthy and powerful man, does he become a king or a nobleman, &c.—he is indebted for all that to merits acquired during former existences. Is another child born in a low, poor, and wretched condition, is he born with bodily or intellectual defects and imperfections, &c., &c.—his former demerits are the principle and cause of all his subsequent misfortunes.

The doctrine of merits and demerits, and of their concomitant influences, has been fully illustrated in the person of Buddha himself during his former existences. He said of himself to his disciples that he had passed with various fortune through the range of the animal kingdom, from the dove to the elephant; that being man he had been often in hell, and in various positions of riches and poverty, greatness and meanness, until by his mighty efforts he at last freed himself from all evil influence, and reached his present state of perfection. He is supposed to have recounted to his disciples on different occasions five hundred and ten of his former existences.

smoke, which he directed at the face of the stranger. Buddha said to himself, " I will do no harm to that Naga ; I will leave intact his skin, flesh, and bones; but I will conquer him with the very same weapons he uses against me." Whereupon he emitted by his own power such a volume of thick smoke as soon to silence his adversary, and oblige him to have recourse to more effectual means of attack. He vomited out burning flames. Phra opposed flames far more active and destructive than those of the Naga. They shone forth with such an uncommon bright- ness as to attract a number of Rathees, who stood motion- less, admiring the beautiful countenance of Buddha, and wondering at his matchless power. The Naga, vanquished, gave up the contest, and left to Buddha the undisputed possession of the cook-room during the whole night. In the morning opening his patta, Phra thrust in the terrified Naga, and brought it to Ooroowela Kathaba, who, surprised, at the power of the stranger, said, " This Rahanda cannot as yet be compared to me." He desired him to stay in his monastery, promising to supply him with food as long as he should be with him. Phra accepted the proffered invi- tation, and fixed his residence in the midst of a grove little distant from the cell of Kathaba. Whilst he was there, four chiefs of Nats of the seat of Tsadoumaritz came at midnight to the spot where rested Phra. They were very handsome, and a bright hue, encompassing their bodies, filled the grove with a resplendent light. Kathaba, surprised, came to Buddha, and said to him, " Great Rahan, the hour of taking your food is at hand ; your rice is ready, come and eat it. How is it that at midnight there was such an uncommon splendour ? One would have thought that the whole forest in the neighbourhood was lined with immense fires, spreading a blaze of light." Phra answer- ing said, " This wonder was caused by the presence of four chiefs of Nats that came to visit me and hear my preach- ings." Kathaba said to himself, " Great indeed must be the virtue of this Rahan, since Nats come to see him and acknowledge him for their teacher. He is not yet, however, my equal." Buddha ate his rice and went back to the same place.

On another occasion, in the middle of the night, the chief of Thagias came to the grove of Buddha, and by his power caused a flood of light similar to that produced by a thousand lighted fires to pour its effulgent rays in every direction. In the morning, Kathaba went to the great Rahan inviting him to come and eat his rice. Meanwhile he asked him the reason of the wonderful light that had been kept up about from midnight until morning, which surpassed in brilliancy that which had been seen on a former occasion. Phra told him that he had been visited by the chief of Thagias, who came for the purpose of hearing his instructions. Kathaba thought within himself: Great indeed is the glory and dignity of this Rahan, but he is not as yet a Rahanda. Phra ate his food, and continued to stay in the same grove.

On another occasion, at the same late hour, Phra received the visit of the chief of the Brahmas. The flood of light that was sent forth by his body surpassed in effulgent splendour all that had been seen. Kathaba came as usual, in the morning, to invite the great Rahan to come and take his food, requesting him at the same time to inform him of the cause of the great wonder that had just taken place. Phra told him that the chief of Brahmas had waited upon him to listen to his preachings. Kathaba wondered the more at the dignity of this great Rahan, who attracted round him so eminent a visitor. But he said within himself: This Rahan is not yet a Rahanda that can be compared to me. Phra partook of his food, and continued his stay in the same grove.

On a certain day, the people of the country had prepared offerings on a large scale to be presented to Kathaba. On hearing this welcome news, the Rathee thought within himself as follows: The people are disposing everything to make large offerings to me. It is as well this Rahan should not be present on the occasion. He might make a display of his power in the presence of the multitude, who, taken up with admiration for his person, would make great offerings to him, whilst I should see my own decrease in a proportion. To-morrow I will contrive in such a way as to prevent the great Rahan from being present. Buddha discovered at a glance all that was going on in Kathaba's mind. Unwilling to offer any annoyance to his host, he conveyed himself to the island of Ootoogara, where he collected his meal, which he came to eat on the banks of the lake Anawadat. He spent the whole day there, and by his miraculous power he was back to his grove at an early hour on the following day. The Rathee came as usual, to invite him to partake of his meal that was ready, and inquired from him why he had not made his appearance on the day previous. Buddha, without the least emotion that could betray an angry feeling, related to Kathaba all that had passed in his mind, and informed him of the place he had been to. Kathaba, astonished at what he heard, said to himself: The knowledge of this Rahan is transcendent indeed, since he is even acquainted with the thoughts of my mind ; his power too is wonderfully great ; but withal, he is not as yet a Rahanda comparable to me. Buddha, having eaten his meal, withdrew to his grove.

On a certain day Buddha wished to wash his dress. A Thagia, knowing the thought that occupied his mind, dug a small square tank, and approaching him respectfully, invited him to wash his tsiwaran therein. Buddha then thought: Where shall I find a stone to rub it upon ? The Thagia, having brought a stone, said to him : " Illustrious Phra, here is a stone to rub your tsiwaran on." He thought again : Where is a proper place to dry it upon ? The Nat that watched the tree Yekada caused it to bend its branches, and said : " My lord, here is a fit place to hang up your tsiwaran." He thought again : Where is a fit spot to extend my clothes upon ? The chief of Thagias brought a large and well-polished stone, and said : " O illustrious

Phra, here is a fit place to lay your tsiwaran upon." In the morning, Kathaba repaired as usual to his guest's place, to invite him to take his meal. Surprised at what he perceived, he said to Buddha: "O Rahan, formerly there were here neither tank nor stone; how is it that they are here now? How is it, moreover, that the tree Yekadat is now bending down its branches?" Phra related then to the Rathee all that had happened, informing him that the chief of Thagias and one Nat had done all those works for him, and ministered to all his wants. Kathaba wondered more than before at the great virtue and surpassing excellency of the great Rahan; but he persisted in his former opinion, that the great Rahan was not a Rahanda that could equal him. Buddha, having taken his meal, returned to his grove.

On another occasion, the Rathee went to Buddha's place, to invite him to come and partake of his meal. "Very well," said Buddha, "I have a small business to do now; go beforehand, and I will follow you a few moments hence." Whereupon Kathaba went back to his cell. As to Phra, he went to pluck a fruit from the jambu tree, and arrived at the eating place before Kathaba could reach it. The Rathee, on arriving there, was quite surprised to find Phra already waiting for him. "How is this?" said he, with an unfeigned feeling of surprise, "and by what way did you come and contrive to arrive here before me?" Phra said to him: "After your departure, I plucked one fruit from a jambu tree, and yet I have reached this spot sooner than you. Here is the fruit I have brought. It is as full of flavour as it is beautiful; allow me to present you with it, that you may eat it." "O! no, great Rathan," replied the Rathee, "it is not becoming that I should eat it, but rather keep it for yourself." He thought within himself: Wonderful is indeed the power and eminent excellency of that great Rahan; but he is not as yet a Rahan that can be ranked to me. Phra ate his rice, and returned to his grove.

On another day, Phra gave a fresh proof of his miraculous power, by bringing to Kathaba a mango fruit, plucked from a mango-tree growing near the jambu tree, and so went on for several days, bringing fruits that grew at the extremity of the southern island. On another day, Phra ascended to the seat of Tawadeintha, and brought therefrom a beautiful water-lily, and yet arrived at the place where his meal was ready before Kathaba himself. The latter, quite amazed at seeing a flower from the Nat country, thought within himself: Wonderful, indeed, is the power of that great Rahan, who has brought here, from the seats of Nats, a beautiful lily in such a short space of time; but he is not as yet equal to me.

On a certain day, the Rathees were busy splitting firewood. They got a large log of wood upon which their united efforts could make no impression. Kathaba thought within himself: The great Rahan is gifted with mighty power; let us try him on this occasion. He desired Gaudama to split the hard log. Gaudama split it in a moment in five hundred pieces. The Rathees then tried to light up the fuel, but they could not succeed. Kathaba requested his guest to come to their assistance. In an instant, the five hundred pieces were set in a blaze, and presented the terrifying sight of five hundred large fires. The Rathees begged the great Rahan to extinguish those fires which threatened a general conflagration. Their request was instantaneously granted; the five hundred fires were extinguished.

During the cold season in the months of January and February, when a heavy cold dew falls, the Rathees amused themselves with plunging and swimming in the river Neritzara. Phra caused five hundred fires to blaze out on the banks of the river. The Rathees, coming out of the stream, warmed themselves by the side of those fires. They all wondered at the astonishing power of the great Rahan. But Kathaba persisted in saying that he was not a Rahanda like him.

On a certain day, a great rain poured in torrents, so that the water overflowed all the country, but it did not reach the spot Gaudama stood upon. He thought within himself: It is good that I should create a beautiful dry road in the midst of the water. He did so, and walked on the dry road, and clouds of dust rose in the air. Kathaba, much concerned regarding the fate of his guest, took a boat, and, with the assistance of his disciples, pulled·in the direction of Buddha's grove; but what was their surprise, when reaching the spot they found, instead of water, a firm dry road, and Buddha calmly walking to and fro. " Is it you, great Rahan," cried Kathaba, " whom we see here ?" " Yes," replied Gaudama, " it is I indeed." He had scarcely returned this answer, when he rose in the air and stood for a while above the boat. Kathaba thought again within himself : Great indeed must be the perfections and attainments of the great Rahan, since water even cannot harm him, but he is not yet a Rahanda like me. Phra, who knew what was taking place in Kathaba's mind, said to himself : Long time has this Rathee kept thinking within himself : This Rahan is great, but I am still greater than he; it is time now that I should inspire him with fear and surprise. Addressing Kathaba, he said, " Rathee, you are not a Rahanda, that has arrived to the perfection of Arahat; you have never performed the meritorious actions of the four ways to perfection ; you are not, therefore, a Rahanda. But I have, during former existences, carefully attended to those practices which have enabled me to reach perfection, and finally obtain the Buddhaship." Astonished at such an unexpected declaration, Kathaba humbled himself, fell on his knees, and prostrated himself at the feet of Buddha, saying: "Illustrious Phra, I wish to become Rahan under your direction." Phra replied : "Kathaba, you have under you five hundred Rathees, go and inform them of all that has happened." Whereupon Kathaba went to the place where the Rathees had assembled, and said to them : " I wish to place myself under the direction of the great Rahan." The five hundred Rathees told him that they were willing to follow his example, since he had been hitherto to them such an excellent teacher. They rose up, and, collecting their utensils, such as the twisted hairs, the forked staff, the hairy girdle, the honey filtre, &c., flung them into the river; then they came, and prostrating themselves at the feet of Buddha, craved admittance to the dignity of Rahans.

Nadi Kathaba, seeing the utensils floating on the water and carried down by the stream, called his followers and said to them: "Some misfortune must have befallen my elder brother; let us go and see what has happened." They were no sooner arrived, than Kathaba related to them all that had just taken place. Nadi Kathaba went forthwith to Buddha's cell, attended by all his disciples. Falling all at the feet of Phra, they declared their readiness to become his disciples, and applied for the dignity of Rahan. Gaya Kathaba, who lived a little below the place of Nadi Kathaba, seeing on the surface of the water the utensils of the followers of both his brothers floating in the direction of the stream, hastened, with his two hundred disciples, to the place of Ooroowela Kathaba. On his being informed of all that had occurred, he and his followers threw themselves at Gaudama's feet, praying for admittance into the order of Rahans. They were all admitted. The conversion of Ooroowela Kathaba was brought about by the display, on the part of Buddha, of no less than three thousand five hundred and sixty wonders.[1]

---

[1] It has been asserted in a former note that the preachings of Buddha were accompanied with miracles, to impart an additional weight and an irresistible evidence to his doctrines. This assertion is fully corroborated by all the particulars attending the conversion of the three Kathabas and their disciples. On this occasion Buddha met with the greatest amount of stubborn resistance on the part of Ooroowela Kathaba. There is no doubt but our great preacher resorted to every means of persuasion to carry conviction to the mind of his distinguished hearer. He had, however, to deal with a man full of his own merits and excellence, who thought himself far superior to every one else. His best arguments proved powerless before a self-conceited individual, who was used to give and

CHAPTER VII.

Buddha's sermon on the mountain—Interview of Buddha and King Pimfa-
thara in the vicinity of the city of Radzagio—Answer of Kathaba to
Buddha's interrogation—Instructions delivered to the king and his
attendants—Solemn entry of Buddha into Radzagio—Donation of the
Weloowon monastery to Buddha—Conversion of Thariputra and Mau-
kalan—The Rahans are keenly taunted by the people of Radzagio.

ACCOMPANIED by his thousand followers, Phra went to the
village of Gayathitha. This village stands on the bank of
the river Gaia. Close to it, there is a mountain resem-

not to receive instruction, and enjoyed a far-famed celebrity. Buddha was compelled to resort to his unbounded power of working miracles, and with it overcame at last the obstinate and blind resistance of the proud Rathee. No conquest had ever been so dearly bought; but it proved well worth the extraordinary efforts made to obtain it. Kathaba became one of the most staunch adherents of Buddha, and one of the most fervent disciples, who laboured hard for the propagation of Buddhism. He is the most celebrated of all Buddhistic monks, and to his name is ever prefixed the distinguished epithet of Maha, which means great. After Gaudama's demise, he became the patriarch of the Buddhists. By his care and exertions, a council of five hundred Rahans was assembled at Radzagio, under the reign of King Adzatatha, to condemn the unbecoming language used by some false or imperfectly taught converts, who wished to shake off, on many points, the authority of Buddha.

In the episode of the conversion of the three Kathabas, the attentive reader cannot fail to have observed one particular that throws some light on the position several heads of philosophical schools occupied in the days that saw the origin of Buddhism. Those sages lived in retired places, far from the bustle and tumult of the world. It is probable that at first they were alone, or with but a few other individuals who delighted in the same mode of life. Their time was entirely taken up with study and meditation. The object of their studies and reflections was the boundless field of metaphysics and morals. Their diet was plain, and their abstemiousness carried to a degree Hindu devotees and fanatics are alone capable of reaching. The fame of the proficiency of some of those individuals in science and virtue soon attracted to their solitude numbers of pupils, eager to place themselves under the tuition and discipline of masters so eminent in every respect. The three Kathabas must have been

bling in appearance an elephant's head. On the top of the mountain stands a large rock, wide enough to accommodate Buddha and all his attendants. He ascended the mountain with his disciples, and, having reached its summit, sat down. Summoning all his disciples, he said to them: " Beloved Bickus, all that is to be met with in the three abodes of men, Nats, and Brahmas, is like a burning flame. But why is it so? Because the eyes are a burning flame; the objects perceived by the eyes, the view of those objects, the feeling created by that view, are all like a burning flame. The sensations produced by the eyes cause a succession of pleasant and painful feelings, but these are likewise a burning flame. What are the causes productive of such a burning? It is the fire of concupiscence, of anger, of ignorance, of birth, of death, of old age, and of anxiety. Again, the ear is a burning flame; the sounds, the perception of the sounds, the sensations caused by the sounds, are all a burning flame; the pleasure or pain produced by the sounds are also a burning flame, which is fed by the fire of concupiscence, anger, ignorance, birth, old age, death, anxiety, tears, affliction, and trouble. Again, the sense of smelling is a burning flame; the odours, the perception of odours, the sensations produced by odours, are all a burning flame; the pleasure and pain resulting therefrom are but a burning flame, fed by concupiscence, anger, ignorance, birth, old age, death, disquietude, tears, affliction, and sorrow. Again, the taste is a burning flame; the objects tasted, the perception of those objects, the sensations produced by them, are all a burning flame, kept up by the fire

---

celebrated throughout the country, since we find them at the head of so many disciples. Humility has never been the *forte* of the heathen sages, either in or out of India. Conceit and self-esteem were fostered in their souls by the consciousness of their own superiority and excellence, by the praises lavished on them by their disciples, and not a little by the se- clusion from society to which they voluntarily resigned themselves. Spiritual pride, like a cunning foe, occupied in the heart the place vacated by passions of a coarser nature and less delicate tinge. The conduct of the elder Kathaba fully bears out the truth and correctness of the above assertion.

of concupiscence, anger, ignorance, birth, old age, death, anxiety, tears, affliction, and sorrow. Again, the sense of feeling, the objects felt, the perception of those objects, the sensations produced by them, are a burning flame; the pleasure and pain resulting therefrom are but a burning flame, fostered by concupiscence, anger, ignorance, birth, old age, death, anxiety, tears, affliction, and sorrow. Again, the heart is a burning flame, as well as all the objects perceived by it, and the sensations produced in it; the pleasure and pain caused by the heart are too a burning flame, kept up by the fire of concupiscence, anger, ignorance, birth, old age, death, disquietude, tears, affliction, and sorrow. Beloved Bickus, they who understand the doctrine I have preached, and see through it, are full of wisdom and deserve to be called my disciples. They are displeased with the senses, the objects of the senses, matter, pleasure and pain, as well as with all the affections of the heart. They become free from concupiscence, and therefore exempt from passions. They have acquired the true wisdom that leads to perfection; they are delivered at once from the miseries of another birth. Having practised the most excellent works, nothing more remains to be performed by them. They want no more the guidance of the sixteen laws, for they have reached far beyond them."[1]

---

[1] The philosophical discourse of Buddha on the mountain may be considered as the summary of his theory of morals. It is confessedly very obscure and much above the ordinary level of the human understanding. The hearers whom he addressed were persons already trained up to his teaching, and therefore prepared for understanding such doctrines. Had he spoken in that abstruse style to common people, it is certain he would have missed his aim and exposed himself to the chance of not being understood. But he addressed a select audience, whose minds were fully capable of comprehending his most elevated doctrines. He calls his disciples Bickus, or mendicants, to remind them of the state of voluntary poverty they had embraced when they became his followers, and to impress their minds with contempt for the riches and pleasures of this world.

He lays it down as a great and general principle that all that exists resembles a flame that dazzles the eyes by its brilliancy and torments by its burning effects. Here appears the favourite notion of Buddhism that there is nothing substantial and real in this world, and that the continual

Having thus spoken, Buddha remained silent. His hearers felt themselves wholly disentangled from the trammels of passions, and disengaged from all affections to material objects, and they who had been but Rahans became Rahandas.

changes and vicissitudes we are exposed to are the cause of painful sensations. Buddha reviews the six senses (the heart, according to his theory, is the seat of a sixth sense) in succession, and as they are the channels through which affections are produced on the soul, he compares to a burning flame the organs of the senses, the various objects of the action of the senses, the results painful or agreeable produced by them. Hence he fulminates a general and sweeping condemnation against all that exists out of man. The senses, being the means through which matter influences the soul, share in the universal doom. Buddha sets forth the causes productive of that burning flame. They are — first, the three great and general principles of demerits, viz., concupiscence, anger, and ignorance. In the book of Ethics these three principles are explained at great length; they are represented as the springs from which flow all other passions. In a lengthened digression the author aims at simplifying the question, and endeavours to show, by a logical process, that ignorance is the head source from which concupiscence and passion take their rise. It is, therefore, according to Buddhists, into the dark recess of ignorance that metaphysicians must penetrate in order to discover the first cause of all moral disorders. Every being has his mind more or less encompassed by a thick mist that prevents him from seeing truth. He mistakes good for evil, right for wrong; he erroneously clings to material objects that have no reality, no substance, no consistence; his passions are kept alive by his love or

hatred of vain illusions. The flame is, moreover, fed by birth, old age, death, afflictions, &c., which are as many *foci* wherefrom radiate out on all surrounding objects fires which keep up the general conflagration. But they play only a secondary action, dependent on the three great causes of all evils just alluded to. What causes birth, old age, and death? inquires the Buddhist. The law of merits and demerits is the immediate answer to the question; it might be added thereto, the necessity of acquiring merits and gravitating towards perfection. A man is born to innumerable succeeding existences by virtue of his imperfections, and that he might acquire fresh merits by the practice of virtue. By birth, a being is ushered into a new existence or into a new state, where the burning flame which is supposed to spread over all that exists exercises its teasing and tormenting influence over him. Old age and death are two periods when a radical change operates upon a being, and places him in a different situation where he experiences the baneful effects of the conflagration. "Blessed are they," says Buddha, "who understand this; they are full of wisdom; they become displeased with all passions and with all the things they act upon. The causes of existences being done away with, they have reached the terminus of all possible existences; one step more and they find themselves placed beyond the influence of the power of attraction that retains forcibly all beings in the vortex of existences, and brings them towards the centre of perfection; they are in fact entering into the state of Neibban."

Whilst the most excellent Phra was enjoying himself in the place of Gayathitha, he recollected that, at the time when he was but a Phralaong, being near the mountain Pantawa, he had received from King Pimpathara an invitation to come to his own country and preach the law. Accompanied with his thousand Rahandas, he set out for the country of Radzagio.   Having arrived at a small distance from the royal city he went to the Latti grove, about three gawots from Radzagio, a place planted with palm trees.   The king, having heard of his arrival, said to his people : " The descendant of a long succession of illustrious princes, the great Rahan Gaudama, has entered into our country, and is now in the grove of palm-trees, in the garden of Tandiwana."   The happy news was soon re-echoed throughout the country.   The people said among themselves : The great Gaudama is come indeed.   He is perfectly acquainted with all that relates to the three states of men, Nats and Brahmas ; he preaches a sublime and lovely law ; the morals that he announces are pure, like a shell newly cleansed.   Pimpathara, placing himself at the head of 120,000 warriors, surrounded by crowds of nobles and Pounhas, went to the garden of Tandiwana, where Phra was seated in the middle of his disciples.   He paid his respects by prostrating himself before him, and then withdrew to a becoming distance.   The countless crowd followed the example of their monarch, and seated themselves at a becoming distance.   Some of them remained conversing with Buddha, and heard from him words worthy to be ever remembered ; some others, having their hands joined to the forehead, remained in a respectful attitude ; some were praising his illustrious ancestors ; others remained modestly silent.   All of them, perceiving the three Kathabas close to the person of Phra, doubted whether Gaudama was their disciple, or they, his disciples.   Buddha, seeing at once what thought occupied the mind of the warriors, noblemen, and Pounhas, addressed the elder Kathaba, called Ooroowela Kathaba, and said to him :

" Kathaba, you who lived formerly in the solitude of Ooroowela, answer the question I am now putting to you. You were formerly a teacher of Rathees, who practised works of great mortification, to such an extent that their bodies were emaciated by self-inflicted penances : what has induced you to give up the sacrifices you were wont to make ? " " Blessed Buddha," answered Kathaba, " I have observed that exterior objects, the sounds, the taste, the gratification of the senses, are but miserable filth ; and, therefore, I take no more delight in the offering of small and great sacrifices." Buddha replied, " Kathaba, if you be no longer pleased with what is beautiful to the eyes, pleasant to the ear, palatable to the taste, and agreeable to the gratification of the senses, in what do you presently find pleasure and delight ? " Kathaba answered, " Blessed Buddha, the state of Neibban is a state of rest, but that rest cannot be found as long as we live under the empire of senses and passions. That rest excludes existence, birth, old age, and death ; the great mental attainments alone lead thereto. I know and see that happy state. I long for it. I am, therefore, displeased with the making of great and small sacrifices." Having thus spoken, Kathaba rose up, worshipped Buddha by prostrating himself before him, and touching with his forehead the extremities of his feet, and said, " O most excellent Buddha, you are my teacher, and I am your disciple." All the people, seeing what Kathaba had done, knew that he was practising virtue under the direction of Gaudama.[2]

---

[2] From the purport of Kathaba's reply to Buddha's question, it may be inferred with certainty that the Rathees were in the habit of making sacrifices or burnt-offerings. These sacrifices again were distinguished into two classes ; the one, including the small or daily ones, and the other, the great burnt-offerings, made on solemn occasions. That these sacrifices were not performed by the killing and immolating of animals, there can be no doubt, as such an act would have been contrary to the tender regard they always had for the life of animals. The institutes of Menu come to our help to elucidate this point. The Brahmin is enjoined, according to that compilation of laws, to make burnt-offerings of clarified butter and other articles to the manes of his ancestors. Agreeably to this

Phra, who was acquainted with their innermost thoughts, knew that they were longing to hear the preaching of the law. As he had always done, he began to preach to them the virtue of liberality in almsgiving, and then unfolded before them, with matchless eloquence, the advantages of leaving the world, &c. The hearers felt an inward delight in all that was said to them. Observing the favourable impression made upon them, Gaudama continued to instruct them on the four laws, regarding the miseries of this world, the passions, the practice of excellent works, and the ways to perfection. At the conclusion of these instructions, the king and 100,000 of the assembly, like a piece of white cloth which, when plunged into dye, retains the colour it receives, obtained instantly the state of Thautapan.[3] As to the 10,000 remaining hearers, they

---

regulation, Kathaba performed those rites, which, in the opinion of Buddha, were perfectly useless, since they could not be the means of elevating the performer to the knowledge and perfection requisite for obtaining what he always calls *per excellence* the deliverance.

Kathaba is rather obscure in his answer. It seems that he intended to acknowledge that, notwithstanding the sacrifices and burnt-offerings he had made, and upon the value of which he had laid much stress, concupiscence and other vicious propensities were still deeply rooted in him; that, through the channel of his senses, exterior objects continued to make impressions on his soul. He had, therefore, become disgusted with practices which could not free him from the action and influence of passions and matter.

In the opinion of Buddha, the observance of exterior religious rites can never elevate man to the sublime knowledge of pure truth, which alone does confer real perfection to him who has become a true sage, and is deemed worthy of obtaining the deliverance. A serious application of the mind to the meditation of the law and the nature of beings, is the only way leading to the acquirement of true wisdom. As long as Kathaba was contented with material acts of worship, and his mind's attention was engrossed with those vain ceremonials, he had not as yet entered in the way of perfection. He had hitherto missed the true path; he had wandered in the broad road of error, encompassed by mental darkness, and deceived by perpetual illusions. His extensive knowledge had served but to lead him in the wrong direction. He wanted the guidance of Buddha to enable him to retrace his steps and find the right way. He had to become sensible of the truth of the great fundamental maxims of all real wisdom, viz., that in this world all is subjected to change and to pain; and that all beings are mere illusions, destitute of all reality.

[3] To complete what has already been stated respecting the Ariahs or venerables in a foregoing note, the following is added. The reader must bear in mind that the Ariahs are

believed in the three precious things in the capacity of Upathakas.

The ruler of the country of Magataritz, King Pimpathara, having obtained the state of Thautapan, said to Gaudama, "Illustrious Buddha, some years ago, when I was but a crown prince of this country, I entertained five desires, which are all happily accomplished. Here are the five desires—I wished to become king; I desired that the Phra, worthy of receiving the homage of all men, should come into my kingdom; that I might have the privilege

---

divided into four classes, named—Thautapan, Thakadagam, Anagam, and Arahats, and, according to the particular position occupied by the beings of those states, each class is subdivided into two: Thus, for instance, Thautapatti Megata means he who has entered and is walking, as it were, in the way of the perfection of Thautapan; and Thautapatti-pho indicates those who enjoy the merits and blessings of the state of Thautapan; and so with the three superior stages of perfection. To obtain the state of Thautapan, a man must have left the direction followed up by all creatures and entered into the direction or way that leads to deliverance. He will have yet to go through 80,000 kaps or durations of worlds, and must be born seven times more in the state of man and Nat before he be a perfected being, ripe for the state of Neibban. Those who have reached the state of Thakadagam shall have to pass through 60,000 kaps, and be born once in the state of Nat and once in the state of man, before they be perfected. Those who have obtained the third step of Anagam have to travel through 40,000 kaps, and are no more to undergo the process of birth; at the end of that period they are perfected. The fourth stage of perfection, that of Arahat, is the highest a being can ever obtain. The fortunate Arahat is gifted with super-natural powers. At the end of 20,000 kaps he is perfected, and reaches the state of deliverance. Those four states are often called the four great roads leading to deliverance or to Neibban. It may be asked whether the state of Thautapan is the first step reached by every one that adheres to Buddha's doctrines, or whether it is the one that requires a certain progress in the way of believing and practising? It seems, from the narrative of the conversion of King Pimpathara and his followers, that the state of Thautapan is the reward of those who have shown a more than common proficiency and fervour in adhering to Buddha and his doctrines, but not the first step to enter into the assembly of the faithful and become a member thereof. One may be a simple hearer, or Upathaka, believing in the three precious things, without attaining that of Thautapan. On this occasion, the king and 100,000 of his warriors and noblemen became Thautapans, whereas the remaining 10,000 became believers and members of the assembly without reaching any further. The first entered into the stream or current leading to perfection. The latter were fervent believers, observed the five precepts, but in no way aspired to the attainment of the doctrines of a higher order.

of approaching him; that he might preach his doctrine to me; and, finally, that I might thoroughly understand all his preaching. These five wishes have been fully realised. Your law, O most excellent Buddha, is a most perfect law. To what shall I liken it as regards the happy results it produces? It is like replacing on its proper basis a vase that was bottom upwards, or setting to light objects hitherto buried in deep darkness; it is an excellent guide that shows out the right way; it is like a brilliant light, shining forth and dispelling darkness. Now I take refuge in you, your law, and the assembly of the perfect. Henceforth I will be your supporter, and to-morrow I will supply you and your disciples with all that is necessary for the support of nature." Buddha, by his silence, testified his acceptance of the offered favour. Whereupon the king rose up, prostrated himself before him, and, turning on the right, left the place, and returned to his palace.

Early in the morning Pimpathara ordered all sorts of eatables to be prepared. Meanwhile he sent messengers to Buddha to inform him that his meal was ready. Buddha, rising up, put on his dress, and, carrying his patta, set out for Radzagio, followed by his one thousand disciples. At that time a prince of Thagias, assuming the appearance of a handsome young man, walked a little distance in front of Buddha, singing to his praise several stanzas. "Behold the most excellent is advancing towards Radzagio with his one thousand disciples. In his soul he is full of meekness and amiability; he is exempt from all passions; his face is beautiful, and shines forth like the star Thigi; he has escaped out of the whirlpool of existences, and delivered himself from the miseries of transmigration. He is on his way to the city of Radzagio attended by a thousand Rahandas." (The same stanza is thrice repeated.) "He who has obtained the perfection of Ariahs, who has practised the ten great virtues, who has a universal knowledge, who knows and preaches the law of merits, who discovers at once the sublime attainments, the most perfect being, the most excellent, is entering into the city of Radzagio attended by a thousand Rahandas."

The inhabitants of the city, seeing the beautiful appearance of that young man, and hearing all that he was singing aloud, said to each other, " Who is that young man whose countenance is so lovely, and whose mouth proclaims such wonderful things ? " The Thagia, hearing what was said of him, replied, " O children of men ! the most excellent Phra whom ye see is gifted with an incomparable wisdom ; all perfections are in him ; he is free of all passions ; no being can ever be compared to him ; he is worthy to receive the homage and respect of men and Nats ; his unwavering mind is ever fixed in truth ; he announces a law extending to all things. As for me, I am but his humble servant." [4]

---

[4] Is not that young man doing the duty of forerunner of Buddha on the occasion of his solemn entry into the city of Radzagio?

The narrative of the donation of the grove or garden of Weloowon by King Pimpathara to Buddha, discloses the manner in which Buddhistic monks have become holders, not as individuals, but as members of society, of landed properties. Buddha and his disciples at first had no place as a body or a society to live in ; hitherto he had taken up his quarters in any place where people were willing to receive him. He must have often been put to great inconvenience, particularly after the accession of new disciples, who daily crowded about him. The pious king felt the disadvantage the society was labouring under : he resolved to give them a place where the assembly might live and remain. The donation was as solemn as possible. It transferred to Buddha the property of the garden, without any condition, for ever. The donation, on the other hand, was fully accepted. This is, I believe, the first instance of an act of this description. The grove and monastery of Weloo-

won is much celebrated in Buddha's life.

In Burmese towns a particular spot is allowed for the building of houses or monasteries for Buddhistic recluses or monks. It is somewhat isolated from all other buildings, and forms, as it were, the quarter of the yellow-dressed personages. Here is a general description of one of these buildings. They are of an oblong-square shape, raised about eight or ten feet above the ground, and supported on wooden posts, and sometimes, though seldom, on brick pillars. The frame of the edifice is of wood, and planks form the wall. Above the first roof rises a second one of smaller dimensions, and a third one, yet smaller than the second. This style of roofing a building is allowed only for pagodas, Talapoins' houses, and royal palaces. The place between the soil and the floor is left open, and never converted to any use. A flight of steps, made of wood or bricks, leads to the entrance of the edifice, the interior whereof is generally divided as follows :—One vast hall designed for the reception of visitors, and used also as a school-room for the boys who go to learn

Having reached the king's palace, Buddha was received with every demonstration of respect, and led to the place prepared for him. Pimpathara thought within himself of

the rudiments of reading, writing, and sometimes ciphering. Except on grand occasions, the Talapoins generally stay in that hall, doing away with their time in the best way they can, occasionally reading books, counting their beads, chewing betel, and very often sleeping. At the extremity of the hall there is a place raised one or two steps above the level. A portion of that place is left vacant, and reserved for the sittings of the Talapoins, when they receive visitors; the other portion, which extends to the wall, is occupied by idols or representations of Buddha, raised on pedestals, and sometimes placed on shelves, with the few implements required for exterior worship. There, too, are to be seen a few trunks ornamented with sculptures and gildings, and containing books belonging to the monastery. The hall and the place as far as the walls occupy just one-half of the oblong-square. The other half, parallel to the first, is occupied by rooms intended for the storing of alms, and as dormitories for the inmates of the house. In some monasteries the ceiling is painted and partly gilt. The cook-room, when there is one, is connected with the extremity of the square, opposite to the one occupied by the idols. It is generally on the same level with the floor of the building. Government has nothing to do with the erection, repairs, and maintenance of these edifices. They are erected and kept up by private individuals, who deem it very meritorious to build such places. Those whose piety actuates and prompts them to undertake such an expensive work assume the title of Kiaong Taga, which means supporter of a pagoda or Talapoins' residence. They are proud of such distinction,

cause themselves to be called by that title, and always make it to follow their names in signing any paper or document.

The above descriptive sketch of a monastery is rather incomplete, if applied to those found in the large places of Burmah proper, and particularly in the capital. Some of them are laid out on a scale of vastness and magnificence difficult to realise by those who have not examined them. A large open gallery runs all round the building; a second one of a rectangular shape, but protected by the roof, forms, as it were, on the four sides the *vestibulum* to the central portion of the edifice. It is the place where the Phongies spend the greater part of their time, either in talking with the numerous idlers that visit them, or in teaching children. Large shutters separate this from the open verandah; they may be thrown all open by pushing forward the lower part, the upper one remaining fixed by hinges, and so may be opened to the height required to protect the inmates from the rain and the sun. The central hall, by far the finest and loftiest of the building, is reserved for the idols and all the implements of worship, and the boxes containing the books of the monastery, commonly put together in a very disordered way. The ceiling is gilt and adorned, often with taste and elegance. A partition divides the hall into two equal parts. The one towards the east is for some huge statue of Gaudama, and smaller ones with many articles of worship. The other, facing the south, is used for several purposes; sometimes as dormitories for the Talapoins. The posts supporting the interior part are six or eight in number, and offer the finest specimens

the thing which could prove acceptable to Phra, in order to offer it to him. He said within himself, My garden, which is situated near the city, would doubtless be a very fit place for Buddha and his followers to live in. As it lies not far from the city, it would be a place of easy resort to all those who should feel inclined to visit Buddha and pay him their respects; it is, moreover, far enough off, so that the noise and cries of the people could not be heard therein. The place is peculiarly fitted for retreat and contemplation; it will assuredly prove agreeable to Buddha. Whereupon he rose up, and, holding in his hand a golden shell like a cup, he made to Phra a solemn offering of that garden which was called Weloowon.[5] Gaudama remained

of teak timber I have ever seen, some being fully sixty and seventy feet high. In some of these monasteries the best parts of the interior are gilt, and sometimes the exterior sides; the ornaments of the extremities of the roof and the space between the roofs are covered with gold leaves. In those two places too are displayed carvings, which reflect great credit on the skill of native workmen, and elicit the admiration of foreigners. One of these monasteries called the kioung-dau-gye, near the place where the Arracan idol is, and another close to the place where the supreme head of Talapoins is living, are the finest and largest specimens of monasteries the writer has ever seen in Burmah.

[5] On the occasion of the presentation to Buddha of the Weloowon monastery, and of the lands attached to it, by King Pimpathara, there was observed a curious ceremony, often alluded to in Buddhist writings. He held in his hands a golden pitcher full of water, which he kept pouring down on the ground, whilst he pronounced the formula of donation. This is a ceremony of Indian origin, which, with many others, has been imported into these parts along with the religious doctrines. It is intended to be an exterior sign of, or testimony to, the offering that is made on the occasion. When it is performed, the parties pronounce a certain formula, calling the Nats, guardians of the place, to witness the act of donation, and, in particular, the Nat that is supposed to rule over the earth; and at the same time the offerer, not satisfied with receiving for his own benefit the merits of his pious liberality, expresses the earnest desire that all men, or rather all beings, should share with him in the blessings he expects to reap from his good deed. The generous and liberal disposition of the donor, it may be observed, exhibits the truly pleasing display of an amount of charity and brotherly love scarcely to be expected from the followers of an erroneous creed. The ceremony, therefore, has a twofold object, conferring unreserved and absolute efficiency on the act of donation, and dividing or apportioning the merits of the good work among all beings.

In perusing attentively the contents of this legend, the reader will easily follow the gradual development of the Buddhist religious system, and, in particular, the establishment of most of the disciplinary regulations

silent, in token of his acceptance of the gift. He preached the law and left the palace. At that time he called his disciples and said to them, "Beloved Rahans, I give you permission to receive offerings."

In the country of Radzagio there was a heterodox Rahan named Thindzi, who had under him five hundred and fifty disciples. Thariputra and Maukalan were at that time practising virtue under the guidance of that master. Here is the way they became Rahans. When they were but laymen, under the names of Oopathi and Kaulita, on a certain day, surrounded by two hundred and twenty companions, they went to the top of a lofty mountain to enjoy the sight of countless multitudes of people sporting and playing in the surrounding flat country. While they were gazing over the crowds of human beings they said to each other, " In a hundred years hence all these living beings

---

in full force in our own days in most of the countries where that form of religion has obtained a long standing and a predominating footing. At first the religious that constituted the body of the followers of Buddha were few, and could easily, in the company of their eminent teacher, procure, in accordance with the vow of strict poverty they had made, shelter, food, and raiment. There was no need for them to accept, in the shape of donation, anything beyond what was absolutely necessary for the wants of the day. We may conjecture that their leader watched with a jealous care over his religious on this point, to establish them in the spirit of poverty and of a thorough contempt for the things of this world. But the society or fraternity growing numerous, the dependence on the daily offerings appeared not to meet in sufficient manner the real necessities it felt, particularly as regards shelter. This want was quickly perceived and keenly felt by the pious King Pimpathara, who came to the resolution of presenting Buddha and his followers with a proper place to withdraw to at all times, but particularly during the wet season, when the pouring of the annual rains puts a check of four months to the religious peregrinations of the preachers. The same motives that induced Buddha to accept the proffered royal gift influenced him likewise to grant to his religious the dangerous, it is true, but the absolutely necessary permission of receiving offerings of houses and lands. From that time, the religious communities have made use of the privilege granted to them in all the places where they have been established. In Burmah this favour has not been abused, and the religious body, though never standing in want of anything required for the daily use, cannot be said to be wealthy. Having not to cast in the scales of the political balance the weight of riches, and the preponderance essentially attending the possession of them, their influence in the political affairs is not, at least exteriorly, felt.

shall have fallen a prey to death." Whereupon they rose up and left the place, but their minds were deeply preoccupied with the idea of death. While the two friends were walking silently together, they began at last to communicate to each other the result of their reflections. " If there be," said they, " a principle of death, a universal tendency towards destruction, there must be, too, its opposite principle, that of not dying and escaping destruction." On that very instant they resolved to search ardently for the excellent law that teaches the way of not dying, and obtain the state of perfect fixity and immutability. In those parts there lived six heterodox teachers who were named Mekkali, Gau, Sala, Thindzi, Jani, and Ganti ; among them Thindzi was the only one who, with his disciples, wore white clothes. They went to the place where lived the Rahan Thindzi, placed themselves under his direction, and put on the dress of Rahan. Within three days they acquired the science, wisdom, and knowledge of their teacher without having as yet reached the object of their eager pursuit. They said to Thindzi, " Teacher, is this all that you know ? And have you no other science to teach us ? " " I have indeed," replied the teacher, " taught you all the knowledge I possess." Finding nothing satisfactory in the answer, the two friends said, " Let us continue seeking for the law that has reality in itself ; the first that shall have discovered it shall, without delay, communicate it to the other."

On a certain morning one of Gaudama's disciples named Athadzi, having put on his religious habit, and carrying his patta on his left arm, went out to receive his rice. Everything about his person was noble and graceful ; his countenance and behaviour were at once gentle and dignified, whether he walked or stopped, looked forward to the right or the left, or sat in a cross-legged position. The false Rahan Oopathi, who became afterwards Thariputra, perceiving the Rahan Athadzi with such a meek and dignified deportment, said to himself, " Such a Rahan is assuredly

worthy to receive offerings ; he has doubtless attained perfection.   I will go to him and ask him, in case he has had
a teacher, who is that distinguished instructor under whom
he practises virtue; and in case of his being himself a
teacher, what is the doctrine that he teaches.   But it is
not becoming to put to him any question whilst he is on
his way to beg alms. I will follow at a distance." Athadzi,
having collected alms, left the city and went to a small
dzeat, where he sat down and ate his meal. Oopathi followed him thither.   Having entered into the dzeat, he
rendered to him the services that a disciple usually pays
to his teacher. When the meal of Athadzi was over, he
poured water over his hands, and with a heart overflowing
with joy, he conversed with him for a while.   He withdrew then to a becoming distance, and addressed him as
follows, " Great Rahan, your exterior is full of meekness
and benevolence; your countenance bespeaks the purity
and innocence of your soul; if you be a disciple, pray
under what teacher have you become Rahan ? Who is
your guide in the way to perfection ? and what is the doctrine he is preaching to you ? "   " Young Rahan," replied
Athadzi, " have you not heard of the illustrious Buddha,
the descendant of a long succession of great monarchs,
who has entered the profession of Rahan ?   I have become
Rahan under him ; he is my teacher; to his doctrine I
cling with all the energy of my soul."   " What is the doctrine of that great master ? " asked Oopathi.   " I am but a
novice in the profession," replied modestly Athadzi, " and
am as yet imperfectly acquainted with the doctrine of my
teacher. The little, however, I know, I will freely communicate to you." Oopathi entreated him to do so.
Athadzi replied, " The law which I have learned at the
feet of Buddha explains all that relates to matter, to the
principles that act upon it, to passions, and to the mind ;
it makes man despise all that is material, conquer his
passions, and regulate his mind."   On hearing this doctrine, Oopathi felt the ties of passions gradually relaxing

and giving way; his soul became, as it were, disentangled from the influence of the senses. He became enamoured with such a pure and perfect law, and obtained the condition of Thautapan. Convinced that he had at last found what he had hitherto searched after in vain, the law of Neibban, he went without delay to his friend, to make him share in the beneficial result of his fortunate discovery. Kaulita, perceiving his friend coming up to him with a rejoicing countenance, indicative of the happiness his soul was inwardly enjoying, asked him if he had found what he had hitherto vainly looked for. Oopathi related to him all the particulars of his conversation with the Rahan Athadzi. Whereupon Kaulita became instantly a Thautapan. Both resolved to leave their teacher Thindzi, and go immediataly to place themselves under the guidance of Buddha. Three times they applied for permission to execute their design, and three times it was denied them. At last they departed, each with his two hundred and twenty companions. Thindzi, enraged at being left alone, died, vomiting blood from his mouth.

When the two friends and their followers were drawing near to the place of Weloowon, Phra assembled all his disciples and said to them, "Behold these two friends coming up to me; they will become my two beloved disciples; their minds are acute and penetrating; they actually take delight in the law of Neibban; their thoughts are converging towards that great centre of truth; they come to me, and they will become my two most excellent disciples." While he was speaking, the two friends crossed the threshold of the monastery, and prostrated themselves at the feet of Buddha, humbly craving the favour of being admitted among his disciples to practise virtue under his immediate direction. On this occasion Phra uttered the following words: "O Bickus, come to me; I preach the most excellent law: apply yourselves to the practice of the most perfect works, which will put an end to all miseries." A suit of dress and a patta were handed to each of the two friends, that were henceforth to be called Thariputra and Maukalan, and they became members of the assembly. Having put on the new dress, they appeared to the eyes of all with the decent and dignified deportment of Rahans that had sixty years of profession.   Their followers became Bickus of the second order.   Seven days after, Maukalan became a Rahanda; but it took fifteen days for Thariputra to obtain the same favour.   The two new converts were elevated to the dignity of disciples of the right and of the left; that is to say, they obtained precedence over all others.

The distinction thus granted to Thariputra and Maukalan excited a feeling of jealousy among the disciples of Buddha. In their conversations they complained to each other of the preference given to those who had just been admitted among the members of assembly.   They went so far as to say that Buddha had acted in this case under the influence of human considerations.   These remarks were brought to the notice of Buddha, who assembled his disciples, and said to them, " Beloved Bickus, my conduct in this instance has not been guided by unworthy motives; I have acted as I ought to have done.   In the days of the Phra Anau-madathi, the two friends were leading the life of ascetics. They paid the greatest respect and veneration to the then existing Buddha, and entreated him, by repeated sup-plications, to hold out to them the solemn promise that they would become the disciples of the right and of the left of some future Buddha.   Anaumadathi replied to them that the object of their wishes should be granted unto them when the Buddha Gaudama would appear in the world. This is, beloved Bickus, the reason that has influenced me in elevating to the first rank the two new converts."   The answer completely satisfied the disciples, and effectually silenced all murmurs.   Further particulars regarding the promise that these two illustrious friends received in the time of the Buddha Anaumadathi may be read, with cir-cumstantial details, in the book called Apadan-tera.

The inhabitants of the Magatha country, seeing that so many persons, chiefly belonging to the first families, were embracing the profession of Rahans, said amongst themselves, " Behold how the Rahan Gaudama, by his preachings, causes the depopulation of the country, and forces countless wives to the unwished-for state of widowhood. A thousand Rathees have embraced the profession of Rahans; all the disciples of Thindzi have followed their example; many others will soon tread in their footsteps. What will become of our country?" With these and other expressions, they gave vent to their hatred of the Rahans, and endeavoured to pour over them all kinds of ridicule and abuse. They concluded by saying, " The great Rahan has come to the city of Radzagio, which is like a cow-pen, surrounded by five hills;[6] he has now with him the disciples of Thindzi; who will be the next to go to him?" The Rahans, hearing all that was said against them, went to Buddha and related to him all that they

---

[6] In his Archæological Survey Report, General Cunningham has supplied us with an accurate description of the position and ruins of the celebrated city of Radzagio. His own measurements of the old ramparts, that are still visible, agree to a surprising degree with those of the two Chinese pilgrims, Fa-Hian and Hwen-Tsan, who visited the same spot in the fourth and sixth century of our era. The city was situated in a valley, surrounded by five hills, which are named Gigakuta, Isigli, Wibhara, Wipula, and Pandawa. It was five miles in circumference. This is meant for the circuit of the inner wall. The exterior one was nearly nine miles. On the southern face of the Wibhara mountain is the famous cave at the entrance of which was held the first Buddhist council, not long after the cremation of Buddha's remains. There is no doubt that the heights were, in the palmy days of Buddhism, covered with Buddhistic monuments. As the place was subsequently occupied by Brahmins and Mussulmans, the Dzedis and monasteries have been mercilessly pulled down to furnish materials for musjids, tombs, and temples. The eminences are now covered with Mussulman tombs, which occupy the places formerly adorned with pagodas. Springs of hot water were numerous in the vicinity of the city. The writer has only met once in Buddhistic compositions an allusion to that natural phenomenon so beneficial to people living in hot climates. The modern Rajghir, both by name and situation, brings to our recollection the celebrated capital of Magatha, so famous in Buddhistic annals. As the extent of Radzagio has been so accurately determined by ancient and modern visitors, one can well afford to laugh at the immensely exaggerated number of houses that are supposed by certain Burmese writers to have composed the city.

had heard. To console them, Buddha said, "Beloved Bickus, the abuses, sarcasms, and ridicule levelled at you shall not last long; seven days hence all shall be over. Here is the reply you will make to the revilers: Like all his predecessors, Buddha is striving to preach a most perfect law; by the means of the truths which he proclaims for the benefit of all, he brings men over to himself. What shall it avail any man to feel envious at the success he obtains by so legitimate a means?" The same torrent of ridicule having been poured on the Rahans, when they went out, they followed the advice of their great teacher, replied in the manner they had been taught to do, and the storm was soon over. The people understood that the great Rahan was preaching a perfect law, and that he never resorted but to fair means to attract disciples round his person. Here ends the narrative of the conversion and vocation of Thariputra and Maukalan.

CHAPTER VIII.

Thoodaudana, desirous to see his son, sends messengers to him—They become converts—Kaludari, a last messenger, prevails on Buddha to go to Kapilawot—His reception—Conversion of the king and of Yathaudara —Nanda and Raoula put on the religious habit—Conversion of An-anda and of several of his relatives—Temptation of Ananda—Conversion of Eggidatta—Story of Tsampooka.

WHILST the most excellent Phra remained in the Weloo-won monastery, enjoying himself in the midst of his disciples and the crowds of hearers that daily resorted thither to listen to his preachings, his father Thoodaudana [1] who

---

[1] In glancing over the episode of Thoodaudana's deputation to his son, to invite him to come and visit his native country, the reader is almost compelled to confess that the motive that influenced the king was only inspired by the natural feeling of beholding once more, before he died, him whose fame, spread far and wide, rendered him an object of universal admiration. Was the monarch induced by considerations of a higher order to send for Buddha? There is no distinct proof in support of this supposition. He was his father, and he but obeyed and followed the impulse of his paternal heart. He entertained a high sense of his son's distinguished qualifications. He had faith in the wonderful signs foretelling his future matchless greatness. He desired, therefore, to honour him in an extraordinary way, on the very spot where he had been born. But he appeared to concern himself very little about the doctrines he was preaching with a success never before equalled.

The king exhibited a great amount of worldly-mindedness, until his mind had been enlightened by the oral instructions of the great reformer.

It is difficult, if not impossible, to form an accurate idea of the effect produced on the mass of the people by Buddha's preachings. We see that eminent and zealous reformer surrounded by thousands of distinguished disciples in the country of Radzagio. These converts belonged chiefly to the class of anchorites and philosophers, already alluded to in foregoing notes as existing at the time Buddha began to enter the career of preaching. But the great bulk of the populations of the various places he visited seemed to have received for a long time little or no impressions from his discourses. The opponents of Buddha, the Brahmins in particular, exercised a powerful influence over the public mind. They used it most effectually for retaining their ancient hold over the masses. It required the extraordinary display of

had ever been anxiously and sedulously gathering every possible information respecting his son, from the time he withdrew into solitude, and performed during six years

the greatest wonders to break through the almost insuperable barriers raised by his enemies. From that period we see the people following Buddha, crowding round him, and showing unmistakable signs of belief in him.

The only explanation to account for this undeniable result is the philosophical method adopted by Buddha in expounding the principles of his system. His mode of proceeding in the gradual development of his ideas ietained the abstruseness peculiar to subjects discussed in schools of philosophy. The technical terms so familiar to scholars prove enigmatical to the uninitiated *vulgus*. It takes a long time before maxims elaborated by scholars are so far popularised as to be understood by the unlearned, which in every age and country have always constituted the great mass of the people. If the mind of the generality of men is unable to comprehend at first a system of doctrines, based on metaphysics, we cannot wonder at the slow progress made by the preachings of the great philosopher: but the working of wonders is a tangible fact operating upon the senses of the multitude, eliciting their applauses, and disposing them to yield an implicit faith to all the instructions imparted by the wonderful being that is gifted with supernatural powers. Feelings, and not reason, become the foundation of a belief which grows stronger in proportion to the mysterious obscurity that encompasses the proposed dogmas, when supported by wonderful deeds.

At the time Thoodaudana sent messengers to his son, the great work of conversion was carried on with a most complete and hitherto unheard-of success. The hall of the Weloowon monastery was too small for the thousands that flocked thither to hear Gaudama. Outside its precincts, crowds stood motionless, listening with unabated attention to the discourses that fell from his lips. So crowded was the audience that the messengers had no chance to make their way to the presence of the preacher. Struck with the intense attention paid to what was said by their master's son, they too wished to make themselves acquainted with the subjects of the instruction. What was listened to from motives of mere curiosity, soon made a deep impression upon their mind. The magic power of the irresistible eloquence of Buddha worked a thorough change almost instantaneously in their dispositions, and they became converts. So perfect was their conversion, that they forgot for the sake of truth the very object of their mission. They became at once members of the Assembly, and took rank among the Rahans. They attained the state of Ariahs, and were foremost among the perfect. The great attainments arrived at by the Ariahs communicate to the material portion of their being such an extraordinary amount of amazing virtues or properties, that it becomes so refined as to partake, to a certain degree, of a spiritual nature. Hence we see the Rahandas going over immense distances through the air, and performing deeds of a supernatural order. The power of working miracles is, therefore, inherent in perfection; and it is greater or smaller in proportion to the degree of perfection possessed by individuals. We find that power expanded in Buddha to an unlimited extent, because his mental attainments were boundless.

the hardest works of bodily mortification, was then informed that his son had already begun to preach the most
perfect law, and was actually staying in the city of Radzagio. He felt then an irresistible desire to see him once
more before his death. He therefore ordered a nobleman
of his court into his presence, and said to him : " Nobleman, take with you a retinue of a thousand followers, and
go forthwith to the city of Radzagio. Tell my son that I
am now much advanced in years, that I long to see him
once more before I die; desire him, therefore, to come
over with you to the country of Kapilawot." The nobleman, having received the royal message, took leave from
the king, and attended by a thousand followers, set out
for Radzagio. When he drew near to the Weloowon
monastery, he found it crowded with an innumerable multitude of people, listening with a respectful attention to
Buddha's instructions. Unwilling to disturb the audience,
the nobleman delayed for a while the delivery of his royal
master's message. Halting at the verge of the crowd, he,
with his followers, eagerly lent the utmost attention to all
that Buddha was saying. They at once obtained the state
of Arahat, and applied for admission into the order of
Rahans. The favour was granted. To obtain pattas and
tsiwarans for so great a number of applicants, Buddha
stretched his right arm, when there appeared at once the
pattas and dresses required. The new converts put on the
dress of their order, when they all appeared with the dignified countenance and meek deportment of Rahans who
had had sixty years of profession. Having arrived at the
exalted state of Ariahs, they became indifferent and un-
concerned about all the things of this material world, and
the king's mandate was entirely lost sight of.

The sovereign of Kapilawot, seeing that his nobleman
did not return from the country of Magatha,[2] and that no

---

[2] Magatha is a country in the north
of India. It occupied nearly the same
extent of territory as that now called
North Behar in Bengal. The Pali or

news was heard of him, despatched a second messenger with an equal number of followers on the same errand. They all were taken up with Buddha's preachings and became Rahandas.   The same thing happened to seven messengers successively sent to Radzagio for the same

---

sacred language of the southern Buddhists is often called the language of Magatha.   Hence we may infer that it was the common language of that country.   It is probable that the Pali language was extensively spoken in the days of Gaudama, and it was the channel through which he and his disciples long after him conveyed their religious instructions to the multitude of converts.   The Pitagat, or the last amended collection of sacred writings, is written in Pali, which is looked upon in Ceylon, Nepaul, Burmah, and Siam as the language of sacred literature.   Except in some old manuscripts, where the old square Pali letters are used, the Burmese employ their common alphabetic characters for writing Pali words.   The words, having to pass first through a Burmese ear, and next being expressed by Burmese letters, undergo great changes.   To such an extent does the metamorphosis reach, that very often they are scarcely recognisable.   The Burmans, however, deserve great credit for having, in very many instances, retained in their orthography of Pali words letters which, though not at all sounded, indicate to the eye the nature of the word, its origin, and its primitive form.

In the southern parts of Burmah the Pali language is learned but not studied, used, but not understood by the inmates of monasteries.   They are all obliged to learn certain formulas of prayers to be daily recited in private, and, on great and solemn occasions, to be chanted aloud in the presence of a crowd of pious hearers. The writer, anxious to acquire some knowledge of the sacred language, often visited those monks, who, among their brethren, enjoyed a certain fame for learning, with the express intention of becoming a humble student, under the direction of one of the best informed of the society.   He was thoroughly disappointed to find those who proffered their services in great earnest quite ignorant, and utterly incapable of giving him the least assistance.

The Burmese have translated in their vernacular tongue most of the sacred writings.   In many instances the translation is not exactly what we call interlineary, but it approaches to it as nearly as possible.   Two, three, or four Pali words are written down, and the translation in Burmese follows with a profusion of words which often confuses and perplexes the reader; then come again a few other Pali words, accompanied also with the translation, and so on throughout the whole work.   The art of translating well and correctly from one language into another is not so common as many persons may imagine.   In a good translator are required many qualifications which are not to be easily met with, particularly in a Burman, to whom we may give credit for knowing well his own tongue, but who, without detracting from his literary attainments, is certainly an indifferent Pali scholar.   These translations may convey, perhaps, the general meaning of the original, but, as regards the correct meaning of each term, it is a luxury ever denied to the reader of such crude and imperfect compositions.

purpose. They, with their respective retinues, became converts of the first class.

Disappointed at seeing that none of the messengers had returned to bring him any news regarding his son, King Thoodaudana exclaimed: "Is there no one in my palace that bears any affection unto me? Shall I not be able to get a person who could procure for me some information respecting my son?" He looked among his courtiers and selected one, named Kaludari, as the fittest person for such a difficult errand. Kaludari had been born on the same day as Buddha: with him he had spent the age of his infancy, and lived on terms of the most sincere friendship. The king said to him: "Noble Kaludari, you know how earnestly I long to see my son. Nine messengers have already been sent to the city of Radzagio to invite my son to come over to me, and none of them has as yet come back to me, to bring information respecting the object of my tenderest affections. I am old now, and the end of my existence is quite uncertain; could you not undertake to bring my son over to me? Whether you become Rahan or not, let me have the happiness of contemplating once more my beloved son ere I leave this world." The nobleman promised to the king to comply with his royal order. Attended by a retinue of a thousand followers, he set out for the city of Radzagio. Having reached the Weloowon monastery, he listened to Buddha's preachings, and, like the former messengers, he became at once a Rahanda with all his followers.

Gaudama, having obtained the Buddhaship, spent the first season (Lent) in the solitude of Migadawon. Thence he proceeded to the solitude of Ooroowela, where he remained three months, until he had completed the work of converting the three Kathabas. It was on the full moon of Piatho (January) that he entered into the city of Radzagio, accompanied by his thousand disciples. He had just stayed two months in that place, so that there were five months since he had left the country of Baranathee.

Seven days after Kaludari's arrival, the cold season being nearly over, the new convert addressed Buddha as follows: " Illustrious Phra, the cold season is over, and the warm season has just begun; this is now the proper time to travel through the country; nature wears a green aspect; the trees of the forests are in full blossom; the roads are lined to right and left with trees loaded with fragrant blossoms and delicious fruits; the peacock proudly expands its magnificent tail; birds of every description fill the air with their ravishing and melodious singing. At this season heat and cold are equally temperate, and nature is scattering profusely its choicest gifts." By such and similar allurements Kaludari endeavoured to dispose Buddha to undertake a journey to Kapilawot. Gaudama hearing all these words said: " What means this? To what purpose are uttered so many fine expressions?" Kaludari replied: " Your father, O blessed Buddha, is advanced in years; he has sent me to invite you to come over to Kapilawot, that he might see you before his death. He and your royal parents will be rejoiced at hearing your most excellent law." " Well," said Buddha, " go and tell the Rahans to hold themselves ready for the journey." It was arranged that ten thousand Rahandas from Magatha and ten thousand from Kapilawot would accompany the illustrious traveller. The distance between the two countries is sixty youdzanas.[3] Sixty days were to be employed

---

[3] It is difficult to ascertain exactly the length of the measure called youdzana, formerly used to indicate land distances. It varies from five to twelve English miles. In measuring the distance from Radzagio to the Brahmin village of Nalanda, the birthplace of Thariputra, which is one youdzana, General Cunningham has found it to be seven miles. This would induce us to hold as certain that at the epoch when Fa-Hian visited the place, the youdzana was equal to seven miles or forty Chinese *li*. But this would not prove that the more ancient youdzana was not shorter than the one used in the time of the Chinese pilgrim. Several authors maintain that such is the case. It appears, likewise, that the length of that measure of distance has varied with localities and places to such an extent that it has been found in some countries to be equal to more than twelve miles. We believe that when that measure of distance is mentioned in this work, one would not be far from the truth in estimating its length six or seven English miles at the utmost.

in going over that distance, so they were to travel at the rate of but one youdzana a day.

Kaludari was anxious to go and inform the king of the happy issue of his negotiation. He flew through the air, and in a short time reached the palace of the lord of Kapilawot. The king, seeing him, was exceedingly glad; he desired the illustrious Rahan to sit in a becoming place, and gave orders that his patta should be filled with the choicest dishes from the royal table. Meanwhile Kaludari related to the king all the circumstances attending his journey. When he had spoken, Thoodaudana desired him to take his meal. Kaludari begged to be excused, saying that he would go and take his meal in the presence of Buddha. " Where is he now ? " replied the king. " Mighty lord," answered Kaludari, " Buddha, accompanied by twenty thousand Rahandas, is on his way to this country, to pay a visit to his royal father; on this very day he has left the city of Radzagio." Thoodaudana was exceedingly pleased; he said again to Kaludari, " Eat your meal here, and please to take another meal to my son; I wish to supply him daily with food during his journey." Kaludari acceded to the king's request. When his meal was over, they cleansed his patta with the most exquisite perfumes, and afterwards filled it with the best and choicest eatables. The patta was then respectfully handed to the aërial messenger, who, in the presence of a large crowd of people, rose in the air with the patta under his arm, and in an instant arrived in presence of Gaudama, to whom he offered the vessel containing the delicious food from his father's table. Buddha received the food with pleasure, and ate it. The same thing was daily performed during all the time the journey lasted. Kaludari went every day to the palace through the air, ate his meal there, and brought that of his distinguished instructor, who during all the way partook of no other food but that which was brought over to him from his father's palace. Every day Kaludari carried news of the progress of Buddha's

journey. By this means he increased in the heart of all
an ardent desire of seeing him, and disposed every one to
wait on the great Gaudama with favourable and good dispositions. The services rendered on this occasion by
Kaludari were much valued by Buddha himself, who said :
" Kaludari is disposing the people to welcome our arrival ;
he is therefore one of the most excellent among my
disciples."

The princes and all the members of the royal family,
having heard of Gaudama's arrival, consulted among themselves as to the best means of paying due respect to the
noble and illustrious visitor. They selected the grove of
Nigraudatha [4] as the fittest place to receive him with his
disciples. The place was properly cleared and made
ready for the long-expected company. The inhabitants
of the country, attended with their richest dress, carrying

---

[4] The attentive reader of this work
cannot fail to remark the general ten-
dencies of Buddhism to isolation, retirement, and solitude. In a retired
position, the mind is less distracted
or dissipated by exterior objects; it
possesses a greater share of self-con-
trol, and is fitter for the arduous
work of attentive reflection and deep
meditation. Whenever Buddha, attended by his followers, reaches a
place where he is to stay for a while,
a grove outside the city is invariably
selected. Thither the great preacher
retires, as to a beloved solitude. He
enjoys it beyond all that can be said.
Alone with his spiritual family, un-
concerned about the affairs of this
world, he breathes at ease the pure
atmosphere of a complete calm ; his
undisturbed soul soars freely in the
boundless regions of spiritualism.
What he has seen and discovered
during his contemplative errands he
imparts with a placid countenance and
a mild voice to his disciples, endeavouring thereby to make them progress
in the way of knowledge and perfection.

In those solitary abodes of peace
Buddha was willing to receive all
those who wished for instruction.
They were all, without distinction of
rank or caste, admitted into the presence of him who came professedly
to point to men the way to happiness,
helping them to disentangle themselves from the trammels of passions.
He preached to all the most excellent
law. The tendency to retreat and
withdrawal from worldly tumult is,
in our own days, conspicuous in the
care taken by Buddhistic monks to
have their houses built in some lonely
quarter of a town, assigned exclu-
sively for that special purpose, or, as
is oftener the case, in fine places
at a small distance from the walls.
Some of those groves, in the centre
of which rise the peaceful abodes of
Rahans, the writer has often seen
and much admired. In towns or
large villages, where the ground is
uneven, the small heights are generally crowned with the dwellings of
religious.

flowers and perfumes, went out to meet Buddha.[5] Children of both sexes opened the procession; they were followed by the children of the noblest families; next came all the persons belonging to the royal family. All went to the grove of Nigraudatha, where Buddha had just

---

[5] The narrative of Buddha's reception in his father's royal city suggests two reflections. The first is, that the saying *Nemo Propheta in suâ patriâ* was as true in the days of Gaudama as it has been in subsequent ages. The mountains of Kapilawot had often re-echoed the praises of Buddha and the recital of his wonderful doings. The splendid retinue of twenty thousand distinguished converts that attended his person, the hitherto unwitnessed display of miraculous powers, &c.,—all these peculiarly remarkable circumstances seemed more than sufficient to secure for him a distinguished reception among his kinsmen, who ought to have been proud of being connected with him by the ties of relationship. Such, however, was not the case. Actuated by the lowest feelings of base jealousy, his relatives refused to pay him the respect he was so well entitled to. Their wretched obduracy was to be conquered by the awe and fear his miraculous power inspired.

The second reflection suggested by the recital of the ceremonies observed on the occasion of Buddha's reception in his native country is the truly pleasing fact of seeing the weaker sex appearing in public divested of the shackles put upon it by oriental jealousy. In Burmah and Siam the doctrines of Buddhism have produced a striking, and, to the lover of true civilisation, a most interesting result, viz., established the almost complete equality of the condition of women with that of men. In those countries women are not miserably confined in the interior of their houses, without the remotest chance of ever appearing in public. They are seen circulating freely in the streets; they preside at the *comptoirs*, and hold an almost exclusive possession of the bazaars. Their social position is more elevated in every respect than that of the persons of their sex in the regions where Buddhism is not the predominating creed. They may be said to be men's companions, and not their slaves. They are active, industrious, and by their labours and exertions contribute their full share towards the maintenance of the family. The marital rights, however, are fully acknowledged by a respectful behaviour towards their lords. In spite of all that has been said by superficial observers, I feel convinced that manners are less corrupted in those countries where women enjoy liberty, than in those where they are buried alive by a barbarous and despotic custom in the grave of an opprobrious and vice-generating slavery. Buddhism disapproves of polygamy, but it tolerates divorce. In this respect the habits of the people are of a damnable laxity. Polygamy is very rare in Burmah among the people. This nefarious and anti-social practice is left to the magnates of the land, from the king down to a petty myowon, who make a part of their greatness consist in placing themselves above public opinion, above moral and religious precepts, for enjoying the unrestrained gratification of the basest appetite. Though divorce be a thing of common occurrence, it is looked upon as an imperfection, merely tolerated for the sake of human frailty.

arrived with the twenty thousand Rahans that accompanied him.

The princes, secretly influenced by pride, thus thought within themselves: This Prince Theiddat is younger than we all; he is but our nephew, let the young people prostrate themselves before him; as to ourselves, let us remain sitting down behind them. This was quickly perceived by Buddha, who said to himself: My relatives refuse to prostrate themselves before me; I will now even compel them to do so. Whereupon he entered into ecstasy, rose in the air, and standing over the heads of his relatives, as a person shaking dust over them, he exhibited to their astonished regards, on a white mango-tree, wonders of fire and water. Thoodaudana, surprised at such a wonderful display of supernatural power, exclaimed: " Illustrious Buddha, on the day you were born they brought you to the presence of the Rathee Kaladewela, to do homage to him; on that occasion, having seen you placing your two feet on the Rathee's forehead, I prostrated myself before you for the first time. On the day of the ploughing solemn rejoicings, you were placed under the shade of the tree Tsampoothapye. The sun by its daily motion had caused the shadows of all surrounding trees to change their direction; that of the tree under which you were placed alone remaining unmoved. I prostrated myself a second time before you; and now, at the sight of this new wonder, I again bow down to you." The example of the king was instantly imitated by all the princes, who humbly bowed down to Buddha. Satisfied with having humbled his proud relatives, Buddha came down and sat in the place prepared for him. He then caused a shower of red rain to pour down over the assembled multitudes. It had the virtue to wet those who liked it, and not to wet those who disliked it. " This is not," said Buddha, " the only time when such a wonder has happened; the same thing took place once during one of my former existences, when I was Prince Wethandra." He went on, relating the most interesting circumstances of that former state of existence. The whole assembly now delighted at hearing his preachings and witnessing the display of his power. They all withdrew when the preaching was over, and retired to their respective places, without, however, inviting Buddha to come and take his meals in their houses.

On the following morning, Buddha set out with his twenty thousand followers to get his meal. When he had arrived at the gate of the city, he stood for a while, deliberating within himself whether he would go to the palace to receive his meal, or go from street to street to beg for it. He paused for a while, reflecting on the course of conduct that had been followed by all the former Buddhas. Having known that they all, without exception, had been in the habit of going out from house to house in quest of their food, he resolved at once to follow their example. Whereupon he entered the city and began to perambulate the streets in search of his food. The citizens, from the various stories of their houses, were looking out with amazement at such an unusual sight. "How is this?" said they; "we see Prince Raoula and his mother Yathaudara going out attired in the richest dresses, sitting in the most elegant conveyance, and now Prince Theiddat[6] is appearing in the streets with his hair

---

[6] Buddhist monks, out of humility and contempt for all worldly things, do not allow hairs or beard to grow. They walk barefooted, wearing a yellow dress of the simplest make. They are bound to live on the alms that are freely bestowed upon them. The regulations of the Wini are, in this respect, most explicit, and leave no room for false interpretation. A Rahan, having renounced the world, and divested himself of all worldly property, is bound by his professional vows to rely for his daily food on what he may obtain by begging. Hence the appellation of Bickus, or mendicants, always bestowed on them by Gaudama, whenever he addresses them in particular on certain points regarding their profession. In Burmah, as soon as the day begins to dawn, a swarm of yellow-dressed monks sally forth from their abode with the patta under the left arm, and perambulate the streets in quest of food. They never ask for anything; they accept what is voluntarily tendered to them, without uttering a single word of thanks, or even looking at their generous benefactors. This action of bestowing alms on the Rahans is deemed a most meritorious one. The offerer, therefore, becomes liberal, not on account

and beard shaved, and his body covered with a yellow
dress befitting a mendicant.   Such a thing is unbecoming
indeed." Whilst they were holding this language, on a
sudden, rays of the purest light shot forth from the body
of Buddha, and illuminated all the objects around his
person.   At this unexpected sight, they all joined in
praising and extolling the virtue and glory of Buddha.

King Thoodaudana was soon informed that his son was
perambulating the streets of the city in the dress of a
mendicant. Startled at such a news, he rose, and seizing
the extremity of his outer garment, ran to the encounter
of his son. As soon as he saw him he exclaimed: "Illustrious Buddha, why do you expose us to such a shame?
Is it necessary to go from door to door to beg your food?
Could not a better and more decent mode be resorted to
for supplying your wants?"   "My noble father," said
Buddha, "it is meet and convenient that all Rahans should
go out and beg their food."   "But," replied the monarch,
"are we not the descendants of the illustrious Prince
Thamadat?   There is not a single person in our illustrious
race that has ever acted in such an indecorous manner."
Buddha retorted, "My noble father,[7] the descent from the

---

of the person he is assisting, but because of the abundant merits he
hopes to derive from the act. This
notion agrees very well with the leading tenets of Buddhism.

[7] The answer of Buddha to his
royal father is a most remarkable one,
and deserves the attention of the observer.   The great moralist does
away with all the prerogatives man
may derive from birth, rank, and
riches. Law alone can confer titles
of true greatness and genuine nobility.
The fervent and zealous observers of
the law are alone entitled to the
respect of their fellow-men. The begging of alms may be, in the eyes
of worldlings, a low and mean action,
but it becomes a most dignified one,
because it is enforced by the law.

This lofty principle boldly establishes
the superiority of virtue upon the
strongest basis, and sanctions the
moral code he was destined to pub-
lish to men and saddle on their conscience. The criterion of all that is
good, excellent, praiseworthy, and
meritorious is no more to depend
on the arbitrary and very often erroneous views of men, but must rest
upon the immutable tenets of the
eternal law, discovered, revived, and
published by the omniscient Buddha.
This truth, like a flash of light, illuminated the king's mind, and, at this
first preaching of his son, he attained
the first of the four states of perfection.

The princes Thamadat and Thoodaudana boast to have descended

glorious princes Thamadat is something that belongs both to you and your royal family : the lineage of a Buddha is quite different from that of kings and princes; it bears no resemblance to it. Their ways and manners must essentially differ from those of princes. All former Buddhas have always been in the habit of thus going out in search of their food." Then stopping his course and standing in the street, he uttered the following stanzas, " My noble father, it is not proper that I should ever neglect the duty of receiving alms ; it is an action good in itself, tallying with truth, deserving of great merits, and productive of happiness in this and future existences." When he had spoken, his father obtained the state of Thautapan. He went to the palace with his father, saying, " Those who go to beg food according to the injunction and prescription of the law, are doing well, and prepare themselves for a state of happiness both for the present and future: those who do go begging, but without any regard to the ordinances of the law, ought to refrain from doing so." He was speaking in that way when he entered the palace. His aunt Gaudamee became a Thautapan.

---

from are, according to Buddhistic sacred books, the princes who were elected to hold supreme power at the very moment the words *mine* and *thine* began to be heard amongst men, after they had eaten the rice called Tsale, and become subject to passions, that is to say, at the origin of society, in the beginning of the world. The kings of Burmah, down to the present occupant of the throne, who are descended, in their opinion, from the Kapilawot line of kings, lay claim to the same distinction. The writer has heard the present King of Burmah very coolly stating as a matter of fact, which no one could think of contradicting, that he was descended from the Thamadat's royal line.

The Princess Yathaudara, mentioned in this narrative, had been the wife of Buddha, ere he had withdrawn into solitude and renounced the world. A son had just been born to him when he left his father's palace. His name was Raoula. The doctrine of the influence of merits gathered during former existences is forcibly illustrated in the case of Yathaudara, who, unmindful of the position she occupied in former years, did not hesitate to fling herself at Buddha's feet, acknowledging him to be worthy of all honour and veneration. Her former merits disposed her to view in him, who had been her husband, the extraordinary personage who was to lead men through the path of virtue to the deliverance.

His father, after this second preaching, reached the state Thagadagan.

Thoodaudana invited Phra and his followers to ascend to the upper part of the palace and partake of the meal prepared for them. When the meal was over, all the ladies of the palace came to pay their respects to Buddha. Some of them urged the Princess Yathaudara to do the same. But she refused to comply with their request, in the hope that a greater deference would be shown to her, and Buddha would come and visit her in her apartments. Perceiving her studied inattendance, Phra said to his father, "My noble father, I will go and visit the princess, and will, without saying a single word, make her pay obedience to, and prostrate herself before me. King Thoodaudana took up the patta, and accompanied his son to the princess's apartments, together with his two disciples, Thariputra and Maukalan. Buddha had scarcely been seated on the place destined to him, when Yathaudara threw herself at Buddha's feet, and placing her two hands on both ankles, touched repeatedly the upper part with her forehead. Meanwhile Thoodaudana mentioned to his son the respectful and affectionate regard she had ever entertained for his person. "Since she heard," added the king, "that you had put on the yellow robe, she would wear only clothes of that colour; when she knew that you took but one meal a day, that you slept on a small and low couch, and gave up, without regret, the use of perfumes, she instantly followed your example, ate but one meal a day, slept on a low couch, and gave up without grief the use of essences." "Illustrious monarch," replied Buddha, "I do not wonder at the practices of late observed by the Princess Yathaudara; in former times, when her merits were as yet only few and imperfect, she was living at the foot of a certain mountain, and knew, even then, how to behave with becomingness, and attend with a strict regard to all religious duties."

This very day, that is to say, the second day after the full moon of Katson, was fixed as the time for the taking place of five grand ceremonies. Nanda,[8] the younger brother of Buddha, was to have his head washed, to put on the

---

[8] Nanda was Buddha's younger brother, or rather half-brother. His mother was Patzapati, the younger sister of Maia. Since Buddha had renounced the world, Nanda had become the presumptive heir to the crown of Kapilawot. His conversion grieved the king much, who, to prevent the recurrence of such an event, exacted from the great reformer that in after times no one could be admitted into the society of the perfect, without having previously obtained the consent of his parents; failing such a condition, the act of admission should be considered as null and void. Hence, we read in the book of ordination, or admittance to the dignity of Rahan, that the person directed by the president of the assembly to examine the candidate never omits to inquire of him whether he has obtained the consent of his parents.

The conversion of Raoula followed that of Nanda. Of this new and distinguished convert no mention is made afterwards in the course of this work. He must, in all likelihood, have become a celebrated member of the assembly, as he was trained up to the functions and duties of his profession by the greatest and most renowned disciples, such as Maukalan, Thariputra, and Kathaba.

In the history of Buddhism, the Dzetawon monastery is not inferior in celebrity to that of Weloowon. Therein Gaudama announced during a certain night the thirty-six beatitudes of the law to a Nat that had come and requested him to make him acquainted with the most perfect points of his law. In the division of the scriptures called Thoots, or sermons, we see that the most important have been delivered in the hall of that monastery.

Here is another instance of a donation of landed property to a religious corporation. In the first case, the gift had been made to him and to his actual followers. But in this circumstance, Phra desires the rich and pious benefactor to make the donation, not only in behalf of self and the present assembly, but also in that of all future members, who might resort to this place. In a Buddhistic point of view, we may conclude that the advice given to the donor was intended as a means of multiplying the sum of the merits of his liberality, which must be commensurate with the number of the individuals to whom it is designed to be extended.

According to the principle respecting property, which from immemorial time has prevailed under almost all despotic governments in Asia, which recognises the head of the state as the sole, real, and absolute owner of the soil, it is evident that the act of donation was, legally speaking, a declaration or a statement of the disposal an individual made of the rights such as he had them, viz., those of use, in favour of a religious body. The landed property, thus conferred, acquired a kind of sacredness which preserved it from the grasp of even the most rapacious ruler. On the other hand, the religious body had no right or power whatsoever to sell or dispose of that property. In a corporation constituted as the assembly of the disciples of Buddha was, and is in our own days, the society alone could have the possession and management of immovable properties given to monasteries. Donations of this kind must have stood good as long as there were members of the Buddhistic religious family willing and ready to maintain their rights. Nothing short

thingkiit, or royal head ornament, to be raised to the dignity of crown prince, to be put in possession of his own palace, and to be married. When Phra was leaving the palace, he bade the young prince take his patta and follow him. Nanda instantly complied with the request, and departed. He was just leaving the palace, when the young lady he was to marry heard the sound of the steps and of the voice of her lover. She was then busily engaged in combing her beautiful and shining black hair. With the left hand drawing aside her hair, and with the right leaning on the window-frame, she, with a sweet yet tremulous voice, eagerly recommended him soon to return. She then continued to follow him with anxious eyes until he could be seen no longer. Meanwhile, resting against the window-side, she had her heart full of ominous forebodings. Nanda would have gladly given back the patta to his owner; but as he felt backward to hand it over to him, he followed Buddha as far as the monastery. Though he had no intention of becoming Rahan on his way to that place, yet, despite of his former dispositions, he entered into the society of the perfect. So that on the second day after Phra's arrival at Kapilawot, Nanda became a Rahan. Some other writings mention that this happened only on the third day.

---

of a complete revolution in the political state of the country, or the prolonged absence of the individuals vested with the right of occupation, could put an end to the effect of those deeds of donation. In Burmah, the Buddhist monks possess nothing beyond the ground upon which stands the monastery. From certain inscriptions found in the midst of the ruins of the temples at Pagan, it is evident that in the palmy days of that city donations of landed properties, such as paddy-fields, fruit-trees, bullocks, and peasants, were made to monasteries and temples. But for the last three or four hundred years, no vestiges of such deeds have ever been found. So far as I have been able to make inquiries, I am not aware that the order has ever become possessor of lands. In Ceylon such is not the case, at least was not when the English occupied the island. Extensive tracts of valuable lands were in the hands of the Talapoins, who thereby obtained over the people the twofold influence conferred by wealth and religion.

On the seventh day after Phra had entered into the city of Kapilawot, the mother of Raoula, Princess Yathaudara, put on her son the choicest ornaments, and sent him to Phra, saying previously to him: "Dearest son, he whom you see surrounded by twenty thousand Rahandas, whose face resembles gold, and whose body is similar to that of the chief of Brahmas, is indeed your father. He was formerly the owner of the four gold vases which disappeared on the very day he withdrew into solitude; go to him now, and say respectfully, that, being at present crown prince of this kingdom, destined to succeed your grandfather on the throne, you wish to become possessed of the property that will fall to you in right of inheritance." The young prince departed. Having come into the presence of Buddha, he endeavoured, with the simplicity and amiability becoming a young lad, to ingratiate himself in his father's favour, and said how happy he was to be with him, adding many other particulars befitting his age and position. Buddha, having eaten his meal and performed his usual devotions, rose up and departed. Raoula followed behind, saying: "Father, give me my inheritance." Buddha appearing neither displeased nor vexed at such a demand, none of his followers durst tell the young prince to desist from his apparently rude behaviour, and go back to the palace. They all soon reached the monastery. Phra thus thought within himself: Raoula is asking from me perishable things, but I will give him something more excellent and lasting. I will make him partaker of those goods I have gathered at the foot of the Bodi tree, and thereby will provide for him a better inheritance for the future. Whereupon he called Thariputra, and said to him: "Beloved disciple, the young Prince Raoula asks from me a worldly inheritance, which would avail him nothing, but I wish to present him with something more excellent, an imperishable inheritance; let him become a Rahan." Maukalan shaved the head of Raoula and attired him with the tsiwaran. Thariputra gave him the first instructions.

When hereafter he became Patzing, Kathaba trained him up to the duties of his new profession.

King Thoodaudana had seen his first son Prince Theidat leave the palace and all the attracting allurements of a brilliant court; despite of all his precautions, he subsequently witnessed his going into a solitude and becoming a Rahan. Next to him, his younger son Nanda, though assured by the promises of soothsayers of becoming a great and mighty ruler, had joined the society of Rahans. These two events had deeply afflicted him. But, on hearing that his grandson had also become a Rahan, he could no longer keep his affliction within himself. " I had," said he, " hoped that my grandson would succeed me on the throne; this thought consoled me for the loss of my two sons. What will become of my throne? Now the royal succession is at an end, and the line of direct descendants is for ever cut and irrevocably broken asunder."

Thoodaudana obtained the state of Anagam. He said to himself: It is enough that I should have had so much to suffer and endure on the occasion of my two sons and my grandson becoming Rahans; I will spare to other parents a similar affliction. He went to Buddha's place, and having paid him his respects in a becoming manner, asked him to establish a regulation forbidding any son to become Rahan, unless he had the consent of his parents. Buddha assented to his father's wish and preached to him the law. When the instruction was finished, the king bowed to him, rose up, turned on the right, and departed. Buddha, calling immediately the Rahans, said to them: " Beloved Bickus, no one is to be admitted to the profession of Rahan, ere he has obtained the consent of his parents : any one that shall trespass this regulation shall be guilty of a sin."

On a certain day, Phra having eaten his meal at his father's palace, the king related to him the circumstance of a Nat, who, whilst he was undergoing great austerities in the solitude, had come and conveyed the report of his son having succumbed under the hardships of mortification ; but he would never give credit to such a rumour, as he was certain that his son could not die ere he had become a Buddha. " My illustrious father," replied Buddha, " you are much advanced in merits ; there is no wonder at your not believing a false report ; but even in former ages, when your merits were as yet very imperfect, you refused to believe your son was dead, though in proof of this assertion bones were exhibited before you in confirmation of the report." And he went on relating many particulars that are to be found in the history of Maha Damma Pala. It was at the conclusion of this discourse that the king became Anagam. Having thus firmly established his father in the three degrees of perfection, Buddha returned to the country of Radzagio.

During this voyage, the most excellent Phra arrived at the village of Anupya, in the country of the Malla Princes. In the neighbourhood of the village there is a grove of mango-trees. To that place he withdrew with his twenty thousand disciples, and enjoyed himself in that secluded and delightful retreat.

While he dwelt on that spot, the seed of the law that he had planted in his native city was silently taking deep root in the hearts of many. His uncle Thekkaudana had two sons, named Mahanan and Anooroudha. On a certain day Mahanan said to his younger brother : " From among the several families of the royal race, many persons have left the world and embraced the religious profession under the guidance of Buddha. Our family is the only one that has not as yet given any member to the assembly. I will make you a proposal : either you will become an ascetic, and leave me your inheritance ; or I will myself take that step, and make over to you all that I possess." Anooroudha at once accepted the proposal.

When the intentions of the two brothers became known, five young princes, their playmates and relatives, named

Bagoo, Kimila, Baddya, Ananda,[9] and Dewadat, desired to join them in their pious design. Having put on their finest dress, they went into the country, having no other attendant but Oopali, their barber. They shaped their course in the direction of Anupya. Being at a small distance from the mango-trees' grove, the young princes stripped themselves of their rich dresses, and gave them all to the barber, as an acknowledgment of his services. The latter at first accepted them, and was preparing to return, when the following thought occurred to his mind : " If I go back to Kapilawot with these fine and rich apparels, the king and the people will believe that I have come by foul means in possession of so many valuables, and I shall certainly be put to death. I will follow my masters, and never leave them." Hereupon he returned in all haste and joined them at the very moment they were disposing themselves to enter into the Anupya mango-trees' grove. Oopali was admitted into their company, and ushered along with them into Buddha's presence. Having paid their respects in the usual manner, they applied for

---

[9] Ananda, whose conversion is here mentioned, was the son of Amitaudana, a brother of King Thoodaudana, and, therefore, first cousin to Gaudama. He is one of the best known disciples of the celebrated philosopher of Kapilawot. He has gained his well-earned fame, less by the shining attainments of his intellect than by the amiable qualities of a loving heart. He bore to Buddha the most affectionate regard and the warmest attachment from the very beginning of his conversion. The master repaid the love of the disciple by tokens of a sincere esteem and tender affection. Though it was a long period afterwards ere Ananda was officially appointed to minister unto the personal wants of Buddha, yet the good dispositions of his excellent heart prompted him to serve Buddha on all occasions, and in every way that was agreeable to him. He became the medium of intercourse between his beloved master and all those that approached him. When he had to communicate orders or give directions to the religious, or when some visitors desired to wait on him, Ananda was the person who transmitted all orders, and ushered visitors into the presence of the great preacher.

Dewadat was both first cousin to Buddha and his brother-in-law. His father was Thouppabudha, Maia's brother. He was brother of the Princess Yathaudara, who had married our Gaudama, when he was crown prince of Kapilawot. Hereafter, we shall have the opportunity of seeing that his moral dispositions were very different from those of the amiable Ananda.

the dignity of members of the assembly. Their request was granted. But previous to passing through the prescribed ceremonies, the princes said one to another : " Great indeed and deeply rooted is the pride of princes : it is extremely difficult to shake it off, and free oneself of its tyrannical exactions. Let Oopali be first ordained ; we will have an opportunity of humbling ourselves by prostrating ourselves before him." Their request was granted. After having paid their respects to the newly ordained convert, they were likewise admitted among the members of the assembly. Their proficiency in spiritual progress was not the same. During the second Lent, which they spent in the Weloowon monastery, Baddya, Bagoo, and Kimila reached the culminating point of perfection by becoming Rahandas. Ananda became Thautapatti. Anooroudha greatly advanced in the higher path of metaphysics. As to Dewadat, he never attained more than the Laukithamabat.

A little while after the conversion of the royal princes, Buddha left Anupya, continued his voyage to Radzagio, and forthwith retired into the Weloowon monastery to spend his second Lent. The time was chiefly employed in training up the new converts in the knowledge of the great truths, and in the practice of virtue. His son Raoula, about eight years old, evinced the greatest dispositions. His attainments were far above his age, and often elicited the admiration of the Rahans. On a certain occasion Buddha overheard them expressing their astonishment at the surprising progress Raoula was making in his studies. Coming among them as if perchance, Phra asked them what was the subject of their conversation. They answered that they were praising and extolling the wonderful abilities of Raoula, and his matchless good dispositions. Thereupon Buddha remarked that this was not to be wondered at. Then he related to them the dzat Miga, by which he showed to them that during former existences Raoula had distinguished himself in a conspicuous manner by his excellent and admirable dispositions. As a reward for his good behaviour and high mental qualifications, he was made Patzin. His mind continuing to expand in an almost miraculous manner, he became a Rahanda with myriads of Nats.

During the same season, Buddha often went to Radzagio to beg his food. There was in that city a flower-seller, who was wont to bring eight bouquets every day to the king, and receive in return from the royal hands eight pieces of silver. On a certain day, as he was coming from the country into the town with his usual supply of flowers for the king, he happened to see Buddha in the streets at a moment when, by a miraculous display of his power, the six glories beamed out of his body. He then said to himself: "I wish to go and offer these flowers to Buddha. But the king will doubtless be much angry with me. He may have me arrested, thrown into prison, and put to death for having failed in offering him the usual present. Despite the great danger that hangs over me, I will go to Buddha and offer him my flowers. Great, indeed, and lasting shall be the merits I will gain; they will follow me during countless existences."

With a heart full of joy, Thoomana, for such is his name, went to the resting-place where Buddha was seated, surrounded by crowds of people, and laid the flowers at his feet. With a marked satisfaction, Gaudama accepted the offer. Thoomana went home and related to his wife what had just happened. The latter, irritated partly by the fear of the king's wrath, and partly by the loss of the money she daily received, began to abuse her husband in the coarsest language. She was so much maddened by passion that she in all haste went to the king, denounced her husband, and instantly sued for a divorce. Pimpathara revolted at such an act of unparalleled audacity, ordered her to withdraw from his presence and go back to her house. Meanwhile he commanded one of his courtiers to order the flower-seller to come to the palace on the following day. As a matter of course, the royal request was punctually complied with. In the presence of the assembled courtiers, the king highly praised the conduct of Thoomana, and instantly rewarded him with great liberality. As Thoomana had offered to Buddha eight bunches of flowers, the king, to acknowledge in a distinct manner such an offering, gave him eight elephants, eight horses, eight slaves, eight bullocks, eight thousand pieces of silver, and the revenue of eight villages. Buddha likewise exceedingly extolled the meritorious behaviour of Thoomana in the presence of the people, and said that during a whole world he would be exempt from the four states of punishment, enjoy happiness in the seat of man and in those of Nats, and finally become a Pitzega-buddha. The value of the offering, though little in itself, became great by the imminent risks he voluntarily exposed himself to. He made his offering, though he was certain of incurring on that account the ruler's displeasure.

When the season of retirement was over, Gaudama travelled through different places. He went to Patzanawonta in the Dzetia country, thence he passed into the Bisakila forest, and returned to Radzagio, in the grove of Yin-daik trees, near the burial-place.

Whilst Buddha was in the splendid Dzetawon monastery, just presented to him, a strong temptation came upon Ananda to renounce his calling and return into the world. He went so far as to tell some of his brethren that he recollected the promise of a prompt return which he made to his young bride Dzanapada-kaliani, and that now he wished to fulfil it by immediately going back into his palace, and resuming his former mode of life. This was soon reported to Gaudama, who resorted to the following expedient to crush in the bud the rising temptation. He took Ananda by the arm, rose with him in the air, and led him in the direction of the Nats' seat of Tawadeintha. On their way, Buddha, by a miraculous process, exhibited to the eyes of his companion the sight of an immense forest in conflagration. On the burnt stump of a tree he showed him a female monkey horribly mutilated, having her tail, ears, and nose cut off. At such a sight the horrified Ananda turned away his eyes in disgust. A little while after this, Buddha exhibited before him the dazzling and heart-captivating sight of a long array of five hundred matchless beauties. They were daughters of Nats going to pay their respects to the great Thagia. Ananda was gazing at them with silent but enraptured feelings. Buddha said to him: "Do you believe those beauties before you to be equal to Dzanapada?" "She is no more to these perfect forms," answered he, "than the bleeding female monkey we have left behind us is to her." "All these celestial damsels," said Buddha, "I shall give to you, provided you agree to remain in the monastery for some years longer." "Willingly do I accept the proposal," replied Ananda; "I will stay cheerfully in the monastery on such favourable terms." Whereupon both returned to the monastery.

The members of the assembly soon became acquainted with what had passed between the master and the disciple, and keenly taunted Ananda with their sarcastic remarks upon the daughters of Nats. Ashamed of himself, Ananda withdrew into solitude. There he devoted himself to reflection and penitential deeds, and finally annihilated the evil desires of his unsubdued passion. When the inward struggle was over and peace had been restored in him, Ananda went to Buddha's presence, and stated his willingness to dwell for ever in a monastery and lead a religious life. Meantime he released him from the promise he had made to him respecting the celestial beauties. Buddha was much pleased at such a happy change. He said to the assembled religious: "Previous to this occurrence, Ananda resembled a badly-roofed house, which lets in the rain of passions; but now it is similar to a well-roofed building, which is so well pro-

tected that it is proof against the oozing of passions."
Whereupon he related the following story concerning a
former existence of Ananda.

A merchant named Kappaka had a donkey which he
used to carry goods from place to place. Having one
day come near a place covered ,with trees, Kappaka un-
loaded his animal, to allow him some time to rest and
graze. Meanwhile, a female donkey was likewise grazing
in the neighbourhood. Its presence was quickly detected
by Kappaka's animal. When the moment of departure
had come, the latter, attracted by the female, kicked furi-
ously at his master, and would not allow the load to be
replaced on its back. The merchant, enraged at this unusual freak, began to threaten the rebellious beast, and
then to hit it with the whip as hard as he could. At last
the poor animal, unable to bear any longer the blows,
mentioned to his master the cause of his unusual behaviour. Kappaka told him that if he would but continue
his voyage, he would give him at the end of the journey
several fine females, much superior to the one he was now
coveting. The proposal was accepted. At the end of the
journey Kappaka said to the beast: " I will keep my
promise with you : but I must inform you that your daily
provender shall not be increased; you will have to share
it with your companion. Subsequently you will have
little ones to provide for and maintain, but your daily
ration shall not be increased in the least; you shall have
to work for me as much as you do at present, and also to
provide for the maintenance and support of your family."
The donkey, after a few moments of reflection, thought it
was better to remain as he was ; and from that moment
he was entirely cured of his inordinate inclination. At
the conclusion of the narration, Buddha said: " The male
donkey was he who has now become Ananda; the
female donkey, Dzanapa-kaliani ; and Kappaka is now
the most excellent Phra, who is the teacher of men, Nats
and Brahmas.

Buddha, whilst at Wethalie, went out through the country, and in all the places that he visited preached to the crowds of hearers. It was during one of his benevolent errands that he met with a celebrated Pounha, named Eggidatta, who with a great many disciples led an ascetic life, after having been formerly, first, the chief Pounha of King Kothala, and next of his son. Buddha earnestly desired the conversion of so distinguished a personage. Maukalan was at first despatched to that famous hermit, to attempt to bring him over to his master; but he utterly failed. The reception he at first met with was anything but pleasant. The work was to be done and perfected only by the irresistible eloquence of the great preacher. Buddha soon came up to the entrance of Eggidatta's cell. He began to upbraid the Rathee for teaching his disciples to worship mountains, trees, rivers, and all that exists in nature. He then initiated him in the knowledge of the four great truths. Eggidatta, seeing the truth, at once became a convert with all his disciples. When this great spiritual conquest was achieved, Buddha returned to Radzagio, and spent the third season in the Weloowon or bamboo-grove monastery. It was during the three months of the rainy season that Buddha imparted, in a more complete manner, to his disciples the knowledge and science which during his peregrinations he had but superficially conveyed to them. At the same time, he carefully trained them up in the practice and observance of those disciplinary regulations which were intended as a means to subdue passions, to estrange them from the world and all its attractions, and to lead a spiritual life.

During his stay in the monastery, among the many instructions that he gave to his disciples, I will relate the particulars that he mentioned respecting the former doings and the final conversion of the Rahanda Tsampooka.[10]

---

[10] The story of Eggidatta gives us an insight into one of the tenets

In the days of the Buddha Kathaba, Thampooka, or rather the being who in the present existence is called by that name, put on the religious dress in the Thawatie country. He lived in a fine monastery, and had for his supporters the best and richest people of the place. One day, a Rahan, belonging to another country, came to his monastery and begged the favour to be allowed to live therein for some time. The heartless Tsampooka denied him admittance into the interior of the building, but tolerated his staying in the verandah during the cold season. The people, however, actuated by better feelings than those

---

which was held by that ascetic. His interlocutor reproached him with worshipping mountains, trees, forests, rivers, and the heavenly bodies. From the expressions made use of by the Burmese translator, the writer is inclined to believe that a direct allusion is made to pantheistic opinions. We know that most of the Indian schools of philosophy have based their various systems of metaphysics upon that most erroneous foundation. According to pantheists, this world is not distinct from the essence of God; all that exists is but a manifestation or a development of the substance of God. This world is not the work of God, existing as distinct from its Maker, but it is God manifesting Himself substantially in all things. Who could, then, wonder at the conduct of Tsampooka? He worshipped God, or rather that portion of the supreme Being he saw in the great and mighty subjects that surrounded him and attracted his notice.

Spinoza, in the seventeenth century, and his unfortunately too numerous followers in this century, have recast into a hundred different moulds the pantheistic ideas of the Hindu philosophers, and offer to the intelligence of their hearers and readers, through an almost unintelligible language, the same deadly food which

has finally produced on the Hindu mind the sad results which we witness. If we were better acquainted with the variety of doctrines which the Hindu philosophers have exhibited in the field of metaphysics, we would be soon convinced that the modern metaphysicians, who have placed themselves out of the pale of revelation, have not advanced one step in that science, and that the divergence in their opinions is but a faithful representation of the confusion which for more than two thousand years prevailed on the banks of the Ganges among their predecessors in the same speculative studies.

It appears that Tsampooka was in his days what the Jogies or Hindoo penitents are up to our time. He remained on his rock, in the most difficult position, for the space of fifty-five years, exhibiting himself to the crowd, and aiming at winning their admiration by the incredible sufferings that he voluntarily submitted to. His apparent sanctity was made up of very doubtful materials. He passed himself off for a man who could remain without eating, and who was gifted with supernatural powers. Plain humility, which is nothing but the result of the true knowledge of self, was not the favourite virtue of our spiritual quack.

of their teacher, brought regularly food for the head of the house, as well as for the stranger, for whom they felt great affection. The spiteful Tsampooka could not bear to see the people showing marks of kindness and benevolence towards his hated guest. On one occasion he forgot himself so far as to abuse him, by repeating the following coarse expressions: Eat dirt, go naked, and sleep on the bare ground. Such an inhuman behaviour soon met with a condign punishment. The wretched Tsampooka had at first to endure horrible torments in hell.

On his return to the seat of man on earth, he was born from respectable parents, but he was always prone from his infancy to indulge in the lowest habits. He would secretly steal away, and actually satiate the cravings of hunger by eating the most disgusting things; he would not wear clothing, but ran about in a state of nakedness; he would only sleep on the ground. His parents, after many fruitless attempts to correct him, resolved to make him over to the heterodox ascetics. These received him; but he would not eat in the company of his brethren, nor go to beg with them. He, from the moment they were absent, went to devour the refuse he could find. His eccentric and disgusting habits were soon found out, and his new friends said one to the other: "Let this man be no longer allowed to live with us. Should the disciples of the Rahan Gaudama hear that one of our company is behaving in such a manner, our brotherhood would become a laughing-stock to them." He was, therefore, expelled from this place. Tsampooka went to take his abode on a rock near the place that served as receptacle to the sewers of Radzagio. On that rock he remained in the most fatiguing posture; he leaned on his right hand which rested on the rock, and also on his right knee; the left leg was stretched and the left arm raised up. He kept his mouth opened. When the people asked him why he remained with his mouth wide open, as a man who is incessantly drawing air into his lungs, he answered that, refraining from the use of coarse food, he was feeding on air only: when questioned about the singular position of his two legs, he answered, that, were he to stand on both legs, the earth would instantly shake. He had been during fifty-five years in that sad position, when Gaudama, moved with compassion at his pitiable condition, went in person to convert him. He began to relate to him all that he had done during former existences, mentioning in particular the sin he had been guilty of towards a brother hermit. At this unexpected declaration, Tsampooka humbled himself. Buddha then preached to him his law. The repenting Tsampooka firmly believed in all that was said to him. He then rose up, and, with a heart overflowing with joy, instantly left his place, followed his new master, and soon became a Rahanda. His proficiency in science and virtue was such that he soon occupied a distinguished rank among the members of the assembly.

CHAPTER IX.

WHEN Buddha was in the country of Radzagio, a certain rich merchant, named Anatapein, came to Radzagio, with five hundred carts loaded with the most precious goods, and took his lodging in the house of an intimate friend. Whilst living with his friend, he heard that Gaudama had become a Buddha. Suddenly, he was seized with an earnest desire of seeing him and hearing his doctrine. On a certain day, he rose at an early hour, and perceived, reflected through the lattices of the window, some rays of an uncommon brightness. He went in the direction of the light to the place where Buddha was preaching the law. He listened to it with great attention, and, at the end of the discourse, he obtained the state of Thautapan. Two days after, he made a great offering to Buddha and to the assembly, and requested him to come to the country of Thawattie. The request was granted. The distance to Thawattie is forty-five youdzanas. Anatapein spent enormous sums that one monastery should be erected at each youdzana distance. When Buddha was approaching, the pious merchant arranged as follows for the reception of the distinguished visitor, and presenting to him a splendid monastery called Dzetawon, which he had made ready for him. He sent first his son, richly attired, with five hundred followers, belonging to the richest families ; then followed his two daughters with five hundred girls, all decked with the most costly ornaments. Every one carried flags of five different colours. These were followed by five hundred dames, having the rich man's wife at their head, each carrying a pitcher of water. Last of all, came Anatapein, with five hundred followers, all wearing new dresses. Gaudama let the crowd walk in front, and he followed attended by all the Rahans. When he entered the grove, he appeared as beautiful as the peacock's tail when completely expanded. Anatapein asked Gaudama how he wished the donation should be made and effected ? " Let the monastery be offered," said Buddha, "to all the Rahans that may come in future to this place from what quarter soever." Thereupon, the rich man, holding a golden vessel of water, poured its contents on the hands of Buddha, saying : " I present this monastery to Buddha and to all the Rahans that may come hereafter to reside therein." Buddha said prayers and thanks in token of his accepting the offering. Seven days were devoted to making this great offering, and during four months uninterrupted rejoicings went on in commemoration of this great and solemn donation. For the purchase of the place, and the expenses of the ceremony, enormous sums were lavished. During the era of former Buddhas this very place had always been purchased and offered to them and their disciples.

[*N.B.*—Here is found narrated in full the history of a celebrated physician named Dzewaka. As such story has no reference whatever to Buddha's career, I will give but a very succinct account of it.]

At a certain time,[1] when Buddha lived in the city of

---

[1] It is impossible to assign the motive that induced the compiler of

Radzagio, the country of Wethalie was made rich, gay, and attractive by the presence of a famous courtesan. A nobleman of Radzagio, who had just returned from that

---

Buddha's life to insert in his work a long episode on the celebrated physician Dzewaka. The story is in itself uninteresting, and throws no light whatever on the history of the supposed originator or reformer of Buddhism. For this reason it has been thought quite unnecessary to give a complete translation of the whole passage. The name of Dzewaka is quite familiar to the adepts of the medical art in Burmah. Many times the writer has made inquiries respecting the works of the Hippocrates of India, but he has never been able to meet with mention of or allusion to such compositions. Hence he has been led to suppose that the father of medicine in these countries has left behind him no writings to embody the results of his theoretical and practical favourite pursuits. Surgery appears to have been no novelty with our great doctor, since we see him on an occasion extracting from the body of a prince, by means of an incision, a snake that put his life in peril.

The numerous quacks who in Burmah assume the name of physicians, and are ever ready to give medicines in all cases, even the most difficult and complicated, are ignorant of the very elements of the surgical art. They possess a certain number of remedies, made up of plants, which, when applied under proper circumstances and in certain cases, work wonderful cures. But the native physicians, unable in most instances to discern the true symptoms of diseases, prescribe remedies at random, and obtain, in too many cases, results most fatal to the unfortunate patient. In medicine as well as in religion, ignorance begets superstition and recourse to magical practices. We may positively assert that

the black art is, with native practitioners, an essential concomitant to the practice of medicine. When a physician has exhausted the limited stock of remedies that he possesses, and he finds, in spite of his exertions, that the disease bids defiance to his skill, he gravely tells the relatives of the patient that some evil spirit is interfering with his remedies, and that he must be expelled ere there can be any chance of relieving the sufferer and obtaining his recovery. Whereupon a shed is erected with the utmost speed on a spot close to the house of the patient. Offerings of rice, fruits, and other articles are made to the pretended evil spirit, who is supposed to have got hold of the sufferer's body. Dances of the most frantic character are carried on by his relatives. Males will only officiate in default of females; preference is always given to the latter. Young girls, say the Burmese, are the fittest persons for the occasion, as it is supposed that the evil Nat is more effectually and easily propitiated by the power of their charms. This exercise lasts until, strength at last failing them, they drop down in a state of complete exhaustion and prostration. They appear as if they had entirely lost their senses. In that state they are supposed to be inspired by the evil spirit. Interrogated by the physician on the nature of the disease, and the proper remedies to be applied for eradicating it, they give answers, or rather they become channels through which the spirit, satisfied with the offerings made in his honour, condescends to declare that he has now left the patient, and that by placing him under a certain treatment, which he fails not to indicate, he will soon

country, narrated to the king all that he had seen at Wethalie, and induced the monarch to set up, in his own kingdom, some famous courtesan, who would be skilful in music and dancing, as well as attractive by the form and accomplishments of her person. Such a person having been procured, she was, by the munificence of the king, placed on a most splendid footing, and one hundred pieces of silver were to be paid for each evening's visit. The king's son being rather assiduous in his visits to her place, she became pregnant. Aware of her state, the courtesan affected to be sick until her confinement. She directed her servant to throw out the newly-born infant, on a heap of rubbish, in some lonely and distant place. The next morning the king's son, going out with some attendants, chanced to pass close to the spot where the infant had been deposited. His attention having been attracted by the noise of crows hovering close by, he went to see what it was. To his great surprise, he saw an infant, yet breathing, half buried in rubbish. Taken with the beauty of this little creature, the prince ordered the child to be carried to the palace, where he was brought up with the greatest care and attention. He was named Dzewaka, which means life, because the prince, when he found him, inquired if he was alive. The young lad, having reached the years of discretion, was unwilling to remain in the palace, not occupied with any business. In order to afford relief and comfort to his fellow-creatures, he resolved to study medicine. He repaired to Benares, placed himself under the direction of a famous physician, and soon became eminent by his extreme proficiency in the profession. Having left his master, and begun practice in his own name and for his own account, Dzewaka worked the most wonderful cures, which soon procured to him unbounded wealth and an extraordinary reputation.

---

recover his health. Occurrences of this nature are exceedingly common. They are called by the natives festivals of the *Nat-pan*, or of the possessing spirit.

Dzewaka was at the height of his fame, when, on a certain day, Buddha happened to be troubled with belly-ache. He called Ananda and said that he wanted some medicine to relieve him from pain. Ananda went to the place where lived the celebrated Dzewaka, and informed him of Buddha's complaint. The doctor ordered first a rubbing of oil, which was to be repeated three days after. This remedy not having a full effect, Dzewaka took three lily flowers, whereupon he spread several powders, and came to Buddha, saying, "Most glorious Phra, here is one lily flower, please to smell it; this will be followed by ten motions. Here is a second one; the smelling thereof will produce a similar effect; and this one will cause the same result." Having handed over the three flowers, the doctor paid his respects to Buddha, turned to the right, and left the monastery.

When he was crossing the gate, he thought within himself, "I have given a medicine calculated to cause thirty motions, but as the complaint is rather of a serious and obstinate character, twenty-nine motions only will take place; a warm bath would be required to produce the thirtieth;" and with this reflection he departed. Buddha, who saw all that passed in the doctor's mind, called Ananda and directed him to prepare a warm bath. A little while after, Dzewaka came back to Buddha, and explained to him his prescription. Buddha was soon restored to his former health, and Dzewaka told him that the people were preparing to make him offerings. Mauka-lan went to the son of Thauna, a rich man, to get some rice from a field that had been watered with milk. The owner gave rice to Maukalan and urged him to partake of it, assuring him that there was some other in reserve for Buddha; Maukalan assented. After the meal, his patta was cleaned with perfumed water, and filled with the choicest food. Maukalan took it to Buddha, who ate it. Afterwards he preached the law to the king and to an immense crowd; amongst them was Thauna's son. They all obtained the first degree of perfection, but Thauna reached at once the state of Arahat.

Dzewaka came again to Buddha's presence, and requested the favour of presenting him with two splendid pieces of cloth, which he had received in present from a king whom he had cured of a most distressing distemper. Moreover, he wished that the Rahans should be allowed to receive clothes of a better sort than those they were wont to wear. Buddha received the two pieces and preached the law to the donor, who attained the state of Thautapan. Dzewaka, rising from his place, wheeled to the right and departed.

A little while after, Gaudama· called the Rahans and said to them, "Beloved Bickus, now I give permission to the faithful to make offerings of cloth for your dress.[2] Whoever is pleased with his present dress, let him wear it; whoever is disposed to receive some other from the people, let him do so. But I must praise you for having hitherto been satisfied with the ancient dress." The people of the city having heard of the permission given to the Rahans,

---

[2] The first followers of Buddha, observing a mode of life much resembling that of the Rathees, had hitherto made use of the dress they had purchased previous to their leaving the world. But when they became professed members of the new society, they were subjected to the observance of the vow of strict poverty, and had to depend entirely on public charity for the obtaining of the required food and raiment. The old clothes brought at the time of their entering the society were worn out and unfit to be put on. Others were to be provided for by some means that would not wound the delicate feeling of absolute poverty. The only one that occurred was the willing and liberal dispositions of the lay members of the Buddhist community. This new source of abundant alms was opened by our Buddha himself, on the occasion of the offering made by Dzewaka. Desiring likewise to do away with the scruples many religious might entertain respecting the lawfulness or unlawfulness of receiving articles of dress, Gaudama laid it down as a regulation that all the religious could lawfully accept all that might be willingly offered them by the faithful. In the foregoing pages we have seen the founder of Buddhism granting to his followers permission to receive houses and landed properties presented to communities. Now the same legislator, adhering to the same principle, gives a fuller development thereto, and extends to articles necessary for dress the leave to receive offerings of this description, proffered by the faithful to the religious. In the book of Buddhist ordinations; or promotion to the degree of Patzin, mention is made of these two sorts of permissions given to the Rahans.

offered at once more than one hundred thousand pieces of cloth. Their example was followed by the people of the country, who made offerings to the same amount.

A little while after this, Buddha received a deputation from the Wethalie people, inviting him to visit their country. Here is the reason of the invitation. The country was very rich and flourishing. The Malla princes governed it each in turn for a certain space of time. On a sudden a terrific pestilence desolated the land, which was in a short time strewed with dead bodies in every direction. In the midst of so great a calamity some advised to propitiate the Nats, by making offerings to them; others said that recourse must be had to the great teachers; a third party insisted upon calling to their aid the great Gaudama, who had appeared in this world for the purpose of saving mankind. The last opinion prevailed. Having ascertained that he lived at Radzagio, a great number of princes, pounhas, and nobles went to Radzagio, with great presents for King Pimpathara, to induce him to allow the great teacher to come to their country. The object of their mission having become known, Buddha agreed to go. He sallied forth from the Weloowon monastery, attended by the king as far as the southern bank of the Ganges. Having reached the northern one, he was received with every possible mark of the highest respect and veneration. As soon as he set his feet in the country, a heavy rain fell which almost deluged the land. The water carried away the dead bodies. The atmosphere was purified, the pestilence ceased, and all the sick recovered. On the fifth day after the full moon of Nayon (June), Buddha having conferred such a favour to the people of Wethalie, left that country and returned to Radzagio, which he reached on the full moon of Watso (July), just in time to spend the fourth season in the Weloowon monastery.

Here is inserted a short sketch of the manner in which Buddha spent his days during the rainy season, as the translator has found in one of the manuscripts before him.

Each day was divided into five parts, and a certain occupation was reserved to each part. 1. Buddha generally rose at an early hour, a little after daybreak, washed his face, rinsed his mouth, and dressed. He then retired into a private apartment. With his all-seeing eyes, he glanced over all creatures, carefully examined the amount of their merits and demerits, and the real nature of their dispositions. The reason for his taking a survey of the state and condition of all beings was to ascertain the dispositions of the various beings, and discern those who were prepared to hear the preaching of truth from those who, on account of their demerits, were as yet unprepared for receiving beneficially for themselves such a great favour. When this was done, he put on his full canonical dress, and, with the mendicant's pot under his arm, he sallied forth in quest of his food. He invariably directed his steps towards those places where he knew that his preachings would be heard with beneficial results. Sometimes he went alone; at other times he was attended with a certain number of his disciples. His countenance bespoke an unaffected modesty and an inimitable mildness. Occasionally he allowed a display of wonders to take place. Musical instruments emitted, of themselves, sweet tunes, which, revealing to the people the coming of Buddha, rejoiced their heart and disposed them to bestow abundant alms, and to hear the preaching of the law. Some of the hearers became Upasakas, others Thautapans, &c., &c., agreeably to every one's disposition. Then he returned to his monastery.

2. As soon as he had arrived, he washed his feet, and during the ablution he had his disciples assembled round him, and said to them, "Beloved Bickus, be ever watchful and attentive, with a mind ever prone to reflection. It is exceedingly difficult to obtain the nature of man,[3] to hear

---

[3] It was at that moment that Gaudama delighted to reveal to his disciples the most startling points of his doctrine, and made them familiar with certain tenets upon which he laid much stress. He wished that what he looked upon as subjects of the greatest importance, should be-

the law, to become perfect, to obtain the state of Rahanda, and to arrive to the condition of a Buddha." He then pointed out to them some subjects of meditation. Many of the disciples devoted themselves to mental labour; some combined together manual and mental exertions; others withdrew to lonely places at the foot of certain trees, and into the caves of neighbouring hills. Buddha then took his meal, and retired for awhile alone into his own private apartment. When he arose a little after mid-day, he anew contemplated all beings, and fixed his attention on those that were to come and receive his instructions. He soon came out, and at once began to impart instruction to all those that had arrived, from what place soever. When the instruction was completed, the people withdrew.

3. After the people's departure, Buddha bathed and took a walk in the open verandah of the monastery. His mat, cushion, &c., were spread in a becoming and open place. The Rahans hastened at that hour to come and communicate freely the result of their mental exertions. When they wanted any explanation, they were encouraged to put

---

come familiar to them. No doubt he intended that those favourite topics should become the spiritual food upon which his disciples' minds should feed during the hours devoted to meditation. Those who are uninitiated in the doctrines of Buddhism will not understand the meaning of such an expression. It is difficult to obtain the nature of man. Such language is, however, in perfect accordance with the principles of that system. A being, who is in one of the four states of punishment, that of an animal, for instance, shall have, in many instances, to pass through an immense number of various existences, ere he can escape from the circle of animal existences, and at last emerge into that of man. To give us an idea of the excessive difficulties a being has to encounter, they make use of the following comparison. Let us suppose that a needle be dropped from one of the seats of Brahmas, and at the same time a man on earth be keeping another needle with the point upwards. It will be more easy for the two needles' extremities to come in contact one with the other, than it will be to a being in the condition of animal to reach the state of man. On the same principle one can easily imagine what mighty efforts must be made during countless existences ere a simple man can obtain all the qualifications necessary for enabling him to become a Buddha. The theory of Gaudama, on this point, resembles much that of some modern thinkers who preach the perfectibility of man to an almost infinite degree.

him questions, which were instantly answered; and they received submissively the answers which he condescended to give to them. This exercise lasted until it was dark. The disciples retired from their master's presence.

4. After their departure, the Nats and other celestial beings were admitted. Buddha conversed with and instructed them until nearly midnight.

5. Buddha then walked awhile to relieve his limbs from extreme lassitude, and went into his apartment to take some rest. He rose very early, and began to review the beings who, during the days of former Buddhas, had distinguished themselves by their exertions in the path of virtue and in the high mental attainments.

During one of his usual benevolent errands through the country, Gaudama converted Ouggasena, his wife and companions. Here is an abridged narrative of that event. Ouggasena was the son of a rich man. In the time of his youth a company of comedians came to Radzagio and exhibited during seven days in the presence of King Pimpathara and his court. Our young man, along with many of his companions, attended the exhibition. On a sudden, he became passionately enamoured of a rope dancing-girl, who performed many feats with accomplished grace and uncommon address. Despite his parents' remonstrances and entreaties, he sacrificed to his ungoverned passion all considerations, and he married the damsel. In his new situation, he had no alternative but to learn the art of rope-dancing, tumbling feats, and standing in various attitudes on the extremity of posts or masts, sometimes sixty cubits high. During his noviciate, he had to bear the laughter and taunts of his wife and of his new friends. By dint of exertion he became proficient in the art of performing tumblers' feats with a surprising agility. One day it was announced at the sound of the drum that Ouggasena was to perform on the top of a post sixty cubits high. An immense crowd of citizens went out with great eagerness to see the performance. When the amusements had just begun, Buddha happened to pass by with a number of disciples. He desired Maukalan to go ahead, and begin to preach to Ouggasena. Soon he came up himself in person, and converted the juggler, who forthwith descended from his mast, prostrated himself before Buddha, and asked to be admitted as a member of the assembly. After further instructions he obtained the science of Rahanda. His wife and all the company became likewise converts.[4]

Buddha had now fulfilled the promise he had formerly made to the ruler of Radzagio, to spend three consecutive seasons in his royal city. He went over to the Wethalie country, and fixed his residence in a fine place, in the midst of a forest of sala-trees, called Mahawon. Whilst he enjoyed himself in that place, a quarrel took place between a portion of the people of Kappila and that of Kaulia, who lived on both banks of the little river

---

[4] The conversion of Ouggasena and of his companions, procured by the direct intervention of Buddha himself, is another instance of the truly liberal spirit which animated the great preacher. His law was intended for all without exception. The profession of these individuals whom he so peculiarly selected was far from being a respectable one. The proud Brahmin would not have condescended to take notice of people who, in his opinion, had degraded themselves so low. But the new teacher, though born from parents belonging to a high caste, entirely free from the prejudices inculcated by the narrow spirit of caste, rose himself to such a high position as to look upon man, whatever his condition or position might be, as a fellow-being fully entitled to the benefit of his instructions. This is one of the most striking features of his preachings, its universality as regards persons and places. It enables us to account for the rapid and astonishing diffusion of his doctrines through so many countries. It constitutes the essential and capital difference between the two great systems which, in days long passed by, have contested for the religious supremacy over the Indian peninsula.

In the subsequent story of Thoodaudana's illness, we see Buddha first, then Ananda, Thariputra, and Mankalan relieving the illustrious patient from his bodily distemper, by invoking, not the interference of a supreme Being, whom they ignore, but a certain power or influence connected with former good deeds. A great, nay, a miraculous, effect is produced by the agency of a cause which no one but a Buddhist can understand. He has recourse to *kan*, or the influence resulting from meritorious actions, as to a mighty agent who has the power to work any desired result whatever. But how a man can by his own will control the influence of his good actions, so as to produce a grand effect in no way short of a miracle, is a thing which can in no rational way be explained or accounted for.

Rauhani. The cause of the dispute was the irrigation of paddy-fields. The small river had been duly barred, but on account of an unusual drought there was not water enough to supply the quantity required for the fields on both banks. One party wanted to have all the water, the other demurred. Hence a dispute arose which, wildfire-like, spread from the banks of the stream all over both countries. A general appeal to arms ensued, and, in a short time, both armies stood facing each other in battle array.

At an early hour Buddha, having risen from his couch, cast, as usual, a glance over all beings. He soon saw the feud that existed between the country of his birth and that of Kaulia. Moved with compassion over the miseries which that people, blinded by a furious passion, were bringing upon themselves, he went through the air, and stood over and above the stream which separated the two armies. Rays of glory, beaming out of his person, soon attracted general attention. Both parties laid down their arms and prostrated themselves, worshipping him. He said to them, " Princes and warriors, hearken to my words. Which is the most valuable, a small quantity of water or the lives of countless beings, and, in particular, the lives of princes ? " They answered, " Of course the lives of princes and warriors are most valuable." " If so," retorted Buddha, " lay aside your passion, conquer your anger, throw away your weapons of destruction, love each other, and live in peace." Both parties, by a low and prolonged tone of voice, expressed their deep regret at what they had done, and their sincere desire to follow his instructions. He preached to them the law in such an impressive and convincing manner that on the spot two hundred and fifty noblemen of Kappila and the same number of Kaulia asked for admittance among the members of the assembly.

The instruction they had heard, and which had determined their vocation, had not had time to cast deep roots in their hearts. They soon regretted their home, their families, and their former gay life. Buddha, who saw what was going on in their souls, said to them, "Will you come with me, and enjoy yourselves on the green banks of the beautiful lake Kontala?" They joyfully accepted the proposal. By the power inherent in his nature, Buddha took them through the air, and soon reached the lake. They alighted on its banks. Delighted with the beautiful scenery that surrounded them, and ignorant of the new objects which they saw, they interrogated Buddha about the names of the new plants and fruits which they perceived. Gaudama condescended to answer all their questions. While thus engaged they saw the king of the birds of the lake resting on the branch of a tree. On a sudden five hundred birds of the same kind came crowding round their chief, and, by their cries and various attitudes, testified the happiness which they felt at being in his company.

The new converts wondered at the admirable instinct of those birds, and communicated to each other their mutual surprise. As an accomplished teacher, Buddha availed himself of the opportune moment, and said to them in a mild manner, "Beloved disciples, what you see now and admire is the lively and true image of my family." So effectually was the instruction conveyed that they all at once became Thautapan, and no longer thought of returning into the world. By the virtue inherent in their new position, they were enabled to fly through the air, and they returned with Buddha into the Mahawon residence.

On their arrival, Buddha began his fifth season in that same place. It was in the middle of that season, in the month of Wakhaong (August), that he heard that his father had been seized with a violent distemper, which left him no rest either day or night. Sensible of his approaching end, Thoodaudana ardently wished to see his son for the last time. In the morning, at the hour when Buddha was reviewing all beings, and examining with a compassionate heart their respective condition, he saw the sad and painful position of his royal father. He instantly summoned,

by the means of Ananda, a select band of disciples, and
flying through the air, alighted with his company in front
of the palace. Without a moment's delay he ascended to
the upper apartments, and sat on a place prepared for him,
near the head of the couch upon which lay the royal
patient.

Buddha, recollecting himself awhile, and then laying
one of his hands on his father's head, said, " By the virtue
of the merits I have acquired during countless existences,
by the power of the fruits gathered during forty-nine days
round the tree Bodi, let this head be forthwith relieved
from all pain." It happened so in the twinkling of an
eye. Nan, or Nanda, the younger brother of Buddha, the
son of his aunt Patzapati, holding the right hand of his
father, said with a fervent earnestness, " By the merits that
I have obtained at the feet of Buddha, let this right hand
be freed from all pain." And perfect cure instantly followed. Ananda, Phra's first cousin, held the left arm.
Thariputra laid his hand on the back, Maukalan grasped
the feet. All of them with a similar faith uttered such
like prayers, and the same happy result invariably followed. Thoodaudana was delivered from all pain. But
he continued to remain very weak.

Buddha, profiting by that favourable opportunity, preached
to his father the law of mutability, and gave him many
and truly seasonable instructions on that most important
subject. With such a persuasive language did he expound
this favourite doctrine that his father became at once a
Rahanda. At the same time he distinctly informed him
that seven days hence the end of his life would inevitably
happen. Thoodaudana, perfectly prepared for the new
change, that is to say, for death, by his son's instructions,
and thoroughly resigned, saw before him the true state of
Neibban, and said, " Now I clearly perceive the instability
of all things. I am free from all passions. I am completely disentangled from the trammels of existence."
Rocking himself in the bosom of these comforting truths,

he spent happily the few days he had yet to live. On the last day, and for the last time, he paid his respects to Buddha by worshipping him. Sitting then on his couch, the royal patient humbly asked pardon in the presence of all his attendants for all offences he had committed by thoughts, words, and deeds. Having performed this act of sincere humility, he consoled his wife Patzati, who sat bathed in tears, as well as the other members of the royal family, and several times repeated before them the great truth—that all beings, when they come into existence, have within, inherent in their nature, a principle of death that hurries them to their end and dissolution; that the same principle that has brought near and united beings together is always opposed, and at last overpowered by the opposite one that tends to separate them. He then placidly lay on his couch, and gently breathed his last in the day of the full moon of Wakhaong, on a Saturday, at the rising of the sun, in the year of the Eetzana, era 107, at the advanced age of ninety-seven years.

Gaudama, after his father's demise, when all the Rahans were assembled round the deathbed, said to them: "Beloved Bickus, behold my father's remains. He is no longer what he was a little while ago. He has undergone the change. No one can offer an effectual and lasting resistance to the principle of death, inherent in all beings. Be diligent in the practice of good works: follow steadily the four roads leading to perfection." After this lecture, he consoled his aunt Patzapati and the other ladies of the court, who, with dishevelled hair, were wailing aloud and striking their breasts. He minutely explained to them the consequences resulting from the great principle of mutability, which pervades all beings and infallibly leads them to destruction by the separation of their constitutive parts.

When the instruction was finished, Buddha directed Kathaba to go and prepare the spot on which the funeral and cremation of the corpse were to take place. Aided

by Thariputra, he washed the corpse, which was subsequently placed in great state, on a magnificent and lofty
catafalco, raised for the purpose. The princes of Thekkara,
Thoopawa, and Weritzara, came to attend the royal funeral and offer presents. The corpse was carried processionally through the principal streets of the city at the sound
of all musical instruments. Buddha, in person, received
the corpse, and laid it on the funeral pile. To no one
else would he leave the honourable and pious task of
setting fire to it. On that occasion there took place an
indescribable outburst of wailings and lamentings. The
impassible Buddha preached the law on that occasion.
He left aside all praises in behalf of the deceased. He
was satisfied with announcing the law; and countless
beings, both among men and Nats, obtained the deliverance.

After the loss of her royal husband, Queen Patzapati,
profoundly impressed with all that she had seen and
heard, desired to renounce the world and embrace a religious mode of life. For that purpose she came to the
presence of Buddha, and asked three times the permission
to follow her inclination and become Rahaness. Three
times the solicited favour was denied her. Buddha then
left his own native country and returned to Wethalie,
fixing his abode in the Gutagaia-thala monastery, in the
Mahawon forest.

Buddha had not been long in this place when he had
to grant the request which he at first refused to his aunt
Patzapati. The wives of the princes of the Kappila and
Káulia countries, who, to the number of 500, had recently
renounced the world, desired also to follow the example
set before them by their husbands. They went to the
queen's apartments and communicated to her their design,
entreating her to help them in obtaining the object of
their wishes. Patzapati not only promised them her support, but expressed the determination to join their company. As a token of the sincerity and earnestness of

their resolution, all the ladies, without the least hesitation, cut their beautiful black hair, put on a dress in accordance with their pious intentions, and resolutely set out on foot in the direction of the Wethalie country.

Unused to such bodily exertions, the pious pilgrims suffered much during their long journey. At last, worn out with fatigue, covered with dust, they arrived near the Mahawon monastery. They respectfully stopped at the gate, and requested an interview with Ananda. The latter, having ascertained from their own mouth the object of their pious and fatiguing errand, hastened into the presence of Buddha, and entreated him to grant the earnest and praiseworthy demand of his aunt and of the other ladies, her companions. On hearing the request, Buddha, for a while, remained silent, as if deliberating on the answer he had to give. Then he said: "Ananda, it is not expedient to allow women to embrace the religious state; otherwise my institutions shall not last long." Ananda, undismayed by that reply, respectfully reminded Buddha of all the favours he had received from Patzapati, who had nursed and brought him up with the utmost care and tenderness, from the day his mother died, when he was but seven days old, and represented with a fervent earnestness the good dispositions of the pious postulants. Buddha's scruples were overcome by the persuasive language of the faithful Ananda. He asked whether women could observe the eight precepts: and added, that in case they would consent to bind themselves to a correct observance of them, they might be admitted as members of the assembly.

Fully satisfied with the answer he had obtained, the venerable Ananda saluted Buddha, and hastened to the gate of the monastery, where his return was impatiently awaited. On hearing the good news, Patzapati, in the name of her companions, spoke to Ananda: "Venerable Ananda, we all rejoice that the favour so often asked for has been at last granted unto us. As a young maid, who has bathed, and washed her hair, is anxiously desirous to put on her fine ornaments, as she receives with delight the beautiful and fragrant nosegays that are offered to her, so we are longing for the eight precepts, and wish for admittance into the assembly." They all promised to observe the rules of their new profession to the end of their lives. Yathaudara and Dzanapada-kaliani were among these converts. They all, owing to their former meritorious works, became subsequently Rahandas.

One of the new female converts seemed to have retained as yet a certain admiration of and fondness for her handsome features, and secretly prided herself on her beauty. Buddha, who quickly perceived the latent enemy lurking in the folds of her heart, resorted to the following expedient to correct her. On a certain day, when the proud and vain woman was in his presence, he created in an instant a consummate beauty, who as much exceeded her in perfection of form as the snow-white swan surpasses the black crow. Whilst she looked on this suddenly appearing rival with somewhat jealous eyes, Buddha caused the beauty of his creation to appear on a sudden very old, with a wrinkled face and an emaciated frame, and to exhibit on her person all the various and disgusting inroads which the most loathsome diseases make on the human body. The change acted as an electric shock on the young religious woman. When Gaudama perceived the change, and that she was so horrified at such a sight that she was nearly fainting, he said to her: " Behold, my daughter, the faithful foreshowing of what shall inevitably happen to that form you are so proud of." He had scarcely spoken those words, when she was instantly and for ever cured of her vanity.

Buddha left Wethalie and went on the Makula mountain, where he spent his sixth season. During his stay in that place thousands of people were converted and obtained the deliverance. At the end of that season, Buddha went to Radzagio, and stayed in the Weloowon monastery.

It was at that time that Kema, the first queen of King Pimpathara, proud of her rank, youth, and beauty, was at last converted. Up to that time she had obstinately refused to see Buddha and hear his doctrine. On a certain day, the queen went to visit a garden which was in the neighbourhood of the Weloowon grove. . By a contrivance of the king, her husband, she was brought, almost against her will, into the presence of Buddha, who worked out the spiritual cure of her foolish vanity by a process similar to the one above mentioned. He caused a beautiful female of his creation to pass successively, in the queen's presence, through the various stages of old age, disease, and death. Her mind having been thus well prepared to hear his instructions, Buddha gave her a lengthened explanation of the miseries attending the body. It had the desirable effect to convert her in so perfect a manner that she entered into the current of perfection, and became Thautapan. After having obtained the consent of her lord, she was, upon her pressing solicitations, admitted into the religious order. She became a Rahanda, and among the female members of the assembly she ranked as the disciple of the right. Such a glorious charge was owing to her former merits.

On a certain day, a rich man of the country of Radzagio went to enjoy himself on the banks of the river Ganges. That man was not a disciple of Buddha, nor did he hold the doctrines of the opposite party. He steered a middle course between both doctrines, with a mind disposed, however, to embrace such opinions as should appear to him based on the best and strongest evidence. Chance offered him a favourable opportunity to acknowledge the superiority of Buddha over his opponents. He saw a log of sandal-wood floating on the stream, took it up, and had a beautiful patta made of it. When finished, he wrote upon it these words, " He who can fly in the air let him take it." The patta was raised on the top of a succession of hampers, tied together, and sixty cubits high. Some heretics living in the neighbourhood asked on successive occasions the rich man to get down the patta for them; he answered them that he would give it only to him who by flight could reach it. The head man of those heretics feigned to prepare himself to fly; but when he was extending his arms, and raising one of his feet, his disciples, according to a preconcerted plan, seized him, saying, " It is not becoming that you should exert yourself for such a trifle." But the wily rich man could not be thus deceived; he persisted in his former resolution, and for six days resisted all their entreaties. On the seventh day Maukalan happened to go to that place in search of his food. He was informed of all that had just happened. He was, moreover, told that the rich man and all his family would become disciples under him who could by flight possess himself of the sandal-wood patta. Maukalan was ready, for the glory of Buddha, to raise himself in the air, but his companion refused to allow him to do it, saying that such an easy work could easily be accomplished by one less advanced in merits. Maukalan agreed to his proposal. Whereupon entering into the fourth state of Dzan, his companion rose in the air, carrying with the toes of one of his feet an enormous rock three-quarters of a youdzana wide. The whole space between him and the bystanders appeared darkened. Every one was half dead with fear, lest, perhaps, it should fall over his head. Maukalan's companion had the rock split into two parts, and his person then appeared to the view of the assembled crowd. After having during a whole day exhibited such a mighty power, he caused the rock to fall on the place he had taken it from. The rich man bade him come down, fully satisfied with the display of such power. The sandal-wood patta was taken down, filled with the best rice, and presented to him. The Rahan received it and went back to his monastery. Many persons living at a distance from the place where the wonder had been exhibited, followed him to the monastery, begging him to show some other signs.

As they approached the monastery, Buddha hearing the noise, inquired what it was. He was informed of all the particulars of the event that had just taken place. He called the Rahan into his presence, took the patta, had it broken into pieces and reduced to dust.[5] He then forbade the Rahan ever to make such a display of his power.

---

[5] The rebuke given by Buddha to the disciple who had, without permission, made such a display of miraculous power, intended though it was for the promotion of his glory, was designed to operate as a salutary check on the pride that might find its way into the heart of even the most privileged beings. Such a lesson was deemed of the greatest importance, since we find in the book of Buddhistic ordinations the sin of boasting of or pretending to the power of working wonders, &c., ranked among the four capital sins, excluding a Rahan for ever from the society of the perfect, and depriving him of his rank and dignity. Buddha, it seems, wished to reserve to himself alone the honour of working miracles, or to give the permission, when circumstances should require it, to some of his disciples to do the same in his name and for the exaltation of his religion.

The following story of Purana and his five associates holds a prominent rank among the events that have rendered Buddha so celebrated. Gandama, as it has been already mentioned in some foregoing notes, was an ascetic who had studied philosophy under eminent masters who belonged to the Brahminical school. In many of his opinions, as well as in his mode of life, there was no perceptible difference between him and the followers of the Brahmins. The writings of the latter, as well as those of the earliest Buddhists, exhibit to us the sight of a great number of schools, where opinions on ontology, morals, and dogmas, &c., at once various, multifarious, and opposite, were publicly taught. Then the human mind, left to its own resources, launching forth into the boundless field of speculative philosophy, ran in every direction, searching after truth. The mania for arguing, defining, drawing conclusions, &c., in those days, prevailed to an extent scarcely to be credited. Many centuries before Aristotle, wrote the rules of dialectics the Indian philosophers had carried the art of reasoning to a great degree of nicety and shrewdness. Witness the disputes and discussions between the Brahmins and the immediate disciples of Buddha. When our Phra began to attract about his person crowds of hearers and disciples; when his opinions on the end of man were understood and appreciated; when the system of castes received the first shock from the new but rapidly progressing doctrine; when the eyes and hearts of the people were slowly at first, and rapidly afterwards, centred on the new preacher and his disciples; when at last alms, that had hitherto flowed into the abodes of the Brahmins, began to enter into new channels and carry their substantial produce to the door of the followers of the new sect, then jealousy and other passions began to agitate the hearts of those who had hitherto retained an undisputed sway over the credulity of the people. They tried, if credit be given to the works of Buddhists, every effort and devised every means in order to oppose the progress of the new doctrine.

In this instance, Purana and his friends, assisted, as the Buddhists

The heretics soon heard of the prohibition issued by Gaudama to his disciples. They thought that no one would dare to match them in the display of wonders, and that they could easily ascertain their superiority over him. The ruler of Radzagio, hearing of this news, went to Buddha and inquired as to his motive for such a prohibition. Buddha told him that the prohibition regarded his disciples only, but not himself. The heretics, informed of

---

pretend, by the agency of the evil one, wished to enter into discussion with Buddha and to surpass him in the display of miraculous power. The contest was to take place in the country of Thawattie, in the presence of the king and of a countless multitude assembled for the purpose. Purana, as usual with Buddhists in regard to those who held opinions different from their own, is styled a heretic. Of the opinions of the enemies of Buddha nothing is said in the present work, but the writer has had the opportunity of perusing another work where a slight allusion is made to those six holders of heterodox doctrines. Their opinions were at variance on the beginning of this world, the eternity of matter, the existence of the soul, and a first principle, creator of all that exists. We may infer therefrom that they were heads or chiefs of various schools, who, though not agreeing among themselves upon purely speculative doctrines, united and combined against the common enemy. A detailed account of the doctrines held by these six heretics would prove highly interesting, as it would throw some light on the very obscure and imperfectly known history of Indian philosophy, in the days when Buddhism assumed the shape of a religious system. To those who are unacquainted with Indian literature, the great progress made by Hindus in philosophical sciences at such an early period may appear somewhat

doubtful : but modern discoveries made all over the Indian peninsula leave not the least doubt respecting this startling assertion. At a period when Greece and the other regions of Europe were sunk in a state of complete ignorance, most of the branches of literature were successfully cultivated on the banks of the Ganges. The study of philosophy always supposes a great intellectual advancement. There would, therefore, be no rashness whatever in asserting that the present state and condition of India, as regards literary progress, are much below the mark that was attained at such a remote period. The epoch of literary decadence began with the devastating expeditions of the fanatical Moslem in the tenth century. It is probable, too, that the religious and sanguinary conflicts between the Buddhists and Brahminists have had their share in bringing about a similar result. The latter, having obtained the ascendancy over their adversaries, became more bigoted. They would no longer tolerate, to the same extent as before, the liberty of elaborating new systems, lest some successful philosopher might hereafter propagate opinions at variance with their own, undermine the mighty fabric of their creed, and endanger the holding of that absolute sway and paramount influence they had recovered, after centuries of a deadly contest with the disciples of the philosopher of Kapilawot.

this, said, "What will become of us? Gaudama himself will show signs." They held a council among themselves as to what was to be done. Gaudama told the king that in four months he would make a grand display of his miraculous power in the country of Thawattie, as it was in that place that all former Buddhas had in former ages showed signs. The heretics from that day never lost sight of Buddha for a moment; they followed him day and night. They gave orders that a large and extensive covered place should be prepared for them, where they might show their power and outshine that of the Rahan Gaudama. Buddha having said that he would select the spot where a white mango-tree stood for the scene of his miracles, the heretics caused the total destruction of all mango-trees in that direction.

On the full moon of Tabaong (February), Gaudama left Radzagio, attended by a large retinue of disciples. He went to preach in different parts. On the seventh of the waxing moon of Watso he entered the country of Thawattie. A gardener gave him by way of present a large mango fruit. Ananda prepared the fruit and Buddha ate it. When this was done, the stone was handed to Ananda with an injunction to plant it in a place prepared to receive it. When planted, Buddha washed his hands over it, and on a sudden there sprang up a beautiful white mango-tree, fifty cubits high, with large branches loaded with blossoms and fruits. To prevent its being destroyed, a guard was set near it by the king's order. Dismayed at such a wonderful sign, the heretics fled in every direction to conceal their shame and confusion. Their head man, named Pourana, took from a husbandman a large jar with a rope, tied up the vessel with one extremity of the rope, passed the other round his neck, and flinging first the jar and next himself into the river, where the water was very deep, he was drowned, and went to the lowest hell, called Awidzi.

Buddha created in the air an immense road, reaching east and west to the extremities of the world. When the

sun began to verge towards the west, he thought the time
had come to ascend to that road in the presence of an
immense crowd, that covered an area of thirty-six youdzanas, and there make a display of his wonderful powers.
He was on the point of crossing the threshold of the building that had been erected for him by the care of Nats,
when a female convert, named Garamie, who had become
an Anagam, came into his presence, and after the usual
prostrations said to him, "Glorious Buddha, it is not necessary that you should take the trouble of working wonders;
I, your servant, will do it." "What wonder will you
work, my daughter, Garamie?" replied Buddha. "I will,"
said Garamie, "fill up the space with water, and plunging
into the water in an eastern direction, I will come back,
and reappear in the west like a water-fowl. On my
appearance before the crowd they will ask, What is this
water-fowl? And I will answer to them, that this water-
fowl is Garamie, the daughter of the most excellent Buddha. This is the wonder I will accomplish. The heretics,
on seeing it, will say to themselves, If such be the power
of Garamie, how much greater and more wonderful must
be that of Buddha himself?" "I know," said Buddha,
"that you have such a power, but it is not for your sake
that these crowds have been gathered together;" and he
refused the solicited permission. Garamie said to herself,
Buddha would not allow me to work this great wonder,
but there is some one else that can do greater things than
I; perhaps Buddha will not be so inflexible with them as
he is with me. She then withdrew to a becoming place.

Buddha thought within himself, There are many among
my disciples who can make a display of great wonders; it
is meet that the crowds should be aware of it, and see
how, with hearts stout as that of the lion, they are ready
to perform the most wonderful feats. He said aloud,
"Who are they that can do wonders? let them come forward." Many came into his presence with a lion-like
boldness and a thundering voice, craving for the honour

of displaying supernatural powers. Among them was a
rich man, named Anatapein; a female child, called Tsera;
a grown-up woman, and Maukalan. They volunteered
their services to perform the most extraordinary wonders,
in order both to frighten the heretics, and make them
understand that, if such a power belonged to the disciples,
what that of Buddha himself must be. But Buddha would
not accept their proffered services, and said to them that
the people had not been assembled there for their sake,
but for his; and that to him alone was reserved the task
of enrapturing the crowds by the great wonders he was
preparing to show. Addressing Maukalan, he said to him
that, being a Buddha, he could not leave to others the
trouble of performing his own duty. In a former existence, when he was a bullock, he drew from a muddy place
a heavily-laden cart, to save a Brahmin's property and
rejoice his heart.

Buddha ascended to the immense road which he had
created in the air in the presence of the crowd, that filled
a place of eighteen youdzanas in breadth and twenty-four
in length. These wonders which he was about to display
were the result of his own wisdom, and could not be imitated by any one. He caused a stream of water to issue
from the upper part of his body and flames of fire from
the lower part, and on a sudden the reverse to take place;
again fire issued from his right eye, and streams of water
from his left eye, and so on from his nostrils, ears, right
and left, in front and behind. The same wonder too happened in such a way that the streams of fire succeeded the
streams of water, but without mingling with each other.
Each stream in an upward direction reached the seats of
Brahmas; each stream in a downward direction penetrated
as far as hell; each in a horizontal direction reached the
extremities of the world. From each of his hairs the
same wonderful display feasted the astonished eyes of the
assembled people. The six glories gushed, as it were, from
every part of his body, and made it appear resplendent

beyond description. Having no one to converse with, he created a personage, who appeared to walk with him. Sometimes he sat down, while his companion was pacing along; and at other times he himself walked, whilst his interlocutor was either standing or sitting. All the while Buddha put to him questions which he readily answered, and in his turn replied to the interrogations that were made to him. At intervals Phra preached to the crowd, who were exceedingly rejoiced, and sung praises to him. According to their good dispositions, he expounded the various points of the law. The people who heard him and saw the wonderful works he performed, obtained the understanding of the four great principles.

Buddha, having completed the twofold work of preaching to the crowds, and exciting their respect and admiration by the most astonishing display of the most extraordinary miracles, began to think within himself as follows: To what place have all former Buddhas resorted after the display of signs, and spent the season? He saw by a stretch of his incomparable foresight that all of them had gone to the seat of Tawadeintha, in the Nats' country, to announce the perfect law to their mothers. He resolved to go thither too. With one step he reached the summit of the mountain Ugando, at a distance of 160,000 youdzanas, and another step carried him to the top of the Mienmo mountain. This was done without any effort on the part of Buddha. Those mountains lowered their summits to the very spot where he was standing, and rose up again to resume their lofty position. Buddha found himself brought almost instantaneously to the seat of Tawadeintha.[6] He took his position on the immense rock

---

[6] The preachings of Buddha were not to be confined to the narrow limits of man's abode; they were designed to reach much further. All beings living in the six seats of Nats were to share with men the blessings of the publication of the perfect law. It has been already stated at length, in a foregoing note, that the condition of Nats is merely a state of pleasure and enjoyment allotted to those who in former existences had done some meritorious work. The fortunate inhabitants of these celestial regions

Pantukambala.   When he lay extended there upon his tsiwaran, the huge mass on a sudden contracted itself to the very narrow dimensions of his dress.

---

remain in those seats until the sum of their respective merits being, as it were, exhausted, they return to the abode of man, the true place of probation for all beings living therein. The condition of Nat, therefore, is not a permanent one ; the Nat, after his time of reward is over, has to migrate to our terrestrial abode, begin a new existence, and endeavour to advance himself in the way of perfection by the practice of virtue.   He is as yet very far from the state of Neibban.   Like man, he has to learn the sublime law, and to become acquainted with the roads leading to the four high perfections.   Buddha, who came to announce the law of salvation to all beings, could not but go to the seats of Nats, and teach them the way to free themselves from the turmoil of never-ending existence.   The preachings of Buddha for three consecutive months were attended with a success that must have exceeded his most sanguine expectations. Millions of Nats were converted, and forthwith obtained the deliverance.   Others less advanced in merits obtained the first, or second, or third state of perfection.

During his stay in the other seats of Nats, Buddha gave a decision on the merits of almsgiving, which is certainly to the advantage of the yellow-dressed Bickus, but appears somewhat opposed to all principles of justice and reason.   In his opinion the inward dispositions of him who gives alms has nothing to do with the merits resulting from such a good work.   Those merits are strictly proportionate to the degree of sanctity or perfection of him who receives alms.   Such doctrine, destructive of the purest and noblest motives that can actuate man to do good, is openly upheld now both in theory and practice by the Buddhist monks.   When they receive alms from the admirers of their saintly mode of life, they never think of returning thanks to those who so liberally administer to all their material wants ; they content themselves with saying, Thadoo, thadoo ; that is to say, Well, well ; and the pious offerer withdraws perfectly satisfied and happy, relying on the merits he has gained on this occasion, and longing for another opportunity of doing the like.   The liberality of the laity towards the religious is carried to an excess scarcely to be credited.   Government do not interfere in the maintenance of the perfect, and yet they are abundantly supplied with all the necessaries, nay, the luxuries, of life.   They live on the fat of the land.

That the crowds of people might be better prepared for hearing the sacred law and obtaining a correct understanding of it, Buddha charges Maukalan to a regular fast, or at least abstinence, carried to a considerable degree.   A free and copious use of nourishing substances unfits man for mental exertions, occasions in him heaviness and supineness, enervates and weakens the vigour of the intellect, and gives to matter a preponderating influence over the soul.   The advice will hold good everywhere, but it becomes particularly pressing and stringent when addressed to an audience of Buddhists, who require the full force of their mind to be able to understand the various bearings of a doctrine resting on the most abstruse principles, the end of which too is to disentangle the soul from the influence of materiality.   Up to this day

The people who had seen Buddha, and who could not now descry him, found themselves in a state of bereavement, as if the sun and the moon had disappeared from the sky. They gave full vent to their cries and lamentations, saying: We are now deprived of the blessed presence of him who is the most excellent among the three sorts of beings, men, Nats, and Brahmas. Some said he has gone to this place; some replied, no, he has gone to that place. Many of the people, who had just arrived from different parts of the country, were exceedingly grieved, because they could not see him. They all repaired before Maukalan, to ascertain from him what place Buddha had gone to. Maukalan knew it, but he wished to leave to Anourouda the honour of satisfying their curiosity. The latter said to them that Buddha had gone to the seat of Tawadeintha to preach the law to his mother, and spend there one season on the rock of Pantukambala. He added, that he would be back in three months hence, on the day of the full moon of Thadin-kioot (October). They came to the spontaneous

---

in Burmah there are some remnants of the observance of fast during the three months of Lent, when the law is oftener expounded to and better observed by religious people. The obligation of fasting during the days of the quarters of the moon is generally admitted, and some few observe it, if not always, at least from time to time. The generality of the Burmese people entirely disregard fasting.

Curious but interesting is the reply Buddha gave to Thariputra, who rejoiced exceedingly because men and Nats vied with each other in paying great honours to him. He unhesitatingly states: Blessed are all those who rejoice on his account. By this joy we ought not to understand the transient and momentary affection of the heart, elicited by some pleasing and agreeable occurrence; but the kind of joy alluded to is a rational, philosophical, and religious one,

having its origin, first, in a full and perfect knowledge of Buddha's transcendent excellence, rendering his person an object of the highest admiration; and, second, in a lively confidence in his benevolence and goodness towards all beings, which urge him to labour for their deliverance from all miseries and their guidance to a state of peace and rest. Such a joy, diffused over the heart, creates an ardent love for Buddha and his doctrine; that affection rests, not on Buddha, as a mere individual, but on him who is the personification of a saviour of all beings. It implies faith in him and his preachings, as well as a strong confidence in his power and willingness to confer the greatest possible benefits. Hence there is no wonder to hear Buddha declaring all those blessed who on that solemn occasion rejoiced in him.

resolution to remain on that very spot, and not to return to their homes, until they had seen Buddha a second time. They erected temporary sheds; and, though the place was small for such a countless multitude, they managed to accommodate themselves in the best way they could. Previous to his departure, Buddha had enjoined on Maukalan to remain with the people and preach to them the law. Maukalan faithfully complied with the request, and during three consecutive months instructed the people, and answered all their questions. The rich man Anatapein fed the Rahans and the assembly abundantly during the whole time.

CHAPTER X.

Buddha's proceedings in the seat of Tawadeintha—His triumphant return to
the seat of men, in the city of Thin-ka-tha—He is calumniated by the
heretics of Thawattie—Eighth season spent in the forest of Tesakala—
Subsequent preachings—He meets with a bad reception in the Kothamby
country—Dissension among the disciples—Reconciliation—Travels of
Buddha—Preaching to a Pounha who tilled a field.

WHILE Buddha was in the seat of Tawadeintha all the
Nats came from more than ten thousand worlds to his
presence ; but the glory that always encompasses their
bodies disappeared, or was completely outshone by that of
Buddha's person. His mother, a daughter of Nats, came
from the seat of Toothita to see her son and hear his instructions. She sat on his right. Two sons of Nats stood
by the right and left of his mother. The crowd was so
great that it covered a surface of eighteen youdzanas. In
that immense assembly two Nats were conspicuous by their
particular demeanour and position. One of them stood
so close to Buddha as to touch almost one of his knees,
the other was standing in a respectful position afar off.
Buddha asked the latter what he had done to deserve the
place he occupied. *I*He answered that, during former existences, he had made abundant alms indeed, but his merits
had been comparatively small, because he had not done
those good works to persons eminent for their sanctity.
The same question was put to the other Nat, who said
that he was, in a former existence, living in very narrow
circumstances, but that he had had the good fortune of
giving alms, according to his limited means, to persons
who were much advanced in merits. With a voice that

was heard by the crowds on the seat of men, Buddha proclaimed the immense advantage of giving alms to and
supporting the Rahans and those advanced in perfection.   They were, said he, like good seed sown on a good
field, that yields an abundance of good fruits.   But alms
given to those who are as yet under the tyrannical yoke
of passions are like a seed deposited in a bad soil; the
passions of the receiver of alms choke, as it were, the
growth of merits.   At the conclusion, the two Nats obtained
the reward of Thautapan.   The crowds on earth had also
the benefit of hearing his instructions.

Whilst Buddha was in the middle of the Nats, he
announced the law of Abidama to his mother.   Having to
go about to get his food, Buddha created a likeness of
another Buddha, whom he commissioned to continue the
preaching of the Abidama.   As to himself, he went to the
mountain of Himawonta, ate the tender branches of a
certain tree, washed his face in the lake Anawadat, and
partook of the food he received from the Northern Island.
Thariputra went thither to render him all necessary services.   When he had eaten his meal, he called Thariputra,
and desired him to go and preach the law of Abidama to five
hundred Rahans, who were present when the display of wonders took place, and were much pleased with it.   In the
time of the Buddha Kathaba those five hundred Rahans
were bats, living in a cave much resorted to by Rahans, who
were wont to repeat the Abidama.   Those bats contrived to
retain a certain number of words, the meaning whereof they
could not understand.   When they died, they were transferred into one of the seats of Nats; and when they became men anew, they had the good fortune to be born from
illustrious parents, in the country of Thawattie, and when
Phra showed his powers, they were much pleased.   They
became Rahans under Thariputra, and were the first to
understand perfectly the sublime law of Abidama.

As to Buddha, he returned to the seat of Tawadeintha
and continued the instructions, where the Buddha of his

creation had left them. At the end of three months' preaching, an innumerable number of Nats knew and understood the four great principles. As to his mother, she obtained the perfection of Thautapan.

The time when Buddha was to return to the seat of men was near at hand. The crowds, eager to know the precise time when Buddha was to come back among them, went to Maukalan to ascertain from him the precise day on which they would be blessed with his presence. " Well," said Maukalan to the people, " in a very short time I will give you an answer on the subject of your inquiry." That very instant he plunged to the bottom of the earth and reappeared, but when he was at the foot of the Mienmo mountain, he ascended, in the view of the crowd whom he had left, and soon arrived in the presence of Buddha, to whom he explained the object of his errand. " My son," answered Buddha, " in what country does your brother Thariputra spend his season ? " " In the city of Thin-ka-tha," replied Maukalan. " Well," said Buddha, " seven days hence, at the full moon of Thadin-kioot (October), I will descend near the gate of Thin-ka-tha city; go and tell the people that those who desire to see me must go to that country, distant thirty youdzanas from Thawattie. Let no one take any provision ; but by a rigorous abstinence let them dispose themselves to hear the law that I will preach." Maukalan, having paid his respects to Buddha, returned to the place where the assembled multitude anxiously waited for him. He related to them all the particulars regarding his interview with Buddha, and conveyed to them the much-wished-for intelligence of his speedy return on earth.

On the day of the full moon of Thadin-kioot (October), Buddha disposed himself to go down to the seat of men. He called a prince of Thagias and directed him to prepare everything for his descent. Complying with his request, the Thagia prepared three ladders or stairs, one made of precious stones, occupying the middle ; one on the right made of gold; and a third, made of silver, on the left. The foot of each ladder rested on the earth, near to the gate of Thin-ka-tha city, and their summits leaned on the top of the Mienmo mountain. The middle ladder was for Buddha, the golden one for the Nats, and that of silver for the Brahmas. Having reached the summit of the steps, Buddha stopped awhile, and resolved to make a fresh display of his power. He looked upwards, and all the superior seats of Brahmas were distinctly descried; on his looking downwards, his eyes could see and plunge into the bottom of the earth to the lowest hell. The Nats of more than a thousand systems could see each other. Men could perceive Nats in their fortunate seats, and Nats saw men in their terrestrial abode. The six glories streamed forth with an incomparable splendour from Buddha's person, which became visible to all the crowds. There was not one who did not praise Buddha. Having the Nats on his right, and the Brahmas on his left, the most glorious Phra began his triumphant coming down. He was preceded by a Nat, holding a harp in his hands and playing the most melodious tunes; another Nat fanned him; a chief of Brahmas held over him a golden umbrella. Surrounded with that brilliant *cortège*, Buddha descended near the gate of Thin-ka-tha city, and stopped there for awhile. Thariputra came forthwith into the presence of Buddha, paid him his respects at a becoming distance, and said, with a heart overflowing with joy: " On this day, O most glorious Buddha, all the Nats and men are showing their love to you." Buddha replied : " Blessed is Thariputra, and blessed are all those who rejoice on my account. Men and Nats love him who is acquainted with the sublime law, who has put an end to his passions, and who has attained to the highest state of contemplation." At the end of his discourse, innumerable beings understood the four great principles, and the five hundred Rahans whom Thariputra was commissioned to instruct reached the state of Arahat. On the spot where all Buddhas set their feet, when coming from the seat of Tawadeintha, a dzedi [1] has always been erected.

Buddha, on leaving Thin - ka - tha, shaped his course

---

[1] The religious edifices that are to be met with in all parts of Burmah deserve a particular notice. They are called dzedis in all the Buddhist writings of the Burmese, but the people generally speak of them under the appellation of Payas or Phras, which, in this instance, is merely a title of honour of a religious character.

Dzedis, in the earliest days of Buddhism, were sacred tumuli raised upon a shrine, wherein relics of Buddha had been deposited. These structures were as so many lofty witnesses, bearing evidence to the presence of sacred and precious objects, intended to revive in the memory of the faithful the remembrance of Buddha, and foster in their hearts tender feelings of devotion and a glowing fervour for his religion.

From the perusal of this legend, it will appear that dzedis were likewise erected on the tombs of individuals who, during their lifetime, had obtained great distinction by their virtues and spiritual attainments among the members of the assembly. Buddha himself ordered that a monument should be built over the shrine containing the relics of the two great disciples, Thariputra and Maukalan. In Burmah, no dzedis of great dimensions and proportions have ever been erected on the ashes of distinguished Phongyies. In some parts, however, particularly in the upper country, there may be seen here and there some small dzedis, a few feet high, erected on the spot where have been deposited the remains of some saintly personages. These monuments are little noticed by the people, though, on certain occasions, a few offerings of flowers, tapers, &c., are made around and in front of them.

Similar kinds of religious edifices have been built sometimes also to become a receptacle of the Pitagat, or collection of the holy scriptures. One of the finest temples of Ceylon was devoted to that purpose. There was also one in the ancient city of Ava, but I am not aware that there is any of this kind at Amarapoora.

Finally, dzedis have been erected for the sole purpose of harbouring statues of Gaudama; but there is every reason to believe that this practice gained ground in subsequent ages. When a fervent Buddhist, impelled by the desire of satisfying the cravings of his piety and devotion, wished to build a religious monument, and could not procure relics, he then remained contented by supplying the deficiency with images of Buddha representing that eminent personage, in attitudes of body that were to remind Buddhists of some of the most striking actions of his life. In many instances, dzedis have been built up, not even for the sake of sheltering statues, but for the pious purpose of reminding the people of the holy relics of Buddha, and, as they used to say, for kindling in the soul a tender feeling of affectionate reverence for the person of Buddha and his religion. If what is put forward as a plea for building pagodas be founded on conviction and truth, we must conclude that the inhabitants of the valley of the Irrawaddy are most devotedly religious, as the mania for building dzedis has been, and even now is, carried to such a pitch as to render almost fabulous the number of religious buildings to be seen on an extent of above seven hundred miles as far as Bhamo.

As Buddhism was imported from India into Eastern Asia there is no

towards Wethalie, and took his abode in the Dzetawon monastery. The fame of the wonders he had performed increased his reputation, and elicited from the people fresh

doubt that the style of architecture adopted in the erection of religious edifices came from the same quarter. To the native genius of the Burmese we may allow the merit of ornamental architecture for the great monasteries, and a few details of the exterior decorations of the religious monuments; but no one will take offence at refusing to the tribes that occupy the basin of the Irrawaddy the merit of originating the plan of such monuments as those to be seen in some parts of the country. It is much to their credit that they have been able to raise such mighty fabrics with the imperfect knowledge they possess and the very limited means at their disposal. The resemblance that exists between the much-defaced Buddhist monuments yet to be met with in some parts of India and at Java, and those now studding the banks of the Irrawaddy, leaves no doubt respecting the origin of the shape and form of such monuments.

At first sight, the traveller in Burmah believes that there is a great variety in the shape and architecture of pagodas. He is easily led astray by many fantastical ornaments that have been added by inexperienced natives to religious monuments. After, however, a close examination of those edifices, it seems that they can be arranged into three distinct classes, to which those presenting minor differences may be referred. The first class comprises those which have a cone-like appearance, though much enlarged in the direction of the base. These are without niches, or rather ought to be without niches, as the small ones to be seen added to those monuments indicate that they are no essential appendage of the building, but rather the fanciful and

tasteless work of some devotees. The pagodas of Rangoon, Pegu and Prome offer the finest specimens of this order of edifices. The second class includes those of a dome-like shape. They are not common in Burmah. The finest and grandest specimen is that of the Kaong-hmoo-dau, or great meritorious work, situated west of the ancient city of Tsagain. In the third class we may place all the pagodas that approximate to the temple form; that is to say, all those that offer the shape of a more or less considerable rectangle, with a large hall in the centre and several galleries running throughout. Upon this rectangle a conical structure is raised, ending as usual with the tee or umbrella. The most remarkable and perfect specimens of this kind are to be seen at Pagan, which may be aptly styled the City of Pagodas.

The cone-shaped pagoda invariably rests on a quadrangular basis a few feet high. The body of the cone in its lower part is an hexagon or octagon, broad at first, then gradually and regularly decreasing to two-thirds of its height. Upon it rises the regular cone, which ends in a point covered with the gilt umbrella.

The architectural ornaments of such structures are circular, bold and round lines or mouldings; above this, to the place where the cone begins, are sculptures, representing leaves shooting from the middle part, one-half upwards and the other half downwards. That part is often divested of such ornaments, as is the case with the Shoaydagon. On the sides of the cone are horizontal lines grouped together; each group is separated by a considerable distance, then comes a sculptured foliage, different from the one already mentioned, but

tokens of respect and veneration. Alms poured from all quarters into the monastery; the liberality of the people towards his person and that of his disciples expanded in

disposed in a like manner. In the middle of the four sides of the base, particularly in the one facing the East, the Burmese have introduced the practice of making small niches for receiving the statues representing Buddha in a cross-legged position. A portico leads to them. On the four angles of the base they likewise place griffins or sometimes fantastic figures of monsters. Small dzedis are often disposed on the lower parts of the hexagon or octagon. This kind of pagoda being naturally destitute of all ornaments, and standing over a tomb or a shrine, as a pillar that has gradually assumed the shape above described, is a very ancient one, and probably coëval with the earliest Buddhist religious monuments.

The second class of religious edifices is that of those that exhibit a dome-like appearance. They are rather uncommon in Burmah. They rest on a square basis. The lower part is adorned with a few mouldings, but the greatest part offers a perfectly even superficies. The umbrella that is placed on them partakes somewhat of the appearance of the monument it is destined to crown. It considerably expands in the horizontal direction, and has a very ungraceful appearance. The Kaong-hmoo-dau in the neighbourhood of Tsagain rests on a basis about 18 or 20 feet high; the dome, according to an inscription, is 153 feet high, the diameter, at the lowest part, is nearly 200 feet. The whole was formerly gilt. The four sides of the square are lined with small niches, each tenanted by a small statue of Gaudama. Separated from the square by an open and well-paved gallery that runs all round the edifice, are disposed in a row eight hundred and two small pillars of

sandstone, about 6 feet high, with their upper part perforated, so as to afford room sufficient to receive a lamp on festival days. Splendid must be the effect produced during a dark night by so many lamps, pouring a flood of light that illuminates on all sides the massive edifice. Whether the monument was built about three hundred years ago, as stated to the writer by one of the guardians, or, as it is most probable, only repaired and adorned at that time, certain it is that this kind of religious edifice is very ancient, and very likely not inferior in antiquity to those above referred to. Another of a similar form, but of much smaller dimensions, is to be seen at Bhamo, not far from the eastern gate.

The third class of pagodas comprises all those that are generally of a square form, not made of a solid masonry, but with openings or doors, a room, galleries, &c., for receiving statues of Gaudama. They are all surmounted with the usual conical structure, which is, it seems, the essential appendage to all dzedis. These edifices, in my opinion, are not to be considered as tumuli or topes, but rather as places of worship, and sanctuaries for the reception of the statues of Gaudama. The monuments are, I suspect, of a comparative modern origin; they have not the plainness and simplicity of the tumuli which agree so well with the simplicity of the religious form of worship of primitive Buddhism. They are not made to answer the purpose for which dzedis were primitively raised. They must have been erected at times when Buddhist worship, emerging from its primeval sternness of form, assumed proportions and developments congenial to

a wonderful manner. The heretics, who swarmed in Wethalie and its neighbourhood, became exceedingly jealous of Buddha's successes. The loss which they sustained in the donations of the people added fuel to the inward discontent. They resolved to devise some means to lower the character of Buddha in the opinion of the people. After a long deliberation, they fixed on the following plan:—A certain woman of great beauty, but of a rather doubtful character, was induced to join them in accusing Gaudama of having violated her. She contrived to assume the appearance of a person in a state of pregnancy, and, covering herself with a piece of red cloth, she went about the town spreading evil reports respecting Buddha's character. She had the impudence even to go into the Dzetawon monastery, and ask Buddha to provide a place for her approaching confinement, and likewise maintenance for herself and the child she was by him pregnant with. Such an infamous calumny did not, however, move him in the least. Conscious of his innocence, he lost nothing of his usual composure and serenity. But by the interference of the Thagia the slander was made manifest. Two mice bit the strings that kept tied up on the abdo-

---

the taste and wants of large religious communities. This class of temples offers a great variety of forms as to the size, dimensions, and details of architecture. But they may be all brought to this general outline. From the square body of the temple diverge, in the direction of the four points of the compass, porticoes; the one facing the east is always the largest and best adorned; sometimes there is but one portico, that of the east, and there are only doors in the middle of the three other sides. From these porticoes the galleries converge towards the centre of the temple, where are statues. In the large and magnificent pagodas of Pagan, galleries with vaults in the pointed style run all round the building. Some of those stupendous structures have two stories, and it is only on the second that the conical part rests, which is the essential complement of every religious building. On one of the middle-sized pagodas rises, instead of a cone, an obelisk, with ornaments that appear to resemble hieroglyphic figures. Some of those obelisks swell considerably towards the middle of their height. Great was the surprise and astonishment of the writer, when he observed in the same place, among the prodigious number of pagodas, in a more or less advanced state of decay, one, not considerable by its dimensions, nor in a much-ruined condition, that exhibited the solitary instance of a regular pyramid.

men the apparatus designed to prop up the deceit, and, on a sudden, the whole fell on the ground, proclaiming at once the innocence of the sage and smiting his enemies with confusion.

Every one present on the occasion gave vent to his just indignation at such a base attempt on the part of the heretics. But Buddha meekly replied that what had just happened was a righteous retribution for a misbehaviour of his own during a former existence. At that time, he was on a certain day under the influence of liquor, when he chanced to meet on his way a Pitzegabuddha. Without any reason or provocation, he abused the holy man with the lowest and coarsest expressions, and went so far as to tell him that his whole life was but a series of hypocritical actions. Turning then towards his disciples, he added, with a grave countenance, that what they had now witnessed was the just punishment inflicted on him under the influence of the demerit created and generated by his former evil doing.

The eighth season was spent in the grove or forest of Tesakala, and when the rains were over, the most excellent Phra travelled throughout the country, preaching and teaching the right way to many. Countless converts entered one of the four ways, and many obtained at once the deliverance.

In the town of Santoo-maragiri, he was preaching to the benefactors who had fed him and his disciples. Among the hearers were two persons, Nakoulapita and Nakoulamata, husband and wife, belonging to the pounha race. During a great many successive former existences they had had the good fortune to be father, mother, uncle, aunt, &c., to Buddha. During the present existence the feeling of affection towards him with whom they had been so long and so intimately connected was powerfully awakened and glowed in their hearts. Under the influence of that natural, kindly, and tender feeling, they came forward, and prostrating themselves before Gaudama, said to him:

"Dear son, how is it that you have been away from us for so long a while ? We are so happy to see you after so long an absence." Buddha, remaining indifferent to such a scene and language, knew at once what were the real wants of that good couple, and in what manner he could acknowledge the great favours he had during former existences received at their hands. He preached to them the most excellent law. They were thoroughly converted. The next morning they had the happiness to supply their great teacher and his company with the choicest food. Meanwhile they addressed to him the following request : "During many existences we both have always been happily united : not a word of complaint or quarrel has ever passed between us. We pray that in our coming existences the same love and affection may ever unite us together." Their request was affectionately granted, and Buddha, in the presence of a large assembly, pronounced them blessed and happy amongst all men and women.

The son of the ruler of the country where these things happened was, to his great affliction, childless. He invited Buddha to come and partake of his hospitality in his house. The offer was accepted. Great preparations were made for the reception of the illustrious visitor. The prince had some of his own clothes laid on the way that Buddha was to follow, in the hope that by treading over them he might communicate a certain virtue, whereby he would have the object of his earnest desire realised. On his arrival near the entrance of the house, Buddha stopped and refused to proceed farther. Meanwhile, he beckoned Ananda to remove the clothes. This was done accordingly, to the prince's deep disappointment. After the meal, Gaudama explained to him that he and his wife during a former existence had lived on eggs and had killed many birds. Their present barrenness was the just punishment of their former trespassing ; but their actual good dispositions having atoned for the past transgressions, they would be blessed with children. Both were overjoyed at this news. They believed in Buddha, obtained the state of Thautapan, and thereby entered into the current of perfection. Their faith in Buddha's word procured for them so happy a result.

During all the time that elapsed after the rain, Buddha travelled through the country, engaged on his usual benevolent errand, and converting many among men and Nats. In the country of Garurit, in a village of pounhas called Magoulia, the head man, one of the richest in the place, had a daughter whose beauty equalled that of a daughter of Nats. She had been in vain asked in marriage by princes, nobles, and pounhas. The proud damsel had rejected every offer. On the day that her father saw Gaudama, he was struck with his manly beauty and meek deportment. He said within himself: "This man shall be a proper match for my daughter." On his return home he communicated his views to his wife. On the following day, the daughter having put on her choicest dress and richest apparels, they all three went with a large retinue to the Dzetawon monastery. Admitted to the presence of Buddha, the father asked for his daughter the favour of being allowed to attend on him. Without returning a word of reply, or giving the least sign of acceptance or refusal, Buddha rose up and withdrew to a small distance, leaving behind him on the floor the print of one of his feet. The pounha's wife, well skilled in the science of interpreting wonderful signs, saw at a glance that the marks on the print indicated a man no longer under the control of passions, but a sage emancipated from the thraldom of concupiscence. She communicated her views to her husband, who had the impudence to go to Buddha's presence and renew the same offer. Buddha meekly replied: "Pounha, I neither accept nor decline your offer; in your turn, listen to what I have to say." He then went on to relate how he had left the world, resisted Manh's temptation, lived in solitude for six years, and freed himself from the net of passions. He concluded by stating that, having become a Buddha, he had for ever conquered all passions. At the conclusion of the instruction, both father and mother became established in the state of Thautapan. The damsel was highly offended at the refusal she experienced, and retained a strong feeling of hatred towards him who had declined her proffered favours. Her father took her into the Kothambi country, where she was offered to the ruler, who, smitten with her charms, elevated her to the rank of first queen.

In the country of Kothambi, there lived three rich men. These three men fed during the rainy season every year five hundred hermits, who came from the Himalaya range for the purpose of obtaining their maintenance. These charitable laymen went over to Wethalie for the purpose of trade. There they met Buddha, and earnestly pressed him to come to their country and preach the law. The invitation was accepted. They returned home, and built for the accommodation of the illustrious visitor each of them one monastery. When all was ready, Buddha went to Kothambi, attended by five hundred disciples. He spent there the ninth season. During his stay he dwelt by turns in each of the three monasteries, and was abundantly supported by the rich man in whose monastery he took his abode.

In the country of Kothambi there were as yet few disciples or believers in Buddha; but the number of holders of false doctrines was exceedingly great. Secretly supported by the first queen, and actuated by jealousy against the new-comer, they reviled him and his disciples in every possible way, and did their utmost to destroy in public opinion his rising fame. Whenever they met Buddha's disciples, they abused them with the coarsest language. Unable to bear any longer so many insults, Ananda, in the name of his brethren, went to Buddha, and asked him to remove to some other place, where they would receive a becoming treatment. "But," said Buddha, "if we be ill-treated in the new place we go to, what is to be done?"

" We shall proceed to some other place," replied Ananda.
" But," retorted Buddha, " if in that new place we be likewise reviled, what then ? " " We shall," replied Ananda,
" remove to some other place." Buddha remained silent
for awhile, and, casting a gentle glance on Ananda, said
to him : " A little patience will save us the trouble of so
many travels, and certainly procure for us here what we
may perhaps vainly look for anywhere else. By patience
and endurance the wise man conquers all his enemies.
Behold the war-elephant; he plunges into the thickest of
the raging conflict, regardless of the darts and arrows flying in every direction, and carries all before him. I, too,
the most excellent Buddha, shall certainly stay here, dili-
gently preach the most excellent law, and perseveringly
labour to disentangle men from the net of passions. In
no way shall I care for the abuses they may pour on me
and my disciples."

Not long after this a trifling accident kindled the fire of
dissension among the members of the assembly. The subject was, as usual, of a trifling nature. It was concerning
a point of discipline of scarcely any importance, infringed
unintentionally by a Rahan. He was accused by one of
his brethren of having committed a sin. But he replied
that, having done an act in which his will had not parti-
cipated, he did not consider himself guilty. Each dis-
putant attracted to his party some religious who supported
his view of the case. The Kothambi Rahans seem to
have been the cause of the disunion which prevailed in
the community, and soon, like a devouring flame, extended
to the female portion of the assembly. In vain Gaudama
interfered, and exhorted the two parties to patience, union,
and charity. In his presence the parties were silent, but
in his absence the quarrel grew worse. At last his entreaties were unheeded, and discord continued to rend
asunder the bond of unity. Disgusted with such a state
of things, Buddha preached to the most distinguished
members of the assembly the blessings of peace and con-

cord. Such men as Baddia, Kimila, and Anourouddha, treasured up in their heart the instructions of their great master. But others continued the dispute. Meanwhile he resolved to separate himself for a time from all company, and to go to a lonely spot to enjoy the happiness of peace and meditation. He shaped his course towards the village of Palelayaka, where he received his food, and went into a grove of sala-trees, to fix his residence at the foot of one of those trees. The villagers, hearing of his intention, hastened to the spot, and built a hermit's hut for his use, and promised to supply him daily with his food.

It was in this place that, delighting in the contemplation of unclouded truth, Gaudama spent the tenth season alone. The rich men of the Kothambi country, hearing that Buddha had departed because of the dissension that took place among the Rahans, became indignant. They openly declared their fixed intent of refusing to give anything for the maintenance of the Rahans, until they agreed among themselves, and became reconciled with their teacher. The timely threat had the desired effect. The disputants felt the unpleasant seriousness of their uneasy position. They could hold on no longer. The Rahans came to an agreement among themselves, and promised that after the season they would go to Buddha and solicit his pardon. In the forest of Paleliaka there lived a certain elephant, much advanced in merits, which went to Buddha, and, during three months, ministered to all his wants, as a most affectionate and devoted disciple would do towards a beloved master.

The three mouths of Lent being completed, the rich man Anatapein made earnest inquiries with Ananda, respecting the place Buddha had withdrawn to, and charged him to invite the great preacher to come back to Thawattie, and live as usual in the Dzetawon monastery. Complying with the pious wishes of the rich man, Ananda took with himself five hundred Rahans, and went to the solitude of Paleliaka. He was likewise followed by the five hundred refractory Rahans of Kothambi, who had come to Wethalie. The ruler of the country and Anatapein had refused at first to receive them. But the prohibition had been removed on account of their repentance. He approached alone the place where Buddha was living. After the usual prostrations, Gaudama inquired whether he had come alone. He replied that there were with him many of his faithful disciples and the Kothambi Rahans. The latter came with the express purpose of asking his pardon, and a firm resolution to yield henceforward a perfect obedience to all his commands. Buddha desired them to appear in his presence. They came, were there well received, and their misbehaviour was forgiven. Gaudama explained to them the great advantage of shunning bad company and of living in retirement. The hearers were fully converted and established in the state of Thautapan. Buddha, on his return to Wethalie, continued preaching in every direction, and led to the deliverance a great number of men, Nats, and Brahmas. The stay in the Dzetawon monastery was not very long. Buddha went into the Magatha country, to a pounha village, named Nala. Not far from that village there is the Deckinagiri, or southern mountain, with a monastery. In that place Buddha spent the eleventh season.[2] His supporters were

---

[2] The few particulars that have been gathered respecting the mode that Buddha followed in disseminating his doctrines, exhibit him in the light of a zealous and indefatigable preacher. We see him passing from one place to another with the sole purpose of instructing the ignorant and pointing out to them the way leading to the deliverance. Behar and Oude appear to have been the seat of his labours, and the scene on which he acted in behalf of all, without any distinction of condition, caste, or sex. Individuals in the humblest walks of life, men engaged in wicked practices, women of an abandoned character, were all, to an equal degree, the object of his tender solicitude. They were all summoned to come to his feet and partake in the blessings that he had in store for them. Gaudama was to an eminent degree an earnest and fervent propagandist. This is a striking feature in his character, which distinguishes him not only from all his contemporaries, but also from all the philosophers that have appeared throughout the Indian peninsula. All these sages aimed at becoming the heads of schools, but none of them thought of promulgating a code of morals intended for the whole human race.

the pounhas of the village. The chief occupation of those men was the tillage of the fields. Gaudama took a particular pleasure during his daily walks in conversing with them, when he met them engaged in their daily labours.

One day Buddha went into the fields, where he met a pounha, with whom he began to converse, in the intention of ultimately preaching to him the holy law. He spoke at first on the subject of his daily labour, his bullocks, his plough, the seed, and the harvest, which supplied the pounha and his family with their daily food during the year. He added: " I, too, am a labourer, provided with the seed and all the implements necessary for carrying on tillage." The pounha, surprised at what he heard, asked Buddha in what place he had left his bullocks, the seed, the plough, &c. The latter coolly replied: " All these things are with me at present. Hearken, O pounha, to what I am about to state. The seed is that fervent desire, that benevolent disposition, which prompted me at the feet of the Buddha Deipinkara to ask for the Buddhaship: it is the science which I have gathered under the tree Bodi. The rain water is that uninterrupted series of good works performed by me, until I have become a Buddha. They

---

Gaudama has the honour of being the first who, with enlarged views, looked upon his fellow-men as equally entitled to the benefit of his instructions. His love of all men prompted him to undergo all sorts of fatigue, to procure for them what he imagined to be a great boon. In making this statement we have no intention to pass an opinion on the doctrines of the founder of Buddhism ; we merely bring forward to the notice of the reader a peculiar characteristic of that sage, which, in our humble opinion, helps to account for the extraordinary spread of Buddhism from the banks of the Oxus to the Japanese archipelago. The tenets of that creed have become popular, because they were intended for all. False though they be, particularly in what has a reference to dogmas, they were accepted by the masses, because there were no other proffered to them. The disciples of Gaudama must have been well received in the various places they went to, for they showed a disposition of mind quite unknown in those days, viz., a lively interest in the welfare of all. This zeal, which appeared so conspicuously in Gaudama and during the first ages of Buddhism, has become all but totally extinct. There is no desire on the part of those who in our days follow that creed to propagate its tenets among other nations or tribes.

have been as the means of watering the good seed which was in me. The knowledge, or science, and wisdom are as the yoke, as well as the plough-shaft. The heart, or the knowing principle which is in me, represents the reins that serve to guide the bullocks. The teeth of the plough represent the diligence that must be used in attending to the eradicating of the principle of demerits and of bad works. The plough-handle represents the guiding principle of the law, which enables me to remove all that is bad, and promote what is good. The food which you, O pounha, derive from your exertions, represents the pure relish which is tasted by him who is bent on avoiding evil and doing good. When you make use of the plough, you cut or uproot all bad weeds. So it is with him who is penetrated with the full meaning of the four great truths; he cuts and uproots from himself the wicked inclinations and low propensities that are in him. When the labour of the field is over, you unyoke your bullocks and leave them to go whithersoever they please; so it is with the wise man. By application to invigorating the principle of good that leads to perfection, he lets go the opposite principle which gives rise to all imperfections. The bullocks have to work hard to complete the work of tillage. So the sage has to struggle hard, to till perfectly and cultivate thoroughly the soil of his own being, and reach the happy state of Neibban. The husbandman who labours so much for bringing his field into a position to receive the seed, and in every way to favour its growth, is imitated by the true sage who endeavours to free himself from the miseries attending existence, to advance in the way of merits by the practice of good works, and who thirsts after the happy condition of the perfect. He who works in the field is sometimes disappointed, and feels occasionally the pangs of hunger. He who works in the field of wisdom is exempt from all miseries and afflictions. He eats the fruit of his labour. He is fully satiated when he beholds Neibban. It is in this manner, O pounha, that I am a true husbandman, and am always provided with all the implements necessary for the tillage of man's soul." The pounha, delighted with such doctrine, became a convert, and professed his belief in Buddha, the law, and the assembly. Subsequently he applied for admittance into the assembly, and by energetic efforts in the arduous work of meditation, he became at last a Rahanda.

When the rains were over, Buddha travelled through the country, preaching the most excellent law, with the happiest results. He went to the town of Satiabia, in the Kosala country. There he received from a pounha of Waritzaba an invitation to go to that place. The invitation was graciously accepted. In that town he spent the twelfth season. A great many pounhas were enlightened and converted by professing their firm adherence to the three precious things. The vile Manh Nat did his utmost to thwart the beneficial results of Buddha's preachings. A great dearth prevailing in the country, he did all that he could to starve the most excellent Buddha and all his followers. But he was frustrated in his iniquitous design by the charity of five hundred horse merchants, who had come from Outharapata, and were then staying in Waritzaba.

Buddha, leaving this country, shaped his course through the great Mantala country; he travelled by the shortest route, a distance of 500 youdzanas. He started on the day after the full moon of Tabodway, and spent nearly five months in this voyage. He reached the banks of the Ganges at Gayagati, where he crossed the mighty stream and went to Benares. He had not been long in that city, when he recrossed the Ganges and went to Wethalie, dwelling in the Gootagarathala monastery. Thence he went into Thawattie, preaching through all the places he visited. When he was in the Dzetawon monastery, he delivered the Maha Rahula instruction for the benefit of his son Rahula, who then was eighteen years old.

CHAPTER XI.

Voyage to Tsalia—Instructions to Meggia—Raoula is made a professed re-
ligious—Manahan's questions to Buddha—Misbehaviour of Thouppa-
buda—Questions proposed by Nats in the Dzetawon monastery—Conver-
sion of a Biloo—Episode of Thirima at Radzagio—Attention paid to a
poor pounha and to a weaver's daughter on account of their faith—In
the twentieth season, appointment of Ananda to the stewardship—Con-
version of a famous robber.

AFTER a rather short stay in Thawattie, Buddha went to
the town of Tsalia. The inhabitants built for him a monastery on a hill not far from the town, and liberally supplied him with all that he wanted. Pleased with the good
reception the people gave him, Gaudama spent on that
spot the thirteenth season. He went to receive his food
in the village of Dzantoo. Thence travelling through the
country, he reached the banks of the river Kimikila and
enjoyed himself in a beautiful grove of mango-trees. The
disciple Meggia, being too much taken up with the beauty
of the place, eagerly wished to remain here for some time.
As a punishment for such an inordinate attachment to a
particular spot, he who had renounced the world and the
gratification of passions, felt on a sudden a strange change
pass over him. A flood of concupiscence inundated his
soul. Buddha, who saw what was taking place in Meggia,
gave him an instruction on contempt for the things of
this world, and entirely cured him of his great spiritual
distemper.

Thence he proceeded to Thawattie into the Dzetawon
monastery, where he spent the fourteenth season. The
great disciple Thariputra, with five hundred religious, was

spending the season in a neighbouring village. The people were so much pleased with him and his company, that they offered to each of them a piece of yellow silk. Some religious, jealous of the great disciple, came to Buddha and accused him of covetousness. Buddha fully justified his great companion and commended the liberality of the donors, who had thus an opportunity of gratifying their liberality and gaining merits.

The Thamane Raoula was then twenty years old. Having reached the canonical age, he was elevated to the dignity of Patzin. The young religious could scarcely defend himself from a certain feeling of vanity on account of his father's dignity and his own personal mien and bearing, which he was very fond of admiring. Buddha was intimately acquainted with what was going on in Raoula's soul. He preached to him the contempt of self and of all varieties of form. The instruction was so impressive that it led the young hearer to the state of Rahanda. On a certain night when Raoula was sleeping near the door of Gaudama's private apartment, Manh Nat, wishing to frighten the young Rahanda, created the likeness of an elephant, which, keeping his trunk over his head, suddenly made a frightful noise. Buddha, who was inside, saw clearly that this was only a temptation of the vile Manh. He said to him, "O wretched one, are you not aware that fear is no longer to be found in him who has become a Rahanda?" Manh, being discovered, vanished away, covered with shame and confusion at the abortiveness of his malicious attempt.

In the same year, Buddha went to Kapilawot, which is in the Thekka country, and took up his residence in the Nigranda monastery, situated close to the banks of the river Rohani. At that place he spent the fifteenth season. On a certain day, his cousin Mahanan, the son of Thoodaudana, came to the monastery, and having paid his respects to his illustrious relative, took the liberty to propose to him the four following questions:—1. In what

consists the fulfilment of the religious duties? 2. What
is meant by the religious disposition? 3. What is the
real renouncing? 4. What is the true knowledge?

Buddha replied in the following manner: "The fulfilment of the religious duties consists in observing carefully
the five precepts obligatory on all men. The religious disposition is but a loving inclination and affection for all that
refers to Buddha and the law that he has published. He
who possesses it experiences a continual longing for the
acquisition of merits. The renouncing is that disposition
a man is habitually in when he finds his pleasure in parting with his riches for the purpose of relieving the needy
and bestowing alms on the members of the assembly.
Finally, wisdom consists in making one's self perfectly
acquainted with what can procure merits for the present
and the future; under its influence man acts up to that
knowledge, and also attends with the utmost diligence to
what may put an end to the law of miseries."

Even among his nearest relatives, Buddha was doomed
to meet with the bitterest enemies. Thouppabuda, who
was at once his uncle and his father-in-law, bore to him
a deadly hatred, and secretly harboured in his heart a
sentiment of revenge, for two principal reasons, because
his daughter Yathaudara had been abandoned by Gaudama, when he left his palace and began the life of an
ascetic; and also for having admitted his own son Dewadat
among the members of the assembly. Having been informed that on the following day Buddha would direct his
steps towards a certain quarter of the town to beg his food
Thouppabuda partook largely of intoxicating liquor, to
nerve himself for the execution of the design he had in
his mind, and went out in the direction in which Gaudama
was expected to come. As soon as he saw him drawing
near, he planted himself in the middle of the road, barring
the passage, and loading his great relative with abuses.
Buddha stopped awhile without showing the least sign of
emotion. Then turning to Ananda, he said, "Great is the

crime of my uncle; seven days hence he shall be swallowed up alive by the earth at the foot of the great staircase of his palace." On this fearful prediction being reported to Thouppabuda, he laughed and stated that he would stay during eight days in the upper story of his palace, and belie his nephew's prediction. Despite the precautions that he took, the fatal prediction was literally fulfilled. The unfortunate unrepenting prince saw the earth burst open under his feet, and he was precipitated to the very bottom of the Awidzi hell. Buddha took advantage of the awful punishment that had befallen a prince of his family to exhort Mahanan to seek a firm asylum in the three precious things, to bear a sincere love and an affectionate fondness to all that related to the law and its practices.

Up to the present period of his life, Buddha had reserved to himself the right of preaching the law to and extolling the merits of those who had brought him his food, after having partaken of their liberal donation. This instruction may be properly called the sermon of thanksgiving. It is called Anou-mau-dana. Now he allowed his disciples to do the like, and repay the generosity of their benefactors by distributing unto them the knowledge of truth.

At that time Buddha preached the four laws of A-sawau, or the four bands that retain a being in the vortex of existences. From Kapilawot Buddha returned to Thawattie in the Dzetawon monastery. At that time a Nat had proposed four questions to his companions which they had not been able to answer. They were subsequently communicated to all the denizens of the six seats of Nats, but no one had been able to solve the difficulty. Not knowing what to do, they agreed to refer the particulars to the most excellent Buddha, then in the Dzetawon monastery. A deputation was forthwith sent to him with the view of proposing to him the puzzle, and entreating him to condescend to give the much-desired solution. The members of the deputation having duly paid their respects, said to him, " O most excellent Phra, which is the best thing to be bestowed in alms ? Which is the most savoury and relishing of all things ? Which is the most pleasurable ? Which is the best and the fittest thing to put an end to passions ? " To these four questions Buddha answered by one word—" The law." Addressing himself both to the Nats and to his assembled disciples, he added, " The giving of alms, though good in itself, cannot introduce a being into the path that leads to the deliverance. The law alone can afford such a benefit. The preaching of the law, and the exertions in communicating its knowledge to others, are therefore the most excellent alms. All that in this world confers pleasure to the senses is but a means to plunge man into the vortex of existences, and thereby into all miseries. On the contrary, the hearing of the law rejoices the heart to such an extent as often to open a spring of joyful tears; it destroys concupiscence, and leads gradually out of the whirlpool of existences. It establishes man in the state of Arahat, which is the end of all passions. The law, therefore, is the most savoury, the most pleasing thing, leading beings to the cessation of all miseries. You, my beloved disciples, exert yourselves in making known by your preaching the said law to all beings. This is the most excellent alms that you can bestow on the beings that inhabit the three different states of men, Nats, and Brahmas."

Buddha soon left Thawattie and went to Alawee. A Biloo was in the habit of eating every day some children of that place. Owing to the ravenous and horrible appetite of the monster, all the children had been eaten up; there remained only the child of the king, who was on the following day to be given over to him. Buddha reviewed, as usual, on a certain morning the condition of all beings. He saw the sad position of the king of Alawee and of his son. He resolved to proffer assistance to both, and also to convert the Biloo. He arrived in the country of Alawee, where he was received with every mark of respect. He forthwith went into the forest where the monster lived. At first he met with a most determined and violent opposition. But, opposing to his enraged antagonist meekness, patience, and kindness, Buddha gradually softened that terrible nature. Concealing affectedly the change which was taking place in him, almost against his perverse inclination, the Biloo said to Buddha, "I have put certain questions to many famous ascetics, but they have not been able to answer them. On seeing their utter incapacity, I have seized them, torn their bodies in pieces, and flung their quivering limbs into the Ganges. Such shall be your fate, O Gaudama, if your science fails you on this occasion. By what means can a man get out of the stream or current of passions? How can he cross over the sea of existences? How can he free himself from the evil influence? How shall he be able to purify himself from the smallest stain of concupiscence?" Buddha replied: " Listen, O Biloo, to my words; my answer shall fully satisfy you. By faith in and affection for the three precious things, man escapes from the current of passions. He who applies himself with a diligent earnestness to the study of the law of merits passes over the sea of existences. He who strives to practise the works that procure merits frees himself from evil influence, and from the attending miseries. Finally, the knowledge of the four meggas or ways to perfection procures perfect exemption from the least remnant of concupiscence. The Biloo, delighted with what he had heard, believed in Buddha, and soon was firmly established in the state of Thautapan. On that spot, where so glorious and unexpected a conversion had taken place, a monastery was erected. Buddha spent herein the sixteenth season. As usual, myriads of Nats and men who had heard his preachings obtained the deliverance.

From Alawee Buddha went to Radzagio, and spent the seventeenth season in the Weloowon monastery. During that season a famous courtesan, named Thirima, sister of the celebrated physician Dzewaka, renowned all over the country for her wit and the incomparable charms of her person, wished to show her liberality to the disciples of Buddha. Every day a certain number of them went to her dwelling to receive, along with their food, abundant alms. One of the pious mendicants, in an unguarded moment, moved by an unholy curiosity, looked at her, and was instantly smitten by her charms. The mortal wound was widened and deepened by a fortuitous occurrence. On a certain day Thirima fell sick. But she did not relax in her daily work of charity. Weak though she was, and in her *negligée*, she insisted on the mendicants being introduced into her room, that she might pay her respects to them. The unfortunate lover was among the company. Her incomparable charms were heightened by her plain dress and drooping attitude. The poor lover went back with his brethren to the monastery. The arrow had penetrated to the core of the heart. He refused to take any food, and during some days completely estranged himself from the society of his brethren. While the intestine war raged in his bosom, Thirima died. Buddha, desirous to cure the moral distemper of the poor religious, invited King Pimpasara to be present when he should go with his disciples to see the remains of Thirima. On the fourth day after Thirima's death he went to her house with his disciples. There her body was laid before them, with a livid appearance, and all swollen. Countless worms already issuing out through the apertures, rendered the sight loathsome, whilst a horrible stench almost forbade a standing close to it. Buddha coolly asked the king, "What is that object which is stretched before us?" "Thirima's body," replied the king. "When she was alive," retorted Buddha, "people paid a thousand pieces of silver to enjoy her for a day. Would any one take her now for half that sum?" "No," replied the king; "in all my kingdom there is not one man who would offer the smallest sum to have her remains; nay, no one could be found who would be willing to carry her to any distance, unless compelled to do so." Buddha, addressing the assembly, said, "Behold all that remains of Thirima, who was so famous for her personal attractions! What has become of that form which deceived and enslaved so many? All is subjected to mutability; there is nothing real in this world." On hearing the instruction, eighty-two thousand persons obtained the knowledge of the four truths. The Rahan who, because of his passion, would not eat his food, was entirely cured of his moral distemper, and firmly established in the state of Thautapan. All this happened whilst Buddha spent his seventeenth season in the bamboo-grove monastery.

When the season was over, he went, as usual, to preach in every direction, and returned to Thawattie, to the Dzetawon monastery. His stay in that place was not long. He undertook another voyage to Alawee. He was received with the greatest demonstrations of joy by the people, who gladly ministered to all his wants. On a certain day, when he was to receive large offerings from the people and preach to them, it happened on that occasion that a poor pounha, who was very desirous to hear his instructions, was informed at an early hour of that very day that one of his cows had gone astray from the herd and could not be found. Hereupon he felt greatly aggrieved. He was afraid to let go the golden opportunity to hear the instruction. However, he trusted that by making the utmost diligence he would be back in time. He ran in all haste until he found the strayed animal and brought it back. It was nearly midday when he returned to the town. Though pressed with the pangs of hunger and overwhelmed with fatigue, he went straight forward to the place where the congregation was assembled. The offerings had been brought a long while ago; the people out of respect stood motionless, with their hands joined, in the presence of Buddha, who, contrary to the general expectation, remained perfectly silent. With his supernatural vision he had seen the perfect dispositions of the

poor pounha. He would have him to share in the blessing of his instruction. As soon as the pounha had taken
his place among the hearers, Buddha, casting a benevolent
glance towards him, beckoned him to come near his person. Meantime, he ordered some of his disciples to bring
the poor man some food, because he was very hungry; and
he would not condescend to begin the instruction till the
man had been relieved from the pangs of hunger by a
good meal. When the preaching was over, several Rahans
ridiculed the attention paid by their master to a common
man. Buddha, knowing their innermost thoughts, spoke
to them by way of an instructive rebuke: "Beloved sons,
you seem to be surprised at my behaviour towards that
poor pounha. But I had perceived at once the super-
excellent dispositions of that man, his craving for the holy
law, and his lively and strong faith in me, which prompted
him to lay no stress on hunger, nor on fatigue, and to make
no account of his personal discomforts, in order to satisfy
his earnest longings for the law." On that occasion an
immense number of hearers were converted.

Buddha went to a monastery built on a hill, near the
town of Tsalia, where he spent the eighteenth season. In
that town there was a weaver, who had one daughter, who
followed the same profession as her father. The damsel
was very desirous to hear Buddha's preachings; but on
the day when Buddha was to come into the town to
deliver instructions to the people, it happened she had to
finish the weaving of a piece of cloth that was urgently
required by the owner. She then said to herself: I will
exert myself with so much diligence that I will be enabled
both to finish my work and listen to my teacher's preaching. She set instantly to work, wound up the thread on
the quill, and took it with her, to carry it to the shed
where her father's loom was. On her way to the shed, she
had to pass near the place where a motionless congregation stood before Buddha, eagerly waiting for the words
that were to fall from his mouth. She laid aside her

quill, loaded with thread, and squatted timidly behind the last rank of the congregation. Buddha had seen at a glance the perfect dispositions of the young girl. It was chiefly for her benefit that he had undertaken a long journey and come over to that place. As soon as he saw her, he made her draw nearer to him. The injunction was joyfully complied with. With an encouraging tone of voice, Buddha asked her whence she came and whither she was going. The damsel modestly answered that she knew whence she came, and also whither she was going; at the same time, she added that she was ignorant of the place she came from, and of the place she was going to. On hearing this apparently contradictory answer, many of the hearers could scarcely refrain from giving vent to indignant feelings. But Buddha, who had fathomed the girl's wisdom, prayed them to be silent. Then, turning towards his young interlocutor, he desired her to explain the meaning of her answer. She said: "I know that I come from my father's house, and that I go to our loom-shed; but what existence I have come from to this present one, this I am entirely ignorant of. I am likewise uncertain about the existence that shall follow this one. About these two points I am completely ignorant; my mind can discover neither the one nor the other." Buddha extolled the wisdom of the damsel, and forthwith began his instruction. At the conclusion, she was firmly grounded in the state of Thautapan. She withdrew immediately, took up her quill, and went to the shed. It happened that her father was asleep, with his hand on the loom's handle. She approached the loom, and began to arrange the thread. Her father, awaking suddenly, pushed inadvertently the part of the loom his hand was laid upon, and struck his daughter in the chest. She fell down and instantly expired. Overwhelmed with grief, the unfortunate father poured a flood of tears over the lifeless corpse of his daughter. Unable to console himself, he rose up and went to Buddha, in the hope of receiving some comfort at his feet. Buddha affectionately received him, and, by his good instructions, relieved him from the load that pressed on his heart, and gradually enlightening his mind by the preaching of the four great truths, he gently infused into his heart and his soul that sweet joy which wisdom alone can impart. The weaver resolved to abandon the world, asked for admittance into the assembly, and not long after became a Rahanda. This conversion was followed by that of a great many others.

Buddha returned to Radzagio, and spent the nineteenth season in the Weloowon monastery. The season being over, Buddha went into the districts of Magatha, preaching in all places. Previous to that time, there lived at Radzagio a rich man who had an only daughter, who was brought up with the greatest care and the utmost fondness. She lived in the upper apartments of a splendid dwelling. On a certain day, at an early hour in the morning, she was looking on the people that flocked from the country into the town. She saw among many a young hunter driving a cart loaded with venison. She much admired his fine, energetic appearance. She was instantly enamoured of him, and made all the necessary arrangements to elope with him. She succeeded, married the hunter, and had by him a large family. Passing on one day through a forest, the most excellent Buddha chanced to meet with a deer which was caught in the net of a hunter. Moved with feelings of commiseration, he helped the poor beast to get out of the meshes. After this benevolent action, he went to rest under a tree. The hunter soon made his appearance, and to his great dismay at once discovered that some one had deprived him of his prey. Whilst he was looking about, he saw Buddha, in his yellow dress, calmly resting under the shade of a large tree. "This," said the hunter to himself, "is the man who has done the mischief; I will make him pay dear for his undue interference." Hereupon he hastily took up an arrow and placed it on the bow, with the intention of shooting dead the evildoer. But despite his exertions, heightened by the thirst for revenge, he could not succeed; both his hands were seized with a sudden quivering, and his feet appeared as if nailed to the ground. He stood motionless in that attitude. Absorbed in meditation, Buddha was not aware what was going on so close to him.

The sons of the hunter as well as their wives grew very much troubled that their father did not return at the usual hour from visiting his nets. They feared that some untoward accident had overtaken him. They armed themselves and went in search of him. They soon came to the spot where they saw the sad position of their father. At the same moment, perceiving a yellow-dressed individual, they hastily concluded, that, by the power of some charms, he had brought their father into this miserable condition. They made up their mind to kill him. But whilst they were preparing to put their cruel design into execution, their hands, suddenly benumbed, could not grasp the weapons, and they all stood motionless and speechless. Awaking at last from contemplation, Buddha saw the hunter and all his family standing before him. Taking compassion on them, he restored them to their ordinary condition, and preached to them. They all fell at his knees, craved his pardon, believed in him, and became fervent Upasakas.

Buddha returned to Thawattie to spend the twentieth season in the Dzetawon monastery. It was at that period that there happened a remarkable change in the management of the domestic affairs of Gaudama. Up to the present time, no one among the religious had been specially appointed to attend on Buddha and minister to his wants. But some of them, as circumstances occurred, undertook the agreeable and honourable duty of serving him. However human nature will occasionally let appear, even in the best of men, some marks of its innate imperfections. On two occasions, the Rahans who followed Buddha and carried his mendicant's pot and a portion of his dress wished to go in one direction, whilst Buddha desired them to follow in another. They had the imprudence to part company with him. Both paid dearly for their disobedience. They fell into the hands of robbers, who took away all that they had, and beat them severely on the head. This twofold act of insubordination painfully affected Buddha. He summoned all the religious into his presence, and declared that, being old, he wished to appoint one of them to the permanent office of personal attendant on himself. Thariputra and Maukalan immediately tendered their services with a pious and loving earnestness. But Buddha declined to accept their offer, as well as that of the eighty principal disciples. The reason was, that their services were required for preaching to the people, and labouring with him for the dissemination of the true science among men. Some of the disciples urged Ananda to volunteer his services; but out of modesty he remained silent. Then he added that, should Buddha be willing to accept his humble services, he knew his heart's dispositions and his willingness to attend on him on all occasions; he had but to signify his good pleasure. As to him, he would be too happy to accept the office. Buddha expressed his readiness to confer on him the honourable employment. He was formally appointed and nominated Phra's attendant, and, during the twenty-five remaining seasons, he acted as the beloved and devoted attendant on Buddha's person. Through him alone visitors were ushered into Buddha's presence, and orders were communicated to the members of the assembly. Gaudama was then fifty-five years old.

On a certain day he went to the village of Dzantoo for the purpose of collecting alms. Manh Nat, his inveterate foe, entered into the heart of all the villagers to prevent them from giving alms to the mendicant. He succeeded so well in his wicked design that no one noticed Gaudama's passage through the street, nor gave him alms. When he drew near to the gate, Manh stood by the side of the street, and asked him, with a sarcastic tone, how he felt under the pangs of hunger. Buddha replied to him, that he could, by entering into the state of perfect trance, remain, like the great Brahma, without using material food, feeding only, as it were, on the inward happiness created by the immediate sight of unclouded truth. Five hundred young virgins, who happened to return from the country into the place, prostrated themselves before Buddha, listened to his instructions, and reached the state of Thautapan.

On leaving the place, Buddha happened to travel through a forest, which had become an object of terror to all the people of Kothala, as being the favourite haunt of Ougalimala, a notorious robber and murderer. The ruler of the country, Pasenadi, had heard from the windows of his palace the cries of his alarmed subjects. Despite the many remonstrances that were made concerning the dangers of such an attempt, Buddha went straight forward to the den of the formidable man, who, enraged at such presumptuous boldness, was preparing to make him pay dear for his intrusion. But he had to deal with an opponent that could not easily be frightened. To his threats and attempts to inflict harm Gaudama opposed the meekest composure, the mildest expressions, and an invincible patience. Softened by the kindness of his opponent, Ougalimala altered the tone of his voice, and showed signs of respect to Buddha. The latter, quickly perceiving the change that had taken place in the robber's soul, preached to him the law, and made of him a sincere convert. Coming out from the forest which had been the scene of so many crimes, he followed Buddha, with the behaviour of an humble disciple. The people of Kosala could scarcely give credit to the change that had taken place in Ougalimala. In a short time he became a Rahanda, and died not long after he had become perfect. The members of the assembly were, on a certain day, talking among themselves about the place he had probably migrated to. Buddha,.

who had overheard their conversation on this subject, said to them: " Beloved Bickus, the Rahan Ougalimala, who died a little while after his conversion, has reached the deliverance. His conversion was at once prompt and perfect. He was very wicked previous to his conversion, because he never cohabited except with wicked and perverse associates, the company of whom led him into all sorts of disorders. But he no sooner had the good fortune to meet me, hear my instructions, and converse with you, than he, at once believed in my doctrine, adhered to me with all his might, and entered into the way leading to perfection. He laboured strenuously to destroy in himself the law of demerits, and thus rapidly reached the summit of perfection."

CHAPTER XII.

WHILE the most excellent Buddha was in the Dzetawon monastery, the heretics of Thawattie made another attempt to lower, nay, to destroy his reputation. They prevailed upon Thondarie, a woman entirely devoted to their interests, to spread the rumour that she had spent a night in the apartments of Buddha. When the calumny had been noised abroad, they suborned a gang of drunkards, to whom they promised a large sum of money, if they would do away with the instrument of the slander. They accordingly selected a favourable opportunity, killed Thondarie, and threw her body into a cluster of bushes close to the monastery. When the crime had been perpetrated, the heretics raised a cry all over the country inquiring about Thondarie. She could nowhere be found. Search was made in every direction, until at last, by the secret directions of their emissaries, the body was found on the spot where it had been apparently concealed. The party hostile to Buddha laid the crime at his door. The king of the country, urged on by them, ordered a strict inquiry to be made. The infamous trick was at last discovered in the following manner. The perpetrators of the deed happened to go into a drinking-place. Heated by the liquor they had taken, they began to accuse each other of having killed Thondarie. Their conversation was

overheard by one of the king's servants, who had them
arrested and led to the palace. The king said to them,
" Wicked men, is it true that you have killed the woman
Thondarie ? " They answered, " It is true we have killed
her." " Who advised you to commit the murder ? " " The
Deitty teachers, who have paid us one thousand pieces of
silver." Indignant at such a horrible deed, the king ordered
the murderers and their advisers to be put to death. Their
punishment consisted in their being buried in the earth up
to their waist. They were subsequently covered with a
heap of straw, which being set fire to, they were burnt to
death. Buddha told his disciples that what had happened
on this melancholy occasion was but a just retribution for
his having in a former existence been drunk, and in that
state abused and slandered a holy personage.

In one of his preaching excursions, Gaudama converted
a distinguished pounha, who asked him, " Illustrious Buddha, what has the great Brahma done to merit the extraordinary glory that encompasses his person and the unsur-
passed felicity that he enjoys ? " To whom he answered,
" The great Brahma, during several existences, has bestowed
abundant alms on the needy, delivered many people from
great perils, and delighted in giving instruction to the
ignorant. Such meritorious deeds have procured for him
the transcendent rank that he occupies, and secured to him
for an immense period of time the matchless happiness
that he possesses."

Two rich men, one of Thawattie, and the other a denizen
of the Ougga city, had in their youth, when engaged in
their studies, promised each other that he who should have
a daughter would give her in marriage to the son of the
other. When they had grown up, the rich man of Thawattie became a disciple of Buddha, but his friend followed
the teachings of the heretics. In due time Anatapein, for
such was the name of the former, had a beautiful daughter.
His friend Ougga had also a fine grown-up son. It came
to pass that Ougga on a certain day arrived from his place

with five hundred carts of goods to Thawattie, for the purpose of trading. He lodged, as a matter of course, in his friend's house. During the conversation Ougga reminded his host of their former promise, and declared that he would be too happy to have it fulfilled without delay. Anatapein, having consulted his wife and daughter, and secured their consent, agreed to the proposal that was made to him. The pious rich man, however, was somewhat concerned respecting the dangers of his daughter's position in the midst of upholders of false doctrines. He gave her a retinue of female attendants, who could, by their advice and conversation, maintain intact in her the faith in Buddha. When the bride arrived, after a long journey, to Ougga's city, she was desired by her father-in-law to go in the company of his wife to pay her respects to his teachers, who were sitting quite naked, with dishevelled hairs, in the midst of the most disgusting uncleanness, under a shed prepared for them. Unused to such an unsightly and revolting display, the modest girl recoiled back with a becoming horror, refusing even to cast a look at them. Enraged at the contempt shown to his teachers, the unnatural father-in-law threatened to send her away from his house, as being an unsuitable match for his son. Firm in her faith, she withstood all the efforts that were made to induce her to alter her resolution and pay attention to such individuals. She went back into her apartments. Having somewhat recovered her spirits, and regained her usual calm and serene composure, the pious young lady began, in the presence of her mother-in-law and other ladies of the town, to praise and extol the glory, modesty, meekness, and all the other qualifications which adorned her great teacher and his disciples. The hearers were delighted at all that they heard, and expressed an eager desire to see them and hear their instructions.

On that very day the compassionate Buddha was at an early hour, as usual, reviewing the beings dwelling on the island of Dzampoudipa, endeavouring to discover those that were well disposed to hear the truth. His searching glance soon discovered what was going on in the house of the rich man Ougga, and the good dispositions of many of its inmates. " Thither," said he, " I shall hasten to preach the law, for many shall be converted." Hereupon he summoned five hundred disciples to attend him. They all took their pattas and other articles. With his company he flew through the air, and soon alighted in the courtyard of the rich man's house. All were rejoiced to see Buddha and his disciples. They lent a most attentive ear to his instructions. The rich man, his household, and a great number of the people of the town were converted. Anouroudha was left at Ougga to complete, perfect, and extend the good work so happily begun. Buddha in all haste returned to Thawattie.

At that time a great noise was made throughout the country on account of a certain pounha whose navel emitted a sort of light in the shape of a moon. He belonged to the party of unbelievers. He was led by them into every village and town, as a living proof of the power they possessed. At last his friends introduced him into the Dzetawon monastery. He was no sooner introduced into Buddha's presence, when the prodigy suddenly ceased. He went away somewhat annoyed at his misfortune; but he had scarcely crossed the threshold of the monastery when the light reappeared. Three times he came before the great preacher, and three times the light was completely eclipsed. No doubt could be entertained that there was in Buddha some secret power superior to the one he possessed. The pounha was at once disconcerted and bewildered. In his ignorance he attributed the accident to some superior magical formula possessed by Buddha, and asked him to teach him the said formula. Buddha said to him, " O pounha! I possess no charm; I ignore all magical formulas. There is in me but one virtue; it is that which I have gathered at the foot of the Bodi tree during the forty-nine days that I have spent there in the deepest meditation.

As to what attracts now the attention of the people in your person, your are indebted for it to the offering of a gold coronet, in the shape of a moon, you made to a Buddha during a former existence. The reward bestowed on you for such a good work is but a transient one. It can afford you no real, substantial, and lasting happiness. Hearken to my doctrine; it will confer on you a never-ending recompense." He went on explaining to him many points of the law. The pounha believed in Buddha; nay, he applied for the dignity of Rahan, and finally became a Rahanda.

N.B.—The history of Buddha offers an almost complete blank as to what regards his doings and preachings during a period of nearly twenty-three years,[1] beginning with the twenty-first season, when he was fifty-six years old, and ending with the forty-fourth season, having reached the patriarchal age of seventy-nine years. So entirely are we kept in ignorance of the important transactions that took place during so long a portion of Buddha's life, that the

---

[1] This short summary of Buddha's life, indicating but little more than the names of the places where he had spent twenty seasons, and leaving us in the dark as to all the particulars regarding the twenty-three other seasons, is another illustration of the assertion, made in some foregoing passages, that the present compilation is very concise and imperfect, supplying us with but an outline of Buddha's proceedings during the course of his preachings. He reached the age of eighty. According to the authority of this legend, Buddha lived forty-five years after he had obtained the Buddhaship. He was therefore thirty-five when he began his public life and entered the career of preaching the law. It is not in my power to say anything positive respecting the antiquity of this work, but the statement of the main facts is borne out by the united testimony of the Buddhistic works existing in various parts and in different languages of Eastern Asia. If it be true that our Buddha lived so long, we must believe that his time during the last twenty-five years was employed in the same benevolent undertaking, viz., to preach the sacred law and point out to beings the way that shall lead them to the deliverance. Many volumes are full of the disputes on religious subjects between Buddha and the heretics, that is to say, his opponents. We may conclude that those controversies took place during the latter part of Buddha's life, as it cannot be doubted that they increased in proportion to the progress the new doctrines made among the people. If, however, we are in great part kept in the dark respecting the doings of the great reformer during a long period of his public life, we are amply compensated by the account of many interesting circumstances that occurred chiefly during the last year of his earthly career.

writer, after having vainly consulted several manuscripts, is reluctantly obliged to come to the same conclusion as that which the Burmese authors have arrived at, viz., that there is a complete disagreement as to even the names of the places where Buddha spent the twenty-three remaining seasons. Out of regard for the rich man Anatapein, who for so many years had been one of his most liberal supporters, Buddha spent the greatest part of the remaining seasons in the Dzetawon monastery. During the few others he seems to have stayed at or near Radzagio, chiefly in the Weloowon monastery. The amount of seasons spent by our Phra from the time he obtained the Buddhaship till his death is forty-five.

I find related, as a fact worthy of notice, the donation by a rich widow of Wethalie, named Wisaka, of the celebrated Pouppayon monastery. It was situated not far from the Dzetawon, in an eastern direction from that famous place. It is mentioned that when Phra sallied from the Dzetawon monastery by the eastern gate, the people of the country knew that he was going to dwell for awhile in the Pouppayon monastery; when, on the other hand, he was observed to leave it by the northern gate, all the people understood that he was undertaking a journey through the country for the purpose of preaching. The epoch of this donation is not certain. It appears from some particulars indirectly alluded to that it must have taken place when Buddha was sixty years old.

In following our manuscript, we find inserted in this place the detailed accounts respecting Dewadat, related by Buddha himself in the Dzetawon monastery, in the presence of a large party of his disciples. The fact of Buddha mentioning the name of Adzatathat as king of Radzagio, leaves no doubt respecting the time when the awful punishment is supposed to have been meted out to Dewadat, on account of the many heinous sins laid to his charge. Adzatathat, having murdered his father Pimpathara, by starving him to death in a prison, became king of Radzagio, and succeeded him when Buddha was nearly seventy-two years old. He was already king, as the sequel will show, when Dewadat was as yet his spiritual adviser. It is probable that the following narrative was made not more than two years after the above date.

When the most excellent Buddha was in the Dzetawon monastery, alluding to the sad fate that had fallen Dewadat, he related the causes that had brought on this dreadful occurrence.

At a certain time, when Buddha was spending a season in the Kosamby country, the people came in great numbers every day to the monastery to bring abundant alms, and pay their respects to him and the assembly. On certain occasions they made inquiries about the most distinguished members of the assembly, such as Thariputra, Maukalan, Anouroudda, Ananda, Bagoo, Kimila, and others, giving utterance to the feelings of admiration and love they entertained towards them. But they never took the least notice of Dewadat. The latter keenly resented the studied slight; the more so, because he thought that in his capacity of member of the assembly and of his royal descent, he was entitled to as much consideration as many others, who in this twofold respect were greatly his inferiors. He resolved to leave the company of Buddha and go to some other place. He went to Radzagio and ingratiated himself in the favours of the young Prince Adzatathat, son of King Pimpathara. The young prince, taken up with the grave manners of the new-comer, acknowledged him as his teacher, and built for him a monastery on the Yauthitha hill, close to the city.

Some years afterwards Buddha came to Radzagio to spend a season in the Weloowon monastery. Dewadat went to his monastery. Having paid his respects in the usual manner and occupied a becoming place, he three times requested the permission of having an assembly or thinga of his own, quite distinct from the other, which was under the immediate management of Buddha. On this point he three times received a direct refusal to his demand. From that day the jealousy he entertained towards Buddha waxed to a base envy, which soon generated in his soul a deadly hatred against him. He made up his mind to break with Buddha all ties of spiritual relationship, and to become the chief of a new religious body. To succeed in his impious design he required the support of the secular arm. The king of Magatha was in favour of Buddha, but his son had warmly espoused the cause of Dewadat. In such a position, the evil-disposed Dewadat advised Prince Adzatathat to compass the destruction of his father, in order to become king. The ambitious son followed the detestable advice, and put an end to his father's life by starving him to death in a prison, in spite of his own mother's exertions to save her royal husband's life.

It was in the thirty-seventh season of Buddha's public mission that Adzatathat ascended the throne of Magatha. Under the new king's auspices, Dewadat carried everything before him with a high hand. Assured of the new king's support, he hired thirty bowmen and promised them an ample reward if they killed Buddha. The ruffians gladly agreed to the proposal. But when they were on the point of committing the crime, they felt themselves overawed by the presence of Buddha. Instead of executing the order they had received, they fell at his feet, craved his pardon, listened to his preaching, and were converted one after the other. Disappointed on this point, Dewadat designed another plan to rid himself of the great preacher. He watched the moment when Buddha was walking at the foot of a hill, named Weitsa-gout. From the summit he rolled a large stone that was to crush his enemy. Fortunately on its way down the hill's side it met with a small obstacle, on which it split into several parts. One splinter alone hurt the toe of one of Buddha's feet, and severely bruised it. On hearing of such a nefarious and cowardly attempt, the disciples hastened to the spot and conveyed their beloved master to his monastery. They offered to keep guard round his person, to prevent the repetition of other attempts on his life. But Buddha said to them that no mortal had the power to hurt him so far as to cause his death. He thanked them for this new token of their affectionate regard towards him, and bade them return to their respective places. The celebrated physician Dzewaka, having been sent for, applied a bandage, which, being removed on the following morning, it was found, to the surprise and joy of all present, that the injured toe was perfectly cured. On another occasion Dewadat made a last attempt on Buddha's life, in the suburbs of Radzagio, by the means of an elephant, infuriated and maddened by strong liquor forced into his throat. The animal was let loose in one of the streets which Gaudama was perambulating gathering alms in his mendicant's pot. But far from doing any injury to Buddha, the elephant, having come into his presence, stood for awhile, and then knelt before him in token of respect. In this manner Dewadat signally failed in this last wicked attempt.

Dewadat differed from his cousin on some points of discipline; and this difference occasioned the schism that he meditated to establish.[2] He had proposed to Buddha to

---

[2] Dewadat, in insisting upon the adoption of regulations of a more rigid character, intended to imitate, to a certain extent, the conduct of the mendicants of the opposite party. He aimed at rivalling them in the practice of austere observances. It does not appear that he innovated in the dogmas that he had learned at the school of his great teacher. As his royal pupil, Adzatathat, had hitherto supported the party of the pounhas, it is not improbable that Dewadat wished to lessen the differences between the practices and observances of the two parties, to render them less perceptible, and by doing so, to prepare the way, by gradual approximation, for a complete fusion. He exhibited himself in the character of a rigid reformer, who was displeased with the too lenient tenor of the disciplinary regulations instituted by Buddha. Be that as it may, it is certain that jealousy in the beginning inspired him with the idea of separating from the assembly. This first step led him farther than he at first contemplated. He wished to set up an assembly, or things of his own, and thereby to place himself on a footing of equality and rivalry with his cousin. Meeting with greater resistance than he expected, and being convinced that he could not succeed so long as Buddha should be alive, he did not shrink from making several attempts on his life. It is a fact worthy of notice that the disturbances which took place subsequently

make it obligatory on all Rahans to live in forests at the foot of certain trees; not to receive food from the people in their own places, but to use only as articles of food such things as they could procure by their exertions; to use robes made up of rags collected in the dust of public thoroughfares, and not such as might be offered by pious laymen; to abstain from fish and meat; and to dwell in unroofed places. Gaudama positively refused to accede to his demands. Meanwhile he meekly warned him against the sin of schism, telling him that the commission of such an offence would throw the perpetrator into the hell Awidz for a whole revolution of nature. Deaf to such a salutary warning, Dewadat precipitated himself into schism. He gained over to his party five hundred inexperienced Rahans of the Witzi country, and with them dwelt in the monastery of Gayathitha. He signally failed in his attempt to draw Ananda to his side. Thariputra, by the advice of Buddha, went to Dewadat's place. Profiting from the time he was asleep at a distance, he prevailed upon the five hundred Rahans to abandon schism and return to Buddha, the centre of unity, who was then in the Dzetawon monastery in Wethalie. Rising from his sleep, Dewadat fell into a paroxysm of rage at the trick played on him. He instantly resolved to start for the Dzetawon monastery, to have his revenge on Buddha for the injury done unto him. He was carried in a litter. Messenger after messenger informed Buddha of the approach of his antagonist. But he calmly said to his disciples: "Beloved sons, do not trouble yourselves. Dewadat shall not see my face nor enter the precincts of this place." Information was, in haste, conveyed that Dewadat had actually reached the

---

in the Buddhist society had their origin, in most instances, in points of discipline of a trivial importance, which were altered or rejected by a fraction of the assembly, whilst they were upheld with the utmost tenacity by the greater portion of the Rahans, as having been established by Gaudama. This observation will be fully corroborated by the particulars that we shall relate on the subject of the councils or meetings held after Gaudama's death.

tank close to the monastery, and was resting a while under the shade of a tree. Gaudama calmly gave the same assurance to his trembling disciples. But the moment of a terrible punishment was at hand. Dewadat, quitting his couch, stood up for a while, to refresh his wearied limbs. But he was seen by his astonished and bewildered companions gradually sinking into the earth, first up to his knees, then to his navel, and finally to his shoulders. At that moment he humbled himself, confessed his fault, acknowledged and proclaimed the glory of Buddha. He then disappeared, wrapt in flame, and fell to the bottom of the hell Awidzi. His punishment consists in having his feet sunk ankle-deep in a burning ground; his head is covered with a red-hot pan, that caps his head down to he lobe of the ears; two huge red-hot iron bars transfixt him horizontally from right to left, two from back to front, and one impales him from top to bottom. He shall have to suffer in that frightful position during a revolution of nature. But, for his tardy and sincere repentance, he shall be delivered, and, by his exertions in practising virtue, he shall become a Pitzegabuddha, under the name of Atisara.

Adzatathat ruled over the two countries of Enga and Magatha. His mother was Waydahi, the sister of King Pathenadi, who ruled over the two countries of Kaci and Kosala. Adzatathat, who was of a bellicose temper, quarrelled with his uncle on account of some districts in Kaci, which he seized by force of arms. Unable to resist the army of his nephew, Pathenadi offered to the invader the hand of his daughter Watzera-komma. The offer was accepted, and a reconciliation followed. Three years afterwards, Pathenadi lost his throne, which was seized by Meittadoubba, a son he had had by a concubine. Pathenadi went to Radzagio to ask assistance against the usurper from his son-in-law. But he died on his way to that place.

It was under the rule of Meittadoubba, in the forty-fourth season, that occurred the total destruction of the

Thagiwi princes of Kosala and Kapilawot by the ambitious Adzatathat.

Buddha spent the forty-fourth season in the Dzetawon monastery. When the season was over, he went to dwell in·the Weitzagout monastery, near Radzagio. While he was in that place, there was spread a rumour that Adzatathat entertained hostile feelings towards Wethalie. Buddha then foretold that as long as the princes of Wethalie would be united and avoid internal strife and contention, they would be more than a match for their enemy; but should quarrel take place among them, they and their country would fall an easy prey to the invader. These words, which fell from Buddha's mouth, were not forgotten by a pounha who was· one of Adzatathat's ministers. He planned, with his royal mother's consent and secret encouragement, the destruction of the rulers of Wethalie, and the conquest of that country, by contriving to sow the seed of dissension among the Letziwi princes. His plan met with complete success some years later, about three years after Gaudama's Neibban, as we shall have the opportunity of relating.

END OF VOL. I.

PRINTED BY BALLANTYNE, HANSON AND CO.
EDINBURGH AND LONDON

www.ingramcontent.com/pod-product-compliance
Lightning Source LLC
Chambersburg PA
CBHW031345070726

47496CB00017B/1772